The Shattered Elements

Logan S. Davis

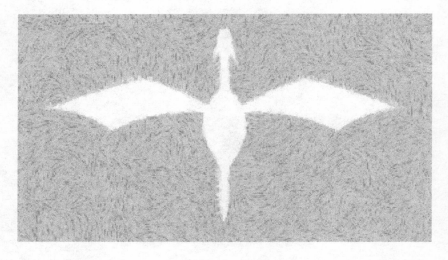

Special Thanks goes to:

Stephanie Martin, Paula Davis,
Scott Davis, Susan Scott, Luke Scott, Bill Harris, Michael Toski,
Jason Hastings, Tom Gamble.

And many others near and far.

For yinz.

Prologue

Epilogue

Prologue

Szakaieh tells of: "A Warning from a Wizard"

"Knowing the ship is sinking isn't the same thing as getting wet." -the Wizard of the Waves

The quotations were never necessary, but neither was I.

So I get the feeling. I've given myself credit for the words above, but I probably saw them in a fortune cookie.

Hold on to your hats, ladies and gentlemen, no matter the headgear or the state of your head. I've failed to address my entire audience, therefore I'll extend an additional greeting to anybody who isn't particularly lady-like and a final salutation to anyone who isn't gentle and manly at the same time. A firm grasp on the aforementioned hat is quite crucial, lest any free-wheeling scoundrel conjure a rabbit as a distraction.

No rainchecks or reconciliations will be made available. The front desk floated away a long time ago. I simply can't pat you on the shoulder and tell you everything is OK whenever the utterly impossible just sort of *happens.* Because first of all, it isn't OK. It's a Guard-damn shit-show, if you want my opinion.

In fact, my friends, the personal recollections I've cobbled together may only be the optimistic fabrications of a few deluded lunatics. I can't concern myself over details like that just because the details are relatively *concerning.* Empirical research, rational analysis, scientific methodology, this bed-of-roses always gets flushed down the crapper eventually, make no mistake. I imagine any Wizard worth shaking a wand at would be inclined to agree.

I also recommend nobody bother conducting any discussions about "what this all means," or "how all these weird names are supposed to be pronounced."

Names are just words, and words are just *made up.* And what this all means is *definitely* made up. One should probably invent meanings and pronunciations of their own, as I'd greet the theft of sincere discernment with crisp disapproval.

If confronted by a true scholar embarked on a quest for facts and information, humbly allow such a personage to forgo the subsequent tome. This old Wizard has regrettably lost the faculties for academic conventions.

I've often received shoddy advice advocating severe injury whenever a performance is imminent. Nobody around here is breaking any legs on purpose, I assure you, Jurisdiction insurance deductibles and so forth.

The wavy fringe of curtain rises faster than the tide, so saddle up and suit yourself and sit your horse and ride.

Book 1: Squires
Chapters 1-8

Chapter 1
Raspho tells of: "The Swarm"

"The tribes of the Low Hills believe that fire is an evil spirit, bent on destruction. Do they forget the warmth, the dancing glow, the countless entrees cleverly composed in the exchange? The flames hold neither bias nor regard for how the world is supposed to be." -the Sorcerer Prodigy

  When I was a boy, I lived on a farm by the coast.
  I begin with an elementary statement, but this raw abstraction of my childhood contains an entire world in the hand-sewn pockets of my mind. I can't remember the exact Sun when I discovered I was a mage. This mundane realization arrived among the earliest Rounds of my life. When I demonstrated I could conjure tiny flickers of flame, my parents remained calm. I felt only the acceptance of knowing smiles. Nothing was amiss with this incendiary phenomenon, in their eyes. My younger brother was a far better swimmer. I thought the trade-off was only fair. Why would it even matter? I still had to carry a flint, even. I was reminded never to reveal I was a mage, nowhere except the beach on our farm. Only my family could know of it. An unusual tone of voice convinced me of the rule. The fires stayed on that beach without much thought when I was a boy.
  I don't recall the name of the town. The proper noun has escaped, and I won't chase an errant title while strolling leisurely through intimate reveries. I need to leave town. I need to travel north, travel four-point-seven kilometers, to the place I recall best. I'll find a place embedded in my memories somewhere. I suppose our farm was named the 'Born' farm, a name distilled without contrivance from the chosen family name. I'm not sure which details matter anymore. At this point in my life, much of what matters lies in the past beneath a fine layer of ash. The events that show how shattered everything is, the ones burning to the core, I recall by my own accord. If anyone feels pulled to commiserate, my desire was never to discourage. The following should be construed as a statement of what happened.
  May hapless words kindle sparks of hope in smouldering hearts.
  Why is the natural place to begin always the place where things went wrong? I need to feel the heat, I suppose, in order to make

sense of myself. I travel back to the salt water and the farm, the sandy corners of my thoughts. I dwell on them as I pull a glass tumbler from the confines of my desk. I've placed the hand-blown vessel on the pages of my latest diagrams. I let nostalgia give structure to the mage that I've become before I pull the cork on the decanter. If I've constructed an arcane tower over the course of a lifetime, then the coastal farm and the kin who dwelled within made the quarried stones of my foundation.

{~}

My family, may the Guards bless them and keep them, grew several varieties of plants in order to survive. The land in our area was staked with claims several generations before I came into being. The farm was crisscrossed with crude wooden fences and low walls of loose stones. I sketched a diagram of the exact holdings, once. The simple barriers created sections of varying sizes. Grazing areas and fallow fields were interspersed with plant life in plots which were constantly changing. Grandfather Born was the last alive from his generation, and the only one of my grandparents I ever met. His voice gently dictated what crops to grow, and when to plow or sow, tend or harvest. Corn, wheat, hemp, and berries are what I recall. A tidy orchard flanked the north-west side of the farm. The rest was surrounded by forest or ocean. The farm had chickens, goats, and a pair of oxen and horses.

We worked the land with a sense of tranquility I'm certain I'll never regain in my life. At planting and harvest, we'd join together with neighboring farms to harvest and celebrate our bounty. I remember the man from across the lane. His name might've been Jim, or Tim, or Slim, but I don't even see a face remaining, just a rough hand and a fading voice.

The burden of sustenance farming was a continuous toil. I recall the blisters and the ache and the sweat. Beans and rice poured forth from canvas sacks when better foodstuffs were in tight supply. I'll hold the farm in my heart, anyway.

A sheriff with a shining silver star on his chest operated a town jail, I suppose, but he rarely had any kind of infraction beyond the usual drunken carousing. Festivals and markets saw strangers gathered in town from the outlying forests. Surely bandits arrived with the outsiders, but even among the press of cobbled streets and dimly lit alley-ways, life stayed predictable for the town. Violence was an unknown realm for any of us. I was as naive as one of our milking goats.

I remember my father and my mother, and how the three of us shared a cabin when I was a boy. The cabin is one of my earliest memories. When my younger brother Jahnny was born the family constructed another cabin with timber hewn from the forest nearby. Gaps were filled with pitch and the slats of the wooden roof were sealed with sturdy varnish. The old cabin was turned into storage and our cluster of cabins grew. Every Sun I can remember Grandfather Born working tirelessly to keep track of food and supplies we needed for winter. He was my father's father and he was aging but nimble and strong. The work was like breathing to him and I recall my mother telling me he loved the farm almost as much as he missed my grandmother. Every now and then he'd stop and light his pipe and a thoughtful look would fall over his face as he studied some plants or fencing or the sky. If you passed him he'd smile and greet you but he rarely had much to say in conversation unless the sun was down and he'd had a couple tankards of beer from the dusty keg in the cellar.

My father got up early every morning to milk the goats and my mother was almost always drying plants or herbs. They hung on racks in the cabin and filled the air with intriguing aromas. My mother planted and tended her tiny green charges and harvested and dried them when they were grown. She was the only one of the adults in my life who could read and write with more than a bare proficiency and she taught me as a child. I'm writing this down because of my mother, seeing how she taught me the value in my letters. She taught anyone with an interest who would listen to her voice, but nobody shared in her passion or her mastery. She read book after book. She read every book anyone could find for her. The most valuable books were ancient and delicate and needed to be handled with care and supervised by the mayor of the town herself. With some of the more practical knowledge my mother gained from books she looked after medical ailments, person or beast. Only the town's surgeon rivaled her expertise.

My father's sister, her husband, and my cousin Violet lived on our farm as well. The cabin they called home was the first one built by our ancestors and the splintery structure was in need of constant repair. My aunt and uncle did the cooking for our family, or orchestrated our efforts at least. Many times I found myself cutting vegetables or jarring pickles after being lured to the Hall by something to eat. The largest cabin on our farm held our kitchen and our dining room and our indoor living area. Adjacent to the Hall was a sturdy building holding our food stores. The Hall contained a matching pair of stone hearths along one wall. The interlocking eye-catching hearths were the most valuable part of the entire Born family holding, in terms of money anyway.

In a town relying primarily on bartering, metal coins weren't seen as particularly useful. The currency exchange was aggravated by the fact that you'd be hard up to find several coins actually matching each other unless they came straight from a smith who was re-minting them. Even then, you'd always end up with a wide array of random alloys where you'd never trust anyone's word about what metals they contained, and the whole thing became a waste of time and effort and raw materials. As a boy, I had an easier time handing over a sack of beans in exchange for a chicken.

In the coldest Moons, we passed the time in the warmth of the Hall gathered by the heat of the hearth. I remember the sound of the kettle. The smooth bricks and the cooking fires always represented aromatic contentment in my life.

Violet fell in love with the family's dairy goats at a tender age. Even when they nibbled her dresses or her hair, she squealed with delight. She named the goats and talked to each of them endlessly. She wasn't much more than a toddler when she insisted on the role of shepherdess. None of us could contain our adoration for the girl. She gave her expert opinions of the goats in a loud voice. In spite of her apparent scorn, they seemed to obey her commands with dancing and tricks. We rolled in the grass with laughter. There were two farm-dogs, Chaser and Claptrap, who helped Violet keep an eye on the goats. The dogs were big, lean, efficient mutts. They kept Violet safe from foxes and coyotes as she spent her Suns playing among the goats. While one of the two dogs kept an eye on the flock and the girl, the other would keep crows away from the crops or rodents away from the food storage. I remember my father counting the seconds it took for one of the dogs to run from the far end of the wheat field to the far end of the grazing grounds, the longest reach the farm could offer.

My brother Jahnny and I adored the ocean. He grew more quickly than I did as a teenager and he nearly matched my height despite being younger than me. He was always skinny. Our mother encouraged him to eat like his appetite was her life's purpose. I was always keener than Jahnny to put flesh on my bones. We both let our hair grow shaggy, but we were unique characters when viewed from any distance. My hair is a a delicate blonde brilliance in stark contrast to the brown of my skin. Jahnny's hair is a shady chestnut glazed with medium gold. The sun baked us constantly and the topical ministrations of soothing aloe plants were a customary evening ritual.

On the eastern side of the cabins, opposite the fields, there lay a rocky dune dropping down to a sandy shore. When I was a child, my father recruited hands from the surrounding farms for a few Suns. They used ropes and iron bars to shift the rocks of the dune and create an angled pathway to the beach. Jahnny loved the ocean more than anyone I knew. He used his time in the evenings crafting surfboards out of planks of malleable timber. We'd sit together on the sand as his whittling knife flashed in the setting sun. The wood shavings fell in scattered piles between his bare feet. He smoothed the wood even further by rubbing the board with rough stones. I sketched diagrams of curves and contours I pictured for his surfboards. When my father gave Jahnny a few coins, he spent every last one on a kind of lacquer to seal the finished surfboards against the harsh moisture of the sea.

He passed nearly as many Marks in the waves of the ocean as he did on land. He'd dash through his farm work salty and damp from his morning swim only to return to the water when he'd completed his tasks.

The ocean was dear to me as well. When my brother completed his second board, I was on the waves along with him, but I floated awkwardly or tumbled under the surf more than I rode. Our aunt would watch us from the shore, peeling apples or shelling nuts or shucking corn. She usually smiled and watched, but the woman was part fish herself, we both knew.

I waded through the water and unfurled curls of fire under the breaking waves, grinning as my creations were enveloped by hissing salt water. If I pushed myself, I could turn patches of the ocean's surface into billows of steam, but I liked to see the flicker of orange against the backdrop of blue-green. Sea and sand made a perfect space to keep the flame from spreading and the isolation from outsiders provided by the rocky dunes meant my privacy was kept. I vented my anger over details of my life in fist-sized bursts of blazing heat at the whitecaps. I burned myself a few times when I lost control, but never badly enough to cause serious damage. Cool ocean water and aloe plants were the medicine I needed.

As I grew older, I wished I could boast to my friends of my power to coax fire from thin air. I wanted to show off what made me unique. When I was sixteen, a girl kissed me at a festival, but she disappeared back to her farm without telling me how to find her, and I never saw her again. I was certain the young women in town thought I was too plain. I remember a different festival night where the teenagers gathered on the beach away from the adults to dance on the sand by the light of our own bonfire. We sang along carelessly as drums and strings and pipes played tunes too fast or brash for our parents. We had hard cider stashed behind a rock on the dune, and we passed the sweet booze around. Nights like those were the closest I ever came to revealing myself as a mage. But in the glow of each manic evening, I took a thoughtful swig from the jug and kept my secret.

I gained momentum with regards to the fire I could inexplicably summon. I began to sear and carve pieces of driftwood in strange and unique ways. The waterlogged chunks of timber were plentiful, and I gathered and sorted them meticulously. I carved the forgotten bones of the ocean with mage flame as a means of practicing the skill. My family kept a careful eye on me, and at some point I was given a more complete lecture about the importance of secrecy. The existence of the Jurisdiction made it imperative that no one ever learn I was as a fire mage. But in truth, such worries were far from the front of my mind. Ultimately my mage skill held no bearing on my life for most of my teenage Rounds. The arcane dabbling was a unique and curious hobby to me. I cultivated myself slowly and casually, but never fully embraced the flame.

{~}

Instead of exposing the fact that I was a fire mage, there was another way I wanted to become my own man. The fire burned inside me and sought a different path to escape. What I wanted most in those Suns was a musket. My father and grandfather each owned one, relics though the devices were, and I was allowed to practice shooting on a limited basis. I was fascinated by the crude guns. My father's closest friend from childhood lived in town, a man by the name of Buscon. He became a blacksmith's apprentice when he was a wee lad. Buscon was one of the few decent gunsmiths anyone in our town knew at the time. Whenever our wagon made the trip to town, Buscon's musket shop was where I wanted to linger. A handful of other villages and clustered farmsteads existed within a few Suns' traveling distance of the farm. However quaint, our town was the most substantial of them. The only true cities were many Suns journey through increasingly perilous territory. Few people ventured to or from the cities in our part of the world. Common wisdom dictated that even if you survived the journey, such places were under the iron thumb of the Jurisdiction. Everyone agreed that the Jurisdiction was nearly as treacherous as the bandits and wild animals and savage tribes you'd face before you reached their sprawling domain.

My father knew of my heady desire for a musket. I wanted to sell my driftwood carvings for the money to buy a musket of my own, but he was dead-set against the idea at first. He told me my carvings could attract unwanted attention and explained how growing food and tending livestock was more efficient and human compared to stalking and slaying animals with a musket. He explained how the Trapper's Guild would compete with me or even object to my presence if I wished to become a fur trader, and even if they didn't, poor stewardship of game populations led to hardship for everyone. He regaled me with his excellent reasoning but I ignored him, drawn as I was like a moth towards the flame. Hand-made muskets, even quality ones like Buscon could make, were notoriously inaccurate, unreliable, dangerous, and noisy. I stashed away every stupid coin I could acquire in the hopes of affording one anyway. My family was a family of farmers, not hunters, but I was determined to become more than just a farmer. I had a longing to stack up the hides and the antlers and the meat. Those things would make me prosperous and attractive in the eyes of the town and I wouldn't let go of my dream of my own musket. My grandfather sympathized more with my desires, I believe. He offered me his recurve bow. I practiced shooting arrows a few times but the twang of a bowstring never held my fervent interest. I ached for the bang and the muzzle flash and the sulfurous smoke.

I continued to create fire-carvings as I watched Jahnny surf, improving my skill and technique with each new project. I learned to channel my energy into white hot rivulets and then coax the rivulets to form searing edges. I grunted and sweated with the focus and the effort the fire-carving required. I ate ravenously to feed the strength I used. Eventually I could mimic the gouges and burn-markings a red-hot chisel left on the wood, insinuating the carvings were made by an ordinary craftsman. I sketched diagrams of my progress to ensure uniformity. The deliberate patterns disguised my mage-made carvings in a convincing fashion. The Sun before my seventeenth birth-Sun my father walked down through the rocky dunes towards the part of the beach where I was working. He pointed to a tear-drop sculpture I'd recently finished. From where I was sitting the body of the piece he was referring to resembled the remains of a broken water cask, discarded and unseen by the eyes of the world. My father nodded at me and dropped a bundle of canvas and twine onto the sand.

And so I was able to purchase my own musket.

{~}

A few Marks later our wagon rolled to a stop. We slid away from the wooden seat and our feet struck packed earth. The town markets nearby bustled with the sounds of passing horses and clips of conversation, but my mind was tunneled towards my sole desire as I tried to contain my excitement. We got a fair price for my carving from an eccentric art dealer. She was curious about the origins of my sculpture, but my father shrugged and said he'd won the piece from a traveler in a game of chance. In spite of the uncertainty, she was eager enough to acquire my artwork and negotiated animatedly from her open-air market stall at the edge of town. When we arrived at Buscon's shop I tethered the horses as quickly as possible while my father opened the wooden door.

The shop of the gunsmith Buscon was dim even though the Mark was nearly noon by the time we arrived. The construction was humble, a curtained window and a short counter. Gun racks covered each of the walls. The only door other than the street entrance led to Buscon's workshop and the smithy beyond. Judging from the faint smell of liquor and tobacco mixing with the gun oil and black powder, I knew Buscon had recently finished a project. He celebrated such occasions with an excess of whiskey, as was his way. Buscon sat beside the counter on a padded rocking chair with his eyes closed, moving ever so gently. He wore denim pants and a plain tee with his leather smithing apron draped over the front. If you caught him working, there were always gloves covering his hands, but they were absent this morning. His brownish tee-shirt was relatively clean. I'd never seen him wear anything else. My father cleared his throat and the husky smith groaned, welcoming us to look around.

I was taking in the muskets and pistols placed out for display when Buscon seemed to find himself. He began a conversation with my father, terse and groggy at first, but gradually words came to him more freely. He made his way to the window and drew back the curtain. Sun streamed in to highlight the precious wares of his shop. Lumbering towards me and blinking, he studied me as if he were sizing up a horse for tack.

"An exciting Sun," Buscon said to me as he approached. "It's my life's purpose, you know, to meet you at this Sun. The Sun where you seek the tool I'm bound by honor to create. These are my solemn aims, to practice accuracy and precision in the art of the musket. Shall we see what speaks to you?"

Buscon showed me several guns and pointed out their features and their flaws. As I studied each gun slowly and carefully, Buscon seemed to find energy in his passion.

"I see you've the eye of a craftsman. I've no doubt you'll select an exceptional piece."

A grin started at the corner of his mouth and slid across his face. He spoke more animatedly with each passing moment. The signs of his earlier lethargy vanished as he talked at length about the details of his work. He was a salesman who wove tales of musket making that captured the imagination and the heart. He knew he had me from the start, as plain as my intentions were. I was grateful he focused in detail on the specifications and the process of making a musket. Shaping steel, shaping wood, these were intriguing tasks to me, and I sketched diagrams in my mind as he gave his descriptions. Buscon confessed that the fancier woodwork on the stocks of his firearms was done by a renowned sculptor and not him personally. His voice grew distant as he admitted to the collaboration, but I found the decorative carvings impractical, especially considering the attached price increase. I think he was pleased when I showed a lack of interest in the fancy aesthetics. Instead, I focused on the barrels and firing mechanisms. The gunsmith swelled with pride as his rich baritone voice filled the room.

I left Buscon's shop with a wide smile on my face and a hand-made musket hanging over my shoulder on a wide canvas strap. I'd chosen one of the sturdiest barrels in the shop. The device would be blasting cartridges for decades, I thought. The musket was unadorned, but Buscon had smoothed the stock well, lacquering and polishing the wood until the natural grain shone through. After choosing my "boom-stick" I was shown the different kinds of powder, wadding, and shot the gunsmith kept for sale. The fresh black powder made me realize my father's supply of the stuff was an inferior quality. Pewter shot could be reclaimed and reused once I had a crucible and a mold. The coins I'd acquired from the sale of my carving ended up in Buscon's leather purse.

I was anxious to go hunting the next Sun. I urged the light to drop beyond the horizon. I'd only ever fired a musket at practice targets. I'd need help to butcher an animal and tan the hide. Sitting next to me on the wagon, I believe my father shared my excitement, perhaps in spite of himself.

"If you can get us a deer," he told me, "we'll have quite the feast."

I don't think I let go of the musket the entire ride home. As close as I placed the gun to my bed frame, I nearly slept with the firearm.

{~}

The following morning I dressed quickly and carefully for my hunt, wearing my best socks and undershorts and lacing up my boots. The trousers and tunic were made from a sturdy piece of canvas which had been a sail in a previous life. My aunt turned the densely woven canvas into clothes. They were a faded yellow-green which would serve reasonably well in the woods. At my hip I had a knife and a length of rope to field dress my game, along with the gunpowder, wadding and shot I'd need for my musket. I greeted my family cheerfully and downed a rasher of bacon. Everyone was present at breakfast to wish me well on my birth-Sun and the best of luck. My mother requested I be back by nightfall. I made plans to record my hunt on a scroll by candlelight that evening while the events were fresh in my mind. I might even sketch a diagram of my first deer.

Unable to contain myself, I thanked everyone and bolted out the door when I finished my eggs. The dogs raced alongside me to the edge of the farm where I told them to stay so they wouldn't scare away my quarry. I set off with boundless enthusiasm in my stride. I was content in those Marks, untroubled. The birds were singing in the trees and the sunlight filtered down through the leaves. The Wilds were a heavenly paradise waiting to offer up their bounty to the wise hunter. I was determined to be the hunter. The weight of the new musket on my shoulder reaffirmed me.

When I was deep enough in the woods and far from any farm or village, I fired a few test shots at tree trunks of varying distances. I was intensely satisfied with my new gun and my heart leapt. The spark and the bang and the punch of the recoil were glorious to me. I primed my musket and reloaded the metal tube with the cartridge which would kill my first deer, ramming down the shot. I reminded myself I should be reloading instinctively. If the animal didn't die from the first hit, I wanted to be able to finish the job instead of watching it suffer. When I finished loading, my fingers wrapped affectionately around the polished wood and I looked around in the wilderness.

I walked a kilometer in order to leave the smell of spent powder from my practice shots behind. I hoped the foreign scent hadn't clung to me. I began to creep carefully forward with my gun in hand. I'd stalked deer in my youth before, just to see what would happen, and the herds were plentiful in these woods. I figured I'd be able to get close enough for a shot without climbing in a tree and waiting. In less than a Mark I spotted a group of whitetails. They were downwind of me and their ears pricked up, heads turning in my direction.

I knew they'd bound away from me if I continued my approach. I withdrew, skirting back and to my right around a hill until I couldn't see the deer. I worked my way downwind around the hill, my feet moving carefully through the woods at a light run. My blood raced and I felt a surge of energy. I tried to feel as a wild predator might feel. I focused on the movements of my body and the weighty balance of the musket in my hand. When the edge of the hill receded, I flanked where the deer were standing. I stayed hunched and I crept up on the spot. A solitary doe was sampling the tender shoots of the undergrowth.

I winced at myself when a stick snapped under my foot but I dropped my stance to a determined crouch and moved forward. My heart raced and thumped in my ears and I hoped the doe wouldn't hear me. I calmed my breathing and tried to quell my anxiety. I didn't want my hands shaking while I was trying to aim.

She'd seen many seasons, that doe, and her appearance pleased me. I tried to judge her age by the sag of her belly and the state of her coat. I hoped I could confirm my guess by studying the wear of her teeth. Her tail twitched and she shifted warily, but she hadn't detected me. I thanked my luck, going to my knees and extending prone on the forest floor beneath a patch of ferns. I rested my musket on a piece of fallen branch and lined up my shot.

I was preparing myself to squeeze the musket's trigger when an odd whining sound in the distance made me hesitate. The sound reached the doe and startled her. I cursed my hesitation, but I was alarmed as well. I ignored the fidgeting doe and sat up, looking towards the sky.

The whining grew, echoing downward from above the treetops. Whatever was causing the noise drew closer and closer. I could tell the sound would pass almost directly over my head. Through the trees I could see what looked like a flock of dull grey birds. When the flock careened past me, I knew with clarity the birds weren't birds. They moved too systematically as they slid in precise paths across the sky. In ranks and columns they whirred, stacked above each other like a three-dimensional parade. They made an eerie sight which was nothing like the natural clusters and V's bird formations would create. I realized the whine wasn't an animal sound at all. I was hearing the turning of electric motors with plastic fans attached to them. The grey birds were compact flying machines, a propeller on each corner.

I was immediately filled with a sense of dread. I stayed motionless under the ferns and paralyzed with fear. I'd never seen the Swarm before, but the stories about it were told around a fire at night to give children nightmares. Around our town in those Suns, anyone could have their guess as to whether or not there was any truth to the matter. If you listened carefully to wise travelers, you might learn that the Swarm belonged to the Jurisdiction. The drones of the Swarm are relatively small, individually. Standing on end, one would only reach my knee. They consist of nothing more than a chassis, a battery, a receiver, four electric propellers, a camera, and a gun. But the strength of the Swarm, of course, lies in numbers. In the sky up above me I saw death pass over the woods. Row after row of them, column after column, layer after layer. I estimated the rigid flock consisted of fifty or a hundred units. I calculated their direction of travel and resisted the urge to cry out in dismay.

When the whine of the Swarm faded in the distance, I began to run. My muscles and lungs screamed at me and nausea followed. I cut through underbrush and raced past tree trunks as I made the straightest path I could estimate towards my family's farm. My musket which seemed so sturdy Marks before felt like an anchor meant to keep me in the forest. The drones pulled away and whirred over the horizon. My surroundings blurred as I rushed through, them trying not to trip. I was only partly successful, but the times when I fell I sprang back to my feet. Bruised, dirty, and exhausted, I neared the edge of the woods after running for most of a Mark. I drew to a walk to catch my breath and prepared for what I might see.

A sound like popping corn alerted me. I ducked behind a tree, sweating, cursing, and fighting back tears. I was only two hundred meters from the nearest cabin, but I wasn't near a road or a path. I could see no movement other than the circling drones and I heard no voices or screams. The Swarm's rectangular formation dissipated, and the drones made strafing passes in intertwining, flowing loops. Watching them bank and maneuver, the machines looked almost graceful, and the pattern they wove had a haunting efficiency which might've been charming in other circumstances. I sketched diagrams in my head instinctively. Perhaps I was shielding myself from the truth. My head spun and I sank against the tree. They could've escaped, I told myself over and over. To expose myself to the drones would mean only death.

I waited until nightfall, too scared to move in any real way. I fixed myself to the tree, my eyes never leaving my family's cabins and the Swarm drones. As the Sun set, the interlopers ceased their circling and landed, perching themselves on roofs and fence posts like lifeless, loitering vultures. After a while my mind went numb watching them, but I stared anyway, letting my eyes adjust to the dying light.

When the surge of adrenaline began to fade, I found myself gazing into the night. An optimistic thought arrived as I tried to rationalize my situation. I had only a rudimentary knowledge of electricity when I was young. I'd seen electric lights and noise-makers, curiosities mostly. One musician in town owned a stringed instrument that buzzing music through wires attached to a magnet and a paper cone. The batteries and generators for powering those objects were cumbersome, but I did know one thing- electricity can run out eventually. This was the thought I clung to for hope, and I waited.

I dozed off in spite of my terror and uncertainty. My body was unaccustomed to the physical and mental strain and my flesh betrayed me. My face leaned against the tree trunk and the bark dented the skin of my forehead. The corner of my jaw was damp from my incognizant drooling and the skin was colder than the rest of my body. I held my musket with a white knuckle grip and strained my night vision to peer through the darkness. At dawn, my strategy paid off. I'd been lucky, or so I thought at the time. The Swarm departed the farm, lifting off in a well-timed cloud before coalescing back to their unnaturally perfect formation. My first sign that something was wrong was a drone trailing behind the pack. My mind lurched. If a drone was damaged, then someone must've damaged it.

Even as near-mad with panic as I was, I hid until the whining faded from earshot before moving. I left the woods at a sprint and dropped my musket by the edge of a fence before vaulting over it. I rounded a corner to get a view of the clearing where our cabins were built. I'd like to simplify what happened next, or gloss over the facts, but I'm writing down every scrap I can recall. My mother taught me the value of such things, even when they're uncomfortable.

I let out a cry of denial when I saw the bodies. Even our horses, dogs, goats and chickens lay lifeless among the dark stains and feathers covering the ground. My aunt and uncle. My grandfather. My mother and father. I saw my cousin Violet last. She seemed to lay peacefully despite the blotches of red staining her frock where the Swarm's bullets struck her. I fell in the grass sobbing. My brother Jahnny wasn't there. I held out hope that he might yet live but dreaded finding his body as well.

The wrecked remains of two Swarm drones lay among my family as a sign of their resistance. My father's hands were wrapped around the handle of a pitchfork. Impaled on the tongs of the farm tool, a third Swarm drone sparked and twitched a propeller. I roared in impotent fury and picked up my father's dropped musket, bashing the drone over and over until the electronics went still. The musket stock splintered under the blows of my futile vengeance. The gun fell from my hands as a wave of emotion struck me. I turned away from the scene and vomited, heaving reflexively even though there was nothing in my stomach.

When I regained control of myself enough to function, I looked for Jahnny. There was no sign of my younger brother anywhere. When I stood on the beach, I suppressed the sobs wracking me enough to drag driftwood around. In the following Marks, I constructed a crude pyre. I had no coffins, and when I thought of digging holes for my family and leaving them covered in dirt the wooden pyre felt better. I resolved to scratch their names in the rocks of the dunes.

The thought of running to town and telling them what had befallen my family crossed my mind several times, but each time I pushed the notion away. I didn't want to draw anyone else to my private nightmare, and I suppose my trust in the town was shaken. If the Jurisdiction was after my family, I was safer remaining hidden. No need to make anyone else a target, or give anyone the opportunity to betray me. But unfortunately, this left me alone with a grisly, arduous task. My sanity and body complained and I forced myself forward one step at a time.

Dusk began to fall as I placed the final body on the pyre. The dogs lay on a lower tier and my family lay on the top. When the layout was set I sketched a diagram. The horses I hadn't the strength to move. The chickens and goats seemed unworthy of the honor of my pyre. I regretted the waste of meat, let alone the milk and eggs and autumn carriage rides which would never be, but as I stared at the pyre I pushed any practical thoughts aside. I was never a particularly devout youth. My mind raced back and forth between anger at the Guards for what happened and pleading with them for the souls of my family members. I bid farewell to my deceased kin, each in turn, and then with a shout of anguish I held forth my hands and unleashed the mage flame.

I drained myself and pushed my limits as I'd never before the evening of the pyre. I could feel the heat of my own blood as the scarlet energy coursed through me. I channeled power to the fire. I gave no thought for who might bear witness to the cremation which consumed so much of my life. The flames leapt high in the falling darkness. I was lucky the Swarm hadn't left a scout behind or the drone would've spotted my display from several kilometers away. The pyre blazed and I added my grief, feeding the flame with every ounce of myself I could throw at it. I lost consciousness as the flickering orange and red danced in my mind's eye.

Chapter 2
Melodie tells of: "The Mammoth's Renaissance"

"A bullet doesn't mean anything without any context. The orderly crates of metal nuggets stacked under our tarps might as well be melted down for scrap if haste or indecision or gravity or moisture or high winds or twitchy hands have a say. A bullet plays by the rules, just like the rest of us." -the Gunslinger Confidant

"None of your cousins knew where you'd gone, but I had a hunch you'd be in here. What are you looking for this morning, Mel?"

The man greeted me amiably at 0900. I'd known him my entire life, and I was un-surprised to hear the Confidant's voice. When I considered the circumstances of the Rose tribe, I knew no other voice I'd rather hear while finishing my morning tea, save perhaps for my father himself. I shifted the clay mug in my hands and considered the man who approached. In those Suns, Flin and the rest of the seven Confidants governed our people along with my father, Generale Sampsen Oakes. Confidant Flin was Sampsen's favorite among the Confidants. Flin wasn't popular because of his physical disfigurement or his drinking habits or his slow moving ways, that was pretty clear. The man might've been an outcast instead, but my father always treated him with respect.

Flin could barely count the number of battles he'd seen. The left half of his face was scarred with a wicked gash that collapsed his cheekbone and destroyed his eye. A similar injury damaged much of his scalp and prevented hair from growing on nearly half of his head. The remainder of his weathered dome he shaved bald, but he was a terrible sight if you caught him removing the bandanas and the wide brimmed leather hat he always wore. He walked with a severe limp and used his bolt-action rifle as a crutch. His left leg was shriveled and nearly useless below the knee, having been crushed by the bite of a titan wolf when I was but a twinkle in the Generale's eye. Titan wolves were said to be the size of horses, but I'd never seen one. Most believed the fearsome beasts had been hunted to extinction during the Tribal Wars. The canine jaws did a number on Flin's leg, though. Apparently he'd threatened to amputate the damn thing himself every time he was drunk for several Rounds after the injury. The severely damaged leg didn't succumb to infection, however, and the appendage didn't hurt, at least not more than the man drank. Confidant Flin called it a "working relationship" with his body. He'd been stabbed in the right shoulder, and his left bicep had been winged by an arrow. He bore the marks of shrapnel across the entirety of his back. The Guards only knew, he'd tell you, if you asked him how he survived his injuries. Despite his flaws and his age, Flin and I had formed an unlikely friendship when I was only a toddler. I'd grown to a young woman under the critical gaze of his keen right eye.

In our tribe of gunfighters, no one was elected to sit among the seven Confidants without support from the people. Flin knew how to gain that support, and he didn't take his duties lightly, nor had he forgotten what fighting meant to us. In spite of everything he'd experienced, Confidant Flin could still dent a thimble placed four-hundred meters down-range.

The morning was the Twenty-third Sun of the Eighth Moon. I stood in a long-house held in posterity for those who raised the banner of the Rose. Our stone long-houses were single-story buildings, rectangular in shape, stretched to varying degrees along an axis as the name implies. This particular long-house was dedicated to the recorded history of the Rose tribe. The Archives of the Recordkeepers was half the size of the Great Hall, and yet the stone walls and floors were the most intricately crafted in the Rose tribal seat. Our home was dubbed 'Sylviarg.' The place was surrounded by a hilly, partially wooded farming region comprising the western edge of the Low Hills. Long-houses framed the Rosean compound with evenly-placed windows and reinforced doors. Wooden trusses decorated the ceilings and supported wooden planks which we treated with resinous liquids to prolong their life. Panels in the ceilings could be opened upward, courtesy of clever hinges attached to the ridge-beam of the roof. Very few long-house windows were actually covered with glass. Most used wooden shutters combined with layered curtains. If the tribe was attacked in Sylviarg, the village functioned as a fort. The walls of long-houses served as cover for our gunfighters.

Until Confidant Flin limped through the door, I was alone in the venerable Archives. A flower icon comprised of blown-glass graced a wooden stand for display, brilliant in shades of red and green and shaped as a stylized rose. A roof panel was opened to the dulcet morning. Sunlight flowed through the room in placid glory. Displayed from hanging fixtures and wall mounts were the expansive canvasses showing the history of the Rose tribe in pictures interspersed with descriptions written by careful hands. From the floor to the ceiling, one wall to the next, they told of the rise of the Jurisdiction. The occurrences remained a mythical tale of uncertainty, even in our official record. The journals were inconsistent, and facts about the Jurisdiction were to be taken with a grain of salt. The Recordkeepers even suggested that the Jurisdiction had always been a part of the world, a lingering scourge upon the earth, like a scarred brand from whatever chaotic crucible the Guards had employed to form the earth from primordial dust. The histories begin with a plague. In the aftermath, the Rose tribe formed by way of unlikely connections, and a healthy dose of desperate necessity. The canvas told of the founding of the long-houses in our tribal seat of Sylviarg. They told of the First Battles, when we seized the precious Mammoth from the Jurisdiction. I touched an image of the City of Old in the High Hills to the west, a place of reverence.

The histories attempted to convey the cost of the tribe's existence in terms of the people we'd lost. Anthems were written so that our people would never forget the past. The founding mothers and fathers sacrificed nearly every pair of hands which could hold a gun to the Jurisdiction battle lines. No description or tale of the Rose is complete without mention of the Mammoth. I paused to study the towering figure, emblazoned in excruciating detail on a wall-mounted canvas vast enough to strain the eyes with its entirety. Tinted light from the blown-glass rose danced on the surface of the Mammoth's hull, and I smiled. The unique machinery was truly the crucial heirloom which sustained the Rose tribe through generations. Familiar as I was with the Mammoth, I didn't linger by the central altar in the Archives.

Canvas after canvas passed before my eyes. Eventually they told of the Tribal Wars. The Low Hills were torn apart by war for nearly seven decades, if you considered the Early Wars and the Later Wars. The Later Wars were the most recent canvasses, and they were the ones I focused on. The paint depicted stories I knew, and the detailed pictures were created by an especially gifted hand. The vivid face of a titan wolf peered back at my jacket. Menacing yellow eyes were surrounded by strokes of fur done in shades of gray paint. I remembered the tales Flin had told me as a girl.

"I wish things could be like they were," I told him.

Flin shook his head and made a whistling sound, exhaling through what remained of his face.

"You don't want that, you know," he grumbled thoughtfully. "Just because things are bad now, doesn't mean they weren't bad then. Look at what the Tribal Wars did, Melodie. I got lucky, they'd tell me. Ha! A lucky man might've ended up the whole way dead!"

Flin smiled at his own dark humor. By the gleam in his remaining eye, I gathered the old man was nearly sober that morning, which was risky from time to time.

The Tribal Wars ended in a series of abrupt ceasefires when I was a child. The unwritten truces hadn't come to pass because any real kind of peace negotiations took place, but because there was a new threat leaving no room for fighting among the tribes. The Slavers sent by the Jurisdiction were the only thing anyone in the Low Hills cared about when the soldiers started showing up. They raided the tribes annually, without fail and without mercy. The Jurisdiction would've been wise to use conflict among the tribes against our forces. The Nobility could've easily gotten us to aid in our own destruction. Instead, they viewed us as a singular savage people at a time when we were bitterly divided. A maddening irony existed that an attacking enemy eased the grievances among the tribes. Grudges were fading as every man and woman and child in the Low Hills faced down the Jurisdiction. I spent my adolescent Rounds wondering if the tribes might unite to fight back against our obvious foe. Despite the apparent cessation of hostilities, I always concluded unity remained no more than a nice thought. Certain bloodstains ran too deep to wash away. I frowned to myself, and I added up numbers in my head for the hundredth time as I considered how much force could actually prevail.

"The world seemed easier to understand in the Tribal Wars," I said out loud, trying to keep my expression neutral as I looked at Flin.

"War is never simple, Melodie. Nothing is simple, if you study it closely enough. Nobody knew who we could trust, or who'd be fighting who from one week to the next one. We lost a lot of fighters back then, perhaps even more than we lose now. At times, we'd be shooting at our own friends, our own family members. The tribes of the Low Hills were a closer sort of group before the Later Wars fucked it all up. I dearly miss the lull in violence when I was young, when we'd come together for trading and festivals. The best times in my memories. I remember a woman, the Begonia tribe I think she was–" I shot him a look. Mischief played over his marred face before he continued. "We were mostly respectful for a few Rounds, the tribes were. Not entirely peaceful, mind you, but the hooligan bandits and skirmishers when I was a boy never toppled the apple cart."

His face formed an edged expression. I was reminded Flin wasn't some senile retiree overcome by nostalgia. He was the Felbane of the West, the Long-Eyed Hawk, the Unseen Ending, a practiced killer of the highest order. When he became a Lieutenant, Flin nearly brought the Low Hills to its knees before his thirtieth Sun. Only his gruesome injuries had prevented him from becoming Generale, an honor he'd essentially handed to my father in the Rounds to come. When Flin shook his head, the gesture was more than a cursory rejection of trivial detail. He was reminding me that life doesn't always go the way you want it to go.

"Cracks and slights got magnified, Mel. Little by little, we turned on each other. Disagreements and animosities became persistent enmity, and where a battle faded another began. Just because the Rose tribe has always made better weapons than the other tribes didn't make the Tribal Wars any easier. The other tribes have always claimed many more families among their ranks. We lost too many people when our ancestors captured the Mammoth. The sacrifice was noble, but we face the pressures of that cost. We were consistently outnumbered. The Jurisdiction is no different, in that regard. A woodcutter's axe or a fishing knife tied to a stick is just as deadly as a rifle if you happen to get the wrong end of it. And don't get me started on the titan wolves. I ask the Guards that no one ever has to see monsters of the sort again." He seated himself in a wooden chair, a pensive look on what remained of his face. "In the Suns now, the challenges we face are different, I'll give you that. We need better EMP charges, Mel. We need artillery cannons, but the bigger problem is making enough shells to load 'em."

"The Mammoth is running full tilt. They're barely pausing for shift changes. She's at capacity, Confidant. We've gotta pray it's enough."

Flin nodded. "Oh, I'm praying," he chuckled. "Prayers are all we've got when it's time to reload."

The saying was ancient, and I smiled. Flin grew grim and spoke quietly. "Last I'd heard, the other tribes in the Low Hills fared even worse than us last Round." He faced me down, suddenly full of energy. "Shouldn't you be cleaning your pistols? Get your clips loaded. We're gonna get hit by sundown, girlie. I can feel it in my bones."

I scowled. "I'm twenty-three and I'm a Lieutenant, now. I don't think you're allowed to call me 'girlie' anymore."

Flin let out a cough. "I'll be callin' you 'girlie' til the Sun I die. As luck would have it, this may be the one. And it's your first fight as your father's Lieutenant, so don't screw it up."

I nodded and tightly controlled my emotions before giving him a salute. I took my leave of the long-house.

The Generale was responsible for appointing four Lieutenants. Each officer took charge of a company consisting of approximately a quarter of the tribe's gunfighters. With every gun accounted for, we had a hundred-and-seven armed women and men serving as regulars in our tribal brigade. Close to a hundred more members of the tribe didn't normally train to fight, but each could shoulder and fire a gun if need arose, down to the last hunched crone and half-grown youth. Three Lieutenants and a slim majority of the gunfighters were men, but women filled our ranks just as eagerly. They had a saying, of course.

"You don't use your pecker to pull a trigger."

The Rose tribe had no dearth of well-worn sayings.

The guns and ammunition which became the hallmark of the Rose were created in the Mammoth. The Mammoth was a high-tech superstructure designed to walk on enormous mechanical legs. After the machine was captured by the Rose, our people buried the entirety of her hull under a rocky hill, leaving only the hatch at the top exposed. The Mammoth made stolen Jurisdiction technology our own. Her interior contained a laboratory, a blast furnace, a forge and a machine shop along with a miniature fusion reactor perpetually delivering a powerful electrical voltage. The production capabilities of the Mammoth enabled us to have precisely crafted firearms at a time when the other tribes of the Low Hills held only bows, muskets and melee weapons.

At the foot of the hill where the Mammoth was installed, a series of cranks driven by horses, oxen, or teams of people combined with wood burning steam turbines in order to charge a bank of crude external batteries. The setup supplied the Mammoth with additional power. Buried pipes were installed for intake and exhaust of air and water. We consistently collected any scrap metal we could find, and recycled nearly every shred within the bowels of the Mammoth. The furnace and forge were always hot. The sound of grinding and hammering echoed through the ends of the air pipes until long past the witching Mark each night.

I greeted the men and women congregating outside the Mammoth's hatch with a solemn nod. The tribe was a close-knit bunch. Many of us were literally family. I counted nearly a score of my cousins among those who might lose their lives in our fight. As for my closest friends, I'd known Corwin and Trenz since I was old enough to remember things. When they became teenagers and started making out all the time, I was eventually asked to be the Maid of Honor in a wedding. Jerro and Verekas were related to me somehow, but none of us could ever clarify exactly what to call our family ties. Second or third cousins? How many times removed? The confusion was hilarious, once.

I thought back to when I was a girl. I remembered the festivals the Rose tribe would host. The celebrations in recent Rounds and Moons were rushed and subdued. The loss of fundamental joys took a toll on the tribe. The childhood I wished could exist for our children was derailed when the Jurisdiction began raiding us. My mother was gone because of their cruelty, and I wasn't alone in losing a parent. There were precious few who of us who didn't see a relation either buried or taken. We mourned our losses and our hearts hardened as we became war veterans before our time. Our fingers wouldn't hesitate when they found themselves at the triggers.

The gunfighters of the Rose were readying themselves for battle, and I did likewise. A bench by the Mammoth's hatch was known as the "loading bench." I stood at the end by the tabled rows of bullets fitting the extended-barrel semi-automatic pistols. I touched my fingers to the rounds, nearly unchanged from the 9 millimeter ammunition in existence for centuries. The bullets rested in padded racks which were easy to access but prevented loose ammo from rolling across the lacquered wooden table top. Distinct bullet types were placed in neat rows on racks further down the table. As I began pushing rounds against the spring mechanisms of my clips, Confidant Terche threw open the Mammoth's hatch with a confirming shout. She clambered through the entrance with another rack of freshly made ammunition strapped to her back and placed the ordnance on the loading table.

{~}

My father stood by the Council long-house talking to Bonder. Bonder was the most experienced of his Lieutenants. Bonder had seen his Suns of combat like Confidant Flin, but he was a reserved man who seldom socialized with anyone save for his surly wife. At my father's other arm was another of Generale Oakes' Lieutenants. Lieutenant Drak was a handsome and fearsome gunfighter. Drak displayed cropped black hair parting perfectly down the center of his head with no trace of a cow-lick. His dark eyes and strong chin were enough of a spectacle for the artists to favor him for their paintings. His armor jacket was crafted with more attention to style and detail than any other and beneath the outer layer he placed a combination of worked suedes, tooled leathers and alpaca wool. I pulled away my eyes and stashed my loaded clips in straps along my belt. I checked the cinches on my jacket. The panels of metal and synthetic fiber sewn into the woven tactical fabric rippled at the touch. When I was ready for battle, I approached the Generale.

Sampsen Oakes wasn't the tallest gunfighter in the tribe, but he was close. He was at least five inches taller than me and his shoulders were broad. Instead of the enveloping trench-coat style armor customary for most of our gunfighters, he wore a fitted suit of true plate armor. The panels were created with care specifically for the Generale and the contoured breastplate was emblazoned with an abstraction of our Rose insignia worked into a medallion of pale aluminum gracing the darker synthetic fiber and carbon-steel. In the crook of his left arm he held a helm to protect his face. A combat knife nearly the length of a man's forearm was sheathed securely at his hip. Resting on the ground at his right side lay Faithful. He liked to joke about how Faithful was my step-mom. Faithful happened to be a multi-barreled, chain-fed, electrically operated minigun. Few gunfighters possessed the strength to carry or fire her accurately by hand, but my dad could call himself one of them. I knew Faithful's sister Honorable was mounted on stationary pivot covering the rear gate behind the Mammoth's hatch. Faithful's ammo chain draped across the Generale's right shoulder in a venerable trail of linked bullets. The deadly accessory glinted in the sun as Sampsen shifted his stance. He nodded gravely in response to Lieutenant Bonder before he looked in my direction.

"Lieutenant Oakes reporting, sir," I said smartly and gave him a salute.

"At ease, gunfighter," he replied. I knew he was trying to remain as objective as possible but I could see how proud he was as he scrutinized me. Sampsen's eyes lingered on the Lieutenant's insignia at my shoulder for a moment. He let a bare smile creep onto his face. Although I spent a great deal of my time with Confidant Flin my father and I shared the painful closeness of losing my mother. She was taken from us in one of the first raids by the Jurisdiction Slavers when I was barely out of diapers. My father often made clear to me I was the best reminder of her that he could ever ask for. His duty as the Generale kept him busy with many tasks, and yet he always found time for his curiously fierce daughter. When one of his Lieutenants retired during the previous season he'd promoted me without hesitation. I knew the gunfighter Verana, who was several Rounds my senior, believed the promotion should've gone to her, and perhaps she was right. Instead, the honor went to me, and a few probably grumbled about how this was because of my family ties. The Generale made his decision, however, and my deepest sympathy went to any who vexed him over it. I consoled myself by winning every shooting competition the tribe could concoct, and my father's unwavering confidence was the rest of the assurance I needed. I'd do my duties as I knew I could. I attempted to assume command with an unburdened mind. Nothing was uncommon about a Generale playing favorites with Lieutenants. I believed myself to be more competent than others who'd been given the title in the past. More importantly, I was determined to meet the confidence of the Generale himself. My father's words drew me from my thoughts.

"Steady, sturdy, savvy?" he said, extending his hand in the customary ready-check.

"Steady, sturdy, savvy," I replied, grasping his armored forearm. I could tell he was mentally preparing for the fighting which was coming for the Rose. The trio of tenets we uttered were the flowing cadence of an ancient prayer, and they'd been with the tribe as far back as anyone could remember. The words surged through gritted teeth, but we found levity in them, too. No one knew if the phrase was supposed to be a question or a response, and it became both. The quintessential Rosean saying was a reminder, a constant admonishment to every gunfighter who wanted to live up to that title.

The wait before the battle was difficult. I knew I'd rather be shooting than wondering what lay ahead.

{~}

Our military records indicate how battle positions were assumed two Marks before Sun-down. We heard the sentries sound warning on their goat-horns as their blowing coursers galloped hard in our direction. The Generale shouted to his Lieutenants, and each of us shouted to our gunfighters. We took vantage points behind the cover of stone fortifications. Bunkers and long-houses gave us superior cover compared to the fields and gentle valleys stretching around the eastern flank of Sylviarg beyond the Mammoth's Hill. In the trenches on the western flank, the rest of the tribe gathered livestock and supplies and prepared for evacuation towards the forest to the west. The Slaver raids had grown stronger every Sun.

My father stood on a wall, exposed to the developing scene. He opened the visor of his helm and lit a cigarillo, striking a match against his gauntlet. A pair of thoughtful drags filled the air around his face with gray haze as he watched the Swarm float across the sky towards his home. The rumble of motorbike engines hailed the arrival of the Regiment. I listened to ambient noises as they rose in volume, and I tried to gauge how serious the Jurisdiction was about our destruction this time around.

When the Jurisdiction Slaver raids began, the Regiment operated covertly, stealing anyone they could snatch from fields or woods before sentries noticed their presence. My mother had been among the first to vanish. We'd nearly gone to war with a neighboring tribe over the disappearances. Only my father's careful judgement allowed the truth to surface to prevent bloodshed. The next Round, when the Slavers tried to kidnap our people, the Rose gunfighters were waiting. That second raid was the only fight where our gunfighters ever defeated a raiding party without casualties. For one hopeful Sun, we didn't lose a single soul as a Jurisdiction Slave.

But the Jurisdiction wasn't about to back down. Nearly two decades passed. Negotiating with an enemy who hid in far cities and high towers was impossible when that enemy was inaccessible and indifferent to the carnage on either side. The Regiment Slavers began waging war, dragging away our wounded amid the fury of firefights. The number of Slaves they gained from the attacks seemed too paltry to justify the losses they took to the raiding parties. The Rose gunfighters fought to the death, avoiding capture by any means necessary, and yet the senseless raids still came. The toll of the repeated attacks, over and over, Round after Round, became an insurmountable burden. I remain uncertain of many facts in life, but I've known my entire life about the Jurisdiction taste for blood. Each raid left us increasingly vulnerable. We knew the current trend couldn't last forever. Whenever the raids hit, we packed supply wagons and readied the tribe for retreat.

The Swarm cloud developing in the distant sky would needle our gunfighters, but the drones could be disabled en-masse with Electro-Magnetic Pulse charges. Specialized payloads were lobbed high in the sky with ballista-style launchers. EMPs were effective against electrical systems, but if the detonations were too close to the Mammoth, we ran the risk of damaging our own equipment.

The darkly clad riders of the Regiment poured over our grazing lands and crops in undulating columns. The guttural patter of engines grew in our ears as the machines spread across the horizon. The loyal Jurisdiction soldiers of the Regiment were genetically altered males, brimming with muscle and designed for combat from the womb. The human war machines stood at least a head taller than even the tallest tribesmen of the Rose, and their bodies were so packed with flesh that they weighed at least twice what our folk would weigh. The Regiment were bloated and grotesque distortions of humanity to my eyes. The enemy soldiers dabbled at further enhancing themselves with potent chemical cocktails and drastic experimental bionics. The Jurisdiction issued synthetic-fiber body armor inside canvas uniforms, and oversized helmets for their oversized skulls. Retrieving and reusing materials after raids had improved the armor of our gunfighters, but as its former owners could attest, the stuff wasn't making anybody invincible. The Regiment traveled on armored motorbikes with wide, knobby tires to match the unseemly bulk and carried high-caliber automatic assault rifles slung over their shoulders along with an assortment of whatever other weapons amused them. When the fighting was thick, they'd throw anyone they could take over their shoulders with ease, as if we were no more than pillaged sacks of grain.

We watched the Regiment advance on our position. The vehicles tore the earth, spraying dirt and kicking dust. The riders cranked throttles in boredom and impatience for the fight. They seemed to take great amusement in smearing crops to crushed bits as they moved in a swerving line. Generale Oakes had seen enough.

"Fire at will!" he roared before tossing away his cigarillo and slamming shut the visor on his helm. He'd barely hoisted Faithful to his hip when I heard a familiar crack of gunpowder from over my left shoulder. I glanced towards Flin lying prone on the edge of a long-house wall. He worked the bolt of his rifle and winked intensely. A puff of gun-smoke fled the breach of the weapon along with the shell casing. I turned back to the enemy and drew my pistols.

High above the field, Flin's bullet lanced through the computerized guts of a Swarm drone and the unit fell from the sky, spiraling downward hopelessly from the ranks of its peers, a dismal signal of imminent destruction.

What followed was a cacophony of gunfire drowning away all rational thought. I focused on aligning the bouncing sights in my hands and straightening the pathways of the bullets they offered. The nose of each pistol coughed in turn, and I kept grips couched and receivers in line with my targets as the machined steel pushed against my arms like a pair of sweaty pistons. The jumping slides ate through the weight of ammunition hungrily, and I reloaded without blinking.

As we opened fire, the front lines of the Regiment halted their advance. I could find no cohesion to their formation as they dove behind their motorbikes or raced to the fringes of the fields. Wooden fences splintered as the riders crashed through Sylviarg's perimeter with the chassis bars of their machines.

A full layer of Swarm drones was decimated by gunfire, and they fell from the sky above the field in a scattered sheet. Despite the gouging losses, the virulent cloud of killer drones seemed undiminished. The Swarm rushed to advance and I felt the Jurisdiction forces return fire. Regiment rifles pounded the stone bunkers protecting our shooters. A few of the enemy soldiers lobbed grenades at us from impossible distances. We shouted and took cover where we could, but grenade explosions and automatic gunfire shook the long-houses. Shrapnel and chips of stone flew in every direction. I glanced around through the smoke of burnt earth and spent powder and saw blood seeping through armor coats. The sound of wounded voices flooded the background when the hammering of weapons reached a lull. Visibility was becoming poor, even in full Sun-light. We regrouped and shouted maneuvers in the oppressive din.

A pair of fallen fighters were dragged back by their comrades in arms, and a couple more lay among the strewn stone. I felt the bullets of the Swarm drones strike me on the shoulders in several places, but my pauldrons held firm. I cried in defiance and shot the purveyors in the air above. One bullet after another, just as you've practiced, I reminded myself. Aim where they'll be, not where they are.

My shots gave away my position to a Regiment soldier, and rifle rounds slammed against my chest armor, knocking me to the ground. I grunted in pain and managed to look over at my father. The man hadn't taken cover. He was unloading Faithful at whoever he deemed most worthy of a timely demise. He leveled the rotating barrels at the soldier who'd shot me and a stream of gunfire bowled the man over. Bullets sparked and pinged against the Generale's plate armor, and he staggered but remained standing. I think the sight of him unafraid gave our gunfighters hope. I surged to my feet and ejected my emptied clips, taking cover as I tried to conquer the dizziness I felt and the pain in my chest. The Generale roared an order. His ammo chain was almost gone. A gunfighter ran to attach more ammunition and gave a triumphant call to his commander before the enemy got him. The remaining Rose gunfighters rallied and renewed their aggression. As if in a distant world, I heard the twang of EMP ballistas and I knew their charges had been lobbed aloft.

The battle turned in our favor for a handful of drawn-out minutes. I rotated through targets and Regiment soldiers behind the frames of their bikes. I darted back and forth behind the trenches and stone walls and chose my angles. The scant steel fairings of the motorbikes were tenuous protection. An arm, a leg, or an eye socket at a time, I went after them as rapidly as possible without wasting ammunition. When the EMP blasts detonated, the horde of Swarm drones was wiped clean from the sky. The immobilized bodies of the death machines rained down on us from above as petty post-mortem revenge. Despite the physical size of the Regiment soldiers, the Rose gunfighters were tenacious and deadly, and our cover was sturdier and more extensive. We spread and flanked effectively enough to drive the Regiment back and cause greater casualties. Just as I began to allow myself hope for victory, a lone Quint appeared at the edge of the trees.

I'd never seen one of the Jurisdiction war machines with my own eyes. Mounted scouts who rode long-range sorties from a neighboring tribe had spoken in hushed rumors of the Jurisdiction's extravagant power. The Quint stood four times taller than any man, a robotic frame striding with callous indifference on hydraulic legs armored with hardened steel. The arms consisted of wide-caliber artillery cannons which dwarfed any armament the Rose tribe manufactured using the Mammoth. My father saw the Quint just as I did. His eyebrows furrowed inside his helm as he released his grip on Faithful's trigger, letting her spin to a stop.

He called his Lieutenants in his booming voice.

"Unearth the Mammoth! Withdraw to the City of Old!"

The command was the final order the Generale would ever give. The Quint opened fire on his position and the artillery shells shattered him like the wrath of the Guards. His breastplate was torn open and he fell, shrouded in metal and smoke and blood. I heard myself screaming. For a moment the battle around me was a scene painted carefully on canvas by a skilled Recordkeeper, and I was staring at the surface as the paint blurred and ran. The image of my father's fallen body burned through me in an instant which echoed in slow motion. I returned to myself with a sensation like a wild animal sank its claws in my gut.

"Pull back! Get to the Wilds! GO!" I heard myself yelling. Was that even my voice anymore? I stayed behind to be sure the flanks withdrew. The Quint spotted me and gunned for me and I dove to the earth. The artillery rounds crushed the stone above me, flinging earth and rock in every direction. A boulder-like chunk rolled over my back and nearly broke my neck, but I shrugged from under the obstacle, tearing the edge of my coat. I knew Sylviarg was falling apart and I lunged for the protection of another damaged stone wall. The artillery fire followed me and I motioned to my gunfighters with desperate hand signals. We abandoned the battle-torn site in a trained pattern, pulling the wounded along with us. I saw gunfighters refuse assistance and remain behind, reloading their weapons in defiance of the Jurisdiction. We honored their valor with words and silent nods as we retreated to the main trench. I saw tears begin mixing with the dirt and dust on our faces, painting them in blackened streaks along with the grim claret of drying blood.

As we passed the Mammoth, she lurched from the earth around her with a pervasive rumble. I saw her girth surge from the face of the hillside she was installed in centuries before. Her folded legs shook free of the earth encasing her and she stepped boldly in the open air. Her appearance was vaguely reminiscent of the prehistoric creature she'd been named for, with two corroded steel tusks ornamenting her head below two panels of grimy bulletproof glass. I assumed there was a Technician in the driver's seat, but I'd never seen the cockpit or the controls. No one had used the forward piece of her in centuries. The rest of her round body held the machinery and equipment which was vitally precious to the Rose tribe. I could see the ports and connections along her sides where the piping and cables were attached. Freed from those constraints, her body breathed wisps of steam in the fading dusk. Until the moment the machine arose, the only reason I'd ever known what the Mammoth looked like from the outside was the canvas in the Recordkeeper's long-house. I thought about the venerable Archive I was visiting that very same morning, ages ago. There was much we'd leave behind in this place. Only our survival mattered now.

I was impressed that the Mammoth retained the capacity to walk after the Rounds of dormancy she'd endured. I gave a silent prayer of thanks to the Guards and another to the Technicians with the foresight to prepare for this event. Blotches of algae and clumps of earth covered the metal body of the Mammoth, but she was beautiful.

As I watched her reclaim her former glory, my gratitude towards her fate became short-lived. The Quint's artillery cannons pierced the Mammoth's back leg with a spray of stinging hits. The entire hull groaned as she stumbled, and for a moment I thought the structure might topple, crashing the Rose tribe's hopes and dreams for the future.

The Quint's armaments were distracted, to our salvation, before they could pierce the Mammoth's vitals. The minigun Honorable ate up her ammo chain and spilled bullets at the advancing war machine in an unbroken torrent. My cousin held down the trigger and shouted every taunt, curse, and obscenity our colorful language could offer. The minigun seemed to hold the advancing Quint at bay for a precious supply of seconds, plastering the robot with dents and sparks and preventing the guns from targeting correctly. A Technician hastily pulled a welding mask down over his face and leapt to make repairs where the Mammoth was hit. To my relief, the Mammoth paced forward, favoring her damaged leg with a limp.

{~}

We moved through the enveloping night as swiftly as the looming Mammoth would allow. I don't know what became of my cousin who took up Honorable. I don't know what became of my father or the Quint which was the death of him. As our march began I pledged in my heart to make the sacrifices of the Sun have meaning. The Technicians made repairs to the Mammoth multiple times and she walked easy now. The thud of her footfalls and the whine of her hydraulics became the rallying guide points for what remained of the displaced Rose tribe. We kept nervous watches and vented our mounting grief with bursts of gunfire in the dark towards the Regiment motorbikes who were foolish enough to pursue us beyond the shelter of the trees.

Confidant Flin joined the fleeing tribe, but he threatened to stay behind and cover us over and over. His limp, he told me. He would only slow us down, he told me. His time had come and gone, he told me. I told him he was full of crap and I wasn't letting him off-duty yet. We were at the rear of the column, but I wouldn't let him fall behind from there. Even as the Mammoth drifted away from us I couldn't stand the thought of losing both my father and my closest friend. I refused to let him stop and gave him direct orders as if he were under my command, half-carrying him in spite of the wounds to his dignity.

"Steady, sturdy, savvy," I said over and over, and the look on Flin's face turned to concern. "Steady, sturdy, savvy."

Clusters of ambitious Regiment soldiers and stray Swarm drones harried us throughout the night, but the countless trees of the forest worked to our advantage and our gunfighters shot them down or drove them off with few additional casualties on our side. The losses we'd already taken in the earlier battle were grave enough. Only about half of the hundred and seven gunfighters who'd begun the fight remained with us in exile. Bonder, Drak and I stood, but my father's fourth Lieutenant had fallen along with Sylviarg and his Generale. We redistributed ammunition and assisted with medical attention wherever we could. Gunfighters discarded pieces of their armor as the night passed and they grew weary from the trek. By dawn, most of the children rode on someone's back and their traumatized sobs were fading to dazed silence. Exhaustion crept over us, but we couldn't stop moving, not yet. The elderly who struggled with traveling volunteered to stay behind as scouts when they felt as though they couldn't continue. We embraced them and handed them guns knowing they went to their deaths.

We traveled vigorously, but the pace couldn't be maintained indefinitely. Around noon the next Sun we stopped at a level clearing in the forest sheltered by the jutting rock face of a ridge we'd taken to following. While the tribe ate and rested, the six remaining Confidants and the three remaining Lieutenants met with each other. The entire tribe kept an eye on us as we formed a loose group. They knew a Generale must be named. The Confidants conferred softly with one another at first, and as the acting Lieutenants we gave them their privacy. Confidant Terche donned her ceremonial stole and spoke for the Council.

"Who among you wishes to be Generale?"

The gravity of the question was like a vein of pure white quartz in a slab of dark granite. The faces of the Confidants showed that they awaited what would happen next. As I was about to speak, Drak cut me off.

"The position of Generale should go to me."

I looked at him with clenched teeth. I'd considered this moment, and apparently so had he. I scowled and returned his gaze with narrowed eyes. He seized the opportunity and spoke to the assembled tribe in a velvet baritone infused with force.

"Melodie wants you to believe the title of Generale should be hers because she's Sampsen's daughter. But she's too young, still too much of a girl. Dozens among us have seen more fighting than her. We can't follow inexperience at a time like this." He gave me a devious look. "Good kisser, though." My face flushed with red. A few of Drak's friends snickered, but I wasn't about to let his tactics go unanswered. I remained expressionless and let an expectant silence develop before I spoke.

"Drak talks to the Rose as if the question is answered. That's because he's all talk."

I unbuckled my holsters and then my armor coat, letting the gear fall in a heap at my feet as I fixed my hazel eyes on Lieutenant Drak. Free of the weight, I felt empowered and I stood tall and straight. My pale undershirt was damp and nearly transparent with sweat and Drak's twitched with the hint of a frown. I let my tightly curled hair out of its utilitarian warrior's tail and the bristle swelled to a mane which framed my dusky face.

"Get the pistols."

Flin limped towards us and avoided my gaze as he held the ornate wooden case. Inside the case were the ceremonial dueling pistols. Each of the flintlock heirlooms had been loaded with a single shot by my father's own hands. The Confidant opened the box and Drak and I chose pistols. I twirled mine to feel the weight and then turned to face away from Drak. I felt his rear end bump unapologetically against mine.

"Twenty paces each. Wait for the signal," Flin instructed us. Our backs separated and all eyes counted the steps. When we arrived at our places, a moment dragged past us before I heard the cough of Flin's rifle.

I rotated my body in a practiced motion. I closed my eyes and depressed the trigger. Drak was in the process of turning and leveling his weapon, but he roared in pain and dropped his gun. The crude shot from my dueling pistol severed the pinky from his right hand. I hoped the watching tribe would know my intent. I didn't want to kill Drak. I didn't even want to wound him. He was part of the tribe, just as I was, and we were gonna need him.

Lieutenant Drak, however, failed to see any sort of charity or wisdom in my actions. He yelled obscenities which seemed to emphasize my gender and then charged at me. I feigned surprise for a split second as he rushed forward. The single-minded gleam in his eye told me that he'd taken the bait. Drak believed he was going to tackle and overpower me. As he closed in on me, I juked away from his outspread arms, whirling out to my left and and smashing the butt of my dueling pistol against the back of his skull. He fell gracelessly in an unconscious heap, his handsome face covered in dirt. I calmly stepped over his body towards where his pistol landed and picked up the dropped weapon. I wiped the blood and bits of severed pinky from the ornate grip using the edge of my undershirt. Looking up at the crowd, I walked to where Lieutenant Bonder stood watching. I held the pistol for the stoic man to take. He gave me a lingering glare and then shook his head back and forth.

Confidant Flin cleared his throat and I looked at him. He saluted, coming to attention. "Generale!" he declared. One by one, the other members of the tribe followed suit. I returned their salute, my face flushed with emotion as they each shouted the word at me. I put every ounce of strength and confidence I could find in my voice.

"Steady! Sturdy! Savvy!" The words rang over the assembled spectators and they began to holler and cheer in response. The Rose tribe wouldn't be defeated this Sun. In a calmer tone, I brought the gathering to a close.

"At ease, children of the Rose. At ease."

{~}

We rested for what remained of the afternoon, but we knew we needed to keep moving. Our scouts located the remnants of an ancient highway. Maps indicated the route would be suitable so we followed where our distant forebears had blazed a trail. The cracked concrete was heaved and uneven, but the wide path made for easier going than the open Wilds, especially for the Mammoth. The road bed cut through the forested hills and saved us many Suns worth of coaxing the Mammoth using guide ropes and oxen.

I felt as if the dark woods held eyes, and I wasn't alone among my people. These were foreign lands to us. We pressed on with collective determination, moving from dawn until dusk without significant respite. Talk turned to the future among the grumbling and weeping, but the Rose tribe was sturdy. The Mammoth stepped forward in mechanical rhythm and the Rose stepped along with her.

No one knew what we'd find when reached exile. The Confidants agreed that the roadway would lead us directly to the City of Old.

There were rumors of titan wolves retreating from the Tribal Wars and taking refuge in the High Hills surrounding the City. If any of their kind had survived, this was said to be their domain. These tales captured the tribe's imagination and set us on edge. Gunfighters jumped at shadows. Guns were drawn followed by apologies and reholstering. Suns passed without seeing any Jurisdiction forces, but our stretched nerves hadn't relaxed yet.

The High Hills rose and fell around us and the quarter-Moon passed us by. The roadway curved sinuously in the wooded terrain. The path was often obscured by erosion or plant life, but the road was broad and easy to trace. We were forced to engage in a substantial detour lasting most of a Sun when the road brought us to a tunnel entrance in the side of a mountain. The tunnel was collapsed, but I marveled at the boldness of digging through such a vast quantity of rock. The scale of the tunnel dwarfed anything I'd ever seen among the ancient ruins I'd come across in the Low Hills.

At the outskirts, the destination didn't disappoint. The Mammoth lurched to a stop at the crest of a hill, and we saw the City of Old. Steel beams clung to deteriorating glass and concrete, jutting towards the clouds, the bony remnants of formidable towers. The dizzying heights made my heart leap with awe at their quantity and scale. My mind was reeling as I attempted to fathom the number of people who might've once called the City home. In and among the valleys of the High Hills, there were rivers running past the City of Old. Two separate tributaries joined at a point near the heart of the City. Ground once meticulously paved with concrete or asphalt now cracked and crumbled as nature reclaimed her rights. The twisted remains of impressive suspension bridges spanned the rivers at different intervals near the horizons. I took note of the bridges which retained their outward shape but I didn't trust them. I doubted they'd be passable by laden wagons or the Mammoth herself.

I called for scouts to move ahead and investigate. The rivers were wide and stubbornly set, and we needed space to maneuver their banks as well as shallow spots to cross them. Horses were dispatched with the scouts to speed their task.

I didn't want to be caught vulnerable in unfamiliar territory. Generations had passed since anyone from the Rose tribe had investigated these lands thoroughly, and what was said about them in the Recordkeeper's long-house wasn't particularly enlightening. Considering the current security issues, I was beginning to see how the City presented a defensible position. The rivers were a natural advantage. The steep terrain of the High Hills only added to the effectiveness of the location. Here the Rose tribe could build a fort that was far superior to the relinquished tribal seat. Here the

Jurisdiction might not bother to come after us. For the first time since the death of my father, I allowed hope to brighten my heart.

The scouts argued over the best place to ford the river when they returned. I rebuffed their clamor and ordered each of them to tell me what they'd observed in careful detail. The Confidants listened to the reports as they were issued and a decision was made. The scouts mentioned no signs of people or bears in the area, and I was thankful. The Sun was drawing to an end, and we'd spend the night outside the City proper. We made camp, and when the moon became visible we heard the new neighbors for the first time.

The howls filled the night sky. They were resonant notes, strange to my ears, and lower in pitch than any timber wolf pack. I lunged from my bedroll to find Flin had already done the same. We looked at each other in the falling darkness. He gave a solemn nod and spoke to me in a hushed voice, his drowsiness erased by his anxiety.

"Titan wolves, to be sure. I'll warn the sentries, but I doubt they'll need to hear it from me. Reassurances would probably be better but I've got none to give."

"Will the titan wolves attack us?"

Flin shrugged and shook his head. "I suppose if they're hungry enough, like any other beast. Let's hope there's plenty of game around here, and they don't think us worth the effort."

"What if we've entered their territory? Would that be enough to provoke them?"

Flin stroked his chin and frowned. I knew he was considering his advice carefully. He thought back on what he knew of the giant wolves and their behavior.

"Titan wolves are smart, Mel. Too smart. Makes them extra dangerous, but it could work in our favor. I don't know if they're as smart as people, but I've seen them do things that would put the brightest trained dogs to shame. Fire isn't likely to deter them. I think we'd better maintain watches and prepare for the worst. If we're lucky those demon wolves will view us as a needless risk. If they know the smell of gunpowder, they'll know to stay away."

Flin and I listened in silence to the titan wolf pack in the distance. Eventually the eerie howls tapered off. The old man's face nodded gravely to me as his hand found my shoulder.

"Steady, sturdy. Savvy, girlie?"

I made sure the sentry rotations were taking place and I requested extra eyes. I don't know if this particular command was truly necessary. The howling ceased but the sound rang in my ears. Sleep would be difficult to come by. I laid in my bedroll, and with dire need and determination I found what I sought.

Chapter 3
Rahn tells of: "The Slave Pens and the Pit"

"Depression sank its teeth in me a few times. My blood decorated the fallen snow." -the Frost Swordsman

Everything was always so Guard-damn cold when I was a boy. My earliest memories hurt with the numbness of it.

I've seen the unvarnished brutality of human desperation first hand, having lived my entire youth in the Slave Pens. And yet I don't think any of the horrors were as bad as the cold. Why we even called them the Slave Pens, I don't know for sure. We weren't even Slaves. Perhaps once we were Chosen and snatched by the Regiment, taken from the Pens, we became Slaves. In those Suns we were like clueless, caged mice forced to exist in idleness until we either vanished or perished in captivity.

And so it went. We were left with garbage, scrap, and debris with which to construct our lives. Even in the fiercest winters we weren't given additional supplies. We burned what we could in the carcasses of steel drums and ate what we could from crude pots placed above them. The Guards knew there was never enough of anything. The Jurisdiction didn't care about suffering. We were livestock of meager value to them. Even in the dark Suns engulfing the planet, humans never exactly became an endangered species. We're a sustainable, disposable, tactical resource.

My scattered impressions of my childhood seem to materialize from emptiness. There isn't a place filled with faces or memories or warmth, only the Guard-damn cold. I don't recall my parents. I don't recall how I arrived at the Slave Pens. There I was, in a makeshift shack in the snow, holding only a thin blanket and a name. From my first Sun, the gangs were perpetually waiting for me outside. They gathered in groups for the sole purpose of teaching lessons in violence. Fighting became like breathing to me, and the gangs tried to claim me as their own. So bereft was my life of real affection that I thought a piece of my heart might've frozen to death during the bleak deference of my childhood. I was utterly powerless against the weight of the world I was placed in. Strength was crude currency, but in the Pens, the gangs bartered with it incessantly.

In my teenage Rounds, I lost count of how many fingers and toes I severed from my fellow prisoners in acts of mercy. Feet, hands, and entire limbs followed on the worst Suns. Infection almost always raged behind. The medical service I took to providing granted me a modicum of independence from the savage whims of the gangs. There were Slaves who pleaded with me to make the cuts, while others whimpered fearfully, unable to fully convince themselves of the necessity.

I had a sharp blade, a prized treasure. I remember the Sun I found the knife among the scrap and rubble dumped out in the snow. The segment of steel bar was about the length of my forearm, hammered flat along most of its length, making a blade. The round end served as the handle, and I kept the grip tightly wrapped with a decent rag. I don't know what my makeshift cutting tool had been in a previous life. A piece of a machine, I suppose. The knife was good steel, or at least good enough for my purposes. I cleaned and sharpened and honed the edge constantly on a set of stones I'd chosen for the task.

When I reached adulthood, the Slaves in the Pens began calling me a word which loosely translates to "The Good Way Out." I was notorious among the Slave Pens for my services. I settled disputes and kept the peace. I made crude attempts at helping the sick and the wounded. There are places in this world where the person who gets called 'doctor' isn't a person who has special knowledge or compassion. A 'doctor' is someone with the stomach to get ugly things done. Few of the babies born in the Slave Pens survived, but I'd watch as they entered our cruel world, coaxing and cutting cords and doing what I could. Along with these babies, frightened children of varying ages were thrown in the Pens to join us. The population declined, but we persisted.

Whenever rations were delivered, the Slaves awaited the moment the gate would open. Wooden crates packed with burlap sacks were left for us inside the fence. Chaos inevitably ensued when the Regiment backed away. The Regiment was Guard-damn cold, and the Pens were Guard-damn cold, and so we became Guard-damn cold ourselves. The gangs fought with each other as they tried to hoard the dried roots and grains. Bland as the fare was, the staples were the only source of food we had. The Jurisdiction added fresh fruit to the crates occasionally, but never enough. I think they planned the scarcity in order to incite us. The Regiment watched and laughed from behind the fence, amused by desperate calculations of how badly we needed sustenance.

I discovered if I rushed in with my blade drawn, the crowd of thin Slaves would hesitate and then defer, usually making the process go smoothly and equitably. Now and then a gang leader grew bold and brandished a makeshift weapon at me. I'd barter with the ambitious leader as we circled, trying to talk them down by offering a slightly larger share of the gains. Most of the time deals could be reached. Anyone who'd been around a while and had a lick of sense knew better than to fight me. I was a formidable opponent and a valuable ally, and I tried to be reasonable in my negotiations. From time to time I was tested. Blood dripped on the snow before things were settled. I tried not to kill my opponents, but fighting to survive is messy business. I stitched back together many of the wounds caused by my own knife. I tried to preserve lives in a place where life is cheap. I tell myself this was the case. Trying and succeeding are two different things.

The sense of community among the Slaves of the Pens was nearly as bleak and bereft as the existence we led. The Slaves congregated in gangs. Few of us attempted to protect the weak. More often than not, those unable to protect themselves or join up with a gang ended up colder and hungrier than the rest. Occasionally a Slave would take their own life, but death visited us often enough without open invitation. The gangs interacted briskly, almost compulsively, and the bits of joy we found were fleeting cover for the biting void we felt beneath the surface. Trust became a rare commodity, driven to become half-animal as we were. Even if you could establish a connection, a friendship perhaps, people were bound to disappear. When people banded together, they did so out of a clear, short-term interest, such as the mob assenting to my equitable distribution of the food.

I know it was nothing short of a miracle that I survived in the Pens. The bruises and harsh lessons of my early childhood are like a primal blur to me. Everything was always so Guard-damn cold. I could never be exactly sure of my own age, but most agreed I'd seen at least twenty winters, making me among the oldest of the Slaves. It was a double miracle that I was never Chosen. The Chosen were shipped from of the Slave Pens, seized by the Regiment and whisked away to Guard knows where for Guard knows what purpose. We were the Jurisdiction's livestock, to do with as they pleased, and the Regiment saw to the task with a perfunctory smile.

Even if my actions went without notice, the fact that I wasn't Chosen gave me status among the Slaves of the Pens. Those who wished to remain in the Pens thought I was the key to salvation, and associating with me might prevent them from being Chosen. Others thought being Chosen amounted to salvation. I tended to agree with the second group. The pain and the hopelessness of the Slave Pens will haunt me until the end of my Suns. I bore witness to tragedy throughout my early life which lurks at the edges of my dreams. I've done things I may never admit to another soul. I've defeated suffering in the darkest way possible, when there was no other way. I've dispensed the crude, unvarnished justice existing among people. Death and I are uneasy friends.
{~}

There was no way I was gonna end up an aging retiree in the Slave Pens. I may've dodged my fate for a while, but I was Chosen in the usual way of things. One Sun, the Regiment came for me, just like they came for everyone else.

The siren blared and the gates of the Slave pen slid open to admit the Regiment. People cowered and hid, but this seemed to have no bearing on who was Chosen. Others knelt and prayed or whispered to themselves. The Regiment soldiers filed in and towered over us. I'd seen a handful of attempts at resistance, but attacking the Regiment was futile. They were created and fed in order to fight. I don't think I ever saw them injured in a struggle. Wiry Slaves would rush at them with blades and clubs and the brutes of the Regiment would cuff them away like misbehaving animals, cracking bones with the careless force of casual blows. The best outcome for such attempts at rebellion was that you might earn yourself a quick death if you could get a soldier to draw his belt knife. Only an officer by the gate had a gun. They didn't need firearms to deal with the likes of us.

On this particular Sun, they came for me. The soldier leading the column pointed down at me from his superior height. My heart began to race, but I nodded bravely and stepped forward. I was determined not to show weakness in front of the Slaves and the Regiment watching around me. Let them see I hadn't been defeated and fearful. The cold steel of my knife burned against the skin of my leg where the weapon was tucked inside my britches. I considered leaving the blade behind, but the eyes of the Regiment watched me intently from above. After sharing a few wordless touches of goodbye, I marched from the Slave Pens in the company of the Regiment without looking back.

I spent many Marks staring wistfully at the gate when I was inside the Pens, and the industrial metal fencing slid open before me. I caught a glimpse of the Jurisdiction compound before a bag was pulled over my head. I felt callous hands grabbing my arms and legs. I was loaded in a military helicopter where I lay on the rubberized traction floor, feeling like a vulnerable piece of cargo.

I was careful not to reveal the handle of my blade tucked inside my belt or the protruding edge running down the outside of my leg under my scratchy trousers. When the aircraft ceased the nauseating lurching, I was hoisted and placed unceremoniously on an industrially carpeted floor. I was hauled to my feet. The bag on my head was removed. I found myself blinking at a bulbous face with beady eyes. His jaw and his neck were unseemingly wide and his breath rushed in and out through flattened nostrils. His ears reminded me of a fungus I saw once. He stood in front of a block of metal which turned out to be a Regiment-sized desk. He looked down at me his appearance struck me as different from the other Regiment soldiers. I tried not to stare at the icon on his uniform, but I guessed he was an officer.

The room was surrounded by off-white walls and the sturdy carpet was a shade of blue-gray. The only electric lights I'd ever seen until then were at a distance outside the Pens at night. The arrays in the ceiling were bright and disorienting to a person who'd never experienced anything like them before. The Regiment office was a cavernous expanse of space to my eyes, and the clean uniformity of the carpet seemed to stretch forever. Two huge door frames, one to each side of the desk, perforated the spacious office along with a lone window. The window covered most of a wall but had blinds drawn over metal bars.

"Well son-of-a-gun, it's Knife, in the flesh." The officer's voice was gruff as he spoke to me in the spacious barracks office room. I said nothing, but I tilted my head back and I looked him in the face.

"Knife's got his knife, even! Give it over, Knife. You had your chance for sport on the chopper that brought you here." The Regiment officer laughed, and tense as, I was I instinctively stepped back from his looming frame. "The boys here are a bit dim," he said, pointing with a thumb to the right.

"But they like you, Knife. Don't we, boys?"

There were general calls of assent from the open door near the officer's right shoulder where I could see several Regiment soldiers eating and drinking at tables in the adjacent room. Without their concealing armor, the flesh of their chests and necks was visibly warped and swollen. I didn't feel particularly sympathetic. I think I saw the looks in the Regiment's eyes. They were always so Guard-damn cold.

"You're the one-and-only Knife, Knife. Highest kill count in the Pens by my reckoning. Though there's been a few disputes over who gets credit for what, heh."

My head felt dizzy. Nausea and fury battled with the self-preserving calm inside of me.

"Highest... highest what?" I managed to say.

The Regiment officer's eyes grew wide but he smiled dismissively.

"Now don't you never-mind none'a that, Knife. Call me Captain Crowbar, just like the boys do. This company used to have what they call a 'discipline problem' before I showed up. Ain't that right, boys?" More calls of general assent met my ears. "I was commissioned to break a few things in order to fix a few things, and you can bet I did my job. Like I said, Knife, you'll have to leave your knife on the floor here for me, now there's a good Knife. We don't want you givin' any of us boys a splinter!"

There was raucous laughter. I reluctantly drew my crude blade from where I'd tucked the apparent namesake inside my trousers and placed the knife on the rug. Apparently I passed for a fine joke. "Here," the Captain said, shoving a Regiment-sized steel machete from the edge of his desk onto the floor in front of me. The implement landed on the carpet with metallic thwack and slid to a stop as the blunt edge touched my foot.

I reached for the machete. The tool was too large to be used as it was intended by a normally sized human. My fingers scraped the rough carpet as I grasped the handle. I could fit both hands next to each other on the wrapped grip. The steel was heavy. The blade was nearly the length of my leg and the weight meant I'd need both arms to move the weapon with any kind of speed. The leading edge of the machete was dull and the entirety of the exposed steel was covered in a rubber coating which made the edge nearly harmless as well as adding weight. Captain Crowbar didn't leave me with time to consider.

"I'm gonna learn ya how to fight, Knife. See the boys here and I, we got money ridin' on you this time around. A fortnight, that's what we got to train you. Well, more like most of a Moon at this point. That's what the Nobs and the Devs agreed to give me so I can get you in the right shape."

The Captain stood and picked up his crowbar, which had been leaning against the wall behind him. The thing was almost as long as I was tall, and nearly as thick as my wrist. One end curved in a hook and the other end bent at a slight angle. The entire bar was cast of iron. He swung it casually in his big hands, pausing to inspect the tip with a frown. The crowbar was painted black, but the paint was chipped away in more places than the finish remained. A brownish combination of rust and what appeared to be dried blood prevailed as the coloration. I clutched the strange machete with a tremble and set my feet. Captain Crowbar burst out laughing.

"Relax a bit, Knife! Wouldn't wanna kill you before you made us rich! Ain't that right, boys?" More agreement from the doorway. "Here, take a load off." The Captain threw a chair at me. I ducked and the chair landed upright behind me with four legs skittering to a stop. Riotous laughter from the Captain and his men. I imagine I was their evening's entertainment. "Nice dodge, Knife! No wonder you're a killer!" He chuckled to himself, but he brought me a gun rack to use as a table and filled a tray with food and ale. It was the first time I'd ever eaten fine food and drink. I have no doubts about my hatred for the Captain and the Regiment., but with my stomach contented by meat and my mind warmed with ale, I thanked my luck as the Sun began to wane. Once the meal was over, the Captain wasn't going to waste any time beginning my training.

"Alright, you dirty limb-nipper. On your feet!" The Captain roared at me with a grin on his face as he brandished his crowbar. He gave me shoes to replace my makeshift moccasins and a set of ill-tailored clothing which was obviously a poorly shrunken version of the Regiment issue 'casuals'. The odd clothing consisted of a t-shirt and trousers with a rope to hold them up. I changed clothes briskly and then picked up the machete with both hands. I placed my newly shod feet carefully on the coarse carpet.

True to his word, Captain Crowbar of the Regiment didn't exactly kill me. I grew to respect his ability to hurt me very precisely. He didn't want any cracked bones or serious bruises affecting my performance later on. He shouted useless commands at me.

"Come on, hit me!" he'd yell. I attacked ferociously, but he stopped the machete with his iron crowbar no matter how I stabbed or slashed at him. In my time with the Captain, I don't think I ever landed a single blow.

"Don't get hit!" would be the next call. I'd inevitably get smacked or tossed around. I remember the way that the iron of the Captain's crowbar felt. Guard-damn cold on the skin, always cold. After consuming weak ale from a tall pitcher, I dared to ask the Captain a question.

"Who am I gonna fight?"

The Captain leaned back in his desk chair and looked down his nose at me. "Shouldn't matter, Knife, should it?" He'd been rolling a cigarette the size of a dead rat. He lit it with a puff and toyed with the smouldering bundle.

"If you must know, it's more of a 'what' than a 'who', Knife." He gave a genuine shrug. "The usual monsters, chances are. Oversized creatures the Devs make in their battle labs. A fine contest, you know. The Nobility sets a handsome prize. We bring fightin' Slaves and the Devisors get their screw-loose scientists to invent new monsters. We get the humans, they get the animals. Poetic, if you think about it too hard. Might be a bird this time, big enough to peck and claw you down." He made hand gestures to illustrate his point. I found them both uninformative and unamusing. "Maybe a beetle the size of a boulder. Maybe a juicy green carnivorous plant, if you're lucky. They haven't done killer vegetables in a while. I should teach you how to use ranch dressing!!" The Captain was overcome by a beefy belly laugh. I tried to digest the strange words and concepts. My bereft existence caused much difficulty with the new information. I could tell the Captain was brighter than his 'boys,' and he caught on to my cluelessness.

"Now don't you be givin' yourself anxiety, Knife. You learn to fight with Captain Crowbar here, and you'll be ready for whatever shit comes your way. Right boys?" The boys agreed wholeheartedly, of course.

Over the next few Suns, Captain Crowbar trained me Sun in and Sun out. My body was always sore. I ate quantities of food which seemed unthinkable in the Pens, and I put on a layer of muscle over my bones. When I became too exhausted for one task, the Captain found another way to train me. In the evening, when it was clear my body needed rest, he'd make me play cards with him after sitting me in a plush chair which was comically oversized for my human legs.

"The mind's a weapon, Knife, don't you forget it. The boys here are fearsome fighters, and they certainly got heart. But it's about as good as they got to follow orders. Times they can barely do that, dim as they are. Eh, boys?" The usual affirmative came murmuring from the other room. Captain Crowbar laughed. "You got soul, Knife. Even if you might be dead meat soon. And you're not half bad at cards, neither. Playin' with the boys loses its luster after the first few hunnert rounds'a victory, heh."

His words sounded like a compliment, but I said almost nothing to my tutor. I hadn't forgotten what happened to Slaves who resisted the Regiment.

The Sun before the fight I was allowed to rest. I ate and sat in the corner trying to make sense of my current turn of fate. I felt queasy from the rich food combined with the constant exertions of my body, and I hoped I wasn't becoming ill. My only chance at survival was to win whatever battle I ended up in. The Captain assured me winning would grant me a life I'd always wanted while losing would be the end for me. In truth the whole idea didn't bother me much at the time. Between an unknown fight and living in the Slave Pens I might've willingly ventured down the path I was on. I was Chosen and I was out of the Pens. For the first time in my life, I felt as if I had a true hold on the handle of my own destiny.
{~}

As evening came in the barracks, I fell asleep effortlessly. My dreams became vivid and surreal. I dreamt of a creature I'd never seen before. A cold magnetism made my weakened steps less and less effective. I couldn't seem to run away from the creature, so I turned and stared at it. The Slave Pens were dark, but green eyes peered at me through the steel fence. When a pair of eyelids closed over the green glow, a gargantuan jagged body floated above me and blocked the moon and the stars. The night-shadow cast by the creature fell across the Pens and surrounded me with a blackness so dark I felt like I was alone in the universe. I was paralyzed, frozen in place. There was a sound like rushing water and cracking ice. I couldn't move. I couldn't breathe. I couldn't-

"Wake up, Knife! You're having a dream! This is the Sun. Need any coffee? What do you want for breakfast?"

When I didn't respond immediately, the Captain seized my head in his hand as if he were inspecting a piece of fruit. His alien face came perilously close to mine. Beady eyes and stinky breath assailed me. The feeling of my head being trapped in his palm made me tense my neck and bare my teeth at him. He frowned as if he wished there were a different melon in the pile. The details of his wide mouth were vivid at his uncomfortable proximity.

"How about some drugs, Knife? No, never-mind, forget the drugs. They might be checking this time. Let's just say your predecessor was a Guard-damn light-weight."

I rose mechanically and I ate what was offered. The panic of my dream must've shown on my face, and Captain Crowbar studied me suspiciously. When I finished my food he led me to the waiting helicopter.

They didn't bother to put a bag on my head, so I looked out the window. The Jurisdiction military compound wasn't much to look at, but when the helicopter lifted away from the ground my heart leapt. The forest viewed from above was more beautiful to me than anything I'd ever seen before. We traveled through the mountains, but the ride was damnably short. Flakes of snow swirled in the chill breeze. As we descended to land, I saw an amphitheater of seats filling with people around a circular stone pit with a wooden door at each end. Butterflies rose inside me. This was where I'd fight for my life. The helicopter landed behind a copse of trees away from the pit and the amphitheater. I was immediately ushered inside a locker room where steel cabinets and racks lined the stone walls. Electric lighting illuminated the cold chamber. Captain Crowbar cleared his throat and handed me a set of clothing.

"Put this on," he said, and I did as I was told, even though I was already shivering. The clothes were a tailored shirt and trousers of sturdy blue fabric, and they fit nearly perfectly. They were finer than any clothes I'd ever worn. There were boots to go with them, real boots of supple leather with rubber soles and when I laced them up I was directed to a wall of armor.

"Now, you can pick something," the Captain cautioned, "but don't carry a lot of weight. These things," he bonked a metal breastplate, "are usually more trouble than they're worth. Could get you killed just as easily as saving you. And you're quick on your feet, Knife. Work that angle instead of getting hit."

I reached out and touched a fur-lined steel bracer sitting on a shelf. My fingers ran over the machined hinges and latches which closed around the wearer's forearm. Captain Crowbar raised an eyebrow.

"Mightn't hurt."

I pulled the bracer from the shelf and donned the metal band with a sense of wonder. With the bracer on my left forearm as my sole piece of armor, I was led to the second armory room. There were countless weapons scattered in disarray, but this time I wasn't given a choice in the matter. Captain Crowbar smartly handed me a Regiment machete, a standard-issue tool. The blade was identical to the weapon I'd practiced with, except this one was razor sharp and slightly lighter because it lacked a rubber coating.

"Don't you be gettin' any ideas," the Captain laughed. "I'd hate to have to waste you before the fight. Twenty-some Rounds of bein' in the Pens, Knife, and for what? Not to mention my excellent training."

I gritted my teeth and measured the deadly heft of the item in my hands. I stretched my legs and shoulders. There was a roar of excitement from the crowd and the gate slid up.

I rushed forward through the entry with my machete held high. The fighting pit and the hard clay floor welcomed me with their contained clarity. Wisps of straw decorated the earthen floor, but they'd been swept to the shadows of the corners. I forced myself to settle. I was alone, the first combatant to take the floor. The crowd reacted with mixed emotion. A few cheered me on. Others were ambivalent, and some greeted my presence with jeering. After a few seconds, I heard the ungainly voices of the Captain and his boys.

"There's our Knife!"

"Knifey-knife!"

"Time'a get sump'n kilt real good, Knife!"

Across the floor from me, a twitching nose forced its way under the rising gate. Front legs followed as the huge rat struggled with her size in the entryway I'd trotted through with ease. The air was Guard-damn cold up here, and I don't think the rat liked the weather any more than I did. Her screeches of displeasure echoed in the stone pit as she was prodded beyond the doorway so that her keepers could close the gate behind her, barely missing her tail as it thrashed at them. I frowned when the crowd cheered, resolving first to hate the spectators and then to ignore them.

The nervous rat began to do her business on the clay floor of the pit, leaving a steaming, slippery rat pile while she kept a wary eye on me. I imagine she was the humble progeny of a trash heap, enlarged beyond all sanity. Creatures like her weren't made to last. Their distorted physiologies meant that they were a temporary curiosity. Regardless of the outcome of the battle, she'd live only a few Suns at most before her body began to fail her. I imagine countless Marks of careful science were funneled into her existence, but I'm glad my mind was free of complex concerns when I faced her down in the pit. She was strange to me as many things were strange to me after I left the Slave Pens. Her yellowed teeth and black eyes hovered above my head as I sized her up.

I considered rushing in to strike her directly in the face, but it was clear to me that her teeth and claws would embrace me. If she wounded me badly, the fight would be over. Her size gave her the ability to move with incredible speed and force. I dodged the first lunge, but on the second she slammed into me with her hindquarters as she turned and I was knocked back. I sprang back to my feet with a burst of panic and adrenaline. The hairs on her body were stiff and they'd scratched my skin, tearing the side of my new shirt.

Horrid rat feces was building up on the clay floor as the rat expelled the contents of her bowels. She advanced towards me, but I'd recovered. When she dashed at me again, I dodged with purpose and slashed at the incoming paws. On her first pass I scored only a glancing blow against her claws which didn't seem to hurt her, but the attack deflected her from lacerating me with her lurching probe. When the second bite came, I roared and swung my machete at the rodent's face. The blade bit. The sensation of sharp metal severing living tissue wasn't a foreign feeling to me, but I gritted my teeth as the machete struck the huge rat. For a split second, I felt panic. My weapon caught awkwardly in the tough fur and skin. If I held on to the machete, the rat would kill me easily.

Before I could retreat, weaponless and fearful, my thoughts refocused and the passage of time began to blur and slow. I felt a sense of energetic calm flow through my entire body. I re-shifted my grip on the machete and gave the weapon a purposeful twist. The edge tore through the rat's right front leg, severing the limb entirely. The clawed appendage oozed blue goo and spasmed mechanically on the ground as life left the flesh. The rat squealed hideous, unholy sounds of displeasure and leapt at me.

I would've died in the lunge if not for the odd battle trance I was experiencing. Only my crisp, controlled reactions saved me. She was a mad flurry of teeth and tail. I dove underneath her and past her, narrowly missing the abundance of fresh rat piles she'd left for me. When we reversed ourselves in the pit, she began to poop on the other side of the floor. I knew time was against me. I had a limited number of chances to attack before a missed step would leave me smeared and vulnerable. I moved forward in a cautious stance. She lunged again, but her movements were defensive instead of aggressive and she was becoming sluggish. Her body began to lack the explosive unpredictability which made her dangerous. I realized I was no longer diving out of the way. Instead I took advantage and hacked purposefully at her neck, deflecting each attack with measured swings and leaving cuts behind. The sounds the rat made were desperate and miserable. When she brought her body close to me, I dared a thrust and shoved the tip of the machete through her left eye. The injury resulted in a bone-chilling squeal. My resolve wavered as pity began to melt my heart. The animal hadn't been given a choice in the fight, but neither had I. She brought her teeth in my direction and her filthy rat claws raked my ankle as I barely managed to wrench myself beyond her reach.

Blue insides were peeking through the mixed browns of the rat's fur. The blood was beginning to drip between the rat piles she'd already left around the floor. The crowd went from excited about the action to subdued and slightly disappointed. I began to hear boos and jeers. I doubted that I was the favorite in the fight, and the smell of rat shit was becoming oppressive. The Captain's voice rang loud and clear from the seats.

"Get 'er Knife! She's right where you want 'er!"

When the rat was battered and broken and nearly helpless, I ended the fight. I leapt and forced the machete through the back of her head. Her skin and her skull were tough, but I was determined to grant her this mercy. I made sure to be thorough. Grunt, stab in. Pull free, grunt, stab in. Pull free, grunt, stab in. Pull free.

A portion of the crowd was leaving their seats. Others were showering me with colorful language. Out of the corner of my eye, I saw Captain Crowbar gleefully accepting a satchel of coins from a man in a red robe. I wasn't focused on any of this, not in any real way. I wasn't even focused on the red blood seeping from my own injuries, or my battered machete coated in blue. I gripped the black tape on the handle with white knuckles and blistered palms and I stepped away from the rat's corpse. A silence fell over the remaining crowd. I was catching my breath as I realized they were looking up at the sky. I joined them almost instinctively.

At the time, I didn't have a word for what I saw. Like I said, I had less difficulty accepting things in those Suns because I'd seen so little of the world. I knew the creature was the one from my dream. Cold, that was what I felt. I knew the creature's blood was coursing Guard-damn cold, just like everything else, and my understanding grew. In retrospect, perhaps I learned the word I was missing as I listened to the shrieking spectators.

"Was this part of the show?"

"Is that a dragon?"

"Oh dear Guards, it's a fucking dragon!"

"Every direction is a good direction- every direction except down." -the Sky Dancer

The wind shifted outside the window, and I silently wished I could join it.

I sat alone in my father's expansive circular office. The chair I was seated in matched one other chair placed in the office for guests. They were both made of a medium-gray slate. The same manufactured stone was featured throughout the room. My chair was plushly padded and comfortable enough, though I doubted many of the occupants experienced much in the way of relaxation. In front of me stood my father's imposing granite desk. Behind the desk was another chair, my father's chair, and the seat dwarfed the one I was sitting in. I stared ahead at the intricate patterns of flames stitched in the upholstery.

The office was free of clutter or decoration to an extreme degree except for the wide stone sconces on the walls which were fashioned from the gray slate. The room would've felt a lot like a medieval cave with the drab gray stone except for six tall windows each consisting of a rectangular pane, stretching from floor to ceiling. The alternation of clear window and stone wall around the perimeter of the office made it an austere concoction of occult past and modern future.

The plateau of granite desk in front of me was marred by only two features. A holographic projector for my father's computer. His title engraved and covered with gold leaf.

Executor Magnare Fleuro.

An elegant, exotic name for a man matching the description. I'd always sort of admired him for his sophistication. My heart ached to forget the rest of him.

The windowed office around me offered a top floor view of the surrounding city. To sit in this place was to be like a hawk perched above the forest. I knew from experience with my father the windows were custom laser-cut from bullet-proof military-grade plexiglass. Precisely coordinated patrol drones whizzed past the windows from time to time, their rotors panning the air as they banked and climbed. The ever-present electronic eyes of the Swarm deliberately averted their gaze from the interior of my father's office. If this isn't power, I remember thinking, then what is?

I heard a clank as the office door unbolted and began to swing inward. Like nearly everything in the office, the door was made of stone. I turned to look towards the sound, unable to stop myself. When the panel was open far enough for my father to retain his dignity, he entered the room and pushed the door closed behind him with a muted click.

He spoke a word which signaled the beginning of the end.

"Daughter."

{~}

The memory skews abruptly like someone has jammed a finger on the pause button of a video. The wind has shifted since then. I try to forget, but details hang with me stubbornly.

I'm told daughters are supposed to adore their fathers. For me, this was barely ever the case. I can only peer at him from a distance as though he were a statue placed on a hill. I've always been like a cautious ship, skirting the edges of a bay but never daring the risk of running aground to seek shelter from a storm. When I was playing with dolls I felt affection for him, but the sensation faded quickly from my life as I entered school and his attention became less frequent and more formal. My father is a tall, thin man. He perpetually dons the vestments of his office, a lengthy robe of dark red velvet. He has carefully contained silver hair with a sheen nearly resembling the precious metal which shares the color's name. His eyes are hazel and carry an intensity like a painful magnetism. The person I've just described carries the power of life and death over every man, woman and child in the entire city of Atlantium, plus a few unfortunate souls beyond it, I'm sure.

The practical side of me wants to argue that Atlantium would hardly be a paradise if my father resigned from his high station. Even the title of Executor doesn't pull the strings of the whole damned Jurisdiction. The nature of that kind of power is difficult to contemplate. Executor Fleuro occupies a position of prestige within the Nobility, and he dons their signature red robes with aplomb. The Nobility in turn rules the Jurisdiction. There was something else I was missing back then. It was the kind of something you know is there but you don't know what the something is. The meager facts I manage to learn about the Jurisdiction only seem to fuel my hopelessness, which if not carefully tended with anger decays towards utter despair. The Jurisdiction created my father. As a young man, I imagine he simply fit their twisted desires like a crimson glove. Executor Magnare Fleuro is a cruel man, one who loves power more than he does his own daughter.

The word feels like a stain now, the surname Fleuro. I'm leaving the title out of my life. I've had a hard enough time keeping my first name. I clung to the idea that my mother was the one who decided to call me "A'Rehia" before she died at my birth. Perhaps those hear my tale may realize why I chose the path I did when the wind shifted. To me, there was never any other way.

Even now, when Rounds and distance have opened up a chasm between myself and the city of Atlantium, I can hardly close my eyes without seeing the blood washing over dark stone. And the fires! Fire like the damnation of the Guards, of course there was fire. With my father and the Nobility, there's always fire. They live and breathe it, they call and cast it where they please. Fire mages that they are, they can't live without. The flames rush forth in jets from their hands.

He laughed a horrible sound as the fire blackened their skin. He smiled as they screamed. My closest friends, screaming.

The wind shifted. Thermals swept upward from Atlantium, blowing the smell of ashes and death. Atlantium was a city like any other city, I'd always assumed, but I'd always known she wasn't quite right in the head. 'Justice' at the hands of the Jurisdiction rarely fits the definition. I have to impress this fact upon whomever I can.

I suppose I've been collecting my thoughts to set the scene for myself. But nothing will likely prepare me to recount the details of how my father killed my friends in a heinous public execution.

I've come to the heart of the matter. If my old man thought to frighten me, he failed, or perhaps being afraid was a sensation which no longer mattered to me.

The wind shifted. The pain and the emptiness I felt outweighed my fears and I fled Atlantium. I tried to leave the whole Guard-damned thing behind me. I'll never forget her, the city. The flawless modern architecture of Jurisdiction buildings and tents and slums filling the rest of her could even be beautiful if you knew them like I did. They were the places I'd explored and lived and grown up, nearly independent of my father. My talent as an air mage gave me a unique perspective on the whole, and in my heart I miss the place.

I was a target from birth. I was always too conspicuous as an air mage. I was only sheltered from reality temporarily by the identity of my father. As I've come to understand, my father's name did nothing to protect anyone, not even the people I cared about. Quite the opposite, in fact. Those nearest to me became the victims. The independent mages of Atlantium came to me, they trusted me. He must've known. He wanted to make an example of them, I'm sure. Jurisdiction law states that mages must be registered as Jurisdiction mages when they come of age. 'Registration' amounts to conscription in the Jurisdiction military. Be where they want you to be, kill who they want you to kill. And so instead, my friends were the ones who got killed. Even after the time separating us, the pain of their execution comes back to me, unrestrained by healing.

I began my journey the next morning when the flames of wrongful death were extinguished. I tasted the air of the sky as the pressure zones swirled, echoing my breezy uncertainty about the future. I paused at the outskirts of Atlantium as I left her. There were trees in the abandoned district, one of the few spots left within the fences surrounding the slums. I couldn't say why I favored the place. At the edge of Atlantium, the abandoned district seemed a sort of refuge with the sparse trees and tall grass. When the wind whipped through the chain links at just the right angle, the entire decrepit fence seemed to shudder with the melancholy of the city. The wild air sang to me before flowing past the edge of my former home. The Jurisdiction didn't end with a city fence. Leaving Atlantium wouldn't make me safe. On the contrary, my self imposed exile probably put me in greater danger. The Jurisdiction would no longer see me as the daughter of the Executor. In a few Moons time, instead of celebrating my 18th birth-Sun with joy, I'd become an unregistered mage. I wouldn't be the first runaway they'd hunted. I'd probably be shot to bits by the Swarm, but I pushed the thought away.

I made my peace with the danger. I refused to burn like my friends did. I don't know if my father could've brought himself to do the deed, but I didn't care anymore. Anything was better than being stuck in the city acting pleasant and demure to a monster.

Certain dangers never pass, even if the Rounds have. I speak of history, but the wolf will always remain at the door. If you've pulled these pages from a corpse, then the Jurisdiction be damned. Mages should be allowed to live free. And Guard damn my father, while I'm thinking of him. My death is on his hands.

I suppose it's important to understand that my skill as an air mage is rare. The Jurisdiction wanted me, and those fuckers get what they want. In reality, every mage is unique. People are different and so are the energy patterns they can manipulate. Many in Atlantium called me "the girl who steps through the sky." This is an equitable enough description of me. My friends and I were dancers in my teenage Rounds. The vibrant outfits and streamers we wore made us resplendent works of moving art. We tied brilliant beads of colored glass in our hair and clothing. People would gather from across the city to see us float and flip and twirl with not a wire or a rope to be found anywhere. People knew I was Executor Fleuro's daughter. This was seen as a tacit Jurisdiction acceptance of the underground mage community. I was supposed to be an olive branch. The number of mages in the city of Atlantium grew continually, every Round I can remember there were more who showed up in the markets and taverns and the peripheral farms and hunting camps. If those free-lance mages decided to submit to Jurisdiction "registration," I'm not sure my father would've known what to do with them all. Mage skills could be valuable on the open market. A free mage guild would've enhanced commerce and trade.

How wrong can a girl be? Such a lethal misjudgement of my father's character will never occur on my part ever again. His brutality seems to defy reason, but I believe I know the reasoning he chooses. He believes frightened people can be controlled.

My friends would never have prospered in the military. This much was always clear to me. I'm convinced that if they'd obeyed Jurisdiction protocol and registered as mages, the process would've only concluded in their deaths eventually anyway. Air mages, as sanctioned by the Jurisdiction, are supposed to be in the Squadron. The Squadron is no place for the soft idealism of budding artists. My dancer friends refused to eat the flesh of living creatures in order to fill their bellies. They were of little use as soldiers under the bloody banner of the Jurisdiction.

Few members of the Squadron can match my passion, but each of them are mages. I'm also sure any number of them are just bloodthirsty flyboys who liked the idea of having an anti-grav pack and a gun. Most of the Squadron uses this technology, along with lightweight body armor and a whole array of advanced tactical gear. There's an exception to the Squadron, however. That exception is their leader, Major Zeyus.

His face is plastered on walls across the city. The varying posters are a decoration throughout Atlantium. The propaganda is a feeble attempt to win people around to thinking that the Nobility actually has their best interests at heart. Even as obvious as the publicity stunt is, after a while Zeyus' countenance grows on you in a familiar kind of way. 'The Major' doesn't wear an anti-grav pack like the rest of his Squadron. This is because his distinguishing characteristic is two brilliant white wings which look as if they were a gift from the Guards. In reality, the wings were the product of Rounds of gory experimentation in the bowels of a Jurisdiction laboratory. He carries a sword at his hip and a quiver of javelins instead of an assault rifle. If you can forget what he represents, Major Zeyus is an amazing sight to behold. He seems to capture your glance with his blonde hair and his white wings and his stylized armor. In Atlantium he became a kind of worn-out joke. His name was usually invoked by people who shared too much anguish to continually speak of it directly. Mumbling "Zeyus will take care of it" was a kind of sarcastic acknowledgement that the Jurisdiction would never take care of anything. In the real world, there was no help coming from above. White wings were for military parades. A man like Zeyus didn't spend his time improving the lives of people in the slums.

We thought Zeyus was a show-thing, a toy soldier. I steeled myself and flew away from Atlantium for what I believed was the final time. The air whistled past my cheeks and pulled my blue-black hair. I was listening for Swarm drones and staying below the tops of the trees. I was keen to leave Atlantium behind, and perhaps I became distracted. Unlike the Swarm drones with their electric whining, Zeyus is stealthy. He's nearly silent, in fact. His movements are those of a practiced flyer. The wind shifted and I had only enough time to turn slightly before he tackled me in mid-air, his shoulder crashing into my ribcage. The impact knocked the wind from my lungs. I might've fallen several stories to the ground, but I was caught in the winged man's grip, a pigeon snatched from the air by a falcon's dive.

Zeyus isn't as perfect as his stylized likeness, but he remains a striking sight to behold. The lines on his face and streaks of gray in his wavy blonde hair betray his age. His picturesque jawline is covered by an unshaven haze and his eyes have a tiredness in them. He must've sensed panic from me, because he spoke calmingly and relaxed his hold so he that held only my outer tunic. He spun me to face him directly and held me at arms length. We floated and his wings stretched to each side in calm undulations. He studied me with a measured frown. His speech was terse and his hold on my shirt made me uncomfortable, but he didn't seem cruel or gloating.

"Swarm does the real work," he said without preamble. "The Squadron is mostly for show. Whole thing's not as bad as they say." He seemed to make up his mind about something, and then he began to calmly drag me away.

I screeched and writhed and tried to free myself. I buffeted Zeyus with blasts of air. I shoved and struck him as forcefully as I possibly could. The air flowed around me in a heady gale, but the struggle was no use. Zeyus's grip and his body were like unbreakable iron. A mage can only do so much, and I lost consciousness from the effort.

Next I can recall, my hands and feet were bound to a cot in the Squadron barracks. The ropes were the first test, I'd come to find out. The tests came with other tests built in, and always with more tests right after. I learned to escape and use a gun. I was forced to kill a rabbit with a hunting knife. I learned how to reconfigure computers and sabotage machinery and transport dangerous materials. The tests made me stronger and harsher than I ever wished to be. I caught myself hoping for a swift death a few times, coerced as I was to become a tool of the Jurisdiction.

Death wouldn't come to me during my time as a fledgling in the Squadron. What came were more tests. Strength, skill, cunning, each of these things add value in the eyes of any military unit. There's no bias involved in evaluating a soldier as a tactical instrument. Every now and then, when Major Zeyus believed the Sergeants were out of earshot, he'd speak words of encouragement to me. In retrospect, those words may've been the only which carried me through basic training as a member of the Jurisdiction Squadron. For a while, I couldn't decide whether the Major was truly being kind or simply being practical. In either case, I survived those weeks because of him. I have scars on my body which speak to both failure and success while

being trained by the Jurisdiction military. The scars on my soul may be harder to sort.
{~}

The Squadron barracks is located in the North-East corner of Atlantium. Even so, I didn't see my father after my conscription. Perhaps it was better that way.

What I did see, as my mind strayed towards my father, was Sergeant Nira's fist crashing into my face. The wind had certainly shifted. I knew within the first Suns of training that the combative woman didn't like me. I also knew by the way she looked at Major Zeyus that she was infatuated with her commander. The blood dripped from my nose and down to my mouth as I lashed back at the Sergeant with my own fists. Her practiced footwork evaded me easily, and she laughed as she circled me in the sparring ring. I floated away from the cushioned floor, a subconscious reaction. This earned me a stiff jab to the ribs which winded me, and I settled back to my feet.

"This isn't where you learn to fly away, fancy girl. This is where you learn to fight!" Nira barked at me.

Major Zeyus watched us throw punches at each other with his arms crossed, neutrality placed on his face. I brought up my guard by raising my fists and I tried to protect my bruised face from Nira's flurried attacks. I exhaled fiercely with renewed determination, spattering blood from my mouth on the strips of white tape around my gloves. I waited and looked for an opening. I landed a couple of jabs before Nira ended the fight. As her hook connected with my head, I happened to see Major Zeyus. The expression on his face betrayed the subtlest hint of concern before everything flashed to black.

I came to my senses where I'd fallen. As I drifted back to myself, Major Zeyus' voice calmly informed me that after basic training was over, the training regimens continued for the Squadron whenever there was no other mission. The process I was hoping was only a hellish boot camp was about to become my entire life. My fight with Nira was a turning point as a Squadron initiate, however. I suppose getting my ass kicked was the closest thing I'd ever get to a graduation. I'd earned myself a uniform as well as a patch for my rank, the stripe of a Private. Major Zeyus stood over me in the sparring ring with my new garments draped over one arm. With his other arm, he reached down and offered to help me stand. I accepted and tried to ignore the throbbing pain in my skull.

"You'll train with me now," he said with the matter-of-fact tone acclimated to giving commands and having them obeyed. "You're on your first patrol in the morning. We've only got a few weeks until your first mission assignment, and you're not ready. So become ready, Private Fleuro."

I was given leave to celebrate and recover for the remainder of the evening, but I didn't have the heart for carousing. I changed to my new uniform frowning at the stiffness of the fabric as well the odd smell of chemicals as I zipped up the jumpsuit. The rest of the Squadron didn't seem to share my bleak mood. They made enough trips to the barracks bar to compensate for me nursing a single drink. They slapped me on the back and thanked me for getting them drunk tonight by becoming a Private. My replies were automatic, and I was blandly glad I could bring them joy. A few of my Squad mates tried their luck at making advances on me. Emboldened by the booze and my new status, they made crude remarks or attempted to embrace me awkwardly. I repelled them with sharp words and sharp elbows, but my heart wasn't in my self-defense. Once I would have been indignant and outraged by the treatment, but at the time the harassment seemed like a minor misery compared to the pain of my headache. Major Zeyus made an appearance with his white wings folded behind his back. The Squadron grew hushed at his entrance, but he gave the order to carry on, grabbing a woman who'd been harassing me by the back of her shirt. He sent my tormentor crashing over the bar with a casual toss, much to the amusement of the inebriated Squadron. I kept my head down, awkwardly frustrated at how I'd apparently warranted a protective gesture.

Sergeant Nira glared at me from across the mess hall. Her frown curved farther downward with every drink, and she tossed them back mechanically. She seemed unfazed by the vast quantity of alcohol even as others swayed unsteadily around her or burst into rambunctious singing. She seemed to think Zeyus favored me as a soldier and perhaps as a companion. I had my doubts. The Major was a handsome man, but he was much older than me. I knew he didn't look at me in the suggestive way that some of the Squadron clearly did. I silently wished he would just shack up with Nira to get her off my case.

Technically, fornication was prohibited by Squadron code, but enforcement of this rule was nearly non-existent. The ranks were a balance of male and female members. Mage skills didn't care about your gender or who you fancied.

I thought about what the Squadron would look like, hundreds of us at once. The thought intrigued me until I began to wonder what we'd be fighting. The Swarm was probably more efficient than the Squadron. Using the Swarm didn't place our lives in danger either, if the Jurisdiction even cared about our safety. If the Swarm wasn't able to kill whatever needed killing, then there were other war machines which surely made a more powerful force than flying soldiers. Machines fell in the domain of the Devisors, who held considerably more sway with the Nobility than Major Zeyus. I thought about fighting in the sky, unprotected with nowhere to hide. I was agile, but I knew instinctively if the Squadron ever saw combat, we'd take significant casualties. Burdened as I was by grief over my friends and despair at my conscription, the thought of being killed in action had no space to drag me down any further.

In lieu of other clearly defined duties, the Squadron was tasked with the general policing of Atlantium. We broke up bar fights and domestic disputes. It was almost the kind of work you could feel at peace with most of the time. Dealing with the Nobility and the Devisors was the worst part of the job. The two powerful organizations pushed around the Squadron with total impunity. Their ruthless curfews and complex contraband restrictions made keeping people in line a fool's errand.

The Swarm conducted an obscene amount of surveillance, none of which was shared with the Squadron. From time to time, the Devisors sent us dispatch orders or arrest warrants. Usually they'd just kill a few people and leave us to figure out why. The Coroners for the Squadron could identify the Swarm's victims on sight. They'd pulled spent ammunition from corpses on a daily basis for as many Rounds as anyone could remember. They'd look at the bodies and wonder what evil deed warranted execution. Had this person truly gotten what they deserved? Was this the result of a computer glitch or an itchy trigger finger or a political assassination?

The ugliness all got swept under red robes. The Nobility came through and destroyed the bodies and the records as a part of their regular routine. Enforcer authority trumped whoever else was on the scene no matter where they interjected themselves. When the robes appeared, everything else scattered. You could usually feel the heat before you actually saw the Nobility Enforcers. If anyone resisted, entire blocks of the slums went up in flame. On nights like these, I found ways to avoid duty. I couldn't stomach watching the blazes. The fire ate people's homes along with everything they had. If the citizenry of Atlantium were unlucky, the fires got them, too, or their children.

Getting a silver tooth became a popular trend among the people of Atlantium. They called the false tooth a "final gem." If you had a silver tooth and the Enforcers got you, your loved ones might still find a substantial piece of your body to remember you by.
{~}

"I want to promote you, Fleuro. Give you a commission. Make you an officer. I don't care what the paper pushers call you, or what your rank is. I'm getting you away from that flying circus of a Squadron."

The Major went through his stretches with a coffee mug in his hand, tilting his torso and fanning his wings. He took a sip of his coffee. "Don't get me wrong, Private. There are mages in the group with courage and talent. But even the best of them have become soldiers, through and through. They love their guns and they'll kill without hesitation. Killing isn't the same as being a mage, much as it pains me to admit." He tossed his empty mug toward a cluster of waiting cadets at the edge of the field. The boy who caught the dirty dish held his prize up like a trophy as the others shoved him and tried to grab it. Major Zeyus watched them absently as he rubbed his chin. "Maybe something about the anti-grav pack stunts their growth." He clasped his hands together in anticipation and poised himself to launch. He looked me dead in the eye. "Mages like you and I are meant to exceed the status quo. We'd be wasted in the trenches, Fleuro."

The Major launched upward before I could reply and I followed him, rocketing through the sky in his wake. The winds were shifting. I shouted at his back.

"But sir! Why don't you promote someone with more experience? Why not promote Nira?" My stomach lurched. I wondered if the sensation was from our breakneck change in altitude or from thinking about the things the Major seemed to be saying. I didn't like the idea of being put in charge of soldiers who would never respect me. I was also suspicious about the supposed difference between a mage and a soldier. Zeyus barked a laugh.

"Nira's gonna get exactly what her heart desires. Well, most of it anyway." I couldn't see the Major's face, but I think a sideways grin resided there. "Sergeant Nira is about to become Captain Nira. She's taking over command of the Squadron. The entire unit will be hers."

I was immediately dismayed at the thought of reporting to a Captain Nira indefinitely without Zeyus around to keep things from getting out of hand. "What will you be doing?" I blurted. As soon as the words arrived, I was sure he'd rebuke me for asking prying questions of a superior officer, but he flew and let the silence grate against my thoughts. I studied the fog draping the woods as the trees rushed below us. The mist settled among the hills like a gossamer scarf fallen from the heavens. The rising sun would sweep the delicate veil away and brighten the earth. I wished my heart would take warmth from the morning, but I knew the rays would only reach my skin.

"Forget about Nira and the rest of the Squadron, Fleuro. You and I are mages. That's my intent, at least. We won't be going back to the barracks. Not until our mission is completed." The words prompted no further comment from me, but I longed to ask more questions. We continued our flight.

I pushed at the air around me, forcing myself to keep pace with the Major's wings. I observed the living white feathers and their enormous surface area. In order to lift dense human bones, the wings were inordinately large. I admired them for a while. Zeyus' torso brimmed with added muscle where the wings met his back. His flight was unlike that of a bird. A bird flew by instinct. The Major Zeyus flew by carefully planned thought and technique. His flight was graceful, but there were hints of hesitation where instinct wasn't entirely developed. I knew he possessed a measure of mage skills similar to my own, which he employed to sense and manipulate the air. I wondered how much he used his body compared to his mage energy. The muscles of his back relaxed as Zeyus dove. He tilted from the dive to a glide, skirting the tops of the trees. I followed him, my hands and feet moving subconsciously as I brought the air pressure against my body to slow my descent. I tried to be efficient about flight without causing myself discomfort. I focused on my feet and my hips and my hands. The defiance of gravity was indescribable, and I bathed in the rush. I knew my head would tire and begin to ache, but I pushed at the air and flew on, willing myself to chase Zeyus.

Another Mark of flight and I'd reached my limit. I called breathlessly ahead of me, and as I saw Zeyus' head turn back in acknowledgement, my focus broke. I let out a yell and tumbled towards the earth. I restored my wits and felt the air around me as I attempted to manage the slippery substance. Don't fail now, I prayed silently. I managed to spin and avoid tree branches before I careened in a landing trajectory. I bounced against mud and dead leaves on the forest floor, keeping my limbs pulled in. I hadn't learned to fly without learning to survive a crash landing. I tumbled to a stop, perilously close to a tangle of brambles and a massive tree trunk. Zeyus floated through the trees and joined me. He paced back and forth when his feet touched down, glancing at me as he worked on the details of his frown.

"You have permission to speak freely, Private."

My head throbbed horribly and I'd sustained several bruises and scrapes. I gave an assessment of the situation as honestly as I could muster.

"My head. I don't think I can fly right now." My stomach joined my head in communicating distress. "I need to eat. I can't take pain medication, either. I've tried it and the stuff just makes me nauseous and totally unfocused. Especially on an empty stomach."

Zeyus considered this and nodded. "We'll stop. I'd like to make our current mission clear to you, Private. We have two objectives. The first is to get as far away from Atlantium as possible. The second is to push your limits as a mage."

I groaned. The adrenaline was wearing off, and I hurt everywhere. I curled in a ball where I'd landed. Zeyus began to pull field rations from the pouches at his belt.

"I'm obliged to report that it appears we've achieved both objectives for the moment, Major," I said weakly.

He gave a half-smile and tossed an item from his belt on the dirt in front of me. In the shadowed light of the forest, I thought he was giving me food. I picked up the object. The belt-food was an oddly shaped knife contained in a leather sheath. A metal handle protruded. I drew the blade.

"You know what that is, Private?" Major Zeyus asked me.

"Yessir. I've seen a knife before," I replied. Whatever energy I might've used for conversation I'd drained in the air. The Major pressed me.

"And what about this particular knife is unique, smart-ass?"

I forced myself to study the knife with a sigh. The tool weighed almost nothing, but this was a common feature of the equipment preferred Squadron members. I pinched the grip awkwardly between my thumb and index finger. I found the handle wasn't substantial enough to hold comfortably, even in my slender hand. The blade was wide and flat and smooth, and the shape reminded me of a leaf. The laser-cut gouges in the center of the blade added to the leaf-like impression. I twirled the handle of the knife as the tip dangled towards the earth. A gentle breeze caught the metal, and in an instant I understood.

"I could push this knife around. Make it fly where I wanted it to go, if I practiced," I said with my eyebrows rising. "It would be difficult, but I could probably get the hang of it."

Major Zeyus was wearing a grand smile. The expression was as open and sincere as any I'd ever seen on his face.

"I'm glad to hear it, Fleuro. I believe you understand the concept. The device is called a kite-knife. I tried to use them myself, but the javelins suit me better. I'm not as good as you, Private. I doubt there's anyone alive who is."

My head was cloudy with pain, but I managed to come to the obvious question.

"Where'd you get this, then?"

Zeyus stared at me, but there was no anger or even irritation in his eyes. He took a bite of his granola bar before he answered.

"The real answer to your question is redacted from any reports of past operations. Black-site confidential security protocol." He looked around at the woods I'd landed in. "To follow regulations, I'd have to scan this whole area for electronic surveillance before I even gave you a name." Zeyus shook his head. He seemed to remember the flask at his belt. The wind shifted. The smell of firewhiskey reached my nose.

"I'm tired of secrets, Fleuro. Tired of hanging onto 'em. You would be, too." The Major swirled the whiskey in his flask.

"So I'm not gonna tell you a damn thing. There's a lot of shit I wish I didn't know in the first place."

Chapter 5
Raspho tells of: "The Cat's Witches"

"I used to think animals were fairly dumb creatures. Over the Rounds, I've come to wonder if animals are actually smarter than us. They're certainly smart enough to not waste energy deciding how dumb humans are." -the Sorcerer Prodigy

I awoke to the light of Sun and a ringing headache. My entire body felt damaged as I groaned and blinked in the glare of morning. I looked at the remains of the pyre . An ellipsis of white ash ringed in cinders of darker gray lay in front of me. This was the Born family beach, but the Born family was gone. I was overtaken by a dull heartache. Such a thing couldn't be properly explained, or conveyed by sketching a diagram. I sobbed as grief pounded in my ears. I barely possessed the strength to stand, but sorrow and loss were at full force within me. I wept freely on the sand.

As my blurry gaze drifted away from the waves, I spotted the cat. Our farm had never kept a cat in residence, but I saw them on other farms. The cats kept mice from barns and cabins and curled up on laps in the winter, but I didn't recognize her. She looked like some of the veteran mousers I'd seen. I guessed that the cat wasn't a tom-cat. Her self-assured posture was confident. Her fur was weathered and coarse, and I doubted she was anyone's pampered pet. She could've been a feral stray. She was lean and dangerous looking. Despite her size, the dogs might've barked at her instead of trying to attack, as they'd done with a rattlesnake they found. I resolved to keep my distance from the wild animal. The minor danger of the cat's presence infused me with a sense of alertness I would've otherwise lacked given the circumstances. As I watched her, she stretched and flexed her paws, digging her claws in the sand as she arched her back. She gave a yawn which revealed a mouth of carnivorous needles before she shook a bit of sand from her whiskers. When she spoke to me, I nearly jumped out of my skin.

"Well?" the cat asked.

I blinked stupidly in the morning light, amazement trickling in at the profound event.

"You're talking to me," I said to the animal.

The cat gave a nod. The gesture was a dignified motion of agreement. I think I found the precise control of her furred chin more unsettling than if she'd spoken a reply. I pushed moved my feet, sliding away from her on the sand, and the cat addressed me like a concerned citizen.

"Have you any idea what to do with yourself next?"

I shook my head and returned the cat's gaze. "I'm sorry. Who- what- how are you talking to me?"

The cat laughed at me in response. I felt sick to my stomach. I checked my forehead to see if I was warmer than I should be. Surely the entire morning was part of a fever dream.

"You can call me Charlie, and I might keep you alive, but I doubt you'll make it easy. May I offer advice?"

I stared at the animal sitting on the beach. The sing-song quality of her precise accent was erudite and foreign. Charlie moved her tail in a graceful twitch and lashed the sand in sprays as she awaited my response. The pattern was hypnotic. When I found the words to speak, the cat managed to convey how thoroughly unimpressed with me she was.

"But you're a cat," I said.

She instructed me casually. "Eat food. Drink water. Gather supplies. Pull yourself together, man-boy. I can wait, but the Swarm might not."

At the mention of the Swarm, I stood abruptly. I glared at the cat, this so-called Charlie. She frightened me as she watched my languid motion towards the dunes. She looked at me as if I were a field mouse she'd found but hadn't decided the best way to pounce for her own amusement. The hair stood on the back of my neck, and I kept glancing back at her. I half expected claws to sink through my hamstrings at any second, but the cat never moved. Nevertheless, the crawling feeling persisted. I breathed a relieved sigh when I cleared the dunes and I resolved that I was far from trusting the strange creature even though her advice for the moment was sound. I half hoped she'd disappear once I'd eaten. I found myself ravenously hungry and I filled my stomach without pleasure or neatness. I gathered a pack and loaded the canvas with food when I finished breaking my fast. I exited the cabin briskly. Charlie was standing directly in my path, and I nearly fell over her. If I'm honest, I also nearly wet myself. She made a sound of annoyance.

"For the love of the Guards, you frightened me," I admonished the cat.

"Then perhaps you should be aware of your surroundings," Charlie responded indifferently. "Come with me."

I was attempting to weigh the logic in following her when she sauntered through the door of my grandfather's cabin.

"Hey!" I called after the cat. "What're you doing in there?" I moved after Charlie. I came around the corner of the open door carefully, wondering if I should've retrieved my musket to defend myself. The cat stood on my grandfather's straw-mattress bed, but her gaze was intently focused on the far wall. Light entered the cabin from a window with tied-back curtains. Just below the rafters, a rack made of antlers cradled a wooden quarterstaff. The staff was carved in a cylinder so straight and smooth that the specifications were nearly perfect. Having been shaped from the branch of an ironwood tree and sealed with a sturdy resin, the staff had survived rot and damage for generations. It belonged to my great grandmother, I was told, a ceremonial family heirloom. I gave the cat a wary look.

"What do you want, cat?"

Charlie gave a growl which surprised me, considering her size. "My name is Charlie, not 'cat.' And take the stick. You'll need it."

"For what?" I retorted. "Where are you taking me?"

"Anywhere is safer than this."

I continued to glare at her for a moment and then sighed. "Fine." I moved forward and lifted the staff. I grew dizzy as I touched the wood. The staff induced a subtle euphoria. I held it with both hands and steadied my balance by leaning on the sturdiness. I realized I could feel the entirety of the wooden form, as if the object were a part of me and we were connected seamlessly. The quarterstaff drew and magnified the energy around me. I began to feel nauseated, and I released the staff, letting it fall against the cushioning edge of my grandfather's bed. The spinning sensation went away.

"What was that?" I asked Charlie, who watched me intently.

"The staff is a mage artifact," she said, idly pawing holes in the down comforter on the bed. "Used by mages. How or why, that I can't say. I might know who can. But these are topics of significance and depth. Best we left them for another time." She tentatively touched a paw to the staff. She gave me the cat version of a shrug.

"Not my cup of sheep, human," she said, jumping down from the bed and leaving the cabin.

"It's a cup of- well, whatever."

I looked back at the staff and resolved to touch the surface again. I grasped the middle with my left hand. The strange feeling wasn't as intense. I tried to adjust to the sensation. I decided I could wrap my hands in cloth or tuck the quarterstaff in my pack if the energy became too much to bear.

As I left the cabin, I felt as though I'd opened my eyes to an entirely new side of myself. The quarterstaff honed my senses to the world around me. I could see pulsing color where none had been before. I blinked in astonishment at the changes everywhere. Charlie had an aura of fiery reds and oranges that made her look far larger than she was. The vivid hallucinations made me more curious about her, if this was possible. I resisted the urge to sketch a diagram as I looked around. My pack was filled, and I knew the cat was right. I couldn't stay here. I steeled myself and walked after Charlie for a few steps before I remembered my musket. I decided to grab the gun on my way to the woods. In fact, Charlie was walking directly towards where I dropped the firearm.

When I reached the fence where the musket lay, Charlie whirled to face me. I instinctively grabbed the quarterstaff with both hands. Charlie's aura swelled menacingly.

"The gun isn't coming with us," she said, pressing a paw against the musket's barrel. I released my right hand from the staff and tried to manage my fear.

"Why would I just leave it here?" I pressed her, totally deflated. "It's my best weapon. I just bought it. The musket is– I'll need it. For hunting. To defend myself. That gun is all I have left." I intended to be stubborn. I eyed the cat, but I was afraid of what might happen if she became belligerent. Charlie made a noise which I realized was a snarl. She shook her head.

"Your best weapon isn't this– *thing*," she bit the word with contempt. "I won't watch you die as you fumble with gunpowder and a metal tube when you should be throwing fireballs." I looked at her shining feline eyes, incredulous.

"But I don't– I don't know what you mean," I mewled. "I don't know what I could do from far away. I've never tried to hurt anything with fire. Why would– would it work against the Swarm?"

Charlie hissed mercilessly in response. "You'd better start practicing and find out! As soon as possible, fire mage Rassspho. The stakes of this game are extremely high, and there are lives including your own to be won in the struggle." The way the cat hissed and stretched my name was jarring to me. I wondered for a moment if I'd ever even told her my name, but the animal wasn't done berating me.

"You may think there's only your own poor life to lose. But think about your family. Think of how the same could happen to another family. If you want to keep more like them from dying ,you'd better step up to the challenge pretty Guard–damn soon. Take me, for instance," Charlie paced the length of my shiny new musket. Her lips were pulled back to expose her teeth. This was more than I'd ever heard the cat speak all together. She seemed irritated that she had to give me a lecture.

"I've been shot by a musket before. More times than I care to recount. I'm sure those weapons were similar. Do I look dead to you?"

I wasn't sure how to react for a few seconds. I peered at the cat, looking for scars. I ached to hold my new musket again. Perhaps clutching the gun would be a kind of comfort. Between my heartbreak, exhaustion, fear, and uncertainty over the cat, I cracked. Tears began to flow and I fell to the grass. "Fine," I said, curling in a pile. "Fine, I'll leave it. I'll leave the musket. I'll practice throwing fire. But for now, I just– I just want to lay here." My tears dripped down along the tall blades of grass.

To my suprise, Charlie walked over to me. She purred and brushed a tangle of hair from my face with a delicate swipe of a furry paw. I gave a groan and attempted to push her away, but she purred directly in my ear. Her whiskers tickled my face, and she let the bulk of her weight rest directly on my ribcage. Despite the intrusion into my personal space, I began to feel better. A cat was better than nothing, I told myself. Better than being alone. I thought about her over and over as I attempted to discern whether she actually existed or if I was hallucinating from grief.

"I'm sorry," Charlie said, in a gentler voice which sounded completely out of character. She spoke at the side of my face. "This is a harsh world. I've learned not to mince words, and I haven't spared much thought for anyone's emotions in a while. You've been through a nightmare, fire mage. But this farm- this isn't the end. It'd be much truer to say you're only at the beginning. I've no intention of letting you get too soft or foolish or dead to carry on." I sensed a certain sadness from Charlie that she'd hidden away under her tough posture. She couldn't conceal the melancholy as she purred, a flickering, broken rumble.

"I know too much, Raspho. I know there's too much at stake to just ignore the world. I can't let you or anyone else escape the truth, not anymore. Come now, boy, get up. We need to get to the woods. Don't make me get my claws out."
{~}

During the subsequent Suns, my conduct was regulated at the behest of Charlie the cat. I could describe her as a teacher or a protector or a guide, but I believe anyone who has ever truly known a cat may understand why I shy away from using those words. In a common cat, I'm sure this brand of innate arrogance can be quirky and endearing. In Charlie these qualities manifested as a unique form of torment. I've written down an accounting of our time together because my mother would've wanted it.

Charlie ignored my pleas to look for my brother Jahnny near the vacant farm, insisting we had no choice but to seek safe ground farther away. I objected to this plan vehemently, rife with emotion as I was, I knew I wouldn't survive an encounter with the Swarm. I couldn't imagine how anyone could. I raged at the cat, swinging the quarterstaff in wide arcs, but my own self-loathing was what I raged against. The Swarm was after me, I knew. My family had died because of me.

I discovered Charlie was too agile for me to ever catch or strike her. Whenever the gap closed between us, I took significant damage from her claws. My green canvas clothes became decorated with ragged tears and trickles of my own blood. I sketched a diagram of where she'd slashed me in order to establish a pattern, but there was no predicting her speed or her experience. Charlie taunted me mercilessly if she wanted something. When I showed weakness, she'd attack, forcing me to defend myself and ultimately do whatever she wished of me. She made me practice throwing fire farther and farther every Sun. I learned there were different mental "muscles" I wasn't using. I began to practice with fierce determination. I harnessed escalating amounts of energy. Charlie purred in praise over my progress.

She assigned me clever tasks. I nearly burned down the entire forest several times with my sloppy flame blasts. Charlie was unfazed by the blazes. She kept the flame from spreading by trotting along the fireline on her padded paws. The orange flickers hesitated and extinguished, leaving a pattern of blackened cinders behind. I made my bursts of fire compact and practiced my control. I began to hunt game. We ate bites of flesh from charred small animals along with supplies from my pack. I tried not to study our dinners too carefully as I tore pieces away with my teeth.

Through a fortnight of journeying we saw no evidence of people, at least not living ones. Highways fallen to ruin and ghost towns showed themselves to us from time to time. We nearly stumbled across a row of decayed and collapsed houses I surmised must've been a pleasant place to live in ancient times. We carefully avoided disturbing the ruins and any other signs of civilization. After crossing sets of hills, we saw a cabin which looked as if the structure might be in use as a home, but the windows and doors were barricaded and there were no signs of anyone inside. We avoided the lone cabin just as we had the rest.

There came an evening sitting by a campfire when I studied Charlie. We'd been going on sparse wilderness rations for our entire journey, and yet the cat looked bigger than when I first met her.

"Have you grown since we left the farm?" I asked her, breaking the silence.

She looked at me. I believe she was considering what to say, but I could never be sure what transpired behind her furred features. When she spoke, I sensed her words were an abrupt departure from whatever she was considering.

"I don't grow the way most cats do."

I raised an eyebrow. "You don't?"

Charlie looked at me. I noticed the red-orange of her fur echoed intensely in her eyes. Her irises flowed with flushes of garnet. Cats don't have eyes like that, my thoughts warned me. I'm not sure I've ever felt so unsettled by an animal. I was no longer sure Charlie could be called an animal. She spoke to me and her words tore through my consciousness like a match falling on spilled lamp oil.

"Fire. I grow from fire, Rasss."

I shuddered. I was beginning to feel nauseous again. I wondered if it was caused by the hapless chipmunk I'd eaten earlier. A half-sketched diagram lay abandoned in my lap. My fears rose in me like a wave, and I willed myself to suppress the emotion. My impression of Charlie shifted. Was I her prey? Did she feed on vulnerable fire mages like a mystic leech? I half-heartedly announced that I was attempting to sleep, but the process eluded me. I could see Charlie with my eyes closed, and she stared at me with her glowing oval cat eyes. She needed me, I told myself as I shivered. I was the source of the fire. She wouldn't kill me or abandon me.

Charlie sensed a shift in my opinion of her. For the next few Suns, she was cool and distant, and she led me forward but spoke nothing else in the way of orders or lessons. I continued to idly craft fireballs as we walked. I cradled them and kept them floating above my hands as I felt the heat touch my fingers and clothing and face, and then I extinguished them safely. I learned that I could throw a fireball about as far as I could shoot a musket. I was proud of myself, but the only one to share in my achievement was a lofty, inexplicable cat.

I began to realize we were traveling exclusively to the west. The Suns fell into a predictable rhythm. We traveled and hunted and made camp when Charlie deemed the Wilds around us were safe enough to do so. If Charlie didn't think it was wise to sleep or build a fire, we moved on until we were clear of whatever danger might be lurking.

{~}

The moon receded below the horizon as the morning claimed us. Charlie paused at the edge of a valley. Her tentative stance and the way she twitched her whiskers made me realize we were slowing down for a while. We'd been moving at a rapid pace, so the change was appreciated. I caught my breath and allowed myself to feel my raised heart rate. I drew my staff from my pack and gripped the weapon in my left hand, leaning casually. I began an exercise which was becoming instinctive and created a fireball in the palm of my right hand. The cat interrupted me. The distraction caused the sputtering flame to singe my sleeve before I could extinguish it.

"Not now," Charlie said. "Not here, not yet."

"Why? What?" I asked as I waved away the smoke. I got no response. Instead Charlie crept forward. The way she was crouched made me think she was hunting, but there was a subtle difference about her. She was watching her own tail. This was no hunting stance, I realized. This was how a cat looked if she thought she was going to fight. This was combat, now. I stiffened at the realization and did my best to mimic Charlie's wariness. She gave me a glance, and I think she approved. With one hand resting on the quarterstaff, I surveyed the valley. The details of our environment didn't feel typical. The plants were paler than usual. There were brown patches where foliage had died even in places where the soil seemed damp and fertile. The trees were farther apart, and their spacing less random. In addition, there were unfamiliar flora and insects that I'd never seen before. Curious lizards with leathery wings looked up at me from munching ferns with unseemly gray flowers. Charlie halted her prowling behind the trunk of a leafless tree which was twisted and weathered. The cat spoke to me between furtive assessments of our surroundings.

"None of the choices are the choices you want," she explained in a hissy whisper. "When our route was in question, we could've ventured through the Low Hills and risked the tribes there. But I think this valley is less dangerous. I don't know if the tribes are at war, but even if they aren't, they don't usually take kindly to outsiders these days."

"What is this place?" I whispered back. If a cat could frown, Charlie was frowning.

"This valley belongs to the False Priesthood. If we get lucky, we might pass through undisturbed. But if the Priesthood has a patrol in this area, we'll have to fight."

My heart sank. "A patrol? You mean soldiers?"

Charlie wriggled her whiskers anxiously. "I suppose." She settled on her haunches. "The False Priesthood were Jurisdiction mages until they broke from the Jurisdiction. The Guards only know what leverage they have against the Nobility. Now they live here, according to rules of their own. The False Priesthood are scientists, though it doesn't feel right calling them that. Their patrols are unconventional, to say the least."

I furrowed my brow. I think I would've kept asking questions, but Charlie's head jerked to her left. A moment later, I heard the sounds. Intermittent clinks of metal against metal and the rustling thuds of footsteps traveled to us in the cool air of the forest. "A patrol," I whispered, and my heart skipped a beat. I ducked, peering past a tree along with Charlie. At first glance, I thought my eyes were deceiving me.

A band of human skeletons was marching directly up the hill at us, elbow-to-elbow in lockstep. The skeletons remained upright and in perfect unison in spite of their mismatched body pieces and awkward joints. The black depths of their eye sockets stared at me unblinkingly, and bony chins jutted forward in defiance of death. The bones were stitched together with silvery thread which glinted in the sunlight. The soldiers of the dead carried spears of bone, tipped and trimmed with steel but showing spots of rust. Several of the skeletons wore decorative capes of differing colors and designs. The horrifying warriors formed an impenetrable line, and my adrenaline surged through me. I counted over twenty in the patrol, and I sensed they were going to try to trap us. Before I could speak to Charlie, she sprang from behind the tree and hissed at the advancing wall of bone. The sound reminded me of a lit fuse.

This was it, I realized. I knew I was going to die on the False Priesthood's front lawn. I felt a pang of sadness about my demise. I should've saved myself the trouble, I thought. I should've just stayed home and died with my family when the Swarm came for them. Instead I'd let myself be led to Guard-knows where by a wholly unnatural cat only to be slain by the dead brought back to life. Hopelessness washed over me for a moment. Then I realized that if I was going to die anyway, I might as well fight. My hopelessness shifted and I was overcome with dispassionate rage. There was no use in holding back if I wasn't dead yet.

I coaxed fire rapidly and steadily. I let the heat collect in dense orbs before mustering enough force and throwing them at our attackers. When the fireballs made impact with solid resistance, they burst into satisfying whooshes of flame. Gaps began to appear in the advancing line. The skeletons tried to roll on the ground to extinguish the fire, but the blasts were causing them to lose pieces of themselves. When one of the skeletal warriors came for me, I deflected a spear thrust with my staff and swung at the side of the unseeing skull. My weapon broke through the bony cheek with a crunch, but the collapsed face was wired to the neck vertebrae with the silvery strands. The skeleton staggered, but it hadn't toppled. Instead the grim soldier brought its spear back up to strike again, but I'd cradled a fireball in the meantime. I threw my projectile directly at the headless torso as vehemently as I could. The attack blew apart what remained of my foe with a rush of expanding flame. I shielded my eyes from the spraying shards of bone and ember.

I looked for Charlie and found her engaged in battle. She struck at the skeletons and damaged their legs to divert their attention. The bulk of the skeletal patrol was busy chasing the cat, and the cat wasn't going to let herself be caught. I grinned a maddened grin in the rising heat of the valley. We were winning, I thought. I tossed another fireball.

"Aw, give it a rest!" a voice called from below us in the valley. "Nobody contacted the Fun Manager to schedule any fun this week!" The skeletons stopped moving immediately. They stood like statues, spears pointed at the sky. Charlie walked around her immobilized adversaries to see who was speaking to us.

"I should've known it was jou," the newcomer said. Her voice remained odd as she walked closer. The woman was dressed in an oversized and strangely cut black hooded robe. The garment obscured her features with flowing excesses of fabric. The material suggested finery and yet the robe had a certain dinginess. The voice was husky but distinctly female. "Flea-bitten fish-bag. Look at this mess. Have jou any idea how much bone-stitching my sister and I will have to do after this? These aren't jour training dummies, Leen. Go find somewhere else for jour games."

"Hello, Duu," Charlie said. The woman stepped closer. Beneath her hood, I could see a pale face with black eyes. Charlie stretched indolently and licked her paw in a masterful display of indifference. "We were just passing through."

"Passing through, my ass. Jou know how to get the patrols to leave jou alone."

This woman's words registered in a flash of anger. I glared at the cat. "You mean you could've kept them from attacking us?"

Charlie returned my gaze unperturbed. "The whole patrol smells like rot. Even more than they're supposed to." The cat pawed at an arm bone on the ground next to her, unwillingly abandoned by its former owner. The bone twitched as though it couldn't decide what to do with itself anymore.

"They're worn. Slow. Falling apart. And you," the cat looked accusingly in my direction. "You needed the practice."

Duu seized on this admission.

"There, jou see? Guard damn it, Charlie. These skirmishers aren't here so jou can show them to every boy-mage with a stick that's dumb enough to let jou kidnap him." She gave me a skeptical glance. "He does seem frightened, though. My soldiers are scary, aren't they?" Her face formed a grin of grimy teeth which made my stomach turn.

"Duu," Charlie started, "You and your sister sew bones together. The whole resurrection complex is an intriguing pastime, I'll give you that, but what else have you got to do? This patrol was terrible anyway. I recognize the lunk-head over there with the purple on him. He was always good for a romp. But I'll wager he's older than Raspho. I'm surprised your associates didn't declare these laggards obsolete. You should take more pride in your work." The cat yawned before recovering her poise and licking her whiskers.

Duu fumed. "Screw jou, jou freaking furball. Oon's been learning to cook cat lately. She's got a sweet-and-sour tempura recipe, wonderful in the fryer. We could sizzle jou up as the appetizer and make an entree from jour side-kick 'stick boy' here. He's got dense femurs, I can tell." Duu licked her lips obscenely. "And it just so happens that we're looking to restock our parts inventory."

The pale woman cackled at my discomfort. I tensed at the perceived threat and grasped the quarterstaff but Charlie was unmoved, and neither Duu nor her skeletons appeared to be readying any kind of attack. The cat answered Duu with the dry detachment she excelled at.

"I'm sure we'd be delectable, Duu. But you wouldn't butcher us, and we both know it. The Wise Witch would eventually hear what you did and she'd hunt you and your sister Oon like the vermin she thinks you are. I'd hazard a guess I'll survive this visit along with the mage-cub here." She gestured towards me with a noncommittal angling of her left ear.

Duu hissed her displeasure. "What a stupid name. 'Wise Witch,' my shorts. That madwoman was a few cards short of a full deck back when she was relatively jouthful and idealistic. The ol' girl's been going steadily senile for a couple of centuries now, at least. 'Wise' doesn't describe Jae-Jae, not in the slightest. 'Wisdom' doesn't make jou think it's jour Guard-given duty to protect every half-witted half-mage who stumbles across jour doorstep." The bone-stitcher's list of gripes became another sickening smile. She stepped towards us again, her black frock flowing in deceptive waves around her knobby knees. Her movements appeared frail, but I could sense power like a rash on my skin.

Duu cleared her throat. "I think I'll let idiot-bag Fleuro have jou, this time around. I don't imagine she's gonna be thrilled to see jou these Suns. I doubt she even knows about this mage-ling jou dredged up. Maybe jou should take her a copy of Oon's sweet-and-sour recipe, jou know, yust in case."

Charlie snorted. "Duu, I hate you. And often." Her voice changed to affectionate familiarity. "And I wish you weren't so Guard-damn right all the time."

I sensed Duu had let go of her irritation. She tossed her head back and released another cackle. "I love this part because I hate jou, Leen. The Wise-Ass Witch. With JOU for a cat." Her face turned serious again. She jabbed a bony finger at us. "But jou both owe me. Yes, the both of jou. Jou owe me work, jou owe me safe passage, and jou owe me target practice. I'll be extrememly inconvenient when I collect, and I WILL collect."

"I don't doubt it," Charlie replied.

"I don't doubt jou don't doubt it, jou silly animal," Duu bared her heinous teeth. "Jou're a useful beastie. It's why I befriended jour scraggly hide in the first place." She raised an eyebrow. "Plus, I'm not the unfortunate soul who has to scoop jour litter box."

Charlie cringed at Duu's verbal abuse of her. She wrinkled her nose and fanned out her whiskers. She seemed to labor through the words of her additional request. "Perhaps as we walk I could trouble you for the news from these parts?"

"Jou want news? Could cost jou extra."

"So be it, Duu. Put it on my tab. News is why I befriended your pasty mug in the first place."

Duu tilted her head. "Are jou sure it wasn't for target practice?"

I could no longer repress the urge to chuckle. Duu seemed to notice my existence after mostly ignoring my presence until then. Her head remained tilted. "Quite a wooden staff jou got there, stick-boy. At least it's a stick jou can be proud to get called 'stick-boy' over." Duu paced away from me and chuckled at her own joke. Her head turned farther than a head was supposed to turn and she inspected me with an anatomical eye. She squinted and evaluated what she saw. The bone-stitcher gave me the jitters.

"I can see jou've been through a lot, kid. It's probably jour pathetic body language. Remember, though," the pale woman said. Her tone of voice mocked a mother's high-pitched lecturing. "Somewhere out there there's a poor lad who doesn't even have a decent stick."

She turned back to Charlie and continued spoke as if I were no longer standing there.

"He's got more of a shine to him than I thought. Maybe he'll even grow a few more whiskers on that baby-face of his before the Yurisdiction decides to cancel his subscription to being alive."
{~}

Charlie and Duu conversed freely as we walked onward. My mother would've told me to write the details down, but in those Suns I was blissfully ignorant of the inner workings of the Jurisdiction. I tried to follow their conversation, but the foreign words and concepts left me confused and my attempts to clarify were ignored. Eventually I studied the landscape more than I listened to the pair talk. The eerie altered colors and life forms which were the mark of the False Priesthood surrounded us. Trees were plentiful, but grassy fields stretched around them and we followed trampled paths as they split and reformed without warning. The rolling hills challenged my muscles and lungs at the pace Duu set, but Charlie was unfazed. The cat maintained a trot, and as decrepit as Duu seemed, she possessed legs which failed to ever tire. We saw another patrol of skeletons as we traveled atop a subtle ridge, but they completely ignored us as they trudged through the adjacent valley with oblivious determination.

From time to time, I overheard mention of the Swarm. These were the only bits of conversation I could follow. Charlie and Duu exchanged other news about the Jurisdiction forces, such as the movements of the Regiment or where the newest outposts might be. I was dismayed to discover that the Jurisdiction had spy-planes which flew so high they were nearly undetectable by human eyes. Along with the Swarm, the spy-planes were controlled by a Jurisdiction faction known as the Devisors. There were places where spy-planes didn't fly, places safe from view, but these places were rare. I imagined a nameless face behind a screen far away, watching my fires on the beach by the farm.

Much of the news Duu passed to Charlie related to the Jurisdiction Nobility and the fickle politics within their ranks. I gathered that the Nobility were generally in charge of the Jurisdiction, but the operation was complicated. The Nobility deferred responsibilities to the Devisors and took orders from another entity or doctrine, a powerful and unspoken mystery. I'd heard enough. I shook my head and focused on hiking to keep up.

"Alright, this is as far as I'll go," Duu announced suddenly. "Almost half my fuel."

At the crest of the hill we were traversing, I noticed the vegetation regained a truer green. The healthy leaves were interspersed with the scattered yellow signs of autumn changes. A wave of relief struck my eyes. I began to breathe more easily. I was looking forward to leaving the False Priesthood behind.

Charlie gave Duu a nod, a friendly farewell, and I performed what I hoped was a respectful bow in the woman's direction. She turned back down the hill and cackled as she walked away. We proceeded without pause. I shuddered as I thought about Duu and the phenomena I'd witnessed in a single Sun's time. Each event was overwhelming for a man who was already struggling to cope with drastic changes in his life. When we were well away from Priesthood territory, I asked Charlie to stop.

"A minute, please."

I was panting, and I tried to regain my breath. I knew my body was hungry, but I didn't have much appetite.

"I need to rest for a minute."

The unyielding animal studied me with a bored, resting cat frown on her face, as if her plaything was stuck. I knew she was weary of dealing with my weakness. I met her gaze and asked the question troubling me.

"Who controls the Jurisdiction?"

Charlie spasmed, a sharp feline laugh which sounded almost like a sneeze.

"You're not dull, are you? Right to the million-dollar question."

I wrinkled my brow. "What's a dollar?"

Charlie shook her head. "Never mind that. The truth is, no-one understands who or what controls the Jurisdiction."

The cat yawned. Seeing the restive gesture allowed me to relax.

"Fate, perhaps, or the Guards themselves, Raspho, for as much as anyone knows. Most would tell you the Nobility are in charge. The Nobility Enforcers are among the most fearsome and sadistic warlocks I've ever encountered. Each and every Nobility is a fire mage, but don't get any ideas. They don't take kindly to unknown applicants. They cloister themselves in their councils and appoint members to positions of leadership. The Devisors hold some sway, seeing as they build and operate the Jurisdiction's war machines, including the Swarm. But beyond what's obvious, things get a lot less certain. I've heard of Jurisdiction 'Sovereigns,' though there's naught except wild theories. A tangible influence is practically untraceable. I haven't seen any credible evidence, but I trust my instincts."

I considered this, and I discovered the sensation roiling my stomach was the resurgence of fear. I shivered. My entire being had been poisoned by the death of my family. Tears were escaping, and I blinked them away. I focused on my breathing and gained a measure of control. I closed my eyes briefly and attempted to clear my mind. In one hand I gripped the staff, and with the other I crafted an orb of flame. The exercise centered me and calmed me, bringing back my appetite. I reached for my pack.

"Not much further, you know," Charlie said to me. She'd apparently picked up on my distress. "The Wise Witch knows how to make everything feel alright. She'll have a bed for you, and a warm bath, and food so succulent-"

"I won't have my family back," I said, cutting her off in a cracking voice with my eyes closed. When I opened my eyelids, the forest around me was scorched. The bark of the nearby tree trunks and the vegetation underfoot were coated with soot. Charlie considered me with a tolerant blink. She was unfazed, and her fur shone brilliantly against the blackened backdrop of mildly damaged shrubbery. Her tail twitched at me, but she said no more. My heart rate began to settle from its racing tempo. I began to accept my trauma. Charlie and I turned as a blue-green flash darted among the trees.

"What was that?" I directed my alarmed question at the cat. The blurry blue-green paused and posed between two trees before my companion could reply. We looked at the anomaly together. The colors coalesced as I stared at them. The figure was a rabbit, at least in shape, although the creature was the size of a wild boar. The entire body appeared to be formed of flowing water, and it glowed with an inner light. The eyes and ears held a darker green, but most of the rabbit's body was a tropical teal-blue. The rippling fur was more finely detailed than the most exceptional work of art I'd ever seen. The aqueous rabbit moved gracefully, and I knew the animal was watching us. Charlie wasn't tense or frightened, so I took in the dazzling sight.

"They call him the 'Lucky Watcher,'" the cat told me in a purring voice. "Nobody has ever touched him, as far as I know, but they say he's a good-luck omen. The Jurisdiction hates him, of course, but he only distracts them and wastes their ammunition. Still, they haven't caught him or destroyed him yet. I'm afraid it doesn't take much in the way of action to inspire hope these Suns."

We continued to admire the ethereal liquid rabbit. After a moment of tilting his head, the rabbit bounded away and I was left blinking at empty space as if I'd awoken from a dream.

In a Sun already filled with strangeness I could've easily been even more shaken by the encounter, but seeing the Lucky Watcher cleared up a few of my doubts. An army of Lucky Watchers wouldn't have granted me the focus I desired in order to sketch a decent diagram, however. I was exhausted and drained beyond comprehension.

"Imunna nap," I announced to the cat with such conviction that I barely cared for her opinion in the matter. I rubbed my eyes. They were probably blood-shot.

I took out my sleeping roll as Charlie settled on a rock overlooking my spot and rested her head on her paws. I could tell from the movements of her tail and her half-opened eye that she kept an anxious watch. True night was still several Marks away, but the time of Sun meant as little to me as anything else did. I forced myself to eat an ungainly bite of food and chewed laboriously as I sat on my unfurled bedding. When my stomach was no longer completely empty, I relinquished consciousness.

{~}

I dreamt vividly of another world. I envisioned vast fields of half-cooled lava. Cracked black slag and orange fissures glowing with heat covered the surface. From time to time, a pillar of roaring lava would burst through the surface and spray sweltering rock in every direction. A cavernous roof above me blocked the sky. The ceiling was riddled with hanging stalactites highlighted by the fiery light of the endless underground. The warmth sharpened the image, and I wondered at the scene. I began to relax and feel at home as I floated beyond myself in the turbulent dream domain.

Voices reached me, whispers at first, but the words strengthened as I listened. I couldn't make out what they were saying. The language was familiar to me and unintelligible at the same time. Periodically a voice would laugh, and the distorted acoustics created an unfriendly atmosphere. The voices became increasingly sinister and malevolent, and I began to panic. Flows of red I thought were lava were turning to blood.

I sat upright in the dark. My body was damp with sweat even in the cool night air of the forest. My eyes immediately met those of Charlie, perched on her rock above me. For a moment, the cat eyes gleamed with a swirling inner blaze, like hypnotic night-lamps. I made myself take a calming breath.

"Do mages ever have um- dreams?" I cleared my throat. "You know, ones that aren't like- normal?" I asked the cat.

Charlie responded in an even tone. "If mages were normal we wouldn't be here, you and I, fleeing for your life in the Wilds. Did your dream tell you something useful, or do you just need to clean your undergarment?"

I turned red and shook my head.

"Think carefully," Charlie instructed. "But don't whimper and whine. Your dreams are yours and they shouldn't control you. YOU control THEM."

I blinked in the dark. "I don't see how that's the case. I didn't feel like I could control anything just now."

Charlie licked her lips with a rough pink tongue. "There are certainly things you and I can never hope to control, Ras-boy." The cat rose and stretched in her usual way. "For the most part, the world around us cares naught for the desires of our hearts. If you're going to be a mage, however," She stared in my eyes, and I knew what fire felt like for a moment.

"You'll have to learn to control your mind, first and foremost. Everything else comes from there."

"Easier said than done," I replied.

Charlie sniffed. "Of course it is, and yet saying remains significant. Any kind of outward change has to begin inside. Instincts and feelings, these things are dangerous animals, but even wild creatures can be tamed."

"And what about the creatures that can't be?"

Charlie licked her whiskers and turned away from me.

"You're looking at one."

I watched Charlie as she flexed her claws. Her tail swayed where it dangled from the edge of the rock. We were both too tense to be comfortable. I was weary, but I decided I couldn't sleep. I tried to lay back down and rest my body even if my mind wouldn't follow. I pulled a piece of dry jerky from my pack and took a thoughtful bite. I'd write down the details of my dream, just as my mother would've done.

{~}

The next thing I knew, morning was upon us. The half-eaten piece of jerky remained in my hand as I squinted at the daylight, slightly confused. I realized that sleep had defeated my efforts at waking rest. At least I snoozed dreamlessly, I told myself. I was left with a slight headache, and my stomach gnawed at me in favor of breakfast.

To my surprise, Charlie already had a fire going.

"Put your porridge in your pot. We'll hunt as we go, and let's try to make good time. The Wise Witch is only two Suns away if we walk efficiently. I imagine she'll greet us sooner than that."

I rubbed my eyes. "She knows we're coming?"

Charlie looked up at me. "She knows more than anyone has a right to know."

I raised my eyebrows. "You sound as if you wished she didn't know so much."

Wiggling whiskers answered me before words did. "No two people have the same passions. I'm a fighter, not a scholar. The Wise Witch has probably forgotten more about mages than I ever care to learn."

I tried to picture her in my head, this fire mage Witch that I'd heard so much about. We'd spent close to a Moon hiking towards her. I remembered how Duu scoffed, but I decided not to let her opinion become my own. I didn't exactly have anywhere else to turn for safety.

"Does this lady have a real name? Or is she just the Wise Witch?"

I put water over the flame and rummaged for dry ingredients. Charlie licked her right paw and wiped her face with it. As I waited for the water to boil, I assumed she was ignoring the question I'd asked. Instead she broke the silence after an interval.

"The true name of the fire mage called the 'Wise Witch' is Madame Director Jae'lin Fleuro."

I shrugged. The words meant nothing to me at the time. Instead of contemplating the Wise Witch, I focused on the food remaining in my pack. I was glad we were almost to our destination because the porridge was growing increasingly bland without any honey or dried fruit. Even my raisins were dwindling. The water placed over the fire gurgled at me, and I answered by dumping my rations in.

When my stomach was as placated as possible, we moved on. I hiked with the quarterstaff in hand. The way in which the artifact altered my perceptions was becoming familiar to me and I studied the changes carefully. We moved swiftly. I took in the sights of the forest when my footing was sound. The hills around us presented substantial changes in elevation. After climbing until my legs burned, we followed a rocky ridge surrounded by trees. The ridge swooped up and down, and the traversable path became wide plateaus and narrow peaks. The elevated path was smoother going than crossing the wide valleys, even if the route was less direct. The ridge also afforded us a view. The sylvan wilderness was pleasant, peaceful even, and looking over the vast natural habitat was comforting. I felt as if the trees presented a place to hide away from the troubled life pursuing me.

By mid-Sun, my stomach rumbled and reminded me I'd need to become a predator in order to eat. Just as I opened my mouth to speak, Charlie purred a warning and pointed with an outstretched paw.

I looked up and a buck stared back at us. He was so close that the sight of him was a shock. I took in the details of his eyes and his antlers and the fur of his coat. I could hardly believe I hadn't seen him until Charlie alerted me. I was also amazed he hadn't decided to flee. His tail and his nose twitched, but his antlers were wide and intimidating. This was his forest, and he was the regent. A boy and a red cat were the interlopers here. Why would he turn tail from such diminutive contenders?

I realized I didn't want to hurt the buck. On the contrary, I felt as if I'd encountered a sacred Guard of the forest, but I had to act if I wanted to make him food.

Until that moment, I'd never killed an animal larger than a rabbit. I only needed a moment. The death of the buck is like a flash of pain in my mind. I pushed energy to a dense fireball in the palm of my hand. The buck snorted and flinched, but my timing was perfect. I threw the fireball at his heart without warning. I willed the fire forward with confidence. My left hand rested on the quarterstaff, and I could feel the heat around me. The fireball raced beyond my reach. The buck's warm body stood in the forest in front of me. I focused, and the glowing projectile collided with my mark. In an instant, the fire tore through the buck's chest and obliterated his vital organs. The elegant creature fell immediately, blood flowing from the fatal wound. The life was gone from the buck's eyes before I could even move to stand over his body.

I shuddered at the gore and the brutality of what I'd done.

"Don't start to cry now, kid. Everything's gotta eat," Charlie said. She wasted no time tearing the buck's belly with a sharp claw, opening the creature from neck to gut.

"Roll your sleeves and find your knife," she instructed me brusquely. "You're about to learn how to be useful."

I swallowed and forced down my revulsion at having stolen the life of such a majestic creature with un-caring violence. The death felt worse to me than when we hunted lesser game, as if the size of the pain I caused increased with the size of the animal. Death had happened, though, a death I'd caused, and I'd deal with the obvious consequence of my hunt. I focused on my breathing and did as I was told.

What followed the killing of the buck was a process requiring several Marks for me to puzzle together. A few seconds of decisive action left me with most of a Sun's work. The vivid redness rang in my eyes as we butchered the deer. I tried to remember what each part looked like so I could sketch a diagram once I washed the blood and fur from my hands. We scraped the insides of the buck as clean as we could and I resolved to preserve the hide. Surely the Wise Witch would know how to tan a deer skin. I wanted to keep the antlers, but they were cumbersome and not terribly practical. I needed to prioritize the space in my pack.

I attempted to smoke as much meat as possible in the confines of a narrow chimney I located in a stony cliff face. Once the smoker was going, I roasted a lean piece of venison loin over a seperate fire and Charlie and I ate as much as we could while the afternoon wore on. The smoking process required many Marks to complete, and I continued stoking the chimney with wood late in the evening, praying the meat wouldn't spoil. I could tell the delay irked

Charlie. I believe she tolerated the impromptu campsite because I killed the buck myself, and perhaps a part of her was proud of me. Besides, we had plenty of meat from the successful hunt, and Charlie was never quick to argue with that state of affairs.

As I packed away the smoked meat, I watched the enigmatic cat. She'd become my constant companion. Her eyes danced as she sat gazing at the dying embers. A mage, I thought. I suppose I'd known all along. A relevant thought occurred to me.

"Charlie?" I asked.

"Yes?" she responded, rising from her spot She began to pace in the firelight. I could tell she was considering whether or not to eat more of the meat, but she spoke to me as she sniffed at the selection. "We'd best keep the fire bright," Charlie instructed. "There might be predators about. They can smell smoked meat from several kilometers away by now. We'll keep watch."

"Were you a human?"

The fire crackled and popped, shooting sparks in the air. The question had startled Charlie. Her fur ruffled as she twitched. She was self-conscious as she calmed herself. Her tongue flicked anxiously across her cheeks in the fire's light.

"I was." Clearly Charlie was content to leave the answer alone, but I decided to dare another question.

"What happened to you?"

She fixed me with unblinking eyes. An odd feeling came over me, and my mouth hung open slightly. I tried to imagine what Charlie might've looked like as a person and not as a cat.

"The Wise Witch made me a cat," she said reluctantly. "Rounds and Rounds ago. These Suns, I barely remember what my body felt like when I was shaped like a hairless ape. I ache in my knees whenever there's a solar eclipse. They're backwards now, you know." She coaxed away a cooked rib from the buck with her paw and began to pull away the flesh. She swallowed and then added another admission.

"Thumbs. I used to miss thumbs the most. But I try to forget the whole Guard-damn ordeal even happened. I prefer it that way."

I sat back and swallowed. "How old are you?"

She responded to the persistent questions with a hiss.

"Old enough to know that curious kittens like yourself are the first to discover what teeth and claws feel like."

I frowned at her, but I kept my mouth shut. My hands traced the surface of a diagram I sketched of the buck. Charlie curled herself in a sleeping spot with a whirl and closed her eyes.

"I've shared enough for several Suns," the cat informed me with a yawn. "First watch is yours, kitten."

Chapter 6
Melodie tells of: "Wolves at the Door"

"This barrel of firewhiskey really buggers the aim and burns the soul. I won't name her 'The Devil' though, not yet. Not without a fair hearing. Let's find out if she can play the fiddle first." -the Gunslinger Confidant

I was drawn out of sleep around 0400 by a burst of air and rumbling growl which made me think that the earth beneath me was shaking.

I opened my eyes and they met a pair of eyes directly in front of my own. Olive green irises with accents of hazy brown framed swollen onyx pupils. There was an iron intellect lurking behind those magnetizing orbs, and I felt as though I was spinning between them. For a moment I believed there was a person returning my gaze. In the next moment, I felt sure I must be dreaming. The person in front of me had- fur. Was it just a beard? Not a beard, no. The hair covered the entire face. This wasn't a person at all. This was a wolf.

"Steady, Guard-damn sturdy-" I began to whisper. I grunted when the eyes blinked. A gunfighter near me raised the alarm. Torches flashed to life around my bedroll and the area flooded with orange light. When I tried to sit up, I was restrained by a paw covering my entire chest. The claws dug against my collarbone and my bicep and I grimaced. The wolf's curving fangs were bare near my throat and I felt delirious. I heard the familiar sounds of weapons being drawn and rounds being chambered.

"Open fire and your pack Alpha dies!" the wolf barked, startling everyone around me. The voice was full of gravel, and my ears rang from the volume. I realized if I wasn't dreaming, then I'd need to survive this encounter. For the sake of my people, I needed to deal with the wolf. She wasn't just any wolf, I gathered. The uninvited beast was undoubtedly a titan wolf.

The canine jaws snarled, and I winced. The growl resumed. My stomach didn't appreciate the pulsing vibrations echoing in my bones. I shook my head and remained unsure if I was dreaming. The beast was the most massive wolf I'd ever seen, and I realized Confidant Flin had been lucky to lose only a leg all those Rounds ago. I motioned for my gunfighters to hold their fire. I didn't know how she'd gotten past the sentries, but an animal the size of the titan wolf wouldn't die without a struggle. I looked at the gray fur covering the paw on my chest and evaluated if gunfire could penetrate her hide. How many lives would be lost in the process? Was there an acceptable number? The outcome wouldn't be pleasant, and the wolf knew it.

"Whaddayu want, wolf?" I said. "What makes you think I'm the Alpha?"

"Do you deny it?"

The wolf looked me in the eye, and I resolved to be as fearless as a warrior can be while planted firmly on their backside. My head wouldn't stop spinning, and my insides hadn't recovered from the growling. I gritted my teeth and bared them. I measured the pressure of the wolf's paw.

"If you'd like to speak with me, perhaps you'd do me the courtesy of allowing me to sit up."

Gunfighters were gathering, and the sentries looked stricken with guilt. My anger at them flared, and I found myself questioning the wolf as she released me.

"How did you enter our camp?"

The wolf snorted through her wide nostrils and broke eye contact with me to look around. Furry lips moved over prodigious canines.

"Easy. Not your camp. Next you can ask the trees how they make their leaves turn green."

"My name is Melodie Oakes, Generale of the Rose tribe," I gestured towards the barely contained gunfighters encircling us with bated breath. The barrels of their weapons were lowered, but they wouldn't require provocation to level their sights. Flin gave me a desperate blink. I forced the expression on my face to remain impassive. I had no doubt the wolf would kill me if anyone dared to break the standoff. Courage was something instilled in every gunfighter of the Rose, but the talking wolf made us question ourselves.

"Lohise," the titan wolf said. The name came with a breathy accent. "Alpha and Den Mother of my pack for now. I'll ask you each to relax. If blood was what I wanted, I'd have it, but I've seen enough blood. Your guns have teeth, but so does my pack. Because of these dangers, I propose peace. Not even humans could be foolish enough to ignore what's coming for us all."

I stared at her and resisted the urge to shudder. Steady, sturdy, savvy, I told myself. Lohise was as captivating to me as she was deadly. The blunt way she spoke and her accent were foreign, but she was adept at conveying sincerity in her words. I kept my features as blank as possible and willed away the panic I felt from listening to the huge carnivore speak to me.

"And what exactly do you believe is coming, Den Mother Lohise?"

Lohise growled again, but the vocalization was pensive and my insides were appreciative.

"Walk with me to the edge of your den, Generale. I have no desire to be shot in the hindquarters as I depart."

I rose to my feet, but I knew there was no sense in reaching for my armor or my weapons. Instead, I faced the wolf directly, measuring every subtle motion of her head and her body. Tall as she was, her eyes met mine squarely. Her physical presence was majestic and imposing. She could've torn me apart like a rag-doll in the space of a breath.

"Let's walk a few paces together, so that these fine marksmen can be at ease." I knew my supposition was unlikely to happen. My gunfighters would stalk the titan wolf and their Generale to the ends of the earth. To their credit, the gunfighters took my hint and allowed Lohise free passage to the edge of where the torchlight fell.

"An uneasy alliance, to say the least." I spoke without preamble, keeping my hands clasped behind my back. "I don't know how the Confidants would feel. I'm not a dictator who rules these people alone."

Lohise kept her eyes on the City across the river. "I understand your concerns. My pack is young. Our numbers were decimated by the wars of the Low Hills." I studied the way her shoulder blades shifted up and down as she walked. "The green-claws wish to slay you as intruders and get their first taste of man-flesh. They imagine glorious victory. For my part, I find your unique flavor doesn't suit my palate." The wolf licked her chops as if to prove her point. "My wolves are inexperienced. In need of guidance." Lohise labored to admit the flaws in her pack. "They've never seen the good side of humans, or sneezed at the smell of gunpowder. All they know is that nearly an entire generation went off to war and didn't return. They harbor resentments over their losses, but I don't want to see my pack dwindle further while chasing a bloody vendetta with no purpose." The titan wolf stopped walking and eyed me. She made her voice formal for the specifics of her offer. "We start simple. I bring you fresh meat as a token of faith. There are fish in the rivers you can string in order to return the favor."

Her body language and her tone projected confidence, but I could sense her apprehension underneath. I drove at the weak point. "Can you assure me that my people won't be attacked?" I asked.

"Can you assure me of the same?"

The question hung between us in a foggy silence. Lohise broke the pause and turned away. She spoke in the darkness and her voice bounced back to me from the cracked concrete of the City.

"Let's hope together, Alpha Melodie. Hope and do what we can."

I watched her go and wondered if I could collect my thoughts before dawn came around. As her figure receded among the shadows, I heard a gun discharge behind me. The bullet struck a ruined edifice and the ricochet angled off in the night sky. I whirled to face the gunfighter who held a smoking weapon and angrily backhanded the woman. My admonishment was more stinging than forceful, and the gunfighter staggered but she didn't fall.

"My Generale- I- I'm-"

"Do you want to start another war when we've barely survived the last one?" I roared at the gunfighter with the undisciplined finger. The tribe stared at me in silence, and I composed myself. I could tell they sympathized with the desire to kill the titan wolf who invaded their camp and captured their Generale. In an instant, my heart went with them. I offered the woman my hand. She grasped my palm and I could feel her tremble. In a softer tone, I growled at her.

"And besides. You missed."

{~}

The Confidants were suspicious. Flin wasn't alone in barely containing his anger. The Generale of the Rose tribe only issued orders when battle was enjoined. Truly, the power for decisions about titan wolves rested in the hands of the Council. The tribe elected a seventh Confidant in order to replace the member who was killed, making the leadership body whole again.

"These are titan wolves we're talking about," Flin reiterated time and time again. "If we let them among us and they decide to turn on us, it could be the end of the tribe. They're killing machines. Fur so thick our bullets may not save us."

Confidant Terche responded to Flin with level words. "If the titan wolves can defeat us so easily, then I find it necessary we respect such a thing, Confidant Flin. This isn't some kind of cowardice mind you, this is a strategic calculation which grants us the best chance at continued survival. If diplomacy has any chance to prevent our destruction, then you can Guard-damn bet I'll talk to the wolves 'til I'm blue in the face. We shouldn't be so hasty to make another mortal enemy."

I said nothing as I sipped my precious ale from a wooden cup. The keg was among our cargo when we journeyed into exile. I planned to let the Confidant's arguments play tonight as they did for the last several nights. The Council was bitterly divided on the issue of what to do with the titan wolves, and so was the tribe itself.

In the Suns following my accosting by the titan wolf Lohise, the Rose tribe forded the river and established our fledgling base camp. We clustered around the shadow of the resting Mammoth among the remnants of the City's ancient buildings. The change of scenery brought no noticeable peace of mind for anyone despite the historic moment of our journey's end. We doubled and tripled our sentries, only to have them jump at shadows in the alley-ways as they pictured giant wolves.

The Council discussion was going nowhere, but even nowhere was progress compared to the bickering which preceded the stalemate. Steady, sturdy, savvy, I found myself thinking. When a simmering silence settled in the Council tent, I dared to venture my own opinion.

"The titan wolves brought us meat. They were pleased with the fish we left in return, which was a lesser quantity. Other than Lohise's unconventional parley methods, they've given us no outright cause to distrust them."

Flin's face flushed to scarlet. "No cause to distrust them?" The comment sent him back to fuming. I don't think I ever saw the man so angry at me. I repressed the urge to flinch away.

"They're titan wolves, Mel! If game becomes scarce in the winter, they'll eat us! And you'll invite them to stroll right up to the buffet!"

I did my best to remain unrattled by the words. I was only partially successful when I tried to speak calmly.

"If they were ordinary wolves I'd agree with you. But wolves don't speak our tongue. Lohise is keen to negotiate to keep the peace."

The Confidants had already heard these arguments. A few of them looked bored listening to us. Flin's anger at me didn't subside, but didn't flare further. The emotion stayed with him as a residual tension while he tried to reason with me.

"Of course the wolf-queen seems keen to negotiate. What better way to get us to lower our defenses? She knows what guns can do at a distance. She wants us to expose ourselves to their teeth."

I considered what betrayal and duplicity could entail. It wasn't the first time I'd wrestled with the possibility. If I precipitated a treaty with the titan wolves and they attacked the tribe, I'd lose my position as Generale, daughter of Sampsen or not. Being stripped of rank would bother me less than the casualties on my hands. The situation was just as Flin saw. The continued existence of the Rose tribe could be jeopardized if we were ambushed by such a fearsome enemy. On the other hand, if the titan wolves proved to be allies or even acceptable neighbors, we could prevent needless fighting and bloodshed at a time when our tribe was weakened. Peace would drastically increase our chances of survival and prosperity in these foreign Wilds.

I thought about Lohise, the Den Mother herself. I could imagine the musky smell of her fur and the way her growl shook me. I spoke to the Confidants abruptly. I saw what was in my heart, and I knew the truth of the matter.

"I don't trust her, Flin. I don't trust the titan wolf, the Den-Mother Lohise. She might as well be a Guard-forsaken demon, for what I know." I scowled and turned to be sure everyone could see my displeasure. The expression wasn't an act. "My friends. Mistrust isn't enough reason to start a war against an enemy we have no measure of yet. Open conflict isn't the wisest course of action now.

This much is clear to me. I suggest we reinforce our position. I suggest we find ways to observe and test the wolves without provoking them."

I looked around to gauge what reaction my words were having, but the Confidants were practiced at these kinds of games. Their faces remained carefully neutral as I spoke, and I did my best to ignore them as I continued.

"The Jurisdiction isn't a friend to the titan wolves. I have no doubts about that. Their pack would gain virtually no benefit from attacking us, and likewise, an attack by our tribe would sacrifice a great deal for an uncertain gain in true security. I'll leave you to determine what's best, Confidants. Know if you choose to initiate open war with the titan wolves, you'll have my guns, but you'll not have my heart."

{~}

My declaration was about as far as I could leverage my power as Generale in the Rose tribal Council. Everyone knew I wouldn't sit out the fighting, including me, but I'd register my dissent now for the formal record. The Confidants looked weary. They seemed to accept my impassioned statement, but none responded to me. Flin looked at the ground. I realized with a pang how his anger had combined with my father's death and left me feeling more alone than I'd ever felt. I'd certainly put up with enough of these endless Council meetings. I rose from my seat at the table and left the tent.

The Sun was ending, and the tribe was beginning to favor heavier fabrics and furs against the cooling air of autumn. The smells of churned dirt and split timbers and hot metal dominated the camp. The men and women of the Rose survived a rigorous journey only to end up doing manual labor. Rations were generous even though winter was coming. The hum of the Mammoth's internal workings would soothe the tribe and their tired bodies to sleep.

I downed my beer before I entered my tent. Eventually permanent structures would be finished. Materials salvaged from the ruins had given us a starting point. The Mammoth needed to be hidden more thoroughly. I imagined my position as Generale would grant me a choice of dwellings. I made a mental note to decline this honor until the tribe was settled. The Generale's travel tent was set up for my use, and I felt it was a fitting place for a Generale to sleep. The exterior boasted a faded decorative fringe and a Rose war banner along one side. A coat rack, a hand-carved wooden chest with a matching chair, a few extra blankets, and my bedroll were everything which occupied the spare military tent. I remembered visiting my father when he made use of the tent at a tribal summit. In those Suns, the sturdy canvas shelter was richly furnished with the fine items a decorated Generale was accustomed to owning. The tribe left much behind in Sylviarg which was too weighty or impractical to bring along. I hadn't distinguished myself enough to merit any kind of tribute from victory or renown. Flowing tapestries and carpeting had to be earned, I reminded myself.

I'd unbuckled the holsters at my hips when a rustle at the tent's entrance caused me to level a set of sights in the direction of the intruder. When I recognized the curve of Drak's jet black hair and his embroidered shirt, I removed my finger from the pistol's trigger and lowered the weapon. I hadn't officially demoted the man following the duel or promoted any other Lieutenant in his place. He and Bonder remained the only two officers by default. His hand was bandaged from the recent loss of a digit, and he saluted with the arm, undoubtedly self-conscious of the gesture.

"Yes, Lieutenant," I said evenly. "Report."

Drak took a step forward and dropped to one knee in a customary show of honor. I tried not to roll my eyes, but as he moved closer to me in the tent, I could smell the man. The scent was like honey and hardwood, like tobacco and spiced vanilla. Memories jabbed at me and I looked at him skeptically.

"My Generale. I come seeking your leave to hunt down the mongrel vermin who attacked you."

I should've interrupted him there, but as usual with Drak, words flowed like wine.

"I give you my promise I'll slay her. A wolf-hide coat will grace your shoulders unlike any the tribe has ever seen. She would serve to grace your title and your beauty, and keep the winter chill from your bones."

I sat down slowly on the tent's lone wooden chair. I continued to look at Drak with my head tilted to the side. The chair was a humble seat, but I was sure to sit up straight. The Sun had already been dreary enough without ex-boyfriends trying to curry favor. I held the pistol in my left hand, but I let the barrel point harmlessly downward between my knees. He moved forward as though I'd given him an unspoken invitation. He went to his opposite knee to bring his face nearly level with mine. I placed my hand against his shoulder and held him away from me. I stared at his eyes with a thoughtful frown.

"Now isn't the time," I told him. A weakness within me prevented me from telling him there would probably never be a time. I warped my gentle frown to a vicious scowl in an attempt to convey how serious I was.

"Dismissed."

Drak stood abruptly and took a step back. I'm sure I knew a refusal wasn't going to be effortless.

"The gunfighters of this tribe aren't mice and rabbits. They aren't going to run and hide and tremble," he stated curtly, his noble deference disappearing.

I looked up at him and twirled the pistol in my hand. "Glad to hear it. I'll always consider carefully the words of my Lieutenants."

He paused and frowned, determined to meet my eyes. He gave a slight nod of his head and left the tent. I relaxed and shook my head, returning the pistol to its holster. I needed to resolve the situation soon, I thought, or take action to quell the uncertainty. Drak was a fool to seek conflict, but he'd given me an accurate assessment of the tribe's sentiment. There were many among us who dreamt of winter cloaks made from titan wolf pelts.

{~}

The next morning was an early start. I was feeding myself buttered biscuits and casually peeling an orange while I sipped a mug of tea. The Engineers explained their plans to me, and whenever my mouth was available I gave my approval with encouraging words. They were the Engineers, not me, and Bonder had already identified our top priorities. When my hands were freed from my breakfast, I joined a team of men and women pulling rope lines lashed to rubble at the edge of the wide square where we parked the Mammoth. New designs took advantage of the corroded steel I-beams and existing concrete wherever we could. As the morning continued, I found myself breaking ground with a pickaxe in my hands. Trenches and piping were planned as we excavated the area. A hearth for cooking fires and a larder for food storage were already partially constructed and put to use. A team equipped with axes crossed the river to get additional lumber. What we couldn't craft from metal or salvaged concrete, we'd supplement with wood. Flammability made timber less desirable, but we could formulate fire-proof coatings inside the Mammoth.

When the Sun reached the pinnacle of noon, the Rose tribe broke from work for the usual repast. I took a swig of watered ale and gnawed on a slice of the venison the titan wolves brought us. Between the rabbit warrens in the area and the fish in the river, we were stocked with a decent supply of meat. Our current stores of food wouldn't last the winter as they stood, but if we could continue trapping and fishing at a modest pace we'd either survive until the spring or our primary cause of death wouldn't be starvation. By the time the earth began to thaw, we'd have a better idea of where crops could be planted.

I sat near the middle of the square, apart from the area with the cook fires where the tribe was eating. A call came through the crowd. The message had been shouted from sentry to sentry before reaching the encampment.

"Wolf! Wolf across the river!"

I shoved the rest of my lunch in my pockets and chugged my beer. "To arms!" I raised the call. Dashing inside my tent, I snagged my pistols and found a saddled horse. Gunfighters around me were in a similar state of motion, but I was the swiftest, and nobody was surprised to see their Generale race ahead. I surged towards the riverbank on the stallion, beckoning the horse to move faster and faster along the avenues of the City even as I was still finding the bouncing stirrups with my feet. I spotted the titan wolf through a break in the ruins. Lohise stood atop the wreckage of a truncated roadway, claiming the cliff as her perch. I didn't cherish the idea of crossing the river on horseback only to have her poised directly above me. I closed the gap between myself and the wolf as much as possible by skirting the water's edge.

"Lohise!" I called to the titan wolf. I took a breath and projected my voice from horseback as my mount shifted to a trot. "Well met, Den Mother. What brings you here this Sun?"

"You ride armed," the wolf stated to me as I reined in the spirited horse. "What if I'd simply been enjoying the sights?" she asked, her voice ringing back across the river. There were gunfighters on horseback arriving behind me to the scene. I held up a hand signal, but their weapons bristled anyway. I spoke my reply.

"A gunfighter always rides armed. If you came here just to look, Den Mother, then we'll strike a pose for you. I imagine you've another purpose in mind for your visit."

Lohise sat down, but her head remained upright and alert. "Bold of you to assume, but correct enough. I have a favor to ask, for which a debt will be owed."

I let my expression remain a neutral frown. I was keenly aware of the presence of my tribesmen behind me. They clustered at the river's threshold. I turned to see a Confidant shake his head and then looked at the wolf across the river.

"What exactly did you have in mind?"

"Cub stepped in a bear trap. Human hands may save her. She needs to be freed from the trap and healed by doctors." Lohise was uncertain of her pronunciation, but her concern required no translation.

There was a muffled buzz of conversation behind me but I blocked out the noise. I needed the separation in order to think. I pulled myself together and unleashed my confident reply before I could be interrupted or preempted by anybody else's loudly stated opinion. The stallion I sat bucked anxiously as he caught the scent of titan wolf across the river. I used the motion of the horse to add drama to my pronouncement. My tone was grave as the mount lifted me.

"I grant this favor and remember this debt, Den Mother Lohise." The horse settled, but I continued my instruction. "Allow us a moment to prepare. Await the crossing of my personal envoy."

I began to ride away, but Lohise offered an instruction of her own, swelling her voice to a snarling roar in order to reach me.

"Too many humans will scare her! Bring only hands you need!"

I selected people in my head as I rode back towards the camp. I wondered if I was choosing a living sacrifice. I decided to give honorary invitations to the assignment instead of direct orders. Gunfighters were grumbling about my decision to help Lohise, and insubordination met the fringes of my ears. I gave sharp commands.

"Return to posts! Form ranks! Steady on!" The discipline I longed to exert would have to wait. The questions about this favor for the titan wolves would probably come from the Confidants as well. I was stretching my authority to the limits as I shouted to the camp.

"I need four gunfighters with a litter. Prepare to swim the river with me. Everyone else stays frosty on our side, Bonder is in command. Doctors prepare to receive a patient. If we don't come back by sundown, then send a sortie, but be savvy."

Flin's eye met mine. "You'd hand yourself over to them," he said with venom as I dismounted.

I seized the lapels of his coat and looked him dead in the face. "If I'm wrong about this, this Guard-damn titan wolf bull-shit, then this is gonna to put an end to any questions about their motives one way or the other. If they kill me you can have your stupid war. Otherwise, you get yourself a hostage. A little puppy hostage. Does that make you satisfied?"

I was being unfair to him, perhaps. There was an edge of aggression in my tone I shouldn't have allowed to slip in there, but I was impatient with the old man's rigid biases. Whatever his perspective might be, I wanted to know how he saw things. He left no room to question his point of view.

"A titan wolf pup is still a titan wolf. The only difference is how many bites it takes to eat a man and how big of coat the hide'll make.

{~}

As I waded across the river, I said my prayers of thanks for the four brave souls who followed me on my risky venture. I kept a close eye on the supplies. We carried a makeshift litter and several clean bandages sealed in wax paper strapped to our shoulders. The water never reached above my chin, but the steady flow landed us downriver from our starting point. I considered Flin's words and his animosity. I couldn't decide if I could chalk up his hatred of titan wolves to the fact he'd lost his leg or if he possessed experience I refused to accept. I imagined a human being eaten by titan wolves. I hoped it would be swifter and preferable to normal timber wolves considering the size of a titan wolf's jaws. They'd make short work of us if this was a trap.

"Jerro. Corwin. Trenz. Verekas. Your courage and your service in this matter won't be forgotten by your Generale. Steady, sturdy, savvy," I told my companions carrying the litter as we reached the other bank of the river. We attempted to keep the firearms dry along with the bandages, and heavy armor was left behind in order for us to

"I need to get the kiteknife," I repeated. "I can't leave it behind."

I shook the cobwebs of sleep away and disabled the proximity sensors around the camp. I jumped away from the ground and floated towards the stone tower, trying to remember the landscape around me. Zeyus thrashed free of his bedding with his weapons in hand and called my name behind me.

"Wait!"

I ignored him. I'd only take a minute. I remembered where the harpy fell. I pictured her mangled body and where it hit the forest floor. Dawn was creeping over the horizon, and fog hung around the trees. I heard the harpies before I saw them.

The opportunistic scavengers were clustered around where my victim had fallen. I touched my feet carefully on a tree branch as if it were a balance beam. The sounds I was hearing made me gag involuntarily.

The harpies were eating their dead colleague. Piece by bloody piece, they were devouring her stiffened body. I saw the kiteknife I wanted to retrieve in the possession of a feasting half-blood. He'd tucked my weapon in a leather strap positioned like a belt, except none of the harpies wore any trousers to speak of. I suppose I should've been thankful my knife wasn't used to butcher the dead harpy. For eating implements, they had gruesome serrated daggers made from bone. Gore and grime coated every inch of the harpies and their possessions. The sounds of rubbery flesh being torn apart nearly caused me to vomit. I drew a kiteknife. I flung the knife with purpose and guided my efforts with confidence. The knife pierced the torso of the closest harpy and lodged in the chest of another. Dark blood sprayed across the fallen leaves of the forest floor. As I was about to draw another knife, a javelin streaked past my shoulder. The throw skewered the heads of the remaining pair of harpies. I walked forward to retrieve my weapons.

Zeyus caught me at a jog. "That was dangerous, Fleuro," he was saying. There was a hint of anger in his voice. The venom faded from his face as he studied the pile of dead harpies. He mumbled words of praise which were the approximation of a military officer. I wiped the blood from the kiteknives and returned the blades to the brace. Zeyus removed his javelin, pressing his boot against the dead avian corpses and pulling the shaft with a grunt. The odor of the harpies was beyond oppressive. Even the spilled blood stank. I hadn't commented, but Zeyus read my thoughts.

"Dirty-ass harpies," he grumbled. "If filthy claws and rusty blades don't kill you, the smell might."

{~}

We moved when the tension of the morning faded, and I found myself considering the world more closely than I desired. My gown I'd worn when I was a girl, dancing around in colorful leggings and scarves. I pictured the artistry of the outfit and the ballrooms. What happened to the outfit and the girl, I wondered? Had she disappeared, only to be replaced by the empty death of a monster in the distant Wilds?

Zeyus slew another harpy before he got honest answers. I saw the death happen, but I knew my mind was starting to protect itself. The harpies were horrible creatures, but murdering them was awful just the same. I hovered in a daze with my awareness shutting down as I stared. I began to twirl through the steps of a dreamy dance. I hummed a ballad to myself.

The next thing I knew, Zeyus was grabbing my wrist. I came back to myself with a gasp.

"Private Fleuro," he was saying. "You weren't responding when I called you." The worry was plain on his face. "We're done here, anyway. Prepare for extraction." I felt his hand grab my arm. I nodded, but my head was spinning, and the tune of the ballad played on a loop in my head.

Later in the evening by the campfire, I was having better luck processing what happened to me. The Major was rigging electronic motion sensors, but he hadn't spoken except to tell me to eat.

"I killed a living thing today," I said, breaking the standing tranquility.

Zeyus nodded at me. "The only way you take it in stride is if you're sick. I know you're dealing with the shock, but you did just fine, Private. Don't shy away from the memory. Don't push yourself to be something other than yourself. That's how you'll make it worse. Think and adjust. You've done no wrong, Fleuro. You did what you needed to do, and you did it well. You protected yourself."

I stared at him. My mind was foggy, but I nodded. He handed me a flask of firewhisky.

"I doubt you feel like celebrating, but do it anyway. Some things only come around once in a lifetime, and pleasure and pain get tangled up when memory becomes nostalgia. So do yourself a favor and have a drink."

I did as I was told. The liquor blazed a path down my throat and I coughed. The action fortified my resolve. I hadn't killed the way my father killed. My head hurt as I thought about my former friends, but the pain was making me stronger. The wind shifted, and my insides warmed from the drink.

{~}

I awoke with a start. An implacable thought surged through me.

"The kiteknife," I said in the autumn morning. Zeyus stirred in his bedroll.

"Hmmf?"

move surely in the flowing river. The place we chose to cross was marked by scouts- a spot where the silt of the river bottom allowed a person or a horse to find footing the entire way across. We waded rather than swam across the river by looking for the red marking of the Rose. Lohise waited for us on the other side examining us as we hauled out. I resisted the urge to reach for the weapons on my shoulders, and I hoped the four behind me would take my cue. Water dripped from our jackets and the litter we conveyed. The titan wolf greeted us with a nod and then led us towards the trees without a word.

The exertion from fording the flowing river and the steep hike which followed warmed my body despite the cool autumn air and the evaporating dampness of my underclothes. My companions were in healthy spirits despite their evident wariness. We saw no signs of titan wolves among the trees. The undergrowth had taken over scattered walls and debris which were the remnants of ancient buildings. Plants burst upward through pieces of cracked plastic siding released from crumbling edifices. Any structure remaining intact undoubtedly consisted of brick or stone or steel and was now only a trellis for climbing vines and the ever-seeking green tendrils of plant life. Rotting wood became nourishment for ferns and flowers as the architectural corpses were reincarnated piece by earthy piece. A broken window winked at us from time to time like a soul-less denizen of the past. Bits of brightly colored garbage reminded us there were Suns lost among historical pages. I surmised the path we were travelling on was a paved street, once. The remains were hefty pieces of asphalt, scored by fissures and angled haphazardly beneath our feet.

Lohise trotted forward in front of us. Without line of sight, she left few signs or sounds for us to track. We hustled along behind her. She stopped abruptly in a dead-end lane. When a rush of breeze died down, whimpering met my ears from the adjacent field of tall grass and wildflowers.

"Over there," the wolf said. Her speech pattern remained foreign to me.

"That's where you'll find Amika, and the trap is biting her leg. I warn you that her mother Couress is close by. She licks the wound more than she should. Couress is young for a wolf mother. Regardless, cubs are rare, and her motherhood was a blessing to us. But Couress has barely seen a human from a distance, much less thought to trust one. I'm going to tell her what must be done. I ask that you refrain from any threatening behavior. She'll undoubtedly be upset."

I gave the titan wolf a nod of understanding and then turned eyes to my gunfighters until they did the same. When Lohise walked away from us towards the field and the whimpering, I instructed my fellow tribespeople in specifics.

"Jerro and Verekas will pull apart the trap. Trenz, I want you to speak to the cub and try to calm her. Corwin, that leaves you to prepare and place the litter and ready the bandages. I'll deal with the mother myself if she becomes a threat. When the pup is free, we'll move her to the litter."

We pressed through the tall grass and came upon the scene in Lohise's wake. Amika lay whimpering with her back left leg caught in a rusted trap just above the paw. I cringed at the wound and the dried blood. The titan wolf cub was about the size of a herding dog, but her exaggerated lupine features were those of a puppy through and through. At the sight of her scared round eyes, my heart leapt for the injured creature. We flanked the pup with our focus consumed by her pain, and the threatening growl of Couress caught us unaware.

We'd been foolish enough to walk between mother and pup. Couress lacked the wide frame and thick body mass of her Den Mother Lohise, but I found the sharp points of the wolf mother's nose and ears and teeth to be threatening as they accented her lean frame. She was wiry and rangy, and her coat looked shaggy and matted and unkempt. Her hackles stood menacingly to match the unbridled fury in her eyes. Her growl ripped through a sequence of snarls before Lohise admonished her in a stern voice.

"I've told you, these humans can help her. They come to free Amika from the bite. They'll treat her injury."

Couress turned her attention to Lohise while we prepared ourselves. She spoke to her Den Mother, but she hadn't been placated. Couress's words were fiercely accented. I could barely understand what she was saying.

"Humans why Amika get bite. What makes trust now?"

Lohise spoke calmly, but she stood as tall as possible and flaunted her size menacingly as she insinuated herself between Couress and my gunfighters. "Not every human is a trapper. Would you say every titan wolf eats mushrooms?"

Couress growled winced and murmured unintelligibly while she growled, but she didn't challenge Lohise. As my tribesmen freed Amika's leg, the pup gave a yelp. The expressiveness of Couress's face when she heard the sound of her daughter convinced me that the titan wolves were beyond beasts. The heartbreak and pity were far beyond the things an animal could feel. I thought Couress would bowl through Lohise regardless of the Den Mother's firmly planted paws.

We shifted Amika to the litter as gingerly as we could. When we wrapped the wounded leg in bandaging, she gave only a couple of cries, but I could tell each utterance was like a needle to the already tense Couress.

"I follow Amika. I not leave daughter in paws of- *humans*," she bit off the word with distaste.

Lohise looked at her pack member and glanced at me before speaking to Couress.

"As your Den Mother, I don't think it's wise. As your Alpha, I could forbid it. But I know you suffer for Amika. If you follow, you follow nice." She turned to look at me. "The human Alpha is before you. There are guns in their pack who are wary of us. Stay nice, and give no reason for them to attack you. If you bite or scratch, you turn over Amika's life as well as your own. And you start a war that kills many more."

Couress bared her teeth. "For daughter I start war."

Lohise snarled and sprang up and wrestled Couress to the grass with a paw. In that moment, when Couress struggled against Lohise's authority, I think I caught my first true glimpse of the titan wolves. The ground shook beneath the weight of their bodies. Lohise gave the wolf-mother an ultimatum through gritted teeth.

"I kill both daughters to prevent it."

{~}

Although Lohise was speaking to Couress, I knew her words were for me. Even her careful pronunciations of our dialect gave a signal to both parties. I gave the titan wolf Den Mother a knowing nod. The four gunfighters lifted the litter at each corner, but not before they'd shifted their guns to where they could be reached with a free hand. I could tell the distraught mother titan wolf unsettled the gunfighters. I found myself tense along with my squad.

We reached the edge of the river with Lohise and Couress following us like looming shadows. The swift pace and the exertions of the Sun were draining for my companions but they pressed forward with a determination naturally present when there are giant wolves who sniff your every footprint. I signaled to them to place the litter on the ground as I turned to Lohise. They caught their breath and stretched complaining muscles.

"When it comes to my tribe," I told her. "A show of unity when we enter the camp will bolster our truce." I glanced at Couress. "They'll give Amika drugs for the pain. They may need to amputate her paw. Can we trust her mother to keep the peace?"

Lohise whirled on Couress with her teeth bared. Unspoken vibrations passed between them and Couress licked her lips in nervous deference. Lohise turned an eye back to me. "I believe we're clear. As for your show of unity, I would shame myself in the eyes of my pack, but only Couress and Amika are here to know of my transgressions." She stretched her back legs and tilted her chin with a disarming sort of charm. She tried to put me at ease as if she were a playful labrador instead of a feral intellectual at least ten times my size. Her moving lips exposed her teeth as she spoke.

"Come on, I won't bite. You can ride a horse, can't you? Just know that I'm swallowing my pride for the sake of my kin, woman. If you try to spur me with your heels, I'll throw you so fast you leave your teats behind."

{~}

The return crossing of the river was surreal. My memory of the event feels like a drunken blur. Lohise was unfathomably sentient and entirely unlike a horse. The forced intimacy of bodies pressing against each other was awkward for us at first. Fording the river was our first challenge, and we were made closer in the struggle to maintain dignity in the flowing water. We came to terms with the positioning of my legs and rear and how much pressure I'd need to exert in order to stay in place on her back. Her fur was denser than any rug. The bristle posed a danger to my crotch, and I thanked the sturdiness of my trousers.

When we reached the opposite bank, I nearly slid backwards off Lohise's rear. Her back hips jarred me as she angled up the bank and regained dry footing. I felt her hesitate as I grasped at fur and recovered my original seat. She paused to look behind us for Couress and the litter carrying Amika. The sentries from the Rose tribe were staring at us, dumbfounded and derelict in their duties. I adjusted my posture and prepared myself.

I don't recall what I expected from the people I was born among when I arrived with the titan wolves. I needed to gauge their reactions honestly. I imagine that the sight of their Generale on Lohise's back was a positive omen compared to a devastating exodus from Sylviarg. I knew Amika's adorable face and her injury were as likely as anything to win the hearts of the Rose tribe. In this, at least, I was correct. The doctors were elbow to elbow with curious onlookers before I ordered non-essential personnel to disperse from the medical tent. Nobody was bold enough to approach Lohise even as I called them by name, but my presence gave the tribe the courage to stand closer to the titan wolf Den Mother than any might've dared otherwise. She greeted the tribe solemnly and followed her words with a rumble and a nod of her head. I could see her status rise rapidly in the eyes of my compatriots.

The immediate events of our return left Couress alone, stressed, and given a wide berth. I wanted to take action to rectify the imbalance but I was hesitant to risk confrontation. Confidant Terche stepped in to rescue me. She approached Couress unarmed and without armor. The Confidant displayed her hands in front of her humble smock. The scrappy titan wolf was tense. I heard the subtle shift of firearms among the crowd.

"I how it feels to have your child in the care of the doctors," Terche said with no introduction. She wrestled for control of the developing scene with a projected voice. "Worse than being injured yourself. The whole ordeal is a trial of pain. To see them suffer as we leave their fate in the hands of someone else. When someone else is the hands of the Guards." Couress and the Confidant began to circle each other. Terche continued to speak unflinchingly. She moved her hands and her steps through expressive patterns of solemn dance as the wolf studied her. "The doctors don't share biases of love or hate. They care nothing about enemies or alliances. Be you friend or foe, human or not, they do their best for whoever ends up in their care. It's their calling, their creed. Imprinted in their existence like a holy scar."

The frazzled titan wolf bared her fangs.

"Sway me not, your sly human words," she growled. In spite of her accusation, the wolf-mother squared her haunches and relaxed towards her buttocks fractionally. Terche continued to tentatively approach the anxious titan wolf. Perhaps Couress wouldn't attack Terche but I gathered the wolf was considering the act. I thought the Confidant was mad to press her luck.

I was interrupted in my observations by the approach of a group of armed gunfighters at the edge of the square. There were almost a dozen men and women, and they had a serious look about them that triggered a response in me. I recognized Drak in the lead. His usual aura of utter self-certainty was abundant, and it caused his steps to take on a marching quality.

"Den Mother," I spoke firmly to the titan wolf beneath me, "Would you kindly position us between Couress and those guns?" Lohise reacted to the group before I even finished speaking. Her stride brought her to the side of her pack-mate in a handful of steps. I hailed Drak from the superior height of Lohise's back.

"Greetings, Lieutenant Drak. I see you've assembled an exemplary detail. To what task are they assigned?"

I was beginning to appreciate the wisdom of Lohise's plan to show unity. Drak's frown was enough to betray his frustration. He'd clearly planned on either provoking or outright murdering the titan wolves when they came among us. My presence had temporarily confounded his ambitions. Drak wasn't a man who'd let himself be caught tongue-tied, however. He cleared his throat.

"We serve only the safety of the Rose tribe, Generale," he said with a partial smile to match his perfunctory bow. I could tell his followers wanted to attack the wolves immediately and without pause. I was generous when I called Drak's friends exemplary. Their stances were sloppy and their hands were twitchy. Behind me, the rest of the tribe seemed to catch on to what was happening. There were mutters of disdain while others held an opaque silence. I imagined there were those who sympathized with Drak. I looked around for Confidant Flin and I realized my old friend was nowhere to be seen this afternoon. Terche's voice was the clearest.

"Shame on you, Lieutenant! We're trying to build a home here, not a bloody mess!"

"Confidant," Drak replied coolly, "I don't doubt it." He fiddled with the edge of his armored jacket near his hip. I sensed he knew the importance of the moment. I didn't agree with Drak, but I didn't think he was a total fool. He was determined to make the circumstances work in his favor.

"Any alliance," he continued, "Needs to come with an understanding. If our allies think we're weak-" he looked directly at Lohise.

"I'm sure you know what I mean, Ms. Wolf. The wise don't seek alliances with the weak."

I conceded the effectiveness of Drak's words. If I wasn't so certain the man would kill any titan wolf he could whenever he got the chance, I might've appreciated his show of force. As things stood, I knew he was a threat to relations with Lohise's pack, and therefore the entire tribe. I needed an effective rebuke and a distracting assignment for him before his minor insurrection could continue.

{~}

The Sun passed and became night. I dismounted from Lohise when my legs grew stiff from straddling her wide ribs. The Den Mother was no worse for the wear, but she took the opportunity to seat herself by the fire. I stayed close to her side as I watched the members of my tribe. I spoke in truncated conversations to those who approached me. As the evening wore on, the tensions became clearer.

An unspoken but physical division had come among the Rose tribe in the City of Old. Drak and his allies who disdained the titan wolf presence congregated apart from the rest of the tribe. It was only a fraction of our people, but the group was substantial enough to cause discord. My heart sank as I spotted Flin sitting among them and nursing his flask.

I could tell the visitors were winning the Rose tribe to their side. Amika was too child-like to be threatening and Couress and Lohise were as much alluring as they were daunting. Shared food allowed conversation to flow freely. The titan wolves possessed amazing appetites. Couress was completely unaccustomed to being served a meal while she lounged about. The tribe peered at the titan wolves with guarded curiosity which our canine guests openly returned. In spite of the progress in relations, there was work to be done.

"Lohise," I addressed the Den Mother. "I have to leave you for a Mark. I'm going to post an honor guard in my absence. I intend to dung out whatever bullshit is piling up. But I don't want to expose my throat." Lohise nodded sleepily. I could tell she was prepared to wait out Amika's convalescence among us. My pulse raced at the thought. This was a delicate test of our friendship.

I walked deliberately over to Drak's side of the camp. I asked questions about the health and equipment of the gunfighters there and did my diligence as Generale. I requisitioned armor and patches for damaged jackets. I made notes for the doctors and provided smoking herbs from my personal supply. I gave updates on the Mammoth's ammunition production schedule. As I performed my inspection, Flin glared at me from his corner with his solitary eye. I didn't want to smooth things with the Confidant. My conversation with Flin would be a difficult task and I was unprepared.

Drak couldn't help himself when he noticed my presence. He spoke to me companionably.

"Preparing to fend off predators, Generale? A noble trait in a commander." He raised a wooden mug in acknowledgement. The fighters around us sensed the confrontation buried in his words.

I spoke and my voice echoed through the ruins of the City of Old.

"I intend the Rose tribe survive and prosper by any means available to us. I intend to encourage you to become the best Guard-damned gunfighters this tribe has ever seen, but make no mistake. I speak as the rightful Generale. If you intend on insubordination, you may speak up now and be dealt with fairly. Otherwise I'll deal with you later and the dealing may not be as equitable."

I studied the faces of Drak's men and women as flickers of wavering loyalty passed among them.

Drak retorted with a vehemence which caught me off guard.

"I intend to put down every last one of those over-grown mongrel savages."

Rage kindled inside of me at the man's stubborn insolence. "Lieutenant Drak, if you harm any wolf under my explicit protection, you'll make Confidant Flin look like a beauty pageant queen when I'm done with you."

I tried to measure the impact of the exchange of words. Drak crossed his arms over his chest. He was lucky I hadn't struck him or demoted him. I couldn't allow the division I was witnessing to take root. Behind Drak, Confidant Flin lurched to his feet, thrusting aside his blanket. Eyes turned in his direction. He walked towards me with the butt of his rifle issuing a dull tap against the chunks of concrete beneath us. A hollowness loomed in my gut.

"The Generale does what she believes is best, gunfighters. You can't begrudge her that. Her judgement has been steady," he began. I breathed a sigh of relief I don't think I completely concealed. Flin wasn't finished speaking.

"I disagree with her. I'll say so to anyone who listens. I'll not disobey our Generale's orders when she gives them, but this disagreement is my right as Confidant. Because, as I'm sure our Generale knows, if the titan wolves betray us-" he began, anger surging through his words. The blood ran cold in my veins and I steadied myself.

"We stand to lose far more than a zealous Lieutenant."

"I've learned a whole slew of different words for a whole bunch of different stuff, and to be honest I don't really like any of it. Words always spin and disguise and complicate. My tongue can barely keep up with their bullshit, let alone my pen. I feel better when I smile or frown. I feel better when I nod or clasp a hand. Please, either wink at me or send an elbow for my ribcage." -the Frost Swordsman

The angular scales covering the dragon were midnight blue in the overcast sky, but they reflected a tinge of metallic green where the muted light of the Sun glanced from their edges. His body and face and wings were distinctly reptilian. His abdomen alone was heftier than a Regiment supply truck, and his neck and tail stretched beyond his torso with snaking sinuosity. He held his rear feet and haunches horizontally in line with his tail as he flew, but he let his muscular front arms hang down to flank the breastbone scales near the base of his neck. He appeared to possess opposable thumbs on each of his digits, tipped with curving talons. He circled in a wide pass and swiveled his head to inspect the scene. Regiment troops among the crowd opened fire with their rifles in pattering bursts.

The sound of shooting caused the spectators to panic. The dragon didn't appear to notice the gunfire, but then his wings flared without warning. He slowed to a hover and inhaled. His wings reached the peak of their stroke and he froze in the sky, a living statue above the pit. A cascade of blue flame poured from his jaws.

The people screaming seemed far away from where I stood in the confines of the stone walls. I braced myself and felt vulnerable, but there was nowhere to run. The dragon paused when he depleted his breath to draw another and unleashed a second plume. As the torrent of blue blanketed the ground, I heard cries of terror fall silent. Newly formed tendrils of frost crept over the edges of the stone pit and gathered in crystalline blankets. Always cold, I thought to myself. The Guard-damn cold is everywhere now, and I'll never escape. I peered upward, trying to get a better look, and I realized the Jurisdiction spectators hadn't burned away to ash. They were frozen where they stood, coated completely in rigid ice, the final expressions on their faces tinted with cerulean until the spring thaw. I looked for Captain Crowbar among the eerie statues of the briskly entombed dead, but I didn't see his mis-shapen mug.

The dragon didn't leave me time to think or observe his morbid work. He landed on the icy edge of the pit and his front claws caused shooting cracks appear as they stabbed the surface. I felt the wind from his wings as he set himself down and folded the two sails behind his back. I braced for my own death, posed in a stance with my crude sword, and I looked up at his huge, green eyes.

The dragon blinked with aplomb and the movement of his eyelids informed me there was more than just a beast to him. I can't say for certain if he intended to reveal himself, but I knew complicated thoughts swam behind those teal eyes. The dragon released a huff of frosty breath and lit the air with a jet of blue before he cleared his throat to speak. His words rebounded throughout the stone pit. Their reverberance made me feel tiny, but I did my best not to cower.

"I don't want to kill you," the dragon stated. His voice carried pitched, harmonic overtones and he squinted at me critically with a slitted iris, tilting his head to the side.

"Tell me why," he implored, as if I should know the answer. He shifted his forepaws and drummed his claws against the ice while he craned his neck to get a better look at me. He carefully avoided getting close to the machete. I could see him study my soiled weapon. He gave the corners of the pit and the corpse of the dead rat a thoughtful sniffing. I tried to prevent myself from being disconcerted when he stepped his front legs down in the pit and swiveled his neck in a calculated curve. He rested his chin on the clay floor, bringing us directly face to face. From the bottom of his jaw to the jagged ridges over his eyes, the dragon's head was as thick as I was tall. The distance from his nostrils to his ears was nearly two of me in length. He refocused his sea-green orbs and his breath pulled the air past my shoulders.

"Water-mage."

I stared back at him, but I didn't sense any aggression. I only realized he was talking about me when he said "water-mage" because of the way he looked at me when he said it.

"May I?"

The offer was ambiguous, but I didn't have the heart to decline. Where would that leave me and what could I possibly do on my own? I wasn't confident of my ability to live in the Wilds. The Captain was supposed to be treating me like a king with the money I'd just won. Even so, I couldn't bring myself to be angry at the dragon for interrupting my life. I wasn't truly disappointed I was no longer the Jurisdiction's pet.

I decided the offer from a magnificent creature was preferable to being completely lost and alone, even if I was only a snack for his journey. I considered the possibility that the dragon might return me to the Slave Pens with a lurch of fear, but the expressiveness of his scaled features and the frozen dead above us made me doubt the possibility. Suddenly I couldn't bear to see the dragon fly away without me. From the changes in his brows, he was attempting to follow my thoughts as they occurred to me. I gave a slight nod. The dragon showed his teeth in a wild grin. His incisors were bigger than my arms.

My heart was racing and I swallowed. I thrust the machete behind my back and secured the metal with the tattered remains of my shirt. The dragon's arm provided an invitation and I saw no reason left to delay. I climbed to his neck and took hold of the scales at the crown of his head to steady myself. I sat on a wide row of scales behind the angular spikes forming hollow curves behind his scaled ears. I found the position behind them was comfortable and the dynamic, shifting motions of his ears were exquisitely expressive. When the dragon lifted his neck up, my stomach was left behind, and I rose above the walls of the pit. I tried to adjust to this new position and I found another row of scales to brace my feet should the need arise.

I clung to the dragon by any means necessary as he launched himself towards the sky. The poorly sheathed machete whipped sideways and bounced against my back, but the blade didn't slip free or slice me. The dragon's ears floated near my shoulders, responding to the tiniest course corrections and currents in the air. I caught a glimpse of the fighting pit below us, ringed with the ice which the recently constructed Jurisdiction graveyard. I shuddered at the thought of the preserved bodies but I found I lacked any warmth for remorse as I white-knuckled my hands around the dragon's scales. When I managed to swallow my fear and find a rhythm in the wingbeats, I was overcome with a sense of exhilaration as I looked down at the world passing beneath me. The wind rushed against my face and my eyes began to water. My breathing felt forced and my stomach lurched when I remembered how far I could fall and be dashed among the trees. Nevertheless, I felt a kind of joy which was imprinted permanently on my being. For a couple of Marks my blood and adrenaline surged through me and brought a rush of euphoria. {~}

We flew south for the rest of the Sun, passing over treetops, fields and wetlands stretching endlessly. As the Sun began to recede from the sky, the solid firmament of landscape ended abruptly at the water's edge. First came a tan band of sandy dunes, and then came the sea. I gazed in wonder at the infinite jewel of the ocean. Tears ran from my eyes and streaked from of my face. The field of rippling blue-green below us was a living work of art, and the beauty was so intense to me the sight was almost painful. The dragon descended towards the surface and the white-capped tips of the waves grew in clarity. The feeling I got from the Regiment helicopter over the forest was magnified by a hundred. I yelled in triumph and lost my grip when a gust of wind caught us. My stomach lurched sideways and I hooked my feet in the nick of time in order to avoid being doused in the surf. The dragon spoke to me again.

"Calm now, man-mage. I go to the Wizard. The Wizard is broken, but the Wizard knows. Broken, but knows."

Suddenly I couldn't contain my exhaustion. My head and body ached. "What Wizard? Where? What does he know?" I asked the dragon sleepily.

I sensed my companion felt there was no ambiguity in his previous statement. He repeated it.

"The Wizard knows."

{~}

I awoke to a foreign sensation. I felt... hot?

The heat wasn't unpleasant, but the stiffness in my body made me moan. The sun beat down on my shoulders as I lay on the sloping sand of a beach. The warm ocean lapped against my toes in soothing pulses. The sand grated against my skin when I shifted. I decided the grains were tolerable, so I let the beach pillow me as I dozed in relative comfort. Eventually my curiosity made me roll over with a groan, and I sat up. The sun was directly overhead, and the piercing blue of the sky was devoid of any clouds. I took in the golden blazing presence of the light above me. Rays struck my skin with a ferocity I'd never felt before. I splashed myself with water from the salty waves as they touched my legs.

I wasn't bleeding badly, and I didn't think any bones were broken. I undid the clasps of the steel bracer on my forearm and let the armor fall to the sand. I was glad to be free of the weight. I removed my soggy shoes and tossed them beyond the reach of the water. My trousers were mostly intact but my shirt was tangled around the machete on the sand next to me. I looked around at the contours of the beach.

The endless ocean was what captured my attention and held it. The water was a vibrant teal blue in the bright sun, and I was enchanted. I stared a the waves falling in their endless rhythm against the shore. When I brought myself to look away from the surf, I saw sunlit detail everywhere. There was sand and a few rocks and a treeline guarding the island's interior. I knew there was more coast to explore, and the beach appeared to be an easier path compared to the dense foliage. My first instincts told me I was on an island surrounded by water, far from where the boots of the Regiment could tread. The thought was a comfort, but the strangeness of the unknown place also filled me with apprehension. My stomach complained and I made myself stand up and take a few steps.

With a grudging thought for potential usefulness, I dragged the machete along with me. The pain of my injuries was significant and my blistered hands didn't want to grasp the handle properly. I stumbled across the sand anyway. I rounded a jutting corner of the island and found myself at the edge of a pleasant bay, a wide band of smooth sand a few hundred meters across. A mangrove tree was perched among the rocks at the other side of the curving cove. The tree stood on a maze of roots like an ensconced sentinel for the tides of the bay, moving gracefully in the shifting breeze. The branches blanketed the area with dappled shadows.

I crossed the sand of the bay with laborious steps. When I was about twenty meters from the tree, I could see the bark on the trunk was formed in the semblance of a bearded face. The tree was a work of art rather than just a plant. I looked at the waves lapping at the rocks beneath the tree's roots and I wondered how many Rounds the mangrove had been keeping watch. I smiled at the leafy greens of vibrant natural life. The tree was as robust as anything I'd ever seen. The looming branches dwarfed me as I entered the shade, and I was consumed with pensive admiration. I'd found a pleasant canopy from the beating sun. I was perhaps not as shocked as I could've been when the impossible happened.

"Can I help you?" the tree said politely. I stared at the face and I realized the pulsing bark and swaying branches weren't simply the product of the breeze or my tired mind.

"I- uh-" I began. I swallowed, and my mind raced for a response. I thought back to what the dragon was saying to me.

"I'm looking for a Wizard," I shrugged. "I heard he might be broken but I guess I'm looking anyway."

For a second I thought the tree ceased to move, and I'd hallucinated the whole thing. Then the tree gave a hearty laugh that stretched the bark of his features to their limits. I nearly fell over his roots from the volume.

"I might know of such a Wizard, Sir. How'd you get to this island? Who told you the Wizard was broken?"

I clenched my teeth. I had no idea if my tale about the dragon would be well-received by the tree. The tree picked up on my indecision immediately.

"Tell you what, Signore. We don't get many visitors here. Tell you what, forget it. You're our first visitor. Literally. ever. Congratulations, sea-faring traveler."

I studied the tree's face as he spoke. I tilted my head to the side.

"Are you the Wizard?" His branches danced above me as I appraised his trunk. "You're pretty Guard-damn amazing, you know."

The tree's posture swelled with pride.

"I sort of am, aren't I? But no, I'm not the Wizard. The Wizard created me to keep himself sane, although it helps to be sane in the first place if you're attempting to stay that way. The name's Westings, Sir. And whom do I make the acquaintance of this fine Sun?"

"I- uh-" I considered what to call myself. I could call myself anything I wished, I decided, free of the Slave Pens. Perhaps a new name would be best for a new life.

"Pleased to meet you Uh," Westings intoned.

"I- no- my name is Rahn," I explained.

"Well why didn't you say so?" the tree boomed. "You can tell me the name you were gonna make up later and I promise to be properly pleased to hear it." Westings shifted his roots and trunk, moving himself in such a way that made the world around me tilt. I carefully watched the many parts of the tree and my footing around his uneven base. Westings tasted the water, the soil and the breeze with careful consideration before he spoke again.

"Rahn, Monsieur. You could be here a while. There's a flint and a striker in my branches over here," Westings squirmed to indicate the location. "Find dead branches from the other mangroves and dig a hollow on the beach over there. I'll see what I can do about food." He dipped a sharp looking branch near the surface of the sea. Fish darted beneath the wavering wooden tips. I smiled and nodded, my mouth salivating at the thought. I abandoned the machete and headed for the treeline. In the Slave Pens, we viewed dried and processed fish-brick as a special treat. My heart leapt at the idea of fresh meat.

Westings and I passed by part of the afternoon in companionable silence as I made a fire. True to his word, he speared three sizeable fish before launching them flying through the air to the beach. After they landed, I ended their wild flopping with my machete. A grin crossed my face as I admired the gleaming color of their scales. Westings hummed melodies as I baked fresh fish over open flame and ate it with my bare hands. The taste was beyond how I'd imagined food could taste. Even the prepared food of the Regiment barracks hadn't come close to Westings' fresh-fired catch. When my stomach was sated and thirst began to chase me, I was directed by a branch in the direction of a spring on the interior of the island. I felt energy returning to my body and I hiked the distance in good spirits.

When I'd hydrated myself, I returned to the bay and strolled up to Westings' face. He was studying the horizon.

"I gather you're not much of a talker, Herr Rahn, but I don't mind doing the talking for the both of us. How'd you like to hear a story?" I nodded in assent. "Take a seat here, Señor. Sitting spots abound. I think I know a story you might enjoy. Maybe this'll even enlighten your current situation. This tale is named after a foolish slacker who also happens to be the main character. I think you may've heard of him. Some of his story might even be true, sprig to the sky."

Westings cleared his... throat?

"I call this particular yarn *The Wizard of the Waves.*"

{~}

Moons passed on the island. The Wizard remained only a character in Westings' tall tales. I was trying to forget the Wizard and the dragon and Captain Crowbar and the Slave Pens. Not to mention the bloated dead rat in the fighting pit. My head hurt thinking about those things. In the meantime, my life was comparatively luxurious, and I began inventing new problems to complain about.

"I'm tired of these stick-shapes you call 'writing,' Westy. Why can't you just tell me stories the way you used to?" I asked the tree for the fifth time. In response he dipped a leafy branch to scratch marks in the sand by my feet.

"There are stories written down in books than I can't possibly recall in order to tell you. You need to be able to read them," Westings replied, not looking away from his writing. "Look here. This is your name."

"I know, I know. Rahn. Like that. So what?"

"Do you have a last name? A surname, perhaps?"

I considered the question. Slaves in the Pens didn't usually bother with family titles.

"Le'Del, I think," I told him. "I don't even know if I'm pronouncing it right. Nobody's ever used it. "

"Your first instinct seems to be a natural one," Westings said. He scratched the letters in the sand and I stared at them.

"Rahn Le'Del," I said. "Why's that thingy in the middle of my second name?"

"That's an apostrophe, joins sounds together to make a single word."

I shook my head. "There are too many shitty rules."

Westings sighed. "If you want to be a mage, you need to nourish your mind. You've had a rough start, growing up as you did. If you want to master yourself and master the arcane, you require sincere academic study. Lucky for you, I can give you that, and we've got plenty of time. You should take advantage."

"But it all so damn useless!" I blurted. "I want to be able to fight! What good is being a mage if it doesn't make me any stronger?"

Westings blinked at me. "I'm going to be blunt with you, Rahn. Your aura isn't a powerful one. Your element is water, like the Wizard and I. We're a bit of a rarity. We really are. Most water mages don't have the power the Wizard has cultivated over centuries fraught with suffering and failed experimentation. So don't expect mage skills to make you invincible. There are more kinds of strength than the strength to kill. If you want to nourish your abilities, it's going to take a lot of thought and a lot of work. I'm afraid some of that work is best accomplished by reading."

I sat down on the beach. The bending lines, the characters, the words, they blurred together. I was exceedingly tired of spelling and grammar. I'd escaped a prison only to find myself in another.

Westings had reminded me time and time again, there was no way off the island except for the Wizard. After the better part of three Moons ,the mythical man remained absent.

"I'm going for a walk," I told Westings. The tree accepted my need for a respite from his lessons.

"I believe you've earned a story later. A saga to set you to rights. Try to let go of your troubles, Rahn Le'Del. I have no desire to make you miserable."

I gave the tree a nod, suddenly regretting my obstinacy. The Sun's heat made me wade in the water and let the waves break over my hands. The warm ocean felt wonderful. How wrong I was a moment ago, I told myself. This place was a far cry from the cold of the Slave Pens. Being trapped here was like being trapped in paradise. I wondered if I might yearn for people eventually. A tree could only offer so much companionship. My thoughts turned to how Westings must feel here. Perhaps we could save each other from solitude.

I rotated my hips and my torso so that I was wading along the bay, away from where Westings stood among the rocks. I'd barely rounded the corner to the adjacent cove when I noticed an object lying on the beach. As I continued to gaze, I realized it was the body of a waterlogged man, washed ashore by the tide. He was shifting around face-down in the shallows like a piece of driftwood with his arms haphazardly strewn to each side. My heart skipped a beat as I realized that he was probably dead. His corpse would become a bloated, rotting lure for scavengers unless I moved him. I drew nearer to him and the aging man sat up with a start.

He pushed himself upright with his hands and whipped his head straight, revealing a pair of bloodshot blue eyes. The white hair ringing the back of his scalp flew up and unleashed a spattered arc of salt water. The sea dribbled over his features and down through his wispy white beard. He coughed and sputtered but he stood up, his knees wobbling beneath him. In his right hand was a length of driftwood inexplicably shaped as a walking stick. He was thin and he slouched forward slightly as he leaned on the stick. His face was wrinkled and weathered. I don't know if I'd ever witnessed a man as old as the marooned stranger. No one stayed around in the Slave Pens until their hair went gray. His exact age was hard for me to guess. As the castaway composed himself, I saw he possessed a wiry strength belied by his skinny limbs and rounded belly. He was completely naked except for a pair of ragged half-trousers made from a pale fabric imprinted with grime. The breeches were held at the waist by a greenish belt woven from plant fibers. The tenuous garment was obscenely transparent in its drenched state.

He saw me standing there and raised his white eyebrows in acknowledgment. The moving wrinkles on his forehead seemed to make words at me.

"Greetings, Muchacho. What brings you to my island?"

My skepticism was undoubtedly difficult to retain. "Your island?" I asked him incredulously. "You're the Wizard of the Waves?"

The bearded man frowned mildly and looked down at himself.

"I suppose I am, aren't I?"

He began to walk briskly away from me down the shore towards Westings. I trailed him like a shocked puppy, emulating his rapid pace even though he'd washed up on the beach unconscious.

"Will you teach me how to be a mage?" I asked him desperately.

He heard me but his mind was clearly elsewhere.

"Hmmm? A mage you say?"

I continued to follow him, but I was puzzled at the man's behaviour. He hummed a tune to himself. He and Westings greeted each other casually. The tree acted like nothing was amiss about the Wizard being gone for Moons and appearing on the beach half-drowned. I paused by Westings and gaped after the Wizard as he strolled boldly towards the mangrove trees of the island's interior. He grumbled incoherently about a 'Bloody Mary' as he passed beyond earshot. I looked at Westings' rugged features.

"Better give him a Sun or two," the tree told me. "Or three. He's usually moody when he first gets back. If he gets sulky, just climb up in my branches and hang on. You know the drill from when that tropical storm passed through."

I straightened my posture and flexed my hands. "I'm gonna go talk to him. I wanna see where he lives."

Westings snorted air through the bark of his nose. "Suit yourself. And don't say I didn't warn you. I hope your swimming lessons stick with you better than your reading ones."

Having lost sight of the Wizard, I nearly missed the entrance to his cave. A clever passageway was hidden by the base of the highest jutting rocks the low-lying island had to offer. I ducked down among roots in order to enter. Shallow pools of seawater covered the floor and I splashed ahead in the dark. When I'd walked several cautious meters under the rock, I saw light leaking down from a narrow shaft above me. The glow pooled against a distant ceiling and I tilted my head up to take in the color. Electric lights, I thought. A ladder in front of me led up to the inside of the loft where the Wizard lived. I gathered the design of his cavern would keep the space from flooding even if the island was inundated with water. I wondered if the Wizard had created his home himself as I finished ascending the ladder.

The Wizard sat there looking at me. A glass filled with an unfamiliar red liquid resided in his left hand.

"Can I help you?" he asked in a tired voice. He took a sip with narrowed eyes.

I nodded, attempting what I thought was respectful acknowledgment before I answered him. "I wanted to see your home. I've heard stories about you."

"Here it is. I hope he left out the boring parts." he stared ahead. Apparently he had nothing more to say for the time being. He took another sip of the red beverage. The smell of liquor became noticeable in the stagnant air of the cave. The electric lighting bathed the place in a foreign glow. The stone walls were abridged by chunks of coral and covered with moss and algae. Trickles of water leaked through cracks in the edifice. The result was a mosaic more detailed than any artist's hand could possibly render. A bed, a humming refrigerator and several shelves of books made up the only furniture other than the padded reclining chair where the Wizard was seated. The carpeting beneath my feet was finely made but grungy with age and salt and moisture. I almost turned away to leave the Wizard in peace, but he spoke to me again. "How's Westings? You two get along?"

I peered at the man in his comfortable chair. "Yes. He's alright. I like his stories. He's teaching me to read."

The Wizard raised an eyebrow. "You can't read?" His tone was condescending, but he found his manners. "My apologies. The world is a mad place, and I suppose it always was. You can see I keep a few books." He gestured halfheartedly at the shelves. As I peered at their spines, the rest of the Wizard's beverage went down the hatch, and he leaned back. His left hand placed the glass on the floor beside his chair.

"Mage or not, you should learn to read, lad. Westings is a wise tree." He gave a sharp laugh. "Probably wiser than me." He groaned and closed his eyes. "I know I'm not much of a host, but I need to sleep. Help yourself to whatever you can find in the freezer. Finest ice cream and liquor and frozen green beans you can possibly steal from those Jurisdiction shit-stains."

The old man started snoring almost instantly. I noticed he hadn't even removed his wet shorts. They clung to him damply in his chair. I spotted a blanket on the bed which was almost clean, and I drew it over of the sleeping man. The perception could've been my imagination, but I thought I saw some tension drain from the lines of his brow. I left the cave.

{~}

When the Wizard appeared the next morning, I got the sense that he'd become thoroughly bored with the island he inhabited. He was even bored with his friend Westings. The Guards only knew how many Rounds he'd been pent-up here, but the state of affairs worked in my favor. Seeing how I was new and interesting, the Wizard agreed to teach me readily and without much ado.

Unfortunately I was a failure at everything over the next few Suns. Music, art, poetry, I was useless as a student and yet the Wizard walked me through each topic with his hand invariably stroking his wispy beard as he spoke. Westings watched us with a detached expression as he felt around in the waves for stray fish. After a particularly painful session that the Wizard called 'yoga' I lost my temper. My teacher and I began cursing at each other in frustration. The Wizard's eyes began to glow.

"Gentlemen! Calm down!" Westings admonished us, wrapping us both with flexible branches. We glared at each other.

"Not a damn flicker!" The Wizard seethed. "Your aura is always the same. It doesn't grow, it doesn't move. Your mind won't expand at all. It's like a chunk of ice!"

The Wizard's words hurt. In that moment I almost accepted myself as unworthy. I looked at the sand. Of course I wasn't a mage. I was a Slave. The Jurisdiction would've known if I had special powers.

Westings added insult to injury. He spoke to the Wizard but my proximity left them no privacy. "Water mages seldom amount to such as yourself, Szakaieh. Rahn doesn't have it in him. You shouldn't hold that against him."

I raged inside at Westings' remarks, but the Wizard's calm dissent gave voice to my anger before I managed to fumble through my own words.

"My dear Westings. I find myself disinclined agree with you in regards to my protege here. Respectfully, of course." The Wizard made a gesture with his hands I didn't understand. The tree released his grip on us. I felt Westings' anxiety grow as I saw the movements of his branches. I realized the Wizard's eyes were glowing blue-green like the tropical sea surrounding the island. His voice boomed and Westings winced. "I'm going to make a mage from Rahn, whatever it takes. I can see him, can't you? The true Mr. Le'Del in there, buried in the ice."

As soon as the Wizard made his assessment, he withdrew. Westings shook his trunk and his branches. The doubt was painfully plain on my reading tutor's wooden face. The Wizard was a regular hermit once again. He leaned on his walking stick and frowned to himself. He let out a friendly chuckle without warning. Or was his laugh the tittering of madness? I'd seen men lose themselves before, in the Slave Pens. A mind could only take so much.

"I was going at this totally wrong, my friend. What does the student desire to learn? What does being a mage mean to you?"

I considered this for a few seconds. I cracked my neck with a casual twist.

"I wanna get rid of the Jurisdiction."

I took a step backwards as Westings and the Wizard exploded with roaring laughter. Tears leaked down the man's face before he could stop himself. I couldn't understand what was so amusing to them. Was I so pathetic that they had to laugh at me like this? The Wizard reassured me as he picked up on my confusion. He placed a hand on my shoulder to steady himself and he tried to catch his breath.

"You and me both, brother. You and me both." The Wizard was giddy, but his laughter ceased.

"So how exactly are you gonna to accomplish this feat? What makes you think you'll succeed where entire armies have fallen? What weapon do you alone possess, hmmmm? Where are you hiding it?"

His face and his raised eyebrows made me realize he actually expected me to formulate a response to his question.

I set my jaw stubbornly. "I suppose I'll need a blade."

A broad smile flowed across the Wizard's face.

"A true swordsman?" He made a few mock slashes at me with his walking stick. His hand came to his chin and his eyebrows continued their dance. "Might limber up these old bones. Westings, do you have my whittling knife? The one I prefer for um... whittling?"

The tree produced the item easily. "Part of the collection."

The Wizard nodded at me. "Toss it to Rahn. Alright, swordsman. Find yourself a stick and make yourself a practice sword. When you're ready we'll start. I'll teach you what I know about sword-play. Westings and I tried fencing once to pass the time. We had ourselves a few epic bouts, didn't we, Westings?"

"If you say so, Szakaieh."

{~}

The Wizard's humble knife brought back memories of the tool which was my salvation in the Slave Pens. I discarded a series of gouged sticks before I managed to shape one to my liking. The wood was a branch about the length of my leg which held a gentle curve. The bulk of the carved stick weighed almost as much as the machete I was given by the Regiment.

I stood across from the Wizard on the beach. He bowed to me. I returned the gesture with uncertainty.

"En garde!" he called, springing to a stance with his walking stick.

I hesitated. "You're going to use that thing?"

He took advantage of my reticence and lunged at me with a thrust. I barely managed to deflect the point of the wooden stick before he was wheeling on me again. I blocked a hail of blows and held my wooden practice sword in both hands like a staff. The only thing I could do at first was awkwardly protect myself. The Wizard moved with uncanny speed and technique. His footwork and posture kept my head reeling. He moved along a single axis, towards me and away from me as if there were an invisible boundary for his feet. He gripped his driftwood walking stick in one hand and placed his other hand near his hip or his back. Nevertheless, the movement of his stick barely left me time to breathe. His movements were effortless and impossible to predict. I took a few bruising smacks and pokes, but I roared back at the Wizard anyway. I went after him with a bumbling swing. He dodged but I turned and charged after him again. His bowed legs juked around behind me. He rained taps on my back and I turned to him again with my anger building, but when I saw the way he was standing my grip relaxed. He'd dropped out of his fighting stance completely. His walking stick was tip-down in the sand as he studied me intently with a hand on his chin.

"Voila. A mage aura," he mumbled to Westings from the side of his mouth.

"Like he'd plagiarized the textbook," the tree agreed.

I felt my aura then. Like a cooling liquid sphere with me at the center. Or was it just my mind, in the center of a dense cloud? The first time I ever noticed the sensation was a revelation. Blue energy hovered around like the power was holding me. Or was I the one holding the power?

"Wonderful, isn't it?" the Wizard said with genuine appreciation. "A bit chilly, though, for my taste."

I swallowed. Air rushed in and out of my lungs. Frost was death. Everything was always so Guard-damn cold, and so was I. Blackened fingers and toes flashed in front of my eyes.

I tried to steady myself and prevent my aura from receding. I survived my past and I was finding a new path.

"Yes," I responded neutrally. My aura pleased me but the sensation ached in a distant way. I twitched, but I wasn't moving my body. The blue around me pulsed. Goosebumps flowed over my skin.

"Can other people see this?" I asked.

The Wizard shook his head.

"Westings and I aren't exactly 'other people.'" He brandished the walking stick with a deft flourish. "Care for another round?"

A wild urge came over me. "You're Guard-damn right I am!"

"En garde!"

We'd finally hit on a skill where I could flourish. The Wizard carefully showed me how to lunge and parry and feint and slash and riposte. He explained that while my weapon might be slower than his, the larger two-handed stick also had advantages as well. While I learned to handle a sword the Wizard made comments about mages. My aura responded when I was pressed hard and my adrenaline was flowing.

As the next few Suns passed, I think I was more content than I'd ever been in my life. We ate fresh fish and fruits and root vegetables and had ice cream and liquor for desert. I was beginning to learn a schedule I enjoyed. The Wizard was in high spirits, and he relished his role as teacher.

Everything changed one morning, out of the blue. The overcast sky matched the Wizard's mood. I wondered if a storm was coming. I walked across the beach from my sleeping spot by Westings' trunk towards where the old man was waiting. I was drinking tea and I hastily downed the rest when I spotted my teacher. He looked impatient and he was pacing. I'd never seen him act in such a way. Even when he was agitated the Wizard was always flowing and composed and precise. When he turned his leathery face there was a different gleam about his eyes. They were more blue than I remembered and there was none of his carefree kindness in them. I gripped the handle of my practice sword involuntarily. The way his voice cracked when he spoke I wondered if he'd even slept.

"You've been learning sword-fighting. Now you're going to learn why you've been wasting your time."

His words were like a dull stone dropped on my heart. I wanted to protest, but he gave a nod to signal he was ready. I rushed at him, bringing my practice sword up over my head. I slashed down. He raised his walking stick to meet my swing. His scowl was filled with so much contempt that the expression made my stomach lurch. Was this even the same man I'd spent the last several Suns practicing with? I stumbled and gasped when my practice sword made contact. An explosive burst of water reduced my wooden sword and the Wizard's walking to splinters. I released my grip before my hands could be sliced by destroyed wood. The Wizard and I faced each other unarmed as the droplets trickled over our faces. The Wizard raised his voice and called over to Westings.

"Toss it to him, Westings."

The tree said nothing, but I turned to see the Regiment machete whirling towards me through the air. The weapon lodged tip-down in the beach by my feet. I drew the blade with a swish of steel against sand.

"Vamos! Andele!"

The Wizard yelled at me as I hesitated.

I was suspicious of this new Wizard. I didn't want to know what might happen if I refused him. His eyes glowed and I tried to avoid looking at his face. I gave a half-hearted whirl of the machete and he smacked the metal away with the back of his hand.

"Don't be a Guard-damn wuss about it."

I gave in and swung my machete at him like an axe. I expected him to dodge or knock the blade away as he'd done before. My attack struck his shoulder with a sickening chop. The blade sank to its breadth. I felt the crack of bone split in twain and the rip of muscle and tendons as they severed. I gasped, stepping back in shock, and I released the handle. Blood was flowing from the wound, but at a critical moment, the unexpected happened. Instead of leaking over his skin and down to the sand, the flowing blood halted, spread over the machete's metal and the wounded shoulder like a viscous red paint. I was overcome with flashbacks to the Slave Pens. I remembered the brutality of knife fights and improvised cauterizations. Blood was supposed to flow away. The Wizard's blood was misbehaving. The Wizard frowned, reaching for the handle of the machete. He worked the blade free from his body and held the weapon at his side with his opposite arm. The blood reversed its course and traveled back through the grievous gash. I watched in astonishment as the flesh of the Wizard's shoulder knit itself back together until only a scar remained. The man made a grunt and even the scar tissue faded. The Wizard was whole again and holding my machete thoughtfully.

I barely saw the wave of water moving across the beach. I think I may've noticed the phenomenon with my peripheral vision if I hadn't been so intent on the Wizard's miraculous healing. Perhaps I thought I'd begun to hallucinate in multiple ways simultaneously. The wave rose up behind the Wizard, washing over the sand. When the water reached him, he relaxed and sat back against the surface as if he was seating himself in a surging armchair. When the advancing wall reached me a moment later, I showed no such grace. The wave was tall enough that I had to look up in order to see the Wizard bearing down on me. Where did all this water come from, I wondered, and how did it get this far up the beach? I tried to run for a few steps before I realized the wave was going to catch me anyway. I turned to dive and swim through the water, but the wave tumbled me, rolling me in painful somersaults and bouncing me against the sand. After a few tumultuous seconds ,the wave coughed me up unceremoniously in its wake. I sputtered and gasped for air, shaking the water from my ears. The wave receded and the Wizard stepped effortlessly back to dry ground at the base of Westings' trunk. He tossed my machete towards the branches and Westings snatched the handle.

"I don't want to be disturbed," the Wizard said to nobody in particular. He turned to walk towards his cave.

I forced myself to stand and began jogging soggily after him.

"But wait-"

He turned and shouted at me.

"I said I'm not to be disturbed!"

My steps halted and I sat down with a thud, dumbfounded. Whatever Westings may've previously said about my mage abilities, he was kinder to me than the Wizard.

"Weather looks dicey," the tree said in his matter-of-fact tone. "Better have some breakfast and make preparations. Batten down the hatches, that sort of thing."

I nodded, but I lacked the correct words to reply.

{~}

The following afternoon a typhoon ripped across the island. I braced myself among Westings' branches, and he clung to my legs and the rocks below him. Rain and wind tore at my tightly curled hair. The raging elements touched a chord within me.

"Stop that," Westings complained over the din of the sky. "Your aura tickles like the dickens."

I grinned and clenched my teeth. Was this an autumn storm? Or was this caused by the Wizard unleashing his fury? Either way, I thought the storm was glorious. I stood up and let the hurricane batter me, knowing Westings would prevent me from being swept out to sea. I knew he was right about my aura. I took the opportunity to feel the energy around me.

When the turbulence subsided, the Marks had crossed over to night. I settled on my damp bedding in the initial glow of the morning. I wrestled with the feeling that I'd learned something important as I tried to relax. I knew I'd changed since I arrived on the island. I considered the ways I'd been shaped. My sleep carried me past the dawn.

The following Sun, there was no sign of the Wizard. Westings offered to help me practice my swordsmanship in his stead. I was mildly surprised, but I gladly accepted the offer. I was even more surprised when he handed me a wooden practice sword. I slapped my hand against his bark in appreciation. The practice sword was a replica of my Regiment machete. The blade wasn't as thin or sharp, but otherwise the proportions were very similar and the weight was well balanced. I stumbled through my thanks for the tree's consideration.

"I have another gift for you. You'll have to thank the Wizard. He does the grocery shopping."

A crate struck the sand behind me, startling me, and I turned around to appraise the package. I looked back at Westings in anticipation before gripping the end of the lid and pulling it away with a splintering crack. Inside the container, a dozen familiar handles offered themselves to me.

"Swords!" I exclaimed, drawing one of the oversized Regiment machetes I'd become familiar with.

"Technically, they're machetes," Winston informed me. "Not actually made as a weapon. Though in the moment when it counts, I doubt such distinctions will matter."

I made a couple of sweeps and jabs with the flawless blade.

"Now we practice," Westings interrupted my revelry. "Wooden sword. I don't want my branches getting hacked off."

I re-sheathed the machete down among its peers and closed the crate lovingly. I picked up the practice likeness and faced the tree. I think he could sense my appreciation. No one had ever given me a present of such grand value before. A branch dipped towards me, and I tapped it to signal I was ready.

I eventually came to learn more about fighting with a sword from Westings than from anyone else. The tree was only willing to fight me casually, as he wasn't a violent sort by nature, but he had a plethora of branches. They attacked from every angle, and I beat them away. The blows didn't harm him much and I didn't bother to hold back. The Wizard failed to appear for the better part of a Moon. In that time, Westings shaped me to a warrior I could be proud of. I know my aura increased. I felt like a mage as I cooled in the ocean after my sessions of sword practice. I began coaxing and taunting the tree to come after me whenever he began to slow down. I'm sure he'd grown bored of trying to do battle with an eager young swordsman. Westings was wise, however, as the Wizard previously noted. His tricks and cheating and changes in strategy expanded my views on combat. He'd slither take hold of me, trapping a limb or my body and tossing me to the sand. He'd slap me so hard with twangy branches I could trace the patterns of his mangrove bark in the welts and bruises.

"You have to remember you can lose," he'd say, as if I'd forgotten.

{~}

When the Wizard finally re-emerged, he was his usual self with an extra dash of calm and composed. He hailed Westings and I with a cheerful greeting and we watched him expectantly. He looked at me, sounding kindly as he addressed me. There was no apology spoken, but I think the contrition was in his tone.

"Well, Rahn? Do you still wish to be a mage?"

My thoughts raced for a moment. I truly hoped the question wasn't a trick or a trap. I realized I wasn't considering the answer to the question. I knew what I wanted. I faced the Wizard with my arms crossed.

"I do."

The bearded man nodded. His thoughts and feelings were carefully guarded.

"Then I'd like you to meet a couple of my friends. Westings here isn't my only creation."

The tree sighed. I gathered these friends weren't his favorite characters.

"Don't worry, bud, you're the most permanent. And certainly the most talkative."

The Wizard made a gesture with his hands and a column of water shot up from the sand. As I watched, the water took on the form of a man. A giant, aqueous caricature of a man. His face was blocky and featureless, and he had no legs. His lower half was comprised of a flowing column of water. His torso and arms were masculine in shape, and his right arm ended in a watery hammer. His left arm supported the translucent curved rectangle of a shield. He was half-again as tall as me, and I stared up at him in awe.

"His name is Blunter," the Wizard said. "When you've defeated him I'll let you meet his sister."

My brow furrowed. "You want me destroy your creation?"

The Wizard shook his head. "Blunter can be re-summoned. You, on the other hand. Worry about your own hide. To defeat a water elemental with physical force alone is a feat beyond any swordsman's grasp. Only a mage can prevail, here. Don't focus on the blade itself. Focus instead on the intent that the blade implies."

Fifteen minutes later, I was laid out on the sand in front of Westings' roots. Blunter hovered menacingly but the Wizard held him back with a gesture. I had a broken finger, a cracked rib, a mild concussion, and water in my lungs.

"Rahn protected himself," the Wizard was telling Westings in a stubborn tone of voice. "If he weren't a mage, he'd be dead right now. I saw him use his shielding."

Westings wasn't having any of this. He was furious. I heard him yelling at the Wizard about abusing me, but I coughed painfully and managed to dislodge some water and a few words.

"I see a path now," I said. "I know how to be a mage."

{~}

Water was everything. Water holds entire worlds in its depths, but water could blur and obscure. Water gave us life, filling up our living bodies, but the substance eroded and chilled and diluted and suffocated. Under pressure or at high speed, water became like stone, stone that slithered around you and wrapped you tightly when it struck. There was of course no way the Wizard's elemental Blunter could've stood upright if he were subject to the normal ways of water. I began to look for the pieces of him that didn't fit. How did he hold himself together? How did the Wizard discipline the water to make it behave?

I ignored Blunter's persistent, labored attacks and studied him. His aquatic hammer bore down and I sidestepped. I'd grown tired of having my blade ripped from my hands whenever I tried to strike him, so I kept the machete at my side and focused on my aura. In order to defeat Blunter, I'd have to undo him. I began to feel where my energy touched his. I knew the way cold felt. A blue vibration tinted my vision and tickled my spine. Instinct overtook me and I slashed forward with the blade in my hands, roaring as the edge tore through the essence of my foe. I was rewarded with a spraying gush of aquamarine. Energy bled from the water elemental in a misty haze before my eyes. Blunter was leaking like a punctured canteen.

It felt cruel to continue the fight. I considered only whether or not to finish my opponent. My purposeful strike had left the hulking form of the water elemental crippled and broken. The only thing

Blunter could do was hold his broad shield between himself and me. I studied his vague features as he sank through the sand and emitted a strange groan as he bled seawater. I was beginning to feel badly for having mortally wounded such a marvelous being when the Wizard appeared beside me. I surmised he'd been watching me but my attention was elsewhere.

"Don't mind Blunter's theatrics. You did splendidly. He doesn't feel pain, lucky son of a gun, but he gets moody when it's his bed-time."

Blunter dwindled to a gurgling puddle. I took a breath, swelling with the pride of my accomplishment. The Wizard beamed. I was glad I'd caught him on a good Sun.

"You've defeated the first of my water elementals, Rahn. Congratulations are in order. Do you remember what's next?" the Wizard asked.

"You said something about his sister?" I responded.

"Was that a question or a statement?"

He'd already begun to pull together the strands of power around him. A new water elemental rose from the sand of the beach. "'This is a different kind of challenge." The Wizard cleared his throat.

"Remand all self-doubting, Sir Rahn Le'Del.
Dear Edges is coming, and she'll cut you to hell.
The blackness in her is like the blackness in water,
though it's not how I made her and it's not what I taught her.
She'll tear off your face, and I'm oft disapproving,
but not an eye is left dry by my daughter's sweet swooning."

"Of course you wrote a fucking poem," I grumbled. I held my blade and prepared to guard against attack as the Wizard chuckled. Edges' differences from her big brother were readily apparent. She was the same height as me and her features were refined and closer to fully human. Her hands and forearms were shaped as sword-like spikes. Like Blunter, she didn't have legs, but her lower body was shaped in a flowing, spiraling skirt. She hesitated a moment before attacking me. In that brief lapse of time, the way she tilted her head and examined me hinted at s superior intelligence. This unnerved me, and my focus wasn't there when the fight started.

The unwieldy machete I chose to arm myself with had never felt so useless in my hands. The only thing I could do was bring the thin panel in front of me to try and deflect some of the spray. Edges let into me without mercy or pause. When my guard was completely dismantled by the flurry of blows, I felt my jaw break and my head rock back on my neck. Next came a cracked rib which knocked the breath from my lungs. My life flashed before my eyes. I knew there was a real possibility I was about to die on that beach. Nausea accompanied the pain in waves. I realized death wasn't coming for me after a few moments had passed. The roaring pain of my injuries almost made me wish it had. The Wizard stood over me with a hand on Edges' shoulder.

"Let's see if Westings can't patch you up, padawan. We're gonna need to practice your shielding before I let her punch your ticket again."

I groaned. The Wizard walked away from me and Edges faded from view. I wondered how much he controlled his elementals. I decided this was rotten and sick. A crazed old hermit was going to murder me by unleashing his sadistic pets. He was only fixing me so that he could hurt me again. Even Westings seemed like an abomination in my injured state. The tree walked towards where I lay. What kind of tree can walk? I felt tears roll down my face. Westings' abstract features drifted in and out as the tree set my jaw. The Wizard returned and handed me a spiced rum drink to sip through a straw. I could tell he was trying to soften my animosity. An energy flow from Westings further dulled the pain I was feeling. My broken bones tingled and I knew they were already being repaired. I closed my eyes and tried to clear my mind.

Still better here, I thought to myself. Better than the Slave Pens.
{~}

The dream I fell to was familiar. The wings, those blue wings like a canopy. The wings were above me again. The dragon moved through the sky, but his stained-glass shadow was the only evidence I could see. Were my eyes even working properly in this place? This whole thing was a dream, obviously. I felt the cold in the dream. The sensation wasn't logically correct when I considered how warm the island had been when I fell asleep. How many Marks ago was that, exactly? I was studying the blue-green mangroves around me, and I knew their familiar contours precisely. The sandy bedding where my actual body was resting nearly jarred me from sleep when I considered the part of myself I'd left behind. The dream world wavered ,but I held myself within it and I rejected what was real for an alternate kind of reality.

"Are you there?" I asked on the dream-island. "What do I call you?"

The reply was too much for my fragile mind to process. A chill swept through the dream and left frost lacing up the bark of the mangroves. I thrashed in my bedding as the voice arrived. My blanket began to stiffen with ice. I felt the distant sting of my knuckles wearing raw. The dragon spoke to me in the dream while I was trying to decide if I was caught in a nightmare.

"Chaeoh," he said, landing quietly on the beach of the dream-island. An energy connection stabilized.

"So... um... how's bein' a dragon? You're a dragon, right?"

A huff of blue breath lit the trees. His voice was large and low, his shrug genuine.

"Maybe."

Chapter 8
A'Rehia tells of: "Recon"

"Nobody likes the Jurisdiction. You won't find a living soul who doesn't think it sucks. Even the Nobility, the Devisors, the Regiment, the Squadron. They may be exporting vast quantities of misery far and wide, but they do enough domestic sales to get high off their own supply." -the Sky Dancer

       I recall an industrial liniment the Squadron slathered on their bodies before they were deployed. The prosaic smell of it brings back a wide array of memories in a bittersweet way. Made en masse by the Jurisdiction laboratories, the stuff came in nondescript little plastic tubes. I always made sure to cover any exposed skin. Without protection, the air and sunlight were damaging over time. The human dermal layer wasn't engineered for the rigors of flight. Whatever alterations occurred in our genetic makeup to make us mages were untested mutations. Perhaps they ultimately left us mentally and physically unsound. There were countless times when I felt like a toddler attempting to grasp a tool sized for a grown-up's hands.
       "Do you have a Prize Mate?" I asked Major Zeyus when the campfire was lit.
       The winged man shook his head almost imperceptibly, but I took the gesture as a negative. We'd been flying for most of the Sun and I was nearly accustomed to the resulting headache each evening. I knew the practice was changing me, and the forced personal growth was a feeling that I had mixed feelings about. I was beginning to wonder about Zeyus, isolated with him with civilization far behind us. He answered my question as he held his aluminum mug in his left hand. The Major was a soldier, through and through, and he kept his right hand resting on his quiver of javelins across his lap.
       "Yeah, I used to have a Prize Mate, Fleuro. Or he had me, at least. His name was Nash. He lived with me for almost ten Rounds. I don't think he ever cared for me much, though, truth be told."
       I frowned. Prize Mates were supposed to be with their betrothed for life. I was always frightened of the flawless custom-made spouses, although I didn't have a reason why. They always appeared harmless enough, obsequious even. Prize Mates were given as gifts to those in the Jurisdiction of sufficient rank and distinction. Mates were genetically engineered for beauty and loyalty, and trained in skills which might please their Mates. The Prize Mates weren't considered Slaves, although the Jurisdiction undoubtedly had plenty of those. I suppose the Prize Mates gained greater autonomy than a Slave by virtue of who their Mate was and how they were treated in this regard. The Prize Mates, like the Regiment, were

incapable of reproducing on their own. They were treated respectfully, lovingly even, and led contented lives, or so it was supposed to seem. Major Zeyus' story reminded me perception wasn't obligated to align with reality.

Zeyus shook his head. He'd become more willing to share details about himself with me. I wondered if the behavior was unbecoming of an officer. I listened.

"I've heard stories. I'm sure you have, too," Zeyus said. "About Prize Mates who misbehave being 'replaced.'" He shook his head. "The Jurisdiction kills plenty of people. I've never had any doubts about that. I just-" The Major gave a manly sniff. "I figured they'd wait 'til I complained. Never had any problems. Didn't think they'd take Nash away from me," he confided.

I realized this wasn't a story Major Zeyus would ever share with the rest of his command. We were off the map now, and not just geographically. He composed himself, but we both knew his restraint came too late. I saw emotion war across his face and his mouth flinched. He felt like he needed to either make a conclusion or change the subject.

"The Jurisdiction, A'Rehia-" he used my first name, and the identifier surprised me. "I don't want you to end up a tool. I've been their tool for Rounds and Rounds. For my entire life. I've gotten over it by now. My Suns are predictable enough. The Squadron is basically obsolete with the Devisors insisting that their Swarm be preeminent on the battlefield. We don't have to kill people as often."

I don't know what part of me ever expected differently from a Jurisdiction officer, but I was shocked to hear his casual confession.

He continued. "You, on the other hand. You're a weapon too potent for the Nobility to pass up. The kiteknives, I wish I'd never discovered 'em. I should've kept the Guard-damn things to myself. If they find out you can use those," he shook his head, unwilling to say what came next. "They'll do anything they can to make you their assassin, A'Rehia. There's no other way to put it."

I looked down at the knife on my belt. My hands closed around the sheath.

"So what should I do?" I asked.

"You listen to me, that's what the fuck you do."

"You'd defy the Nobility because of me?"

Major Zeyus inhaled and looked me dead in the eye. "To defy the Nobility implies that the Nobility has a clear and present intent I'm violating. Given my rank, I'm at liberty to expand certain definitions." This was the Zeyus I knew. Back to business. "For now, we're gonna train you. Kiteknife practice you'll have to do on your own. I have another exercise for us. Keep the sheath on your knife for this game." Zeyus lifted off and hovered above the trees. I followed him reluctantly. He floated towards me with his sheathed knife held expectantly.

"Three dimensional tag." He rushed at me. I shot backwards beyond his reach. He came at me again and I flipped upside-down and over his head, passing between his white wings. Time hesitated, and I realized the sheathed kiteknife was in my hand. I tapped him on the shoulder. He wheeled to face me and barked a companionable acknowledgement.

"You got the rules. I'm not gonna let you win, now."

In spite of his assertion, I won the next two rounds by tagging him on each of his vast white wings. He quickly realized his weakness and attempted to compensate. He began to tuck the feathery appendages away from my reach or roll his body so that I couldn't stretch for them. He baited me and manipulated my expectations. I knew my advantage was in close spaces, and in order to get near to Zeyus I was contending with his superior reach. There were situations where Zeyus's wings gave him improved aerodynamic maneuvering, but I could manipulate greater volumes of air with considerable force. Having already flown for most of the Sun, I depleted my mage energy and found myself losing repeatedly. I landed awkwardly on a branch as I lost focus. Zeyus circled me in mock triumph. I struggled to catch my breath as I clung to the tenuous perch. When the throbbing in my head let up, I floated the rest of the way to the ground, rocking back and forth like a falling leaf before I came to rest with a grunt. I was exhausted and my head hurt. I gave up thinking and feeling and listening and looking. I had no reason to do otherwise.

I passed out.

{~}

I didn't record Marks in a journal like Zeyus, but I'll wager we traveled north for nearly a Moon. The last fortnight was spent playing complicated games of tag. When I slept, I dreamt about ancient dogfights with their primitive wooden planes. Hadn't my theatrical friends worked with me to display what we knew of the histories, complete with battles in the sky? The Suns where Zeyus and I tested each other felt like rehearsal for a deadly performance. We faked one direction, and then another, and then another. There was no angle too steep and no tactic too dirty. We began clashing with knives instead of trying to tag each other. The leather sheaths slammed against each other as we vied for leverage and momentum. I found myself working on my war whoop. What was left of the sparrow in me was becoming a hawk.

{~}

"There's something I need to show you," the Major informed me. "There are things you need to understand."

I was dabbing liniment on my hands and face, but I was listening.

"I'm going to tell you about my history. I'm not keen on feelings, but you need to understand this stuff before you do any fighting." He shifted his wings. The nervous motion displayed a trepidation I'd never seen from Zeyus. We'd stopped under the cover of a grove of trees near the base of a crude stone tower. The odd tower dominated the horizon and loomed before us like an eavesdropping giant. I caught a whiff of the shifting wind and the unsavory stink it carried. I was suspicious of our surroundings, but I listened carefully.

"I used to be completely dedicated to the Squadron. Unflinchingly loyal, a passionate military man. There were two events in my life that changed that. The second event I've already told you about. The Sun when Nash disappeared was truly the last Sun of my career as a soldier. My first spark of doubt arrived Rounds before, right after I got my wings." He flexed the feathered appendages to illustrate his point.

"I was proud of them, Fleuro, when they were new. I'd never give them up willingly. Even now. The Devisor who oversaw the research team used an intricate robotics rig. I didn't know much about the man. Our relationship didn't exactly involve drinking beer and shooting the shit. The Devisors aren't much for social skills under any circumstances. He was a pioneer and an eccentric, and when my body was healed up, the man went out and got himself murdered. I suppose if he hadn't, you'd see more wings like mine. They're conspicuously short on volunteers for the procedure these Suns." He allowed himself a smile. "After the original scientist was murdered, the other Devisors couldn't get the artificial wings to work again. They put prototypes on a few Slaves, but a flying Slave isn't particularly useful compared to how costly the whole project became and the subjects kept getting disfigured or worse. Mixed results didn't inspire anyone else in the Squadron to sign up for extra appendages." He was particularly self-conscious about his wings as he was speaking. He placed his hands on their surface and preened wayward feathers.

"I got the assignment of discovering what happened to the Devisor scientist who made my wings. On the surface, the mission was easy." Zeyus paused and swallowed. His adam's apple bobbed. "But there are things you can't un-see."

I heard a screech coming from the direction of the stone tower. The sound made my stomach turn. A desperate wail was blended with a hefty dose of agony. The creature who'd issued the screech dropped from the tower's edge. Peering through the leaves, I saw purple wings that spread and then folded against the gray stone of the tower. The figure began to glide towards the copse trees where we were crouched. Zeyus drew a javelin, but the creature banked away, apparently unaware of us. I peered up from behind the leafy cover and shuddered at what I saw. The creature was mashed together from the bodies of a human and a bird. As I stared, I realized my instinct was exactly right. The creature had a stunted torso and legs and would stand at least a head shorter than most grown humans. I wasn't sure if the mis-shapen frame was capable of standing upright. The feet had opposable thumbs and claws. The arms were feathered and extended as wings featuring clawed hands. The face was narrowed and the lips protruded forward. I couldn't determine if the greasy strands on the creature's head were hair or feathers. Zeyus interrupted my thoughts.

"They're half-bloods, A'Rehia. People call them 'harpies.' They're the reason I'm able to have these wings. Before my procedure could be accomplished, the Devisor ran experiments." He caressed a wing with a loving touch. He squinted at me as he folded the wing and continued.

"The Devisor scientist, he started caring for the half-bloods as if they were his children. They suffer from mal-formed organs and a host of other problems. They're more animal than human, and they have a sadistic streak." Zeyus shook his head. An empty look was in his eyes. "I found the body of the scientist I was looking for eventually. Or what was left of him, anyway. The harpies tore him apart. Bits of him were scattered across a square kilometer. He brought them treats and jewelry and music and art, and they murdered his ass. Their creator and their caretaker." He released a huff of air which reminded me of martial arts training. Perhaps feelings were like combat to Zeyus.

"The strangest part was, I couldn't blame them. I'd like to say I have absolutely no idea how they felt, those awful bird-animals, but somehow I do." He braced himself and gritted his teeth. He knew his statements were against protocol, too far for comfort, but he said the words anyway.

"The Jurisdiction filled their lives with inescapable suffering, and yet without it, they wouldn't exist at all."

Above us, I saw the harpy pause. His head twitched, turning backwards over his shoulder. He caught a scent, and his eyes bulged. When the avian gaze fell on us, Zeyus threw a javelin. The projectile struck the half-blood in the neck. A spray of blood diffused in the air as the shaft pierced flesh and the harpy fell. My heart raced. I looked at Zeyus. He frowned back at me.

"No reservations, Private, no hesitation. Put those things beyond their misery. I might empathize with these cursed bird-brains, but I've also seen them eat."

I heard the sound of half-human shouts from the top of the tower. Harpies were gathering, and I dreaded the moment they might appear. Zeyus spoke to me urgently.

"The reason we're here is information, Private. In addition to your training, we have a mission." He glanced at the stone tower. "An unknown combatant around here kills the harpies on a regular basis."

I raised my eyebrows. Zeyus spoke in a matter-of-fact tone. "The population is kept in check. Otherwise they would've taken over more than just a couple ruined stone towers over the Rounds. Whatever kills them might also be interfering with the Swarm and the high-atmosphere recon drones. As to how it's done," the Major shook his head, "That's beyond my paygrade. Even with oxygen tanks, I doubt either of us could safely reach that kind of altitude." Zeyus cleared his throat. "So it's back to the harpies. I'm gonna discover what the foul critters know. Which means I'm gonna have to kill a few of 'em." He tilted his head to study my reaction, which I'm sure was fairly skeptical. "That's just the way this works, Fleuro. Care to join?"

I nearly shook my head 'no' right away, but I managed to hold my neck in place. I was puzzled by the question. Major Zeyus gave orders, not invitations. He acted like he was asking me to dance rather than help him slay as many half-human abominations as necessary to get the information he wanted. He sensed my hesitation, and his smile was genial, but the man was morbid and unyielding.

"Oh come on, Fleuro. Sun's gonna come in your life when you gotta kill by circumstances less handsome than me. I'm sorry, but there's no way around it. You can watch this time. You can keep your distance if you want. But ain't no creatures I know of in this world that crave and deserve death the way the harpies do. Easier chance at first blood than most soldiers get."

I gritted my teeth. I nodded acknowledgement to my superior.

"You didn't lose the kite-knife, did you?" he asked. My emotional hurdles were already forgotten. Zeyus undid a strap on the side of his javelin quiver to reveal a brace of additional blades. "Here you go. Should've made you carry 'em sooner. Almost brought you a pistol, but the saturday-night-specials they got layin' around the armory weigh too much, and to be honest, you're a lousy shot. These'll do for now." There were three kite-knives in the brace and a conventional dagger for keeping on my person. I thanked the Major and strapped the brace of blades to my waist above my left hip. I took a breath and nodded. Zeyus gave me instructions.

"Stay high and away. Watch for harpies moving towards you or throwing objects. Don't worry about watching my back. If you get more attention than you can handle yell 'Bear'. That's the emergency word to remember. Repeat it back to me."

"Bear," I said, frowning at the simplicity.

Zeyus continued, unphased by my reaction. "If you're set, I'll press to the fray on the top of the tower. They should be focused on me since I'll be challenging them. If you hear me call 'Marco,' it means I'm asking for your status. If I hear nothing in return, I'll assume you're in trouble. Otherwise yell 'Polo' or 'Bull,' and I'll know I'm clear to continue. What's the code?"

I raised an eyebrow at him. "What happens if YOU get overwhelmed and need MY help?"

Zeyus drew his sword with his right hand and a javelin with his left. The were no emotions left on his face.

"Then I don't deserve these wings, and I guess the harpies are gonna get 'em back."

He launched himself with fervor and intensity which were far beyond what I was feeling at the time. I followed him at a pace that was dreamy and demure in comparison. I drifted higher. I pumped my legs and pushed against the pressure of the air. The exertion gave me the boost of adrenaline I needed. My hand went to my knives. When I could see the top of the tower, I looked for a target.

The harpies were in disarray. There was no organization in the way they responded to the presence of the threatening intruder who interjected himself in their midst. The closest harpies lunged at Zeyus immediately. He cut and stabbed them without hesitation or pageantry. I saw him dodge rusty knives flung by clawed feet. I felt a rising panic knowing the flocking harpies could crush Major Zeyus with their numbers. I repressed the urge to yell 'Bear,' hoping he'd retreat, but the harpies weren't attacking immediately. The flapping mob kept their distance as though the Major secured a place among them by killing its previous occupant. He spoke to the harpies, but I couldn't understand what he was saying. The replies were jumbled and the dense beaks spoke clipped words. I hovered closer to listen. A mistake.

A harpy spotted me, and the hungry look in her eyes told me her intent. I gained altitude while cursing under my breath, and I felt the kiteknife handles on the unfamiliar brace attached to my side. She was fast, I thought to myself. I could hear a raspy, muted scream of a sound as she increased her breathing. A kiteknife slipped to my hand and I released the weapon, pushing away from me with the surrounding air as the kiteknife fell. Too slow, I thought. Too weak. The knife fluttered, and I willed the blade to fly towards my target. My heart pounded in my ears as I concentrated. My hearing was keen as I sensed the air. The harpy was closing the gap between us. I drew a second knife. I knew the first knife wasn't moving fast enough, but perhaps I could get my attack in the right spot to distract my enemy. I managed to increase my air pressure against the slippery metal.

The blade spun and struck the harpy in the eye. The impact echoed against my mage senses, but the noticeable effect of the knife's impact was silence. The wingbeats and ragged breathing stopped. The harpy fell from the sky as a bundle of frayed feathers.

I don't know what I'd thought that killing the harpy would feel like, but I expected to feel something, anything. I figured there'd be a sensation when the life left my enemy. Instead, there was almost no difference, no change. I found myself thinking about my favorite commanding officer informed me of our mission's final checkpoint before we could return to base.

"There's a remote village in these Wilds," he said. "We need to get a look. With any luck, we can get in and out undetected. If we're spotted, we could be in danger. Worse than the harpy tower. So if you hear me call 'Bear,' regroup to the south. I'll meet you at the river bend where we stopped a few nights back. If you make contact, I want you to call 'Bear' as well."

I nodded, but my imagination was already running away. What could possibly be dangerous about a village in the middle of nowhere? My heart rate increased. I could tell Zeyus was cautious and observant.

"Stay under cover of the tree canopy, as far from the ground as you can," he told me. "There might be traps, so take your time and be careful."

I began to dance from tree trunk to tree trunk like a stealthy grasshopper. Zeyus kept his wings compact. We moved through the forest as a duo. We passed over a herd of deer who flicked their ears but failed to spot us above their heads. I grinned about how sneaky we were, but my confidence caused me to lose focus, and my feet struck a branch with too much force. The brittle branch split near the trunk and a crack reverberated through the trees. The Major paused and directed a scowl at me. I lowered my head in contrition, but I knew better than to speak an apology.

I kept my footing light as a feather after that, floating rather than stepping on anything. As I began to wonder if we were going the wrong direction, I noticed subtle signs of human activity.

A trees had been cleared of dead branches. The markings of an axe were visible on the trunk. I spotted a pit trap and a deadfall trap, cleverly disguised by shrouds of undergrowth. There were clusters of mushrooms and edible plants which were too intentional to sprout naturally. When a cabin became visible, Zeyus hid behind a tree and I followed suit.

We spent several seconds observing the forest by the edge of the remote village. I saw no signs of danger. In fact, the only people I saw were just children.

I watched Major Zeyus. He was tense. My curiosity beckoned me to investigate. Before I could move, Zeyus tipped his head in an unmistakable gesture meaning we were done here. I shrugged, letting myself hover away from the tree. I twirled in a flip and followed the Major back the way we came.

As we departed, Zeyus moved with a sense of urgency I emulated in order to keep up with him. When he pointed to a group of grey panthers moving through the woods below us, he accompanied his gesture by barking a word.

"Bear!"

Those are cats, I almost replied, but then I remembered the importance of the code word. Zeyus rocketed away in the clear sky. He moved as fast as he could, and I did my best to follow. My endurance was improving, but I knew I couldn't sustain the breakneck pace for Marks at a time. Zeyus stole glances back at me as he tried to gauge how much energy I had left. We traveled to the prearranged meeting spot by the river before I had to stop.

"Why'd you say 'Bear'?" I asked between huffs when we landed, trying to catch my breath.

Zeyus shook his head. "You heard my briefing, Fleuro. That village is more dangerous than the harpies. Harpies lack intelligence. Whatever lives in that village doesn't. Did you see the panthers?"

I nodded.

"Panthers are solitary creatures, Fleuro. They don't form a casual entourage like drunken football players. May the Guards take me if those beasts were wild animals. Whatever's killin' off harpies certainly isn't."

The recognition that I was in danger and wasn't aware of it caused a dense knot to form in my gut. The wind shifted, and the sensation left me light-headed. I sat down. Zeyus grabbed the water flask from my belt and handed it to me along with a field-rations bar. The dense food made my stomach churn, but I ate as much as I could anyway. I began to contemplate the remaining Suns before I could eat real food again.

{~}

I don't recall the return trip to Atlantium. Perhaps the daily flying was uneventful considering the turbulence I'd experienced and the overall circumstances of my life at the time. The games of tag and the kiteknife practice we'd engaged in previously were omitted in favor of speed. We traveled as far as we could each Sun. I learned to coerce the air around me with uncanny efficiency. I was nearly able to maintain a pace with Zeyus and his wings. I found he was calling for us to stop and rest almost as often as I did.

After a Moon away from the city of my birth, we found her on the horizon in the middle of an afternoon. For the second time in my life, the view of Atlantium from a distance reached my eyes. To this Sun, the memory of the view carries an uneven mixture of familiarity and disgust. I suppose her architecture was admirable. The buildings owned by the Jurisdiction, that is. The rest of her was an acquired taste.

The people of Atlantium formed different reactions to the ongoing decay of urban commerce. The decline was accepted by part of her residents, while others never adjusted. Each generation saw life become more difficult than the last. They saw the concrete cracks run further and deeper while available supplies of lumber and fuel dwindled. The Jurisdiction could've assisted the populace, of course, but they seemed to prefer actively killing anyone who exhibited open signs of discontent.

Speaking of killing, our innocuous return to the city merited the illustrious attention of none other than my father, the Executor himself. He stood regally in the midst of the Squadron's green landing field, flanked by a pair of Nobility Enforcers. The imposing fire mages wore the velvety finery which was the usual custom for the Nobility. I wondered if the tailoring of the robes held any armor. I'd certainly considered shooting or stabbing them often enough. I remembered the kiteknives on my person and I shifted the brace behind my back. I was facing enough of a challenge landing gracefully in front of my father without him noticing the weapons immediately. I tried to suppress my anxiety and focus on the air, but I'm sure my hands began to tremble. If the Executor was here to greet us, he must have a reason. Perhaps he had special orders or a rank he wished to give me. Hadn't Zeyus said that he wanted me to be promoted? My mind wandered to darker thoughts. What if he knew about the harpies? What if he knew about Zeyus? What if he already decided we were traitors?

My feet touched the ground and I stumbled. I took a couple steps to catch myself, but I didn't fall. My insides felt like they dropped lower than the rest of me as I grappled with the presence of the earth under my shoes. Magnare Fleuro's silver hair and intense eyes appraised my clumsiness. I saw his gaze move to Zeyus, who landed with confidence and aplomb. The Major hailed his commander with energy and dignity. My heart went to him in gratitude. He folded his wings with military precision.

"You've been gone a while," my father began without preamble. His words fell like stones dropped on the ground. "I trust your reconnoitering was productive."

Major Zeyus frowned. "Indeed, Executor. Do you require a full debriefing?"

My father shook his head. He stepped to the side and then turned to face the other direction. The Enforcers behind him stood like statues. The three fire mages brimmed with barely concealed power. Their auras made the air around them waver with warping pulses of heat. Wisps of smoke materialized in random fashion. I wondered how Zeyus could stay so calm. They could roast him like a goose. Executor Fleuro gave the Major a smile which might've seared the eyebrows from a lesser man.

"Formalities can wait for the Devisors," my father said. He made a dismissive gesture. I suppose he decided he'd kept us wondering for a sufficient length of time. He had a flair for the dramatic he felt entitled to as the Executor.

"I came here to speak to you about the promotion request which reached me after your departure." He looked at me. His gaze wasn't malicious but I wasn't going to let myself be fooled. "The mission you flew was unusually lengthy for a recent graduate of basic training," my father said. His hands were clasped behind his back and I heard his knuckles crack. "I find this request unusual. I don't recall promoting any novice in the Squadron this early in her career." The Executor gave Zeyus a pointed look. He made clear by his posture that he expected a satisfactory answer from his officer.

Zeyus kept his expression neutral. I wondered what thoughts his face was carefully disguising. "Private Fleuro is an exceptional mage, Executor. She's deserving of the extended assignment and the early promotion."

My father looked as though the compliment meant nothing to him. I doubt the reaction was an act.

"Is that so, Major? I must ask. What role do you foresee in the Squadron for Private Fleuro? Are you proposing she be given her own command?"

Major Zeyus issued a measured shake of the head. "Not yet, Executor. She'll require experience and leadership training. But as an air-mage, she's unmatched in the Squadron."

At this claim ,my father raised his silver eyebrows. "Not even by yourself, Major?"

Zeyus appeared to consider this. "Her maneuverability would have to be categorized differently."

Fires appeared in Magnare Fleuro's eyes. "And how exactly did you test her 'maneuverability'?"

Zeyus managed to stifle his discomfort with the question, but he inhaled through his nose and he stepped back a few centimeters. In the past couple of Moons, I'd become a fool, and I'd heard enough.

"Father," I said. The Enforcers turned when I broke protocol. The grass around the hem of my father's robe turned from green to brown, from brown to charred black, from black to white ash, but the grass was as far as his anger traveled. I sent my thanks the Guards.

"Enough for now, Major. I insist Private Fleuro be given remedial instruction in proper discipline for her station. As for the specifics of your request, we'll discuss after you recoup. Dismissed."

The end of the encounter arrived, and we saluted before walking to the barracks entrance under the searching eyes of the Executor and his Enforcers. We exhaled relief when the gazes of the Nobility were no longer on us. Zeyus looked as if he'd aged entire Rounds in the preceding Marks. His hand contacted my shoulder in a companionable gesture, but his mind was already somewhere else. I gave him a nod and headed for an overdue shower.

**Book 2: Knights
Chapters 9-24**

Chapter 9
Raspho tells of: "Village Meditations"

"Light it up, burn it down. You'll find music in the curves if you extrapolate correctly." -The Sorcerer Prodigy

The next Sun saw us moving with an efficiency bordering on haste. My actions felt automatic as I worked the stiffness from my muscles. I harbored only mild resentment towards Charlie's brisk pace. We hiked relentlessly, and I munched on smoked meats, satisfied with the previous Sun's accomplishments. My pack was absurdly burdened from the deer hide and meat. I shoved the antlers into the pack despite my misgivings. Stronger, I reminded myself as I shifted under the weight. I'm getting stronger from this.

The trees broke at a clearing when noon was a few Marks behind us, and we stopped to rest at the side of a deer path. The tall grass formed fickle blinds around as we sat. After we'd eaten strips of meat and followed up with drinks from the water flask, I leaned back against the springy shafts, aching from my overburdened pack already. Charlie rolled onto her back and stretched nonchalantly.

"We're surrounded," she said.

"What?" I replied, sitting up straight.

Charlie yawned and blinked, as if she'd simply commented on the weather. Before I could think of my next question to ask, the gray face of a panther appeared in the grass.

The sheen of dark fur was like polished charcoal. The panther was patterned with subtle hints of smoky gray among deeper black. The beast growled a warning pitch. I heard three more growls, identical in nature, and I knew Charlie was correct. We were surrounded. I tried to relax, but in truth, I was terrified.

"Ahh, nice to see you, Deba," Charlie began. "I know, I know, I'm naught but a wee-tabby these Suns, but I still smell like me. Go on, you can check."

I glared at the reddish cat frantically as she spoke. "You know these panthers?"

She gave a casual nod. "It's a shame you don't speak cat, kid. Bunch of pussies, though, if you ask me. The Wise Witch is their master. Pets, scouts, lost spirits- who knows. Jae'lin calls them Ash Cats because that's what she uses to conjure their muscular bods. This one, Deba, I guess you could call her an ex-girlfriend."

Charlie tilted her head, appraising the looming panther in front of her.

"Or are you her sister?"

Deba didn't appear pleased with this assessment. I clenched my hands around the Keenwood Staff as the feline bared her fangs and studied us. Her claws dug through the topsoil only a paw-span from Charlie's tail. Despite her menacing demeanor, Deba settled on her haunches in the grass with the other three Ash Cats to keep watch. I realized I'd never been less inclined to make a run for it in my life.

Charlie displayed a total lack of concern about the presence of the Ash Cats. She was clearly bent on showing them she wasn't afraid. I began to wonder if her extreme indolence was an act. I tried to relax as much as I could. Maybe Charlie knew something I didn't. I decided the best way to look unafraid was knowing you could win a fight. I realized I'd need to find another way to appear brave. I could picture the Ash Cats pouncing on me in vivid detail.

The approaching personage could only be the Wise Witch. I figured this was the case when she appeared on the horizon. The hem of her skirt whipped about in a wild tail as she flew directly at us. I could tell she was a woman of advanced age, but her slight frame betrayed only the barest signs of a hunch. Fire mage though she was, she floated through the air sitting side-saddle on a carved branch. The smoothed wood was inlaid with a floral pattern wrought in delicate silver. Her earthy full-length dress was wrapped at the waist by a belt and pouches made of the same material. The suede grip of a wooden wand protruded next to her hip. To accent the fabric, she'd stitched everything in a forest-green thread which was nearly black. The garb was practical, evenly woven, and kept clean despite subtle signs of prolonged use. The Witch's clothing did nothing to pull attention from her face. She was striking even from a distance. Her dark eyes contrasted violently with her wind-blown silvery-white hair. She gazed at us over the front end of the levitating branch.

"You shouldn't be here, Gunny," the Wise Witch warned.

The branch hovered to a stop above an Ash Cat. I gaped at her countenance, feeling as though she'd settled among us from the heavens. The energy of her aura was like the face of the sun, and it did nothing to dissuade my awe of her. I released my grip on the staff involuntarily. The Witch aura drove against me like a physical pressure. Heat filled my lungs and drove the air away. I couldn't breathe. I looked up at her, feeble and desperate.

"Shield yourself, mage!"

She cried a warning, but I was already on the verge of fainting. The pressure ceased abruptly. I coughed and swayed, returned to my senses, but the burning in my lungs remained. I was glad I was sitting down.

"He doesn't know how to shield," Charlie told the Wise Witch. "Your aura is too much for him."

The Witch turned to my traveling companion, fury plain on her face.

"I bet he doesn't know a damn thing! Poor boy's been kidnapped by a murderous parasite devoid of morality!"

Charlie snarled. "Jae'lin, look how small I am. If he was feeding me fire don't you think I'd be larger? I can still fit in his lap!"

The Wise Witch crossed her arms and made a tsking sound.

"Urnstead, please. We've been down this road before. If I tried to document your ruses, my paper-making would clear-cut the Guard-damn forest." She turned her head.

"What did this cat do to you, young man? Did she insist you provide her with fire? Did she steal you from your kin?"

I found the courage to use my voice. I had to carefully transfigure the concepts floating in my head so into noises with my mouth.

"My family- um. They were killed by the Swarm. She probably saved me. She taught me things. We fought skeletons. We-"

The Witch interrupted, jabbing an accusatory finger at Charlie.

"You took him to the False Priesthood?" The cat said nothing, but her ears and tail froze in place like a statue. The Witch and her gaze swung fell on me again. "Young man, what's your name?"

"Raspho," I replied dutifully.

"Raspho. Did the Priestess slatterns put any needles in you? Did you eat or drink while you were there?"

Charlie responded before I could confirm a lack of abuse.

"No, Jae'lin. It's not like that. You know it's not like that anymore."

I was shocked at the vehemence with which the Wise Witch admonished the cat.

"It's been like that before! Nobody nicknamed you 'Hellcat' because you're so Guard-damn cuddly, Gunny. You drink too much fire and it could be like that again. It's like a drug to you, Urnstead. You're an addict. You need more and more of it, and with each lick you become less and less human. Last time your appetites ran away with you it was a miracle you didn't raze the Low Hills to the ground! It's a double miracle your best friend ever grew his feathers back."

Charlie's voice sounded meeker than I'd ever heard her. She mumbled towards the tall grass.

"That was ages ago, Lin." Sadness cracked her tone. Her voice faded to a hissy whisper.

"Besides, I'm not getting any less human. You turned me into a fucking cat."

The Witch gave an exasperated sigh. Her face softened. "Ages ago, indeed. Charlene Urnstead, I don't have the energy to be angry at you right now." She crossed her arms, but her hand rested near her wand. Charlie's pupils grew wide for a brief instant.

"Alas, I won't soon forget the things you've done. Please leave here in peace. I'll take Raspho to the village."

I'm not sure what I expected Charlie to do next. I guess I expected her to go her own way. I don't imagine she was particularly attached. She'd accomplished her self-imposed mission, and the Wise Witch didn't want her around. Instead she surprised me. She spoke to the Witch and argued her case. Her voice became the resonant lament of mournful meowing. I'd never felt sympathy for Charlie before. The change in roles was a new sensation.

"Please, Lin. I need to talk with Steffen. Only a few of us left. I can't bear the thought of total solitude from everyone. Nobody understands. You and Steffen are the only ones who know." She swayed, and I watched the Wise Witch study her. The woman's brows furrowed as Charlie mewed her sorrowful notes, crying the same phrase over and over again as she rocked back and forth. The display was the most unsettling thing I'd ever seen the cat do.

"I still fight back, I still fight back, I still fight back, I still fight back..."

The Wise Witch made a gesture with her hand. Charlie ceased her repetitions. The cat licked her lips and shook her head, standing straighter. She glanced around at the Ash Cats, concealing her weakness.

"But mostly," Charlie said as she cleared her throat and resumed, "I'd like to see my closest friend. I won't let you keep us apart."

The Wise Witch retained a coldness to her gaze which would've cowed anyone.

"For Guard-sake, Charlie, I know you still fight back. That was never in question. Come on, woman! Can't you see how it became your curse? Those of us who know and understand you have gotten weary of the bloodshed. You get yourself tangled up, over and over." The Witch shook her head. "I'll honor your request to see Steffen, Urnstead. Please make yourself useful while I show Raspho to the village. A nasty rabid creature has been killing songbirds in the valley for sport. The beast might've been a boar once, but Guards know what to call it now. I don't want the Ash Cats to get bitten, but I have no such concern for your flaming hide. You do this and I'll consider the favor a down-payment on your penance, Charlie. After that we'll see about what else is to be done around here. The Defiance hasn't existed for centuries, you know that, don't you?"

Charlie was purring in a way I hadn't heard since my family's farm. Deba rose to her feet and looked at Charlie anew, her aggression gone. The panther's tail swayed with idle anxiety as she sniffed the red cat.

"The Defiance still exists, Jae'lin. It exists until the Nobility have me stuffed and mounted in a trophy case."

{~}

Truth be told, I'm not sure anyone can ever know what they're capable of doing in the reddest parts of their flesh. I try not to picture myself as a pile of complex chemical reactions, but the imagery of chaotic systems sticks with me, and I channel the idea. There are moments, as conscious organisms, where we think and act on separate wavelengths. Other times we take Rounds, decades even, to know the contents of our own hearts. Extreme circumstances bring forth the best or the worst from within us. We hide entire worlds within ourselves through buried traumas and biologies. Our hopes and fears about the world around us rarely meet up with reality in an orderly fashion.

Despite my reservations about predicting my own future, the village of the Wise Witch was almost exactly as I imagined such a place might be. The bulk of her territory was nestled in a forested valley, concealed by a sea of trees and the rocky hills of the surrounding terrain. I might've missed the domain altogether had the Wise Witch not indicated the site to me with a weathered index finger. As we drew closer, I saw patches of exotic gardens placed cleverly in the sunlight and mushrooms in the dappled shadows. Narrow paths of carefully placed stones wound through the undergrowth. The trees took pride in the lush moss around their roots, and ferns abounded in a furtive ornamentation across the loam.

A cluster of wooden cottages lay at the heart of the village. The structures reminded me with a pang of my family's cabins, alone and silent, a world away on our farm by the sea. Perhaps Jahnny had made his way back to them. Perhaps he'd left for places unknown, just as I had. Perhaps the town would reclaim the farm. I could picture the tan beams of treated wood that made up the cabin walls. The Witch village cottages were spattered with earthy dyes, and the contrast jarred me from my nostalgia.

The Wise Witch didn't say anything as we crossed the final bushel of cat-lengths to her village. She floated above and ahead of me. Her pensive frown and her buffer of altitude discouraged idle chat. I walked with purposeful energy and felt pedestrian compared to the flying crone I was following. Her aura relaxed as her anger at Charlie subsided. I viewed her as I thought a mage might view her. Her aura was bright, but I could keep the pressure from touching me if I focused on my own energy. She rippled like a flame as her thoughts shifted. My subconscious flinched away. I knew physical frailty wouldn't prevent the Wise Witch from destroying me. Her aura made me feel like a gnat in a bonfire.

Despite my anxieties, the Wise Witch invited me to make myself at home in a hospitable tone when we reached the village. She floated away to determine what transpired in her absence. I had no need of her guidance after I reached the cottages, however, because I was immediately greeted by a cluster of children eager to know my name. A half-dozen faces came right up to me. I could see more youngsters behind them, playing and performing various tasks. None appeared any older than my brother Jahnny. I was the oldest person in the village apart from the Witch herself.

My heart was struck again by a sharp ache as the youthful community reminded me of the home I lost. A boy with glowing eyes stoked the fire beneath a kettle with outstretched hands. I heard a girl call him Briin. A few scraggly logs of split wood rested on a hearth in front of him beneath a pot. Briin was actively coaxing the kindling to defy its meager, smouldering limitations. By the wall of the closest cottage, a scrawny girl pulled a wooden lid from the top of a stone box to reveal the winter chill she'd captured within. I grinned with pleasure, and I couldn't help but look inside. The milk, meats, and cheeses seemed to grin back at me. The girl placed her hands on the side of the box. I squinted at her. A trickle of blue light was leaking from around her hands. When she spoke to me, I was taken off-guard.

"For a mage, you're kinda dumb, aren't you?"

I frowned back at her. "Why do you say that?"

The girl smiled and laughed, or giggled, at least.

"Don't worry. The Wise Witch can teach you." She shut the lid of the cold-box. "My name is Erixe. What's yours?"

I told the girl my name, but before I could ask her another question, the Wise Witch appeared in the sky on her branch and landed among the cottages, voicing her approval of the bubbling cauldron. If my presence had drawn the children to gather, the Witch drew them to riot. She greeted them all with hugs and names and questions. I smiled a sad smile, overcome with emotion at the sight. Perhaps I'd found a new home in the village of the Witch.

Her charges each noticed, the Wise Witch came to inquire after me. I saw Briin point in my direction, eyes wide, and the Witch caught me in her gaze. I was seated on a carved log, but I stood as she approached, leaning against the wooden quarterstaff which was becoming my constant companion.

"So, Raspho," she said. She eyed me with her head tilted, her discernment piercing. "I think I've seen this staff before. What did you say your family name was?"

I shook my head. "I didn't, Ma'am. Name's Born. I'm Raspho Born."

The Witch's eyes lit up. "Ha!" she laughed. I was taken aback by her open mirth, but she gripped my shoulder in reassurance. Her hand was uncannily steady for an elderly mage. Her smile beamed.

"Born indeed, Raspho! Would you like to know what your real name is?"

I looked back at her suspiciously. "Erixe told me I was dumb, but now you're telling me I don't even know my own name."

The Wise Witch nodded. "Erixe is usually correct. Your family changed their name to avoid the Jurisdiction, as many did. Your surname wasn't 'Born,' Raspho. It was 'Kilnborn.' The Keenwood Staff is proof of that."

Understanding kindled in me like a spark in sawdust. My eyes widened. "So that means my family was fire mages."

The Wise Witch nodded. "Not everyone, of course. I don't know what became of the Kilnborns I once knew. I can only tell you I've seen that staff. Not exactly a recent memory."

I thought back to my Grandfather Born on a festival night, a few Rounds before. He'd quaffed all his firewhiskey, and he cornered me at the edge of the festivities. I think that night was the only time in my life when the old man ever frightened me. He wouldn't stop sobbing against his empty flask. He wouldn't stop saying 'it wasn't fair.' I tried to stop him. 'It wasn't fair,' he wailed, over and over, stumbling in the dark. He said I reminded him too much of my grandmother. 'Why couldn't I just be normal,' he kept asking me. His words started to slur together. Why did I have to have blonde hair? The evening was strange enough for me to recall vividly. His wife was gone, and the pain was overwhelming. He poured his words at me and I wasn't prepared to hear them.

I spoke hoarsely to the Wise Witch. "I think my grandmother was a mage."

Her eyes were sunken in their sockets and baggy with weariness when I looked closely at her face. Her skin bore the wrinkles of age, and for the first time I was concerned for the health of the Wise Witch. I wondered if her appearance had changed in the brief moments I looked away. I considered the chances she met my family once, in a past before my time. I was unsettled by the mage, but she continued to treat me with unwavering kindness.

"I never met your grandmother, Raspho." She cleared her throat and cocked an eyebrow. "I'm afraid the Witch you're looking at hasn't been a fair maiden for quite a few Rounds."

I knew I had to ask her the obvious question which might not otherwise be polite. "How old are you?" I blurted. I withdrew, as if to soften the interjection. I knew my question was the logical continuation of our conversation, and this fact emboldened me. "Charlie wouldn't tell me how old she is."

At first, I feared I'd harmed the Wise Witch's dignity, as one might by asking a proud lady her age. The look crossing her face was a visage I'm not entirely certain I could describe. She was the kind of forlorn you only get if you're filled to the brim with unwanted knowledge. I could see immediately how the woman had probably earned her title many times over.

"A millenia, I suppose."

Time hesitated around me. I felt the molecules of my body vibrate, and the sounds around me rattled to a halt. The Witch spoke on as if nothing were amiss.

"I stopped celebrating my birthdays. They get depressing, you know. I could probably give you the exact figure if I studied my records."

I was stunned by her frank assessment of her own longevity. The revelation would've kept me reeling, but Charlie trotted through the village from the woods. The Witch eyed the newcomer skeptically.

"That was fast," the woman addressed the cat in a dry tone.

"You expect me to toy with my prey?" Charlie replied evenly. She continued. "Don't let her fool you, Raspho. Director Jae'lin Fleuro has seen eleven-hundred and thirteen Rounds, and she recalls every Guard-forsaken Mark of it."

The Wise Witch rubbed her chin with a pensive look on her face. I wondered if she forgot I was standing there. Her demeanor indicated she wasn't going to reply to Charlie. She looked as if she'd made up her mind.

"Briin, Erixe," she called to the mage orphans. The boy and girl presented themselves from nowhere. I wondered if Charlie had coaxed them to eavesdrop along with her. The Witch gave instructions. "I need to attend to present affairs. See Raspho is settled in here." She turned back to Charlie. "Let's go, Ms. Urnstead. Steffen is far afield. The latest Suns have proven unkind to your friend. If you want to see him, we'll have to go find him first."

I think Charlie might've given me a meaningful look before she left, but I couldn't decode it. She receded among the forest with the Witch. My focus was freed of a target, and I took in the village around me. As the mages led me through the cottages, a sensation of tranquility and welcoming were present in tangible fashion. Briin was shy, only speaking when he indicated the available bunks in the cabin. Erixe, on the other hand, chattered away at me constantly.

"We're protected here," she said with bubbly enthusiasm. "There's the Witch, of course, with her cats. But Leon and Jeriah are my favorites. The Trapper and the Woodcutter, we call them. I'm sure they're making new defenses for us. Maybe you'll meet them later if they finish their patrols."

Her fervor reminded me with a pang of my cousin Violet. Erixe was older than Violet by a handful of Rounds, and certainly taller, but her enthusiasm mirrored the vanished innocence which left a hole in my heart.

"What's wrong?" Erixe asked. I stopped walking. I hadn't realized my feelings were so obvious. Erixe shook her head. "I can tell when people are upset. I just can." She crossed her arms, insistent on sympathy.

"I-" I began. I didn't want to tell my story to a girl I just met, but I couldn't avoid her presence or her frown. "I lost my family," I said.

Erixe gave a knowing nod which made her appear wiser than a child. The gesture reminded me of the Wise Witch. I decided the tutelage of a mage-woman who'd lived a thousand Rounds would be an interesting way for any child to grow up.

"Don't worry," Erixe told me as she patted my arm. "You're not alone in the village, you know. Briin didn't speak to anyone for over a Round. My parents are alive, I think. But when they discovered I was a mage-" She didn't have to finish her statement. The sense of betrayal and loss was plain on her face. "If you ever feel like you need to talk, or even just hide away, you can do that here. No one will judge you any worse."

I gave a gruff nod. I swallowed, clamping down on the true extent of my troubled spirit in spite of her comforting words. Erixe took the opportunity to change the subject.

"The Witch is gonna teach you how to shield," she said matter-of-factly. She reached towards me with bony finger and a blue spark stung my skin.

"Ow!" I said and drew back from the touch with a scowl. Erixe giggled and chased me with her finger. I found myself gritting my teeth, squeezing flames inside my clenched hands. I let her catch me, thinking perhaps I could shield myself. I understood the concept, didn't I?

Fire whooshed around me in a turbulent burst when Erixe prodded me with a blue-white zap. The girl fell back, startled. She swiped her smouldering clothing, and I could see her eyebrows were singed. Wisps of smoke dissipated to a thinning haze. The pungent smell of burnt hair reached my nose. I was appalled at how I'd almost hurt her, and I stammered a panicked apology. For a moment she looked shaken, but then a wide grin appeared on her face.

"Boy, oh boy, you need training alright! That's exactly what the Wise Witch says not to do! 'Power without control is weakness.'"

I must've looked forlorn, because Erixe gave me a friendly shove and pointed towards the cook-fire. "Don't worry about me, Mr. Kilnborn. I'm not a journey-mage yet, but unlike you I DO know how to shield myself. I wasn't expecting you to be so fiery!" She tugged at my sleeve, energetic as ever despite her damaged eyebrows and sooty hands. "Let's go!" she said. "Dinner's almost ready!"
{~}

The flavors of the food were rich and exotic, but Charlie was correct. The Witch served real food and I'd missed the experience. As for the differences, I decided I could expect no less from a Witch's cauldron. The children sat on carved logs and stools by the fire as they ate. There was a wooden table with benches to the sides, but this dining arrangement wasn't a popular spot. I sat down on a three-legged stool with a woven cushion, and inertia held me there. I ate a final slice of roasted mushroom in savory sauce and set my wooden bowl aside so I could take in the view of the sunset. I could hear Erixe's laughter as she played a game with her friends. She left me to digest my food in peace, but I saw her glance in my direction several times. My hand rubbed my chin as I gazed at the flickering flames of the outdoor hearth.

My belly was full and my head felt weighty as the sun fell past the horizon. I rose from the stool and cleaned my bowl in the wash tubs before I made my way to my cabin. I gave a tired smile to the kids who peered at me with curious eyes and laid down on my new bunk in the dark. The other children were intent on passing their free time around the fire. I wondered if they had any supervision at all. I exhaled and pushed my concerns from my overburdened mind. I certainly wasn't in charge of them. My thoughts were already conflicted by comfort and anxiety as the two battled within. I suppose consciousness was the true loser in the fight. I slept soundly.

{~}

I knew I'd slept because the other bunks in the cabin were filled when I woke. In addition, a bulky red cat took up more than her fair share of my mattress. I grunted and tried to shift Charlie away using my shin, but she stretched her feline body and put holes in the bedding with her claws. I surmised she must've found her friend the previous evening, but not her own bed. I sighed and left the warmth of the straw mattress behind.

A folded set of clothes had been placed on the wooden trunk my bed. I picked them up gratefully, resolving to examine my tattered and road-worn garments to see if they were still serviceable. An adjacent room was obviously a bath house, and I slipped inside to change. I considered the Sun when I dressed in the faded green canvas, and the events the clothes had survived. I shuddered as I pulled the dirty garments off of me. Not the time to think, I told myself. Maybe after breakfast. I found a washcloth and soap and drew water from the cistern to scrub the worst of the dirt from myself. I didn't feel clean, but I didn't feel dirty either, and I didn't want to take the time for a bath. I was feeling rather brisk from the combination of exposed skin and cool water. No sense in being a chilly fire mage, I thought. Steam began to rise from the surface of my body.

Ahhhhh. Much better.

I unfolded the trousers by my bed. They were made of a tightly-knit cotton fabric. I realized the fabric was manufactured by a machine. Rustic as my life was, the uniformity of mechanically manufactured material inspired awe in me. I wondered if the Wise

Witch stole the brownish cloth from the Jurisdiction. The shirt left for me was actually two shirts. The first was a long-sleeved cotton shirt also made of manufactured cloth, but snug and soft and gray, unlike the trousers. The second was a tunic knit by hand from a yarn which appeared to contain every shade of green imaginable. I appreciated the new clothes in the dimness of the cottage even though the apparel felt foreign to me.

I exited the cottage and blinked at the dawn. I decided to answer nature's call. I found a likely looking tree and I was fumbling with my belt when I heard a voice above me.

"First off, there's an out-house for that."

I was mortified and looked over my shoulder, not daring to turn around or speak. The Wise Witch hovered with a smirk. "Get your oatmeal and meet me by the tanning racks. If Erixe's eyebrows are any indication, we've got work to do."

I gave a contrite nod. My cheeks were reddened from the awkward encounter and the morning chill. I did as I was told and relieved myself in the proper location, washed up and found a boy distributing mugs of oatmeal with nuts and berries. The mug was a meager breakfast, and Erixe pressed a second hot mug in my hands. The coffee was braced with cream, but my first experience with the beverage was decidedly bitter. The liquid smelled pleasant enough, and since there wasn't much oatmeal, I sipped at it anyway and tried to adjust to the flavor.

The Wise Witch didn't hold any hard feelings after her morning greeting, but she didn't waste any time with small talk before launching to her subject matter. We walked away from the cabins towards a space where the trees were farther apart. There was a distinct lack of clearings or fields near the village. I gathered this was intentional, for concealment or defensive purposes. The soil the sun reached wasn't for frolicking, but for growing food. This meant our lessons and our practice would take place in the forest, where there were flammable obstacles around. The Wise Witch didn't show concern as she drew her wand. I realized with a pang I'd left my staff with my pack in the cabin where I slept. Ever perceptive, the Wise Witch shook her head at me.

"Artifacts aren't for beginners. You need to learn to be a mage without the staff before you understand the capabilities of a mage-made object. Here, sit down." She pointed to an inviting rock pristinely padded with moss. I complied, and she proceeded to instruct me in breathing and meditation.

"Your aura isn't your shielding," she intoned when I was relaxed and in a heightened state of awareness. "And yet, everything about the arcane is interconnected. Of this, you can be certain. You must feel it. Know it's there. Know your own presence is a part of the world around you. Know you have the capacity to project power into this world. Projected power coincides with an ever-present desire to resist your own destruction. You can feel your shielding now, can't you? Your skill as a mage isn't solely pushed outwards as you exchange energy for fire. The energy is entangled with the very essence of your being. Just as you conjure flame, you can protect yourself from harm. Don't think of it as a wall or a barrier. You don't want to be shut off from your aura or the energy around you. Instead, realize you wish to assert yourself in this reality. Your manifestation has a physical form, and you must consider yourself inviolable. Shielding must become instinctive for you. We can't hope to predict with any kind of certainty what might strike us, or when. Therefore shielding should be like breathing. As with breathing, there's intention, but also a subconscious element. Your body breathes to protect itself. These Suns, Kilnborn, it may need more help than that."

I listened and adjusted. I could feel the heat radiating through my clothing as my aura flickered around me. The Wise Witch was speaking to me from several meters away while her hands gingerly inspected her wand. She walked towards me and raised the wand. Her motion was the only warning she gave, and yet something in her aura telegraphed her intentions clearly. The first shielding test began, and I passed with flying colors. The Wise Witch showered sparks on my upturned palms, but the bright flecks fizzled before they did any damage to my skin. She upped the ante, and I could feel the surge of energy. The sparks thickened until they were molten embers. I wavered and sweated from the effort as I watched the embers fall towards my palms, but I didn't flinch away from her. My effort at shielding held. The conjured embers died as blotches of ash. The Wise Witch nodded.

"Remember my lesson. The exercise may have ended, but the embers never cease. I'll check on your progress, Mr. Kilnborn. You need to practice carrying the burden of staying alive until it becomes part of you." Her modicum of praise was short-lived. "We're going to practice an active mage-craft, now. Let me begin by asking you a question. You're a fire mage, so to speak." A grin slid across the Witch's lips and lit her entire face. "What IS fire, Raspho? Physically? Sure. Scientifically? Why not. But also spiritually. Metaphorically."

She made her statement and paused. I rose to my feet along with the woman. I was taller than my teacher, but I didn't feel taller. Even when the Wise Witch stood on the ground instead of hovering on her branch, I felt diminutive in her presence. I was considering her question when her words started to echo in my ears and the Witch began to glow. Everything was happening at once. I was swimming in flame. I was drowning in flame. Why was there fire everywhere? What happened to the Witch? What happened to the forest we were standing in? What was her question again?

I spun to the left to figure out where I was. As my feet broke their stance, the hallucination vanished almost as quickly as it took me. I was right where I'd been all along. I turned to the Wise Witch and found she was wearing an amused look. Her arms were crossed. After a moment, I recalled question she'd asked me.

"I- I don't know. What just happened to me?"

To her credit, the Witch didn't laugh or deride me. She answered me with a calm assertion.

"You did that to yourself."

I was puzzled. "What? How?"

The Witch held a passion for the subject of mage-craft. Her enthusiasm became obvious to me from the musing look in her eyes. Her eyebrows arched as she considered her reply. "Much as I've seen, Raspho, there are questions I still can't answer. Each and every mage is unique. There's plenty about us which will never be understood, even by brilliant scientists, or by a dedicated practitioner like myself." She rubbed her chin.

"Your hallucinations are complicated. I won't guess at the specifics. This is dangerous territory, advanced studies. You're pushing energy inward on yourself, Mr. Kilnborn. You may conjure a flame in the space around you, but a mage can affect the inside of their own head in a similar fashion. Mages engage in this practice intentionally for a variety of reasons, though I wouldn't recommend un-guided exploration. I suggest that after we're done here, you spend the afternoon meditation in order to consider the phenomenon. I don't imagine you wish to suffer repeats."

I shook my head and tried to make sense of my confusion. The hallucination left me drained and disoriented. I tried to focus on her lessons, but the Wise Witch could see I was taxed. She grilled me once again on the nature of fire. My half-hearted and speculative answers were less than satisfactory to her. She made me conjure a fireball. As my creation floated before me, she told me to relax and feel the mass and the energy independently. I did as I was asked, completing the exercise. The Witch spoke in general terms about principles of energy transfer before she dismissed me. The coffee rumbled in my belly and I exhaled with gratitude.

"Lunch. Rest. Meditation," the Witch told me. "These are your tasks, now. When dusk approaches, I'll find physical labor for you. Until then," she dipped her head and stepped behind a tree. I blinked at the forest, but I was too hungry to puzzle through where she'd gone.

Lunch consisted of cheeses, breads and roasted root vegetables with a variety of sauces. There was a cool herbal tea to wash the food down. I gathered there wasn't usually meat in the village by prodding Briin with questions. The Witch herself didn't care for meat preserved in the usual ways of smoke or salt that I was accustomed to. She was a careful steward of animals and kept no domestic or captive livestock save for the dairy goats occupying a pasture several kilometers to the west. This meant meat in the village was fresh but erratic. I thought about my pack, laden with the pelt and smoked meat, and I wondered where my belongings had ended up. Briin offered me a hard-boiled quail egg. I shook my head and declined. The boy told me about harvesting the eggs. He was competing with a fox to collect. Briin came to know the signal of a red-orange tail vanishing in the Wilds as the sign of an empty nest. His companionable silences endeared me to him. He began to juggle the eggs, tossing three of them in an elliptical pattern in front of him. I commended his stunt with genteel applause.

The Sun passed the peak overhead. I headed to the cabin and tried to lay down, but I was restless. I decided I wanted to meditate instead of sleeping. I wondered if the Witch knew how I'd feel. Such was the hazard of having an exceptionally talented teacher, I decided. I doubted there was any feat beyond the mysterious abilities of the Wise Witch.

I wandered away from the cabins of the Witch village and I chose a path I'd never traveled before. I was rewarded with a vivid view of nature devoid of other people. I looked for a likely sitting spot and decided to rest against the bottom of an ancient tree. I looked to where the trunk stretched above its peers. Was the tree just a seedling when the Wise Witch was a girl? The curves where roots stretched through the soil seemed a perfect fit for my backside. I wondered if the tingle against my spine was my imagination. I pushed the thought away, absurd as the notion was. I needed to think about magecraft. Trees were only trees... right?

I took in the sense of the forest around me. The detail shifted as I focused on the reaches of bark and leaves. The breeze flowed through the area, setting the scene in motion. I closed my eyes after a while, but they held the image of the forest despite my drooping eyelids. I became accustomed to the subtle rush of heady air and the rushing sounds of the plants. My acclamation with my surroundings betrayed the pulse of wingbeats in the distance.

The noise was wrong. The frequency was too low and the amplitude had too much force. I measured the pace of the flapping and decided the wings belonged to a rather large bird, indeed. My interest was piqued, so I pulled myself from my meditative stupor and peered around.

The source of the sound eluded me, but my eye caught a beguiling figure. A woman stood delicately on the outstretched limb of the tree in the canopy far above me. Her black hair was tied in two flowing ebony tails. She wore a form-fitting utilitarian gray jumpsuit on her lean figure. Her facial features were exotic and her cheeks were twinged with a flawless rosy flush of mild autumn and exertion. I blinked and her presence jarred my thoughts. After the events of the morning I was having difficulty trusting my own eyes, and I rubbed them purposefully. I pondered whether the spell-binding woman was real. The sound of wing-beats stopped, but the earlier event was unimportant to me as I gazed at the raven-haired vision. She crept forward with subtle grace. My heartbeat hammered in my ears, reverberating through the tree at my back. There was nothing else in the entire world but the woman and the tree.

I was beginning to wonder how she'd climbed so high when she leapt from the branch. I caught a sharp intake of breath and barely contained my cry of dismay. The woman spun through the air in a perfectly controlled tumble, her hair trailing behind her. The air mage hadn't fallen. She floated as if she'd leapt from a dock, only to swim in a sea of emptiness.

I felt dizzy. My head was at war with itself. This was exactly the kind of thing I was supposed to be meditating in order to prevent. I did everything I could to avoid passing out on the forest floor as I considered the alluring mage who levitated flawlessly above me. Was I messing with my own head again?

The tolling of a bell from the village disrupted my speculation as I attempted to settle my thoughts. I was beginning to feel my aura and I groaned. I hadn't seen a bell anywhere in the village, but by the sound it was a fairly difficult thing to miss. The metal resonance sent a constant tone thrumming through the trees as the bell rang over and over again. I stood with a stiff lurch. It was a few Marks too early for the evening meal. I began to walk, and then I began to jog as I watched my footsteps carefully along the unfamiliar path. Children were gathering in the village, and the Wise Witch hovered with concern written on her face. Her lips moved as she counted kids and supplies. Briin hauled downward on a rope trailing to the eaves of a cottage. I gathered the bell resided inside. When we were each accounted for, the Wise Witch nodded to the boy. He released the rope and the ring faded.

"We're going on a journey. We'll be leaving the village for a fortnight," she said in a wide voice. "There are a handful of you here who have traveled with me before. First, we're going to pack the things we need. The older ones help the younger ones. Every set of hands. We leave tonight. Yes, Jeanie, you may bring your dolls, hush now. The Ash kittens will go with us as well. They'll need you to be brave and look after them, sweetie. Everything is going to be alright. I have sugar treats for each of you if you walk with me, do you understand? This will be our camping trip to the City of Old. Leon and Jeriah will tell us when we should come back home."

When she finished addressing the children, the Witch floated over to me. She spoke in a tired voice.

"I wish I knew when I was bull-shitting them," she began, but her uncertainty wasn't the point she wanted to get across. "If you see a flying man with white wings," she cautioned ardently, "I want you to burn them black. Knock him from the sky. Take the life from him if you must. Can you do that for me?"

I looked at her with wide eyes. I hadn't expected violent requests from a woman who'd acted so warm-hearted only seconds before. What choice did I have? I nodded and assented to her gravely. When I saw her expression, I knew she meant business. When she handed me the Keenwood Staff, I knew she meant war. The Wise Witch gave 'Ms. Urnstead' a scratch behind her ears.

"You heard my concern, cat. If you sack the Winged Man first, I might even forgive you."

{~}

Preparations happened in a flurry. Questions about my mage skill were tossed aside. Charlie insisted I was already an instrument of death, shipped to the Wise Witch intentionally by the Guards themselves. A Mark later, and we were on the march. The whirlwind departure was so intense that our hike away from the village felt like a respite from the efforts of packing. I heard whimpering and complaining from the children, but I marveled at their obedience and resolve. Each of them carried a pack adjusted to their size, no matter how diminutive their person. The Witch walked with us, her branch floating placidly under her left hand. When we settled to a pace, she spoke to me.

"Perhaps you wondered why my village has only children," she began, shaking her head. "A few grow up and move on, lead peaceful lives later in life." Her fingers rapped against the branch. "But my protections fails. I've lost more than I care to contemplate to circumstances beyond my control. More than a couple lifetimes worth."

I looked at her. A realization was setting in and the idea numbed me to the core.

"You'd sacrifice me to save the children."

We stopped moving, the Witch and I. Charlie was leading the way, capturing the children's attention by playfully jumping across the trail. The footsteps continued to carry the children of the village past us, but the Wise Witch looked me dead in the eyes.

"It isn't something I don't ask of myself. What would you have me do?"

I considered how the death of a child compared to my own death. Hadn't I thought to myself over and over how I'd take Violet's place if I could?

"I- I don't know," I answered. "I think you're right."

The old woman put her hand on my arm and turned back to our path. "Good." she said, her voice gone gravel with emotion. "That's good."

"Nobody would hand a lit blowtorch to a toddler. So don't hand people guns who don't deserve the honor. Because otherwise you're gonna have about as much fun as a square-dance in an out-house. You're right, Amika. Sounds shitty, doesn't it? Does your Den Mother know you say that?" -The Gunslinger Confidant

When the matriarch of the titan wolves sought the favor of a Doctor, bringing Amika and her mother to our settlement, she knew exactly what she was doing. Lohise had such cunning and keen senses that I even suspected her of having a role in the pup's injury in the first place. I shook the suspicion away, and then I suspected the Den Mother of planning my own acceptance as well. I reflected on the dispirited Rose tribe's fondness of the titan wolves in their midst. A few loyalists clung to Lieutenant Drak and Confidant Flin, but the number of gunfighters rallying to the rebellious faction had decreased dramatically, making the few remaining members appear less and less reasonable.

Part of me admired the principled stand of the disgruntled gunfighters. I didn't begrudge them their wariness about our titan wolf neighbors. In fact, I actively encouraged the trait in our sentries. I wasn't going to trust our deadly guests to the point of foolishness.

Yet I longed for a return to tribal unity. I hoped improved cohesion would come sooner rather than later. I'd hoped the process would go smoothly, but I underestimated Drak's determination to see our fledgeling alliance fail.

Lohise's pack howled through the night when their Den Mother first came among us. We could hear them positioning their chorus directly across the river from our camp. Those who weren't sleeping were suited and strapped. The titan wolf leader didn't hesitate to reply from the midst of our settlement. She answered her kind with crooning sounds, melting hearts among the Rose tribe in addition to reassuring her pack. When the next morning dawned, Drak's side of the camp was all but abandoned.

Another Sun of titan wolf company passed in the wake of that first night. Lohise and Couress made themselves the perfect guests. They spoke politely, eating what was offered to them and answering curious questions which bordered on the ignorant and rude. When the wolves expressed irritation, they only further tantalized their audience. Amika's whimpers kept Couress close, but the wolf mother remained calm. I believe she wanted to project reassurance to her daughter despite her misgivings with the humans surrounding her.

The following night the titan wolf pack across the river was silent, but canine voices made their way to my dreams nonetheless.

{~}

The Rose tribe was drinking tea and rubbing their eyes when the stuttering cracks of gunfire broke forth from our side of the riverbank. The sharp sounds were from the same model of submachine-gun Drak favored. My adrenaline spiked and I dropped my mug.

There was no time to do anything other than sprint. When I heard yelps from the other side of the river, I feared the worst. I knew I was facing an event which could be the Rose tribe's undoing. I pictured the deaths which were imminent when Lohise and Couress realized what was happening.

I bolted through the ruins and drew a pistol as I ran. I spotted Drak. He stopped firing and he was preparing to move. To my dismay, Lohise appeared before I could accost him.

Blindsided as he was, Drak was lucky to survive the attack. The titan wolf hit him like a battering ram. She broke the gun he was holding with her paw, and his arm along with it. I heard myself shouting. I imagine Lohise heard me. She knocked Drak to the ground and opened his belly with her claws. To her credit, she hadn't slain him outright, but I knew Drak wouldn't stand a chance without medical attention and a dose of luck. As I waited on the runners with their stretcher, I knelt over the fallen man. Blood leaked from his arm and abdomen and the corner of his mouth. My heart twisted in my chest, and I think he saw the pain in my eye. The shock from his wounds was probably setting in, but he managed to hurl a few words at me just to twist me up.

"You side with the beasts over me?"

I frowned and said nothing to the man, waiting for gunfire around me. The tense situation remained blessedly free from the sound. Lohise circled Drak's closest allies, daring them to shoot with bared teeth as they huddled in formation. In earlier days, before my father fell, before I became Generale, before we left Sylviarg, I might've lost my composure under the pressure I was feeling. I frowned and clasped Drak's unconscious hand. Even if he lived, I'd be replacing him as a Lieutenant. If he lived, he'd continue to be a thorn among the Rose tribe. I could've hoped he died. I could've even sought capital punishment with the Council and given him what he rightly deserved for his violent insubordination, but looking down at the gravity of his wounds, I pushed the thoughts aside.

Drak's friends dispersed as the stretcher arrived. I stared them down with my arms crossed. Lohise sat on her haunches nearby to wipe the blood from her claws. She stared across the river. I nodded my head towards her in acknowledgement. I wanted to tell her there was no ill will over Drak's injury since she acted in defense of her pack. I opened my mouth to speak but she cut me off.

"The care of Amika is no excuse for bullet wounds," She growled.

I bristled back at her. "This wasn't my doing, wolf. You see how I operate. I'm not going to turn against my own when they're trying to protect the tribe."

"They lack discipline, hairless ape!" Lohise barked. "What was this aggressive male protecting?" The muscles and fur of her shoulders moved as she grappled with her disgust. "Every action falls on you, Generale. You humans think you're so much better than other animals, like you're extra-special. But of course you aren't. You're just animals with thumbs, same as any wolf."

"You're wrong!" I insisted, arms crossed. "We have a code! We have a Council! We're not going to oppress our people if their dissent doesn't turn to violence."

"Tell that to the members of my pack who lick blood from their fur!" Lohise roared. My heart raced. I knew this was becoming a dangerous conversation. Lohise's control of her temper was the only barrier preventing my swift death. The Den Mother let her furred lips sink and cover her pale fangs, but her growl rumbled from within and rang against my bones.

"This won't be smoothed over. I'll end up fighting my pack as you do yours, except my fight will be bloody. Less silly posturing." She paced, rumbling pensively to herself as her anger faded to remorseless calculation.

Lohise continued speaking when her facial expression shifted to weariness.

"I'm going to eat one of your oxen, Generale. I'll share bits with Couress and Amika, of course. Consider the meal a payment on this incident. I'm going to need strength to repair your mistakes. Besides, I already know which ox to slaughter. He's been giving me the eye since I got here, chewing on grass and staring at me like a facile dullard. The time has come to remind him which link he is in the food-chain."

{~}

I counted it as beyond lucky that a hapless draft animal and a mutinous Lieutenant's health were the only losses the Rose tribe sustained from the diplomatic incident. The ox was valuable, and the labor would be missed as we fortified our new home, but he was a paltry price to pay to avoid a war. I offered Lohise the further service of doctors for whatever wounds Drak might've inflicted. She barked back a pointed question about what herbs I'd like to season them with before I sent them across the river, so I dropped the matter.

The construction of a new home progressed. Upon seeing the foundations taking shape, the Confidants decided the time was right to mourn the dead. A ceremonial bonfire was built as wide and ambitious as could be managed in our main hearth. When dusk fell, the dancing light flickered over the Mammoth and the rusting steel beams at the edges of the ancient intersection. We roasted spits of game while bread was baked in the new stone ovens. The precious booze remaining among the tribe was raised in toasts to the fallen Generale and every fighter who lost their lives in the battle which resulted in our exodus. Even Lohise honored the Rose tribe's sacrifices by grabbing a wooden mug with her teeth and downing the contents in a gulp. Moons would pass before we tasted anything alcoholic again. Fermentation setups weren't a high priority compared to food and shelter and defense, but they were probably next in line.

I spoke of my father, but I kept my words brief and I spoke of him as a daughter rather than a gunfighter. Lieutenant Bonder surprised me by giving an impassioned accounting of his Generale's deeds in battle. I think the eulogy was the most words I'd ever heard the man say in succession.

Drak hadn't regained consciousness. He lay sweating and pale on a pallet beside Amika. I knew the doctors had done what they could for him, but when I asked about Drak, they shook their heads and shrugged and said it was the Guards' turn to decide. By contrast, Amika was healing admirably. Her bandaged stump wasn't infected, and the doctors were using less medicine for the pain. Even Amika's mother Couress appeared to relax and study her daughter's caretakers with interest as they gingerly examined the missing limb and made plans for a prosthetic. When a doctor named Killie begin carving a titan wolf paw, the woman earned a rare nuzzle from Couress. I felt the act of compassion in the hardened chambers of my heart and I channeled the emotion. The loss of my father ran together with a steady surge of hope.

Flin remained surly with me. This wasn't a surprise given Drak's recent fate, but I sensed an aura of defeat in him which worried me. He knew Drak had gone too far and probably ruined his hope of regaining support against the titan wolves. I tried to speak to him of other things and remind him he was part of the tribe. No disagreement over politics was going to defeat our friendship. Maybe I couldn't find the words, but Flin stayed distant and distracted. Perhaps he was concerned about remaining a Confidant. The possibility existed that the Rose tribe could vote to replace him. I knew the loss of his position would further devastate him. I resolved to speak to him in depth the next Sun, when the night's festivities drew to a close.
{~}

The morning after started slowly. I knew a restful day was in order. The construction crews began later and their duties would be light. Picked-over bones and empty mugs were dealt with straight-away as nutty breakfast bread and greasy spiced sausages occupied the ovens. The camp was relatively subdued, and I didn't need to rely on the sentries to realize that the titan wolves across the river were howling again. This was no pensive evening wolf song. The sounds I heard were the excited calls of the hunt. Lohise beckoned me to join her, and I leapt to her back without much thought. I hadn't donned my armor, but I had my pistols at my hips. For a moment I considered staying with the tribe to prepare myself and establish a squad of gunfighters, but I realized time was of the essence when a bright red signal flare went up in the sky across the river. Lohise's urgency reinforced my own, and I shouted orders before clinging to her fur as she surged through the water. I wondered when my gunfighters would arrive. I also wondered if I was about to be eaten by the pack of titan wolves. The latter speculation was becoming familiar. The rogue signal flare crackled, leaving a smoky trail before bursting as an intense firework. Lohise needed no guidance from me, and her pace left me breathless. Her legs ate up the distance with the explosive bounding of a predator. There was no chance any horse in pursuit of us would ford the river or rocket through the trees of the Wilds with such velocity or abandon.

We arrived at the source of the signal flare with fortuitous timing. A few moments later and the scene would've been an unbridled ruckus, complete with scorched fur and half-devoured limbs. A group of frightened children huddled around a blond young man with a wooden staff. The teenager was brandishing a floating fireball with menacing intent. I drew my pistols instinctively, knowing fire mages were the province of the Jurisdiction. In the brightening sky above the man, a woman with silver hair floated inexplicably on a carved branch. She reprimanded the menacing titan wolves in a formidable voice. I heard her warning them to stay away, lest she show them what she was capable of. Fear shone on her face, but I gathered personal safety wasn't her concern. A glowing red line encircled the group of children. The elderly woman appeared to sustain the supernatural light. When she wasn't cajoling the wolves, she hummed an old warrior's ballad from the Low Hills. She held a slim wooden baton in her hand as if she was conducting a musical ensemble. The titan wolves tested the invisible barrier, yelping when the heat burned them, but they were getting bolder. The fire-ward wouldn't withstand a full rush if the titan wolves engaged.

Lohise barked at her pack. Her words were accented and foreign. I realized I'd become accustomed to hearing her speak for humans and not for her own kind.

"Step away, wolf-brethren! Keep those mangy paws in line!"

For a moment, I thought the titan wolf pack would attack Lohise instead of the children. The first time I witnessed Lohise's pack, I feared I'd made a fatal error in appearing among them. They eyed me atop their leader with open disdain for both the Den Mother and her new human associate. I brandished my pistols, trying to look as powerful as I could. I pulled the slides back on the weapons, making the resulting clicks were apparent. The pack growled and paced as they considered whether attacking any of the available targets was worth the effort. None of the titan wolves were fully grown, at least not as fully as their Den Mother. Many of them reminded me of the wolf-mother Couress and her rangy build. Their voices were strongly canine and difficult to understand. Two males emerged to confront us.

"You make nice chair for hairless ape?

"What a *dog.*"

I gathered from the huffing noses that this was a dire insult among the titan wolves. Lohise circled her challengers with confident indifference. "Perhaps I'll let her teach you a lesson about 'hairless apes'. Be grateful I consider the substitution. Bullets would be kinder than my teeth." Lohise addressed the pair by name. "Khuper and Hassadi. Couress and Amika rest comfortably. The human who started shooting yesterday may-never-wake-up. Leave these humans be, lest they decide to confiscate your flea-ridden pelts for their own use."

Hassadi gave a snort of derision. He was barely forming his words but his intentions were clear.

"Mage-sting but... tender morsels," he argued.

"And if they decide to eat your daughter? In vengeance for these pups? What then?" Lohise countered.

Khuper snarled. "Why would gun-monkeys care what happens to other-pack? And for the last time, Amika is MY daughter. Not his!"

Hassadi and Khuper's jaws faced each other as they snarled. I suppressed a grin. The division among Lohise's pack was clear to me now.

"Amika is a pup of the pack."

Lohise's annoyance was plain as she strode forward. She was pressing an uncertain advantage. "I don't care which of you Couress chooses. If I were her, I'd be sick to death of you two yipping mutts. Neither of you will ever become Alpha by crying under your paw about the whims of a fickle mate."

"But she's MY mate!" Khuper protested.

"She could mate with a briar bush, for what I care! Neither of you have greater claim to Amika. She is a member of this pack!"

By the way the titan wolf raised his hackles, I was certain Khuper was going to attack, but I couldn't decide who was most likely to get the worst of it. He glared at Hassadi and then Lohise, and then towards the terrified children. His fur bristled and his muttering made my blood run cold. These two males would kill each other, I realized. Hassadi was shorter than Khuper, but his chest and his haunches were thicker. There was no clear winner in the dispute. Scars crisscrossed the shoulders of the two titan wolves as signs of the ongoing struggle. Fur was slow to regrow over the damaged skin.

Khuper withdrew as reluctantly as possible. Hassadi departed soon after, heading in a different direction. The pack began to disperse. The wolves trailed after the would-be Alpha males and spread among the trees, weighing divided loyalties. I exhaled with relief. Within the protective red mage-circle, a boy began to cry. The woman on the floating branch landed gracefully and comforted him with soothing words. I climbed from Lohise's back and walked to the edge of the ward. The glow retained a cautionary intensity. I had no desire to test the mages, and I cleared my throat. My hand was wrapped around the grip of a pistol, and my palm was beginning to sweat.

"The Rose tribe greets you, mages. Do you hail from the Jurisdiction?" There was steel in my voice, and I was prepared to defend my tribe.

The reply was unexpected. A laugh reached my ears.

"Ha! Guards forbid I ever end up THAT senile!" The woman walked forward. I could see she was aging, but age hadn't diminished her tenacity or the intensity of her dark eyes. The breeze stirred up her skirts, but they rippled from an energy beyond just the wind. I squinted and tilted my head.

"Hail, gunfighter of the Rose. The children of my humble village are sworn enemies of the Jurisdiction, same as you." She performed an odd curtsy which was clearly directed at Lohise.

"And I've an esteemed Den-Mother to thank for saving these mage cubs-" She glanced at her frightened charges and mouthed the remaining three words in silence.

"-from being lunch."

{~}

The fabric of the Council tent tinted the sunlight, casting the interior in greens and yellows. The government of the Rose tribe sat around an oval table which was the central feature to the tent. The afternoon was warmer than average, and the insulation of the tent created a pleasant atmosphere. I removed my armor jacket and draped the cumbersome layer on the back of my chair when I arrived. The table had been set for us, and the clinks of our soup spoons prevented oppressive silence.

"Mages," Terche said, putting down her spoon and shaking her head. "Who would've thought?"

The mood among the Confidants was pensive. I found myself grateful for the fact that they weren't fighting. The Council seemed to accept our latest guests magnanimously. The children huddled together in the City and tried to dry their clothes by the fire after crossing the river. The tribe greeted them with mixed success. The newcomers had kept to themselves and exchanged frightened whispers. I suppose in contrast to the titan wolves, the Witch and the orphaned children appeared less consequential. Flin stayed silent as the sparse discussions of the Confidants progressed. My worries about him were only compounded by the latest development. The last Moon was a whirlwind of change for any old man.

The Witch strolled through the flaps of the Council tent like she owned the whole Guard-damn City. She was greeted with frowns of annoyance, but we'd planned to summon her after another Mark anyway. We allowed her to speak without voicing any substantive objections.

"There's only one thing I came here to say," she began as eyes trained in her direction. "I want you to think on my words for a while. You may think we're foreign because we're mages. You might think only the Jurisdiction employs such people." The Witch looked around the Council tent.

"Your entire tribe consists of earth mages. Each and every petal of your Rose, meek and mighty, down to the last member. And your Generale, of course, is the strongest mage of all. Consider what I've said, and please look after Raspho and the others. I'll return in two-Sun's time."

The Confidants looked at each other and blinked in confusion. They turned back to the Witch, but she was already gone, having vanished with a swiftness I found disorienting. A twinge of energy remained behind, swirling in the tent where the woman was standing moments before. I forced myself to look away.
{~}

I tried to forget the Witch. I tried to forget what she said in the Council tent. I spent the Sun contemplating the art of forgetting things as I sat by the side of Drak's sick-pallet. He remained unconscious. For a minute I almost envied him. I'd be able to dodge the truth if I could stop considering it. Try as I might, I couldn't escape the Witch and her words about mages. But more than that, I couldn't escape the feeling. I knew the Witch was correct. I couldn't explain everything, but a lack of logic didn't change facts. I sighed. The Moons ahead would bring us a winter, mages or not.

I set myself towards practical matters. I braved Lohise's anger to ask her about the area around the City. I sent scouts to ride patrols in three directions, but I didn't dare to send them to titan wolf territory. Even so, I dreaded discovering a gunfighter was slain during an encounter with Lohise's divided pack. Lohise wouldn't make assurances, but when the Sun passed its peak she departed the City of Old to negotiate with her pack personally. I was beginning to see how common interests might serve to bring us closer. Human or otherwise, nobody wanted to fall prey to the Jurisdiction.

Lohise's absence was brief. Only the night passed before the Den Mother made the return trip across the river to rejoin Couress, Amika, and the Rose tribe. Her fur was wet and bedraggled. I pulled a hook from the mouth of a fish I'd been fighting with and tossed the catch by her foot. As Lohise sank her claws through the scales, her half-contented sighs told me our alliance would hold for the remainder of the Moon.

{~}

The Jurisdiction loomed in my thoughts. I was overcome by recurring dreams about the mechanical Quints. Steely, robotic footfalls rupturing the soil began to haunt my dreams. Lifeless, hollow eyes pierced concrete and earth and stone. Artillery barrels yawned like cavernous portals to a black abyss. No heartbeat, no feelings, only machine parts. Obsequious, gargantuan tools of death and destruction, leveled directly towards the sigil of the Rose.

That Witch, Guard damn her, she brought my nightmares to life with her when she returned. She came in hot, screaming at us like a banshee.

"The Quintish are coming! The Quintish are coming!"

She'd seen them herself. Their presence had pushed her to the edge. I'd never witnessed such a profoundly strained countenance or heard such ghastly sounds from a human. The Witch was a bad omen if you ask me. A glowing cat appeared along with the Witch and touched a nerve with Lohise. The Den Mother bared her teeth. The cat crouched in response as the titan wolf circled the gathered gunfighters. The Rose tribe gathered to watch as I sent my Lieutenants to prepare our defenses.

"What are you doing here, Hellcat?" Lohise asked, her eyes locked on the feline associate of the Witch. "Is there nobody left alive in the Low Hills for you to torment?"

I knew the bared fangs meant confrontation. For her part, the cat seemed less keen on conflict, but this was unsurprising considering she was comically undersized for the fight. I was chagrined that the titan wolf even cared about the odd red cat at all. How dangerous could she be compared to the Quints headed our way?

"Den Mother, is it? I've only ever had one goal," the cat began. Her voice sounded tiny compared to the booming of the titan wolf.

"One goal?" Lohise shot back. "And what goal is that? War and death?"

"I fight the Jurisdiction. That's all I've ever done."

Lohise wasn't having any of this. Her snarl crescendoed to a roar.

"So you're a liar as well as a vicious fool! When you couldn't convince the tribes to follow you, you set fire to their homes in the night! Were you fighting the Jurisdiction then? Did each and every one of the Tribal Wars start because of you? Was one wretched cat the sole perpetrator? Were you all it took?"

"Enough!" the Witch interjected. "Den Mother Lohise, I understand your objections. Charlie may be a wretched cat, but there are Quints out there. Can't you feel them? The earth shivers and shakes. We've no time for this vendetta. Rally your pack, bring them to the City. The only chance we have is if we're united."

Lohise sneezed and shook her head. "Our last conversation wasn't exactly cordial. They'll think it's a trap. And if they don't, then they might decide it's safer to run away. Can you tell me that isn't the case?"

Apparently it was the Witch's turn to snarl.

"Now you listen here, wolf! I hid from the Jurisdiction for decades. Centuries even! When the Defiance fell, when my second husband fell, running was the best possible course. We never had a hope of fighting back in those Rounds without precipitating needless suffering and death. Gunnery Sergeant Charlie Urnstead here couldn't give up on the fight, and I'm sorry to say, but it drove her to madness. That doesn't mean I've avoided conflict with the Jurisdiction," the Witch paused to utter a sharp laugh. "Hiding isn't as peaceful as it sounds. I've seen the Jurisdiction attack villages and strongholds I cared about. I've countless lives destroyed as they made a stand. But stand they had to, and stand they did! When every other option fell away from them, they died as martyrs, heroes, legends. The Jurisdiction isn't going to stop with the City of Old. We're seeing a new undertaking which is likely to be our undoing. Your pack will be next, Lohise. I imagine they've sumptuous pelts among them, and the Regiment will hunt them for sport without a second thought. Bring your pack. Bring as many as you can. Convince them this is the time to fight a bitter enemy. Our options have been whittled down."

Her eyes began to glow with the fire in her blood.

"The banner of the Defiance deserves a final farewell."

{~}

We tried to buoy our spirits, but our prospects were grim. Even if Lohise managed to rally her pack to our aid, what could the titan wolves do against such un-Guardly technology? I was skeptical of how much cover fire the Rose tribe would be able to provide them. Our guns weren't powerful enough to pierce that kind of armor.

Thinking about the Quints and their armaments brought me to the problem we faced first and foremost. The huge machines wouldn't need to come within range of our weapons to attack us. They'd bombard the city from a distance, hitting us from behind the cover of trees and hills. This was the entire purpose of artillery. We'd be under siege, shelled with no reprieve. Courageous sorties would be no match for what was coming. We'd try to hold the City, despite the odds. We were better off in the ancient refuge with rivers and sturdy walls around us than on the run in the Wilds. Packed wagons weren't waiting for us this time.

My train of thought converged with the other tracks in my mind as I saw to the final preparations. The Quints would bear down on the City at any minute. The Rose tribe took shelter underground in a basement tunnel we'd discovered, dusty and forsaken beneath the ancient ruins. We'd be cramped inside, but the bunker was the only way we could be guaranteed any kind of protection. If the Quints attempted to cross the rivers, we'd surface to engage and make a stand. The pressing issue on my mind was the Mammoth. We'd concealed the machine with earth and concrete, but a sustained attack on her position was likely to damage or destroy her. Branches and gravel were added to the site to cover up telltale metal panels.

A crude hatch groaned in place over the concrete frame at the entrance to our hideaway. The tribe looked around at each other in the torchlight. I knew the Witch and her mage children were among us. Even Amika and Couress were huddled below, fighting their discomfort at the press of humans around them.

The first mortar explosion shook our compound, and gasps and murmurs swept through the bunker. Verikas and Trenz lit up a couple of smokes. I think some folks might've complained about the lingering haze of cigarillos if the situation hadn't been so tense. We listened to the crackle of torches in the gaps between the hammering of artillery above us. The scant construction we'd begun was being obliterated. I heard weeping in the depths of the tunnel.

A brief pause in the consistent shelling caused me to rise to my feet. I was about to go check the surface when a series of purposeful barks sounded beyond the steel door.

"Vamos, gunfighters!" I yelled, injecting my voice with the confidence I longed to feel.

"Join our allies and Cover them! Throw back the Quints! The rivers make them vulnerable! To battle!"

The Witch flew over our heads as the door opened. She shot through the air and was immediately beset by gunfire. She dipped and dodged, her shielding glowing orange. The other fire mage who decided to fight with us was a teenager called Raspho. He joined the ranks of our gunfighters, but he had a green look to his face I recognized all too well. I reset my focus. This was no time to be worried about an untested recruit. We needed every hand to survive.

Armed gunfighters poured from the bunker with their adrenaline surging. We were immediately surrounded by Lohise's pack of titan wolves. I kept a wary eye towards them despite the dire circumstances of the battle. They appeared to have a grudging acceptance of us. The comfort of their presence was an unsteady feeling. I saw Khuper and Hassadi snort in derision of each other. No doubt they eyed the bunker and awaited Couress and Amika, but I didn't have the time to manage an awkward reunion. I had a counterattack to lead.

We formed up and advanced with practiced determination. I estimated the total number of enemy Quints at around a dozen. I saw no signs of the Regiment or the Swarm. The Quints fired on our position and we warned of incoming mortars as they struck the earth and fortifications around us. I'd given Lieutenant Bonder a promotion in the form of an armor-piercing bazooka. He was a steady hand. As we reached the riverbank, we dove behind the sandbags we'd placed for cover and sighted on the closest Quint. The machine was about to ford the river and I saw no reason to delay. I signaled to open fire, and we hit with everything we had. The machine stumbled on the gravel beneath the moving water and struggled to aim its cannons as our bullets pinged against its arms. I was about to give the signal to take cover and reload when Lohise rushed the Quint from the left flank. As the left cannon of the war machine began to recover, titan wolf teeth sheared metal and wires and hydraulic tubing. A shot went off haphazardly before Lohise released her grip and the gun arm dangled twisted and useless. The Quint's remaining arm caused me to duck as the robot unloaded. I heard a snarling wolves crash against metal legs and a splash which could only mean one thing. I dared to look above the sandbags to confirm what I heard. The Quint struggled uselessly in the shallow water, unable to maneuver itself upright. Dark fluids leaked from the machine and polluted the river's flow with the stench of mechanical death. A gunfighter lobbed an improvised firebomb in the direction of the downed Quint's face and the homemade napalm cracked and popped as it cooked cameras and circuitry. The hydraulic movements grew sluggish.

We were triumphant for a moment but the moment wasn't fit to last. I cautioned against preemptive celebration as I gave my orders. The smoke rising from the burning Quint reduced visibility and made regrouping difficult for Lohise's pack. Gunfighters flanked in three different directions. The titan wolves barely returned to cover before the next Quints tore up the river bank with artillery cannon fire. We tried to repeat the tactic we'd used to defeat the first Quint, but the increased danger of dealing with multiple targets resulted in the loss of precious life. Our forward position was hit especially hard when a third Quint closed in on us, and we tried to drag the injured back. A titan wolf was slain when a Quint swung the barrel of its arm towards her belly.

I fought back the rising panic. There was no chance we would destroy all of the Quints. Bonder crippled the war machine closest to us by hitting it in the crotch with a rocket, but the firefight was alright becoming untenable as artillery leveled everything in sight. Trees, concrete, sandbags, steel, nothing mattered. With a seemingly endless supply of oversized ammunition and an utter lack of empathy, nothing stood in their way. The Jurisdiction would remake the entire surface of the earth as they saw fit. When the Quints were finished here the City would be lifeless. The Jurisdiction liked things simple. People were never simple.

There wasn't a question about what came next for the Rose tribe. We'd fight to the death, of course. The gunfighters who stood to lose their lives knew what would happen to the people protected by the bunker should they fall, and I believe each and every one of them refused to accept that outcome. No doubt the titan wolves felt a similar understanding. I didn't need to convince anyone to fight, only guide the task at hand.

Any strategic discipline I could muster was falling apart at the seams as the odds turned cruelly against us. There were no orders I could give which would mask the desperation. We began to fight like cornered animals. Lohise was fearless in her guerilla rushes to defeat our foes, but I could tell she was losing blood. Each fallen wolf was a precious cub lost to her.

I grew detached from myself, as if I were looking down at the battlefield from afar through smoke and pain. I felt guns in my hands. The steel devices perched precariously on my arms. I squeezed triggers, and I was yelling something, somewhere. But inside I was wondering if anyone would live to tell of our stand. I wondered if we'd be the stuff of anthems, or if a bard would ever learn to sing them after the Quints were through with the City.

Moments like these might end in tragedy and defeat. Even great victory is often drenched in sorrow. But a turn of fate can amaze and astound, and bring a sense of hope and wonder. I try not to think of the Guards playing dice with our lives.

A beast appeared in the sky. I believed it was an illusion cast by the Witch who battled from her flying branch. The creature was surely beyond the realm of actual flesh and blood. A lizard the size of a mountain had too much mass to truly be floating above the trees. I was inclined to think the dragon was conjured for show because the alternative was utterly irrational.

And yet there he was, breathing blue flame and circling for a second pass. I remained keen to discount the evidence of my own eyes until I saw a human figure slip from the dragon's neck and drop to the earth.

There was a man there. A man was riding atop the dragon, a man who ran through the forest with nothing except a pair of blue pants and a sword. He moved reflexively as he deflected artillery shells with the flat of the blade.

"What the fuck," I heard myself muttering.

Despite the cool autumn air, he wasn't wearing a shirt, and my eyes were drawn to the dark skin of his broad shoulders and his chest. I watched him jam the weapon through the leg of a Quint and the clash of steel jostled me back to myself. I gave a whoop of encouragement to the fighters around me and reloaded as I leapt forward. The sound of artillery was already tapering off. I rounded the edge of the bunker and stopped dead in my tracks.

The Quints were frozen. Thick blue ice incapacitated them down to the last by the time the dragon finished his final pass. Angular heads seemed to glare at me in confusion. In the distance, the winged lizard landed and folded his wings. Vapor billowed from his nostrils as he spoke to the man with the sword. I could hear the booming pulse of his reptilian voice. The resonance made me repress a shiver. I sheathed a pistol and inquired about casualties as I tried to locate my Lieutenants. I needed to attend to my fighters in the wake of this near catastrophe. Despite the pressing concerns, I happened to spare a curious glance towards the dragon's landing site.

The man with the sword was staring back at me.

Chapter 11
Rahn tells of: "A Dragon's Whimsy"

"If you're choosing between survival or an honorable death, then I don't presume to know the answer. But you should probably keep a blade in your boot." -The Frost Swordsman

Westings and I had our chilly spots between us, but the tree became a close friend anyway. I think eventually we were more honest with each other than the arboreal being could've been with his creator. To say the Wizard was unstable would be putting his state of mind mildly. Westings accepted the Wizard for who he was, but he'd never been given a choice in the matter.

The Wizard didn't want me to leave the island. I was convalescing on a woven mat at Westings' insistence, and I hadn't defeated Edges yet. I'm not sure any test I passed would've left the Wizard at peace with my departure.

The eccentric old man submerged the entire island with a tsunami when Chaeoh appeared, forcing Westings and I to brace ourselves desperately in the towering surge of water rushing over us. A storm began to percolate between the Wizard and the dragon Chaeoh which snagged at the fibers of reality itself. I looked deep into Westings' woody eyes as water swirled in chaotic vortexes around us. Chaeoh tested the humidity by releasing spurts of blue flame from the sides of his maw. Szakaieh conjured a blade of water like a rushing whitecap. Westings and I felt the fear of knowing that we might not see the dawn. We focused our shielding as we said fare-wells to each other.

The Wizard abandoned his aggression before the tension broke wide open and things got completely out of hand. He briskly stated that leaving the island was my decision, and no dragon was going to kidnap me. I decided to fly away on the dragon's back. The Wizard was furious with me, but affection had begun to soften his eyes. As the water levels receded and the light faded, I imagined him hoping I'd return.

Despite Chaeoh's obvious intelligence, the dragon wasn't much for conversation. When he did speak, his sentences were oversimplified or cryptic or without proper context. I'd never met another dragon to compare him with so I assumed it was normal. When I climbed on his neck, he didn't exactly hand me a map and a flight plan.

I expressed my desire to free the Slaves of the Pens several times to the dragon. The Regiment would be no match for the size of

Chaeoh or his claws. I realized my true obstacle would be getting the obstinate beast to listen to anything I said.

I berated him for a while. Sometimes he'd grunt or swivel his head if he thought he could calm me with a short reply. When I began to lose my patience, I lashed out. A cold fist against a hardened scale made him notice me.

He launched me through a cloud by swerving his neck and his shoulders. I rocketed through the water vapor for a moment and then I was falling. Never have I felt so vulnerable or so alone as I did when I was tumbling through the air looking desperately for Chaeoh. The dragon was nowhere to be found. Death approached me with the frank certainty of a flipped hourglass. Chaeoh was too far away to do anything about my rapid descent, too far away to care. The piece of forest I was going to die in rushed to meet me.

I barely felt the dragon claws slip around my waist. They did nothing to slow my descent until they dug in painfully. My fall wasn't arrested completely until I was about to be skewered by an evergreen. Chaeoh tossed me again, back out to the sky, and I grabbed frantically for his neck as he passed beneath me. I managed to get enough of my fingers around the edge of a scale.

"Not a flyer?" the dragon asked me as I hooked my feet and attempted to breathe.

"Oh NOW you want to talk," I retorted, trying to relax. The overdose of adrenaline left me nauseated, but a barrier inside me was shattered by the dragon's reprimand. I no longer cared where we were flying. I lay my face against the smooth surface of the scales on Chaeoh's neck. Onward to a new world. I noticed the dragon aura around me for the first time. Blue-green energy pooled like a molten stew of emeralds and sapphires in his heart and in his belly. Where my aura made contact with his, I felt as though icy crystals had caught the winter sun's light. I experienced a brief moment of absolute confidence, as if I were completely indestructible. There was no task too formidable for me to accomplish. I'd bring the Guards themselves to their knees, and the Jurisdiction would bow in the process. Chaeoh's pitched rumble showed his appreciation.

In the next moment I felt I was a total fool. A drained, lost fool who'd entrusted his life to a gigantic lizard. How could I ever be so stupid? I was a Slave, escaped from the Pens, and my only weapon wasn't even a weapon, but a farming implement. Perhaps Chaeoh was taking me to a field of plants which was better suited to a Slave's work with a machete. I was already beginning to feel hungry. My rations and fresh water wouldn't even last another Sun.

When I was growing up in the Slave Pens, I wept infrequently. The tears would've only frozen on my cheeks anyway, just as they did while Chaeoh flew to an unknown destination. This time, the cold came from within me. I'd seen too much of the world. I knew there were forces I had no hope of rivaling. Was I destined to be a rag-doll, tossed about by the whims of the powerful? Was there freedom to be found in any of this?

{~}

Perhaps Chaeoh knew my melancholy. The empty coast was sheltered by the trees and the surrounding terrain. Although the sand wasn't as warm as the Wizard's island, autumn hadn't marched far enough south to take hold of the cove. Chaeoh grabbed fish and I found fresh water and built a fire in the sand using dead wood from a dense forest nearby. The insects were malevolent but my aura and shielding kept them at bay. The cove was a tranquil site to camp. We listened to the animal sounds of the forest and the rushing pulse of the sea as night descended. I slept by the coals of the dying fire while Chaeoh stretched out on the beach. He was thoughtful enough to move away from me so his lurching tail didn't kill me in the night when he shifted in his sleep.

My dreams were troubled, and I awoke in the morning with a sense of foreboding. Perhaps I sensed a sign in Chaeoh's body language, because the dragon was preoccupied in the light of dawn. I made coffee before he spoke to me. The mug obscured my nose and mouth as I sipped, but I met the dragon's eyes when his giant head craned towards me over the surface of the sand.

"Are you ready?" Chaeoh asked me.

I stiffened. I could feel where the steely weight of the machete was slung to my back. Other than my trousers, the makeshift sheath was the only piece of clothing I wore. The coolness of the air against the bare skin of my torso heightened my senses. My blood was beginning to flow like the rush of melted snow. At first, I was unaware what the dragon meant when he asked if I was ready, but after a few moments, my intuition informed about the work we'd be doing. Chaeoh shifted away, stretching purposefully, as if he knew I'd discover his intentions. His claws dug trenches in the sand. His tail bulldozed the beach as he performed his calisthenics. The force of his weight created thuds I could feel through my feet. He was enormous. I shielded my face and took a step back while sand flew in my coffee. The dragon's rituals left every inch of him coated in grit. As I was beginning to wonder if my thighs would chafe against a sandy dragon, Chaeoh charged towards the water at full gallop, plunging himself into the ocean. I swirled the last of the gritty coffee in my mug as I watched him swim beneath the waves.

When Chaeoh emerged, he glistened in the sun. The dragon carried a ferocious amount of speed as he broke forth. The salt water streamed from his scales in vivid patterns. He helped the brine depart by tucking his wings back and shaking them. The midnight blue center of his broad scales soaked up the light, while metallic green highlighted the edges of his living armor. He trumpeted a battle call,

and the harmonics echoed in my blood. My soul's response was involuntary. I have no trust in my memory of the event. My coffee mug is probably still lying on that beach. I leapt up, far higher than I'd ever jumped before. At the zenith of my leap, Chaeoh calmly placed his paw beneath my feet. He couldn't smile without showing his teeth.
{~}

Part of me understood intrinsically what was happening in the fight below us. I didn't need to be told the Quints were the enemy and the human gunfighters were our allies. Certainly the dragon made the situation obvious enough when he started spewing blue everywhere. I discovered Chaeoh's scales took an unpleasant chill when he was breathing frost-fire. He was kind enough to swoop low so I could jump to the ground.

The Quints looked manageable from the air, but they were a fearsome sight to behold from the forest floor. They towered over me with their metal exoskeletons and minds full of silicon and wires. They were horrible and unfair, and I was enraged. I hated them even more than I hated the Regiment. A part of me acknowledged there was a crumpled bit of humanity remaining in the Regiment. With the Quints, there was no such concern.

A battle trance came over me rapidly. By the time one of the ugly war machines decided to shoot at me with artillery cannons, my inner mage was frozen with disdain. The shells came at me, and I brushed them away with the machete. I was blinded by determination and my enemy didn't possess the firepower to stop me. In fact, I began to doubt if any gun or machine was up to the task. I was a mage, not the victim of their sadistic science projects. I was annoyed that Chaeoh was freezing the Quints before I could vent my anger.
{~}

Chaeoh landed behind me. His head drew close to mine and he made soothing sounds. I realized I was shaking. I tried to steady myself. I placed a hand against the dragon's elbow when the scales appeared in my peripheral vision. My pulse began to stabilize, but Chaeoh spoke to me.

"Fight's not over yet," he said.

I thought he was speaking metaphorically, but I followed his gaze past my shoulder, where I caught the eyes of the gunfighter woman.

She raised her pistol and fired at me three times. I managed to deflect the first two shots, but the third struck me in the shoulder. Ice spread across my skin from the impact site, and blood pooled beneath. I plucked the bullet free with a grimace and flicked the slug away like a dead insect.

"Was that your usual greeting?" I called to the woman.

I think I saw her smile briefly before she could hide her reaction.

"Nice party trick," she said as she walked forward. Beside her ,a wolf which was huge enough to be the stuff of nightmares sat down as if the creature could listen to us speak. The woman continued and appeared to take her time in spite of the battle's aftermath around her.

"I met a few mages just the other day," the woman said with a shrug. Her confidence brought an understanding that she was their leader. I swallowed and felt weak. If she ordered her gang to kill me, I wouldn't be able to block the bullets forever. Eventually they'd accomplish exactly what they intended. I shifted my stance closer to the dragon at my shoulder.

Chaeoh remained calm, but I could feel the tension in his aura. I wondered what he thought of this woman and the immense wolf, and if he'd fight on my behalf. The dragon interrupted my speculation.

"They'll help free Slaves," he said. My heart leapt at remembered desires and I smiled. The organ sank after he spoke again. "I'll return. Be careful." He gestured subtly with an errant claw. I knew where he'd indicated, but I turned my head a few degrees to see a single turquoise eye wink at the edge of my vision.

I didn't dare take my eyes off of the woman, not with all those guns surrounding her. Battering gusts of air kicked up the dust and the enormous blue shape which was my backup vanished when Chaeoh took wing and abandoned me. I did my best to look as though I'd expected the departure, and his absence didn't concern me. The gunfighters ooh-ed and aah-ed over Chaeoh as he unleashed a musical blast of sound and stretched his full length in the sky. Their leader studied me intently instead. I nodded to her in acknowledgment.

"Yes, I'm a mage," I offered. "I'm Rahn Le'Del, and what of it? What gang is this? "

"My title is Generale Oakes of the Rose tribe. This titan wolf-" she gestured adjacent to her, "-is Den Mother Lohise. We're grateful for your aid. I doubt we've means of repayment acceptable to a mage such as yourself or his- dragon. Which leaves us uncomfortably in your debt."

"Is that why you decided to shoot me?"

Generale Oakes turned to the side on her heel as she frowned. "Too many fronts. Too many battles. If you were inclined to fight us, I wanted it over with sooner rather than later." She faced me again. "I apologize for the lack of hospitality. These are trying times." As I studied her the strain she was under became apparent. This was wrong. I shook my head.

"There's no need to repay me," I assured her. Her expression remained neutral, and I couldn't stop the flow of words. "Or the dragon. He brought me here," I confessed. "He's not my dragon, by the way. I'm his human, more likely." I attempted a smile, but the expression felt thin. Generale Oakes looked entirely unamused. Her facial features barely shifted. I cleared my throat, attempting to defeat the tension. "I'd be grateful for warm fire and a meal, and thread for this bullet wound."

The Generale holstered her pistols and walked across the space between us. I was most of a head taller than her, but I felt like I was overly exposed in front of a powerful gang leader. I shivered, knowing I'd probably collapse here and suffer from exposure if she refused to help me. The Generale placed her hand on the ice where she'd shot me. The cold crispness began to melt under the warmth of her touch, and I drew a sharp breath as the numbness left the wound. She pulled her hand away and looked at the blood on her fingers.

"Were you expecting blue? Here," I said, and I removed the sling from my back with my uninjured shoulder. I tossed the sheath aside along with the battered machete. "You can take the sword if it makes you feel any better."

"It doesn't," she said. She met my eyes briefly and began to walk away. Her gunfighters withdrew. I sagged and exhaled. I began to contemplate a cold night of solitude but her steps stopped abruptly. Her head turned just enough for me to see a cheek, but her voice was firm.

"Our home is your home."

I didn't recognize the greeting, and her words confused me for a moment before relief dawned. She turned back to her gunfighters. "Give our guest a shirt," she said. I collected my dignity, determined to make camp under my own power. I was handed a loose-fitting rough-knit blouse, and I put the garment on with a nod of thanks. The shirt was stained with someone else's blood, but I was grateful. I knew I was going to bleed on it too. The clothing restored warmth to my body, but only for a few moments before we reached the bank of the river. The water sucked away the energy I had left through the frigid skin of my legs. I almost succumbed to the thought of giving up and letting my head slip beneath the surface. The only thing keeping me moving was the memory of the Wizard and his water elementals. I wasn't the victim of the water anymore. I was the water's equal. I grunted and took another silty step.

I desperately wished I hadn't surrendered my machete. In hindsight, disarmament felt like an error on many levels, tactical, diplomatic, and others I couldn't name. I longed to have a blade on my person as I entered the camp of armed strangers. They were weary and traumatized, and they viewed me with curiosity clouded by suspicion. I studied the faces, unsure of how to greet them, and I thought about their Generale.

A group among the tribe was unlike the rest. Children of varying ages stood clustered together. Their clothing and appearances weren't particularly unusual, and yet they had a different sort of energy. I had only a feeling to go on, but the part of me which was a mage didn't doubt the way that I felt. The children made me think back to the Slave Pens. They gathered around an older woman with a hefty ornate branch as well as a determined looking young man with a wooden quarterstaff. The weapons were unique among the guns of the Rose tribe. I realized they were mages, free mages living here instead of working for the Jurisdiction. The Wizard wasn't alone. His choice of island solitude wasn't even necessary. I was thrilled and perplexed with the revelation.

I wanted to travel back to the island in order to tell the Wizard what I'd found, but Chaeoh wasn't at my command. He'd chosen to leave me immersed in the culture of the Rose tribe instead of ferrying me around with him. The Slave Pens left me without an understanding of established community. The Rose tribe may've fallen on hard times, but they were a free, proud people with traditions and camaraderie. I had difficulty remembering names, but I found nothing lacking in their hospitality. They all lamented the tribe's short supply of alcohol. This seemed like a dire breach of celebratory protocol to them. I tried my best to assure them that I didn't mind. What precious liquor remained was used to treat the wounded, so I was given a jot of the stuff to send to my gullet when the doctor with the bottle saw my shoulder. I gathered that the Rose tribe wasn't going to mourn on the evening after battle. Instead they put together a victory celebration with the available resources. We ate meat and side dishes and drank earthy teas. The air was filled with the sound of singing. I smiled in the firelight and listened intently to a never-ending stream of stories told in the tribe's precise, expressive accent. I became self conscious of the character of my own voice, and when I spoke I found myself sounding like a foreigner with gruff, lilting sentences.

As I revealed the details of my life in conversation, the tribe's opinion of me changed. I entered their midst as a visitor and found myself becoming a hero. The tales told by other gunfighters recounting how I'd fought the Quints with nothing more than a machete furthered the change in attitude. As my standing in the eyes of the Rose tribe grew, I felt the Generale's opinion of me go in the opposite direction. I began to wonder if she'd ever stop scowling. The night was supposed to be a celebration.

When Trenz and Corwin learned I'd never shot a gun, they nearly had a fist-fight over who would get the honor of lending me their piece. A crowd gathered by the improvised gun range and a woman named Verekas explained the parts of her rifle to me. The barrel was this part, the breach was that one, the bolt, the safety and the sights all had a role. She showed me how to load it and hold the butt against my good shoulder, and I squeezed the trigger for the first time. The metal tube kicked like a mule, and my shot went high and wide even though the target was only a few paces downrange. The crowd around me roared with laughter. Even Generale Oakes let her frown crack at the corner. My face was flushed from the rush of recoil and my own utter incompetence with the weapon. I worked the bolt and had another go. This time, the shot slammed through the wooden target. I turned around and offered the empty rifle back to Verekas. She raised my fist with her hand in an expression of mock triumph. I couldn't help but smile. The tribe laughed and hooted and spattered applause.

When the commotion died, I found a curious woman standing in front of me. I recognized her as a mage I'd seen earlier. Her hair was pale, and the branch she used as a walking staff was taller than her. The silver inlay was a work of art, and the glint immediately captured my gaze. Admiration was plain on my face. When her handshake sent a jolt of power through my palm, the unprovoked injury hurt like hell. When she introduced herself as 'the Witch' I nodded. I stated my full name curtly, remembering Westings and his lesson about the apostrophe. Her aura swelled, and I immediately thought of the Wizard. The Witch had seemed so kindly towards the children and the Rose tribe earlier. Why did she treat me with such venom? Her eyes glowed with fiery power. Her gaze was intent on cutting to the core of me. I don't think she wanted to make a scene, but perhaps it was inevitable.

"Who trained you?" she asked, her voice muted and conveying her age with a humble warble.

I shrugged. "A Wizard." I clenched my jaw. I felt protective of him. I had no desire to give up the identity of my friend to this woman's intimidation. My resistance, however, was bound to be futile. Just as the Wizard who trained me was my superior, so was this Witch. Shackles of flame appeared, grabbing my ankles and wrists. I screamed at the burns and poured power towards shielding myself. Ice formed around my skin, hissing and steaming as I tried to keep the restraints from searing me.

"Who trained you?" the Witch asked again, brandishing a slim wooden baton like a gang initiate's shiv. Answering the question was no longer optional. In a separate plane of existence, Generale Oakes and the gunfighters around us pointed guns at the Witch, but she ignored them with such conviction they could've flinched from the tangible disdain. The titan wolf watched as she rested her chin on her paws, but she made no attempt to intervene. The canine queen had decided where the scales of power were levered. I tried to clear my mind of everything and maintain my shielding. I defied the Witch by silencing the urge to yell as I strained against her chains. I spat the words rebelliously. I wasn't a Slave of the Pens anymore.

"The Wizard of the Waves trained me, ma'am. The Soaking Soothsayer, the Soggy Conjurer. The Lucky Watcher or the Demon Rabbit. An old hermit named Szakaieh. Guard-dammit, call him whatever you want."

The Witch's aura vanished so abruptly I feared for her life. My restraints were gone and she crumpled to her knees with the silvery branch clattering to the ground beside her. I knelt along with her, afraid she'd pushed herself too far. For a moment I thought the Witch might die right there in front of me. When she spoke, her voice was only a whisper, but I know the entire tribe heard her. The entire forest heard her. The titan wolf began to howl. The Generale herself dropped to one knee in acknowledgement.

"My Kai. He's alive."

{~}

For the next several hours the Witch was an ordinary woman. The lines on her face were pronounced and her eyes darkened further as they welled with emotion. She spoke in a voice which was strained, but the City was listening. Even the crackling of the fire grew quiet when she spoke.

"When the Jurisdiction first appeared, people fought against it. How could they not? The Jurisdiction was always a monster." She looked around at the audience gathered for her as if she was trying to see each and every person she was speaking to. "When the first mages began to appear, they were beholden the Jurisdiction. The Jurisdiction may even be responsible for the very existence of mages. I'm relatively certain that the early Jurisdiction employed biological warfare on an unthinkable scale. Governments split and countries fell apart at the seams and the world was thrown into chaos. The Defiance was created as a response. What remained of the world's militaries that hadn't succumbed to the struggle or joined up with the Jurisdiction tried to band together. They lacked sound strategy and cooperation was often difficult."

She paused. I could see this tale was remembering a past wound for the Witch.

"In the early days, there were times when I wondered if the Defiance wasn't almost as horrible as the Jurisdiction. The Defiance captured mages and tortured them. Called it part of the war effort. Civilians, too, if they thought you'd 'gone J-D.' The Jurisdiction was even more synonymous with mages back then. I was one of the first mages to ever work with the Defiance. I risked everything. So did Gunny Urnstead, here. She was human, then."

"No wonder," Lohise grumbled.

I realized the titan wolf was listening intently. The red cat purred and curled up next to the Witch. Her shining fur echoed the flickering of the flames. The story brought whispers and murmurs to the Rose tribe, but they faded as the Witch continued. She cleared her throat, but her first word cracked anyway.

"Sza-kaieh was barely a mage when I first met him. Neither of us were youthful optimists at the time. I was a scientist, and my first husband was a soldier. James died when the Jurisdiction took over. When I learned what had happened, I blamed myself. Kai listened to me as I was trying to piece together how everything went wrong. Nobody paid much attention to him at the time. He was basically just a drifter, and as I said, barely even a mage. He sat down on a park bench next to me one Sun, and I told him to take a shower. I could always tell he was different. A few Rounds later, when his hair was going gray, he showed me he could make raindrops dance in patterns on a glass window pane. We started to connect, and we discovered we were about as close to perfect for each other as we were likely to get. We married on a beach and danced in the moonlight. We had a daughter. Her name was Chrysanthemum. She was an air mage."

Her voice wavered, but the Witch wasn't going to be deterred. Tears appeared in the crowd, and I could feel them. Even Lohise looked as though she were suppressing a howl.

"Everything escalated. The war, the Defiance, Kai's talent as a mage, they all blew up on me. Before I knew what was happening to us, I felt like a gear in the war effort instead of a human being, and Kai was right alongside me. His waves were an effective tool against the Quints, the Regiment, the Nobility. For my part, I perfected the art of destroying machinery of every description imaginable. A spark here, a surge there, I could disable the drones. Chrysanthemum, Guards bless her, found herself raised by her nannies in a bunker. Sun and Moon the Defiance struggled. We hit a peak in those Rounds. If the Jurisdiction was a conventional enemy, we would've prevailed."

The Witch sighed, and our hearts broke along with hers. "But the Jurisdiction is a kind of evil I've yet to comprehend. When they were finally cornered, we'd discover our forces had defected and turned against us. The rate of betrayal and desertion became so high we suspected foul play, but what could we do? Nobody could determine the cause or how to stop it."

Jerro handed the Witch a steaming mug, and she accepted gratefully. She took a sip. The fire popped and a log shifted.

"A battle came which ended everything for me. Certainly that battle ended the Defiance. I saw no sense in continuing to fight when the only possible outcome was more death. So we ran. We hid. Those who wanted to fight," her glance cast shade at the cat, "They were left with almost no operational capacity. And my Kai," she choked up. The Witch fortified herself with another sip from the mug.

"My Kai was hit with a torpedo." She paused. The word 'torpedo' was unknown to me and I wasn't alone. As explanations were muttered she continued.

"The explosion was catastrophic. The detonation of the Jurisdiction warhead would've destroyed an entire city. Kai was in the ocean, and the sea level surged for kilometers around him. A tidal wave bore down on the Jurisdiction forces. I thought that was fitting, but-"

The Witch stood. Her aura returned. "I'd always suspected Kai had his hand in the Lucky Watcher. I never dared hope the illusion was actually him. Now I know Kai's alive," the Witch frowned. She took a deep breath.

"If he's been off sulking this whole Guard-damn time I swear to the Guards-" A few people in the crowd began to chuckle. The Witch lifted her mug with a smile and a gesture of toast to diffuse the tragedy. The tale was over, but as the attention turned away from her ,the old woman's frown returned.

I hadn't lost focus. As the others left the Witch, I stood in front of her.

"What about your daughter?" I asked.

The Witch cocked an eye at me. "You're a close listener, aren't you Rahn? Maybe too close." I suppressed the urge to smile or nod and remained impassive instead.

"I can't help but wonder how much of this tale you've heard before." She continued to sip from the wooden mug. She was in no rush to deliver her words. "I apologize for my treatment of you earlier. I'm going to need your help."

I shook my head. "You need the dragon. I don't know how to get back to the island."

The Witch appeared to consider this. "So Kai lives on an island, then? And the dragon will return to us here in the City?"

I nodded, feeling cautious around the Witch. "He didn't say how many Suns."

"So the dragon speaks," she said in a cunning tone. "Then I should like to have a word with him."

"You didn't answer my question," I said.

The Witch froze.

"My daughter is dead," she said tersely. Her tone was defensive and I was taken aback. "You won't convince me otherwise."
{~}

The following day, funerals were held. I helped in tangential ways, mostly staying in the background. I enjoyed a light lunch before being summoned to the Confidant's meeting. I knew Trenz by name and she nodded when the time arrived.

Throughout the morning, Generale Oakes gave last rites to the fallen dead. The titan wolves were included. I observed an alliance brimming with tension in lieu of a battle. A wrong move by man or wolf would prove disastrous. On the other hand, the recent victory against a common enemy could solidify a relationship. There was no doubt the titan wolves felt uneasy about their kind being buried in the ground by human hands. Lohise had insisted, however, and her word was law among their kind. The requiems were new to me. With all the death I'd seen, I felt I should be immune, but the ceremonies struck a note in me.

When I stood before the Confidants, my mood was grave. I didn't really care about the fluff of casual conversation. There were more important things which needed saying. Generale Oakes was seated at the head of the table, and she motioned for me to sit down. I grasped a rough hewn chair and took a seat. I found the abrasive wood offered an identical level of comfort to the Generale's gaze. I shifted the chair legs to a better position on the earthen floor. The Confidants were silent. The urge to speak nagged at me, but I observed the gathering instead. A second chair was placed beside me. My suspicions were confirmed when the Witch entered the tent. She took the chair, mindful of the splinters, and seated herself, smoothing her dress.

Confidant Terche addressed us. "I'd like to formally welcome you to this meeting of the Rose Council. Your exploits have woven imaginative tales." A couple of the Confidants snickered. A couple others frowned opaquely. "I wish I could tell you that we as Confidants are united in the matters at hand, but I cannot. However," Terche looked towards Generale Oakes, "the Generale has argued she wishes to make a personal request of you. It isn't our custom to deny this to our Generale. Perhaps I'll allow her to explain." She gestured towards Generale Oakes. The transition went smoothly and I wondered if the two had conspired together.

"I want you to train us," Generale Oakes began. "Not everyone, mind you. A few of my honor guard. You're both mages. The Witch tells us the Rose tribe has mages. I want to learn. I want to do what you do."

The Witch and I looked at each other. Her lips wrinkled together. I intended to let her field the question.

She cleared her throat. "Perhaps this could be done, Generale Oakes. In a few Moons time. That's the best I could offer you. You have to understand, my priority is finding my husband. If I'm not mistaken, I believe Rahn has other priorities as well."

If looks could kill I may've been slain right there in that Confidant's tent by Generale Oakes. Her face told me her fears about me had been confirmed. The Witch handed me the floor with a gleeful jab of a glance after setting me up to fail.

In the first few Rounds after I was freed from the Slave Pens, I don't think I was capable of enlightened strategic maneuvering. The mage intertwined with my nature was guiding me, however. I believe I needed to let the world know who I was and what I was doing. It's pretty much the only way I can describe the feeling. I needed a channel for the energy. The mage inside me was going to use my own ferocity whether I desired the phenomenon or not. I didn't want to be like other people I'd seen, venting anger at the world and hurting other people. I wanted to be a force for changes I cared about.

"I'm going to free my people," I found myself saying. "I grew up a Slave. I don't want anyone to live that way, so I'm going to make it so they don't have to anymore." I shook my head and I bared my teeth as well. "I don't know how far I'll have to travel. Only the dragon knows. But I'm gonna need help. The Slaves will need a place to live. People to guide them. The task won't be easy."

Generale Oakes narrowed her eyes. "You want the Rose tribe to assist you?"

"Yes." The word came easily despite my conscious reservations. I've never had more conviction in my life. "Yes. I want everyone to help the Slaves. You've much to gain. The people I speak of are young. They could bolster your ranks."

The Generale rubbed her chin. Around her, the Confidants conversed in hushed tones, but their conclusions were obvious from the sideways looks they gave me.

Terche cleared her throat. "I regret to inform you that the Rose tribe doesn't deem it wise to offer assistance in this matter. What you propose is too vague. We don't have people or resources to spare on a gambit."

I swallowed. Generale Oakes studied me. I spoke my suggestion in a neutral tone. "Perhaps the dragon will be able to point me in the right direction."

Generale Oakes raised an eyebrow. "Is this before or after the dragon shows the Madame Witch here where to find her lover?"

"Husband," the Witch corrected her. Before anyone else could speak, we heard a ripping noise. Claws like curved daggers slashed through the side of the tent. Hands went to hips, but nobody was prepared to shoot the Den Mother herself.

"Let's forget for the moment that I wasn't invited to this important meeting," the wolf began. "I'll back this human. The one with the sword." She nudged me with the side of her muzzle and the wolf whiskers brushed my face.

"Generale!" Lohise barked the word in the tent as she stepped through the rip she'd created. Oakes sat straighter in her Council seat. I could've sworn that the Generale growled at the wolf and not the other way around.

"If you're proposing these mages teach you, I suggest you aid them. Look after the children while the Witch searches for her mate.

Help the frost mage free his pack. Thusly are alliances chosen. The banner of the Rose flies higher, and the cubs prosper beneath."

Chapter 12
A'Rehia tells of: "Notes in an Archive"

"Don't let the pressure build up in one spot. You gotta spread that shit out or else you're gonna break something. Your body and your mind weren't made for this, in case you'd forgotten." -The Sky Dancer

Sun after Sun, my presence was requested in my father's office. He was obviously trying to test me to see if I'd slip up and reveal a rebellious thought or deed. I became a player in the game myself. I knew the danger, but as my father judged me, I was judging him back. I told him as much of the truth as I could manage. I evaded any mention of kiteknives or the village. I play-acted for my life through his countless stupid loyalty oaths. What I discovered was that my father was becoming anxious. His irritation was frightening, considering the power he wielded. I was certain his anger was going to blow up on something. By the time we had our final "debriefing and strategy" session together, I think the man was nearly as stressed as I was.

The rumors from the Squadron barracks contained details I hadn't learned from my daily sessions with my father. I tried to connect the facts to the state of things around Atlantium and the Jurisdiction complex. The panic was apparently spreading throughout the whole of the Nobility.

Government instability was never a pleasant state of affairs for the residents of Atlantium. Whenever the Nobility felt threatened, people died. Wind shifted like clockwork.

The Enforcers remained absent from the streets for nearly a fortnight. No doubt they were holed up in a boardroom, re-hashing plans as they adjusted their battle robes. Reports had come back from a Jurisdiction installation in the north, and they painted a grim picture. An entire barracks of Regiment soldiers had been assassinated. Suffocated, according to the medical examinations. No signs of a struggle and no smothering objects or mechanisms. A hundred-something corpses rotting in their bedsheets. I wagered the official report about the incident was released to preempt the rumors and promote diligence and solidarity among Jurisdiction troops. I don't know if the plan worked. Combined with less-than-official stories of an entire division of Quints being destroyed, the Squadron and the Regiment soldiers stationed in Atlantium were tense. Fighting among the units became common. Major Zeyus sent a half-score of drunken brawlers to the infirmary before things settled down.

I knew the Devisors would be running their Devastators full-bore, now. The earth-eating machinery harvested vast chunks of the earth in order to manufacture replacements for the Jurisdiction's lost forces. Devastators ate anything and everything. Trees, plants, dirt, rocks, it didn't matter. Slithering jaws used massive amounts of energy to harvest the planet by disassembling whatever material was in their path. In the labs and factories, the matter was reconstituted as whatever minerals or compounds were required to wage the Jurisdiction's endless war against anyone who didn't toe the line. Quints, Swarm drones, Regiment embryos, Squadron gear, the Devastators provided for everything. Death was well supplied.

I was becoming depressed, and Major Zeyus could see it, I'm sure. Being part of the machinery of the Jurisdiction was taking a toll on my mind. I could no longer tolerate the gentle dissuasion of my conscience I'd used as armor throughout my childhood. I no longer had the possibility of distracting myself from the truth of things.

{~}

The anxieties of Atlantium came to a crossroad when the dragon attacked.

I never imagined such a fantastic creature could exist, that night I first saw him. Was he created by the Jurisdiction? Had he turned against us? He flew in an evasive arc but there was no mistaking his gargantuan form blocking the stars or the unearthly blue fire pouring from his maw. His greenish eyes lit the clouds. Alarms went up across the city, sounding urgently in the barracks section where I was stationed. The Regiment started motorbikes and funneled from the Atlantium garage, slinging rifles across their backs as they rode.

The Squadron was gearing for battle as well. I cinched the straps on the body armor I was issued. My comrades gathered in the landing yard to watch the creature, framed in haunting glory by the purple evening sky. The dragon's tail cut wide swaths through the flurry of Swarm drones attempting to surround him. Looking around, I saw members of the Squadron shaking their heads with uncertainty, but Captain Nira shouted at us to get in line. She had only gleeful anticipation on her face as she shoved a clip in her rifle and adjusted the scope. I tried to convey useful intel to Major Zeyus by focusing on the air. I described the smell, the charge of static, the sound traversing the emptiness. A chaotic system of compression and rarefaction. What was it all trying to say?

The Squadron was only seconds away from liftoff when the wind shifted and the thundering began. I thought we were experiencing a minor earthquake. The turf of the landing yard was shaking beneath us. There were flashes of orange alerting me and I pictured Atlantium's artillery in my mind. The shells were the size of a Regiment soldier. The cannons themselves were like steel towers tilted on their side at the foundations. The guns of Atlantium had spoken, and the dragon broke his silence in order to roar in pain and anger. The flashes of gunpowder revealed wrecked scales and torn wings as the flying reptile attempted to rush the colossal artillery battery.

The ensuing salvo drove him off. He was falling, and dying probably, by the sound of him. His groans were otherworldly as they echoed through the Wilds beyond the limits of the city. I yearned to investigate. The wounded dragon was gliding away in a final retreat, putting leagues between himself and Atlantium. I pictured him crashing to the ground. I couldn't say why I felt a pang of sympathy for the creature, but I hoped his suffering would end quickly. I knew the Regiment would probably find a way to amuse themselves by making trophies.

The call to stand down came from Major Zeyus. Captain Nira's expression matched my own, but her disappointment stemmed from frustrated blood-lust rather than empathy. Zeyus shook his head back and forth at both of us, but he didn't betray what he was actually thinking.

{~}

Given the level of scrutiny we both faced, the Major never told me about his plans. I'm sure my father had been grilling Zeyus at least as much as he grilled me. I wondered if torture was involved. Zeyus hadn't told me about his treatment. He probably didn't want me to accidentally make a mess of things. I recall the bags under his eyes, but if the Major was placed under physical duress, I saw no outward signs. Regardless of whatever ongoing struggle he faced, the Major wasn't the type who gave up or failed to act.

One night, within a week of the dragon attack, I lay down in my usual bunk after a shift on patrol. I was thinking about my mother, and about what her life must've been like with my father. I wondered what she would've thought about her air-mage daughter. I heard the wind shift outside the barracks window. I went to sleep and didn't wake up.

{~}

To the Jurisdiction, I was officially dead and gone. Just notes in an Archive, like a discarded crate of moldy fruit. Zeyus undoubtedly concocted a proper cover story. I wonder what my military funeral had looked like, or if the Major faced repercussions from my father.

{~}

The rest of me woke up, eventually. I was several hundred kilometers from where I'd allowed my body to fall asleep. The remains of improvised cloth bindings were tangled around my wrists and ankles, and I was lying on my hip on a thatched roof. My heart raced at these waking realizations, but I kept myself from shouting. Instead, I wiggled and slid and rolled around clumsily despite my loosened restraints. The thatch creaked and crunched underneath me and I cursed about the noise I was making. I rolled gracelessly to the edge of the roof and fell to the muddy ground with a thump. Air-mage though I was, I was unprepared for the drop, and I was winded. Stars swam before my eyes, but the adrenaline induced by fear brought me back to my feet. A nondescript cloth sack filled with supplies tumbled from the roof and plopped over me, causing me to snatch at the items in annoyance.

I took a few staggered steps and recognized where I was. This was the forest village Zeyus and I had visited on his recon mission. The place was deserted now, devoid of the children and panthers we'd seen. The main hearth was completely cold, and the ashes were damp below the surface from a recent rainfall. I listened intently to the Wilds around me, but I heard no human sounds anywhere. Only the birds of the forest busied themselves in the village on the empty morning.

I bore witness to a pair of sparrows chirp in conversation to each other above a stone well. The cawing of a raven startled me. He was perched atop the cottage near the rumpled thatch where I'd awoken. I'd never seen a bird of his size or color before. To say he was gray would be technically accurate, but this constitutes a vastly insufficient description. The blend of dark and light reminded me of graphite melting with steel. He was trimmed in bright chrome along the edges of his feathers. I didn't need an ornithologist to know I wasn't looking at an ordinary bird. A sinking feeling came over me as the raven blinked and cocked his head to the side. I slumped against the muddy earth as he took flight, departing directly over my head with a handful of feathery wingbeats.

I had the distinct impression there was danger around me, but I was at a loss over the exact nature of the threat or what to do about it. The overcast sky clouded my mind. I drew the lone kiteknife I kept tucked in my bra with a trembling hand and clutched the blade in front of me. Sitting against the wall of the cottage, I stared at the trees.

{~}

For the next few days, I was sick as a dog. I don't know if my illness was caused by whatever Zeyus slipped me to keep me unconscious, but I couldn't keep food in my stomach. The rapid onset of the sickness made me too weak to even stand.

The raven came to see me often, sitting beside the bed I'd appropriated in an open cottage. He brought me herbal beverages or water in clay bowls. He made me biscuits with jam and butter, but I refused them more often than not. Faces swam inside my mind, but the raven kept the bad faces from coming too close to me. The wooden bucket next to my bed smelled like flowers and bleach when I wasn't fouling the bottom of it. The animal hides and artwork on the walls were rapturous and terrifying when I opened my eyes.

I sweated and tossed, delirious with fever and nausea. My head pounded a rhythmic dirge. I wondered if I'd pushed my mage skill further than I could go. I could barely feel the air energies, and yet my mind was aflame. My dreams became wild visions I was unable to escape from. The reveries took turns comforting me and tormenting me. The raven pressed a cold compress to my forehead. I know he spoke to me, but his words were distant noises.

My fever broke and my appetite returned with a vengeance. I devoured biscuits and the raven's words materialized in a comprehensible fashion.

"I told you before, but I don't think you were listening. You're experiencing a mage-sickness. I wish I could tell you what caused it. Here's to recovery, my dear." He watched me eat, a concerned look on his avian face.

I groaned in resurgent pain. A clawed bird leg handed me a glass of water. I brought the vessel to my mouth, and a waterfall poured over my inflamed tongue and down my gullet. When I'd sated my thirst, I pulled the covers back over my head.

{~}

The dreams came with renewed force. Why were they always so clear and complex? The vividness made me angry whenever I woke. When I was inside the dreams, I felt like I basked in the glory of the Guards. The worlds were too lush and inviting. I lost myself in a foreign land. My other life began to feel like a dull chore. I fell in love with the vibrant characters inhabiting the dreams. I wanted nothing more than to remain with them, and with the exotic landscapes we traversed together.

My eyes cracked open to reveal it was evening. Was this what the evening actually looked like? The dim light in the cramped cottage was enough to make my head begin to ache again. I just wanted to sleep. Perhaps, I thought, if I slept enough, I'd become a skilled sleeper and I wouldn't need to be bothered by the annoyance of waking up anymore.

I think the smells of food finally tempted me from the cottage. I'd subsisted on so little that my stomach demanded my limbs transport the tummy towards an aroma.

Outside of the cottage, a marinated flank of lamb was roasting over a fire in a stone ring. The succulent meat sizzled and beckoned me with its decadence. The raven saw me, and he smiled a handsome smile. The gray bird had spent a Sun at the bird-office, and he was removing his jacket and loosening up his tie. He welcomed me by asking my name. He lit a pipe and thoughtfully scrutinized my pale face. He handed me a mug of warm, spiced apple cider. I thanked him in a daze, but he was already putting on his apron and carving off an irresistible slab of meat before handing me the wooden plate.

I ate like an animal. The raven laughed, in his friendly way, and his bird-voice crooned as he reclined in his comfortable chair next to the fire. Gray-raven was wearing his pressed slacks and his polished dress shoes. I decided he was handsome. He ran a silver comb through his perfect head of feathers as I ate. I was famished and the food tasted better than anything I'd ever eaten. When my stomach was full, I started to become sleepy. I realized I was tired from all the sleeping I'd been doing.

I never realized how wonderful sleep can be without dreams. I don't think I ever appreciated the value of rest for the mind until the raven tucked me in freshly washed sheets after a hot bath. I don't recall anything except blackness, and I'm grateful.

The next morning, I almost felt like my old self again, but I should've known. We're never our old selves again, especially in the morning.

{~}

Clothes were hanging on the wall across from my bed. The dream haze hung with me, but I was starting to forget faces and names and scenic vistas. Part of me felt a sense of loss about the fact. A desire to go back to the dreams clung to my soul. Instead of giving in, I washed myself with a basin of clean water and a cloth. I put on the sky-blue trousers and a shirt that tempted me with their normalcy. To my surprise, the clothes fit wonderfully. The cut was flowing around the cuffs and tapered to fit my body. The new clothes raised my spirits. A few ribbons were left along with the new garments. I discovered a genuine smile on my face. I tied my black hair in two tails and tied ribbons around my neck and ankle. I floated from the cottage, reveling in my return to a reality which didn't feel terribly unpleasant.

The Sun was brilliant in the sky. The omnipotent orb highlighted a handful of clouds and betrayed the hue of the atmosphere. The glare of the open outdoors was both piercing and soothing. I inhaled, shuddering before looping in a lazy backflip above the ashes of the previous night's roast. The ribbon on my left ankle fluttered in the breeze. I took in the village and the forest. Beyond the subtle cottages, the treetops stretched for kilometers in every direction. I saw no signs of human life or Jurisdiction interference. The sudden thought struck me like a stone. Was I free? Had I accomplished my goal of escaping the Jurisdiction? I wished I could grant my late friends the same chance.

My thoughts were interrupted by the raven as he startled me. He rose to greet me and then swooped and landed on a branch. I returned his greeting with a reply, hiding my surprise. I studied the raven as if I was seeing him for the first time. The bird was a sturdy creature, I could tell. Perhaps not with muscle and bone, but I knew there were other kinds of strength. His uniqueness felt as though it was deliberately difficult to explain.

"You're a mage, aren't you?" I heard myself saying before I'd processed the information. I asked him the question, but my words were a statement.

"Not in the slightest," the raven said. His beak didn't lend itself to expressiveness. There was a grin in his eyes, but his tone stayed flat. "It's Saturday, kid. I don't start repentance until tomorrow."

My head spun, but I think my brain ended up pointed in the right direction. The jests pulled me to and fro. I considered what his raven humor might mean about the bird's disposition towards me, and I tried to maintain my composure. I wasn't sure how well I'd be received in this village. Did he know who my father was? Was I a prisoner here?

"You don't seem like other mages I've met," I said with a bland shrug.

The raven adjusted his feathers with an air of patient idleness. "Yes, I imagine I'm a bit different from the Squadron or the Nobility."

The raven was frightening, even if he hadn't meant to be. He bristled with power. My eyes picked up the aura, and his image echoed in my temples. "Are you a messenger from the Guards?" I asked him. I had an edge to my voice.

The raven shook his head, becoming sympathetic and tame. He was testing me, I realized. He spoke in a kind voice, but I sensed a careful press in his words.

"The Guards? You should know better, Ms. Fleuro. I was a Pastor, back in the day. Before the Jurisdiction banned religion. Outlawed the very Gods themselves. The only reason people say 'Guards' is because a few brave chumps from the Defiance made a low-budget action movie about superheroes. The Jurisdiction killed the would-be film-stars, of course. Even saying 'the Guards' is technically illegal. And I wouldn't break the law now, would I?" Wicked sarcasm danced in his calm words.

"No, Miss, I'm not sent here by any particular deity. Not one that I know of, anyway. I'm just a disillusioned man-of-the-cloth stashing stunts under my stoles." He whirled on the branch and opened up his wings, putting himself in motion. Static crackled through the air around him.

I wanted to ask more, but Steffen beckoned me to follow him.

"This way," he said. "The cottage by the vines. We've a couple people I'd like you to meet, and we can talk about your 'mage lessons.' I know you've got questions, and I've got my own. Especially pertaining to that knife you showed up with."

I frowned, remembered the kiteknife I'd hidden in my underwear. The weapon hadn't exactly been a helpful survival implement thus far. Steffen must've taken the knife from me when I was sick. My irritation at its absence was placated by the memory of my sickness. The fact that the raven was offering to discuss the confiscated item argued in favor of guarded trust on my part.

Leon and Jeriah were blessedly normal when I compared them to the talking bird. The so-called Trapper and Woodcutter couldn't have been more different from each other, but I could see they were close partners. Leon was short and slight, and he spoke in a gregarious way that put me at ease. He dominated the conversation by deftly removing the burden of speaking from anyone else's purview. Jeriah, on the other hand, was easily the tallest man I'd ever seen who wasn't a member of the Regiment. He had a gentle intelligence about him which almost made me forget the oversized sledge of an axe he carried strapped to his back. As the two woodsmen introduced themselves, flashes of my convalescence returned to me. How exactly had I assumed that a bird was taking care of me? I shook my head. My assistance must've come from these two.

"Hey now, don't let the bird get your head turned around," Leon began when he sensed my confusion. "They don't call it 'bird-brained' for nothing. He's liable to perpetuate your delusions just to see if you squirm." The Trapper set up a trip-line as he talked. His knots were practiced and automatic, and he didn't break his stream of words. "This village belongs to the Wise Witch, but perhaps you knew that, eh Ms. Fleuro?" He pinned me with an accusatory glance, but he moved on rapidly, and I didn't have enough time to become defensive. "S'alright. Don't worry about it, eh Jeriah? Nothing we can't handle. We know you're J-D, of course, but we don't think you'll gonna fly off and sing. How about it, breezy?" Once again I felt a twinge of animosity behind his genuine smile. Leon's voice and hands moved artfully and relieved the tension before the strain could trigger a reaction. "Whew. Too much serious-talk there, I'll wager." He shrugged and smiled. "To be honest, we don't really care. You gotta be hungry. I know that I am. How do you cook your rabbits down there in Atlantium? Jeriah here is partial to basil. Can't say I agree with him, lass. I'll wager the herb pairs betters with squirrel. Shall we check the traps?"

{~}

Changes exist which take centuries to happen. Other times, the words themselves are too lengthy to convey a correct sense of brevity. I had my suspicions about Steffen and how the raven might test me. I don't know if my sickness was the raven's doing. If I'd been given a choice, I don't know if I would've come back from the dreams.

I was seeing the world, now. My mind was accepting the totality of my life. My mage skill grated painfully against my senses.

The air felt differently, tasted differently even. Part of this sensation I chalked up to the foreign environment of the witchy woods. I knew there was more to my transformation. I'd been altered. Or had I altered myself? For a brief moment, a memory of sickness assaulted me. I pushed the thought away.

Leon was talking to me at length about the culinary peculiarities of wild game. Jeriah was gently removing a recently deceased squirrel from a trap with a sympathetic frown on his face. He witnessed my dazed expression, and his frown turned to true concern. I drifted away from the ground, and tears streamed down my face, but I didn't know if I was feeling joy or sadness. The inside of me was broken, and I was never going to recover it.

I wanted to push myself. I rose in the sky, higher and higher, returning to what I was. I reassured the Woodcutter by calling towards his outstretched arm, telling him I was alright. 'd just be a moment. I spun in the air. Not easy, but good. I was weak, but I knew my life as a mage would continue.

Steffen sliced past me in an aggressive fly-by. The sudden rush made me flinch. He fanned his feathers and banked his glide, circling back around to face me. I was becoming light-headed from the sustained levitation.

"You're not ready, A'Rehia. When the time comes, you still won't be ready, but the time will be here and that'll mean you're ready. Nobody leaves this life alive, missy, but I gotta tell you. The afterlife has a special seat for your skinny rear end."

Chapter 13
Sunderah tells of: "An Egg-Shaped Bomb"

"Who hasn't felt a flare of anger at the world around them? Who hasn't wished for wanton destruction, if only for a fleeting moment? Dragons may be the ones breathing fire, but the desire to do so is nearly universal."
-The Bright Dragon

Being a human was painful.

I know there was joy, too, back when my name was Sarah. I had my loves, before they were taken from me. I remember them in my arms, my human arms. The appendages seem thin and soft as I recall them now. Teeny-tiny, my little loves! Even when they were grown, the girls would've been such dainty things, like their mother. Or any human. Crumbs on the countertop to the Jurisdiction, swept aside carelessly.

We lived in the woods. Considering the oppressive Jurisdiction cities and the tribes of the Low Hills, we didn't have much of a choice. My girls had a father, of course, but my memory of him is hollow compared to the girls. By the time the summer solstice came around, he'd already been missing for a few Moons. I'll never know why we lost him. Perhaps a pretty tavern wench stole him from me, but I doubt it. The wolves who lived in those Wilds probably got him. Furry ones weren't much of a threat, but the ones in Regiment uniforms we avoided with desperate necessity.

If luck held, the girls and I would've gotten through the winter without a man. I knew the best spots for fishing. I made rabbit-skin boots to keep feet warm. I kept my campfire hidden and my knives sharp. I trusted the neighbors as much as anyone could. We constructed lean-tos in the safest spots in the valley and moved to another valley when danger became apparent. We never formed a tribe or stayed put enough to call ourselves a town or a village.

The others were like me, trying to survive with what they had. But in my experience, people turn thief if their belly is empty enough. Any animal can be dangerous if you starve or corner it. Grace and mercy are luxuries among the traits of humanity. My nimble loves were diligent about hiding. I learned to draw a bow and nod towards the pot of stew.
{~}

When the Sun of death arrived, a bomb fell in the valley. I figured the entire world was being destroyed. I guess I didn't have time to think. If I were to describe everything transpiring inside my mind in a sentence, I'd say without surprise:

"I guess those Jurisdiction assholes decided to finish us off."

An imperceptible flash was imbued with yellow and orange. A universe of smoke followed the colors. The explosion didn't hurt. I didn't feel a thing, at least not until I woke up later. The Guards saw fit to take my loves from this world without causing them any pain. If I hadn't been spending my morning walking along the fishing trails, I would've departed along with them. When I picture the bomb in my mind, I feel as if the Sun itself fell directly on top of us.

Perhaps one of my ruddy neighbors spotted the packaged ordinance as the bomb fell from the sky. Perhaps a forest-dwelling pauper pointed to the device slipping through the air when nothing at all could be done. The Jurisdiction bombers flew at unthinkable heights. Folks like us didn't exactly have radar arrays or wireless communications networks.

After the blast, I found myself alone in what remained of the forest. My memories of being human are strongest in the tragedy. My loves were gone, and I speak of humanity reluctantly. I was tossed among uprooted trees by the shockwave of the bomb. A part of me was already changed. My body was damaged on the surface, but my mind was something else entirely. When I began the desperate trek that followed the fall of the bomb, perhaps my transformation was nearly complete.

I'd been taken from my loves. I jettisoned the need for food or sleep like an overloaded supply truck. I hiked without fatigue, knowing my body was nothing more than a disposable instrument and I'd be done with squishy flesh soon enough. The mountains were on the horizon, and I turned my feet with unwavering purpose.

There was no consideration of strategy, no calculation of tactical odds. I didn't care what damage might befall any part of this world anymore, including myself, save I might also damage the Jurisdiction which took my loves from me.

I laughed to myself as I walked. I thought about the maneuvering of Jurisdiction leadership. Rigid ideology and patient discussion were hot air compared to the flames of passion in my heart. Preening simian oligarchs, the lot of them. I was burning to show them how foolish they'd become. The Jurisdiction destroyed my loves, and I would destroy them back, a tally as ancient as the Sun.
{~}

The air around me grew cold and thin as I ascended. By the time I reached the snowy peak, my abused human body leaked red fluids on the icy white powder. For a moment, I panicked. I was fearful that I wouldn't arrive at my destination, and my frail ape-based biology would prove too weak. The trepidation passed by like wet leaves on a bonfire. I was driven forward by the Guards.

I spotted the dragon egg at the top of the highest peak. The vessel was lit by fiery, flowing shades of orange within. Heat melted the surrounding snow to expose tendrils of rock cradling the egg like a

terrestrial scepter. I struggled up the final slope to meet the egg. The bones and muscles of my legs became a mess of useless tissue. I dragged myself up the final lengths with my arms alone. As the final breath left my lungs, I placed my hand on the surface of the egg.
{~}

The pain of humanity was gone, replaced not by peace or comfort or acceptance, but by wrath. I seethed in the dimness of the eggshell. I began biding my time until the day when my strength outgrew the parameters of my confinement.

When the Sun reached a peak, I jabbed sideways with a sharp elbow. I was rewarded with an audible crack. Next, I flexed my wings. I could feel them brimming with impatience, but the eggshell held firm, and I made a frustrated grunt with a toothy, elongated maw. I pushed using the muscles in my legs and claws on my feet. The first chunk of the dragon egg gave way. Light struck my scales for the first time.

I pushed my head through the hole I'd created. The rays of light gleamed as they reflected from my bronze body. I cried in pain until I realized I needed to close my pupils and my eyelids. The bright white energized me and I thrashed about, demolishing the remains of my shell. The pieces of dense casing tumbled down through the snow and faded to a dull ochre. I roared and clung to the jutting rock underneath me. Cold air pushed against my raw wings. The sound I unleashed echoed through the surrounding mountains. I blew a jet of flame with a purposeful exhale.

The pale bones of my human body lay abandoned on the mountaintop, scoured of flesh by the passage of time and bleached clean by the elements. I studied them with a moment of reverence before the wind scattered them away from me.

I launched myself from the mountain, diving from the sky like a meteor plummeting to earth. I spiraled to look for prey and I spotted a ram. The horned animal tried to leap away from me, but he wasn't accustomed to evading airbourne predators. I completed my descent, crushing the life from him with my hind limbs. The meat filled me with heat and power as the blood flowed through my flesh and scales. I sniffed at the air and licked my messy chops.

The sense of discontent I felt was profound. The loss of my loves was acute, but I could also feel the planet wasting away beneath me. There was too much heat trapped in the air, like an infection raging on a wounded animal. I lifted off and floated above the earth as I frowned at the dark gouges the Jurisdiction made across the landscape. The remaining spots of green ended in swaths of careless destruction everywhere I looked. Where the Devastators passed through, life struggled to re-exert a presence. The machines ate everything until only dirt and rock remained. They dragged snaking tubes behind them like parasitic worms on an organism they hadn't quite killed.

Perhaps I could travel east, I thought to myself. Perhaps to the north as well. Maybe even out over the seas when I reached the water. I wanted to get away from the mountain where I made my transformation. I had no intention of returning to where my loves were killed. I needed to hunt to build my strength. My stomach growled at me. I'd eaten the ram only Marks before, but my golden belly didn't remember. I turned my head and flared my nostrils as I flew. The Jurisdiction was everywhere I went. The smell of smoke and sweat and cooked food prevailed even at higher altitudes.

I spotted a barracks. The ill-fated Jurisdiction outpost was a stranger to bloody conflict. I didn't care about the fate of Regiment toughs. I licked my lips as I ruddered through the air with my tail.

I chose to dine. There were no reinforcements and no reprieve. I devoured the outpost entirely over the course of three Suns.

None of the Regiment knew what was happening when I first attacked. The meat was bland, I must say. I hit them at night, moving through the air like a hot breeze pressing from the south. The sentries were the taste-test, snapped up in my bronze jaws and swallowed with an efficiency you can only accomplish if you incinerate the gristle and the bones in your throat as you swallow. The Regiment soldiers have an earthy quality to their flesh and the food immediately bolstered my spirits. By the time the other entrees started shooting back, I'd already warmed up my appetite. The Regiment had no shortage of guns or senseless bravery. They clung to a disbelief which prevented them from being afraid of me. The flavor wasn't seasoned properly with flowing juices. I reached casually and grabbed one by the leg. I brought him to my maw and bit down experimentally. His armor had a pleasant crunch, but I decided I didn't need the extra minerals in my diet. I removed his protective coating like I was shelling a nut. I had to pull his gun from my mouth before I swallowed him, but even cherries have stems.

I flew away with an extra Regiment soldier in each hand. I had to flex my claws to get them to stop squirming. I figured a snack to tide me over would go nicely with my nap.

{~}

The second time I showed up for dinner, the barracks got a hospitable frenzy going. I think they even switched to bigger guns on my behalf. I yelled in pain, but my yells of pain tend to have a lot of flame involved in them. Being shot isn't my favorite kind of exercise. The bruises and holes in my wings were a reminder to keep my wits sharp. In any case, I was rewarded for my efforts with a gourmet selection of barbecue.

The third and final time I raided the Jurisdiction outpost, the personnel were on the verge of utter disarray. I grinned, realizing I must've already eaten the officers in charge. A few Regiment soldiers fled the barracks when they sighted me, running towards the forest.

No safer out here, I thought. I dipped a wing and banked before scooping up a sprinting Regiment meat-pie. His terror was a fulfillment to me. I gave a dragon-sized laugh, but the noises the man made were annoying. I was glad to be done with him. I wondered how many other snacks had made it to the trees. In the structure behind me, a final handful of soldiers took shots from the lower floors of the building.

What foolishness they possessed that kept them defending the outpost wasn't my concern. Their chance to escape had passed. Even if they acted in bravery, I could smell the fear emanating from them. I landed on the barracks and called them by name. My breath ignited splintered wooden beams on the damaged roof below me. I pulled with my claws and the construction came apart in my mitts. I tossed away the roof, pieces at a time, like hunks of stale bread. I tore downward through the edifice and reached further and further with my claws. I could hear the Regiment making sounds below me. I could smell the stink around me as I thrust my head in the gaping hole I made in the barracks. Three stories deep I struck concrete and steel.

Bursts of fire and gouging claws were useless against the bunker. I growled in frustration. The basement was stubborn. I couldn't break through. The futility of my rage only made me depressed. I withdrew and spewed flame through the barracks above the holdouts as I tried to rekindle my vengeance. Whether or not any members of the Regiment survived after the burning building collapsed is anybody's guess. By then I'm not sure their deaths would've improved my mood.

I snagged another late runner for the woods. He made for a reasonable consolation prize. With my appetite sated, my mind turned to seeking what comfort I could find in sleep. The air was growing colder, and the urge to rest was suddenly overwhelming. My wings and limbs drooped and I struggled to remain aloft.

I was fortunate when I found a cave in the forest. Perhaps I sensed the warmth of shelter. Everything was vivid to me when I first awoke as a dragon. My muzzle began to tingle as I landed at the entrance to the cavern. I smelled a faint whiff of campfire, but I couldn't bring myself to remain alert. The natural enclosure was spacious enough to suit me. Here I could shelter from the outside world for a while. I peered through the darkness with a fiery orange eye. A tiny creature scurried between my legs and startled me. I bared my fangs before I realized my teeth were larger than the threat.

The creature was only a little girl. A little girl like my girls. I grunted and drew my head back, bumping awkwardly against the roof of the cave. My scaled lips fell over my teeth and I tried to make them smile instead of sneer.

The expression didn't work. I was scary. I wondered if I'd ever be tender again. I'm sure there was dried blood around my maw. The girl screamed. A moment later, her family arrived behind her bearing knives and sticks and pathetic expressions.

I surprised myself when I spoke to them. Perhaps I thought I'd forgotten how.

"I won't hurt you."

I tried to sound human but wisps of flame ignited when the words came out. The rumble of my voice betrayed me.

I didn't want to force the family from their cave. I'd gladly have shared or gone elsewhere. The humans made desperate whispers and fled my presence so rapidly they nearly fell over themselves. I was tired and I decided not to insist. I shrugged my wings, circling my footsteps before laying down on the sandy floor. I shifted towards the warm embers of the family's abandoned fire.

My loves, I thought. My loves were warm once, weren't they?

Chapter 14
Vilkir tells of: "The Iris Princess"

"Listen, kid, I know you think diplomacy is for wimps. You ever see an infected arrow wound before? You ever help the Sage with stitches? Didn't think so. You wanna be a warrior? Your main mission objective is to keep Ms. Tehsyn's hands making cookies. Got it? No-one else is gonna make cookies like those, kid, believe me. Stitching bad. Cookies good." -The Warrior Shaman

When the Tribal Wars raged through the Low Hills, the Iris tribe chose to remain aloof.

I meditated on my tribe as I adjusted my doeskin leggings. Aloof was a word you could call it. Detached and forgotten was probably more accurate. The vibrant tapestry of Iris culture was woven without the strands of warfare. The things we were famous for, the music played on reeds and skins, the dancing, the colorful artwork, these were bargaining chips in times of peace. When the time came to survive the Low Hills and the Jurisdiction, we needed to look elsewhere.

The Turns were warm even though autumn was drawing near. I donned a vest to match my leggings. The Confidants generally wore robes and stoles in greens and browns and earth tones, and the artisans chose this style as well. No one would deny there was beauty in the intricacy of the clothes and songs and creeds. The purple flower accented with yellow was stitched everywhere you looked, marking us each as its own. Iris flowers we were, and just about as useful in a fight.

The tribe was nomadic, thank the Spirits and the Guards and the Elements and whatever else might be listening. Our herds, our mobility, our versatility, these were the traits which sustained us through the hard times. The connection to nature couldn't be denied. My passion for my tribe stemmed from it. Whenever danger grew near, we fled like dust on a passing windstorm. We had herds of horses and fleets of agile wagons. We knew the fields and the intrinsic pathways of the Low Hills more intimately than the deer of the fields. We could relocate at a full gallop with no more than a moment's notice. I used to joke that a member of the Iris tribe could live for Moons at a time without ever setting foot on solid ground if they were determined to do so. The artisans sat in the back of their wagons at their looms and hummed melodies about picturesque stoles. The goats and the alpacas could be intractable when they lagged behind or strayed outward, but the herding dogs looked after them with little fuss. Whenever the Iris tribe was in flight, the sense of urgency spurred wayward animals to coalesce with the column.

Nobody in the Iris tribe was interested in archery. It simply wasn't in fashion. The few bows the tribe possessed varied in shape, make and condition. The bowyer and fletcher from the Iris tribe itself had died when I was a boy. Despite the fact that his longbows were weightier and more difficult to shoot than the recurves of the other tribes, I preferred the Iris craftsman's yew bows for power and range.

I was a hothead in my youth. I've no doubts about my sins. In a community where any violence was total foolishness, I was like an infected hoof on a prize horse. I started fights and acquainted myself with the bruises a wooden herding staff could cause me. By the time I was an adolescent, I could shoot a longbow with more accuracy than anyone in the tribe except for my mother, Keysha.

I'm sure the tribe always blamed her for my wild ways. She made tents from the skins of hunted animals instead of the woven textiles the Iris tribespeople normally traded in. We placed our tents at the edge of the wagon circle, away from the heart of the tribe. To acquire wealth or rise in status, you were best seen as a craftsman, a writer, or an artist. The more skilled, the better. My mother and I were viewed as none of those things, and therefore of lesser value. We didn't even own a wagon, just a pair of old coursers.

She usually stood up for me. The times when she didn't, I think she reached her limit. Whenever I found myself in trouble for a new infraction, she'd either be standing there jawing at the tribal Council with her staff in =hand or she'd disappear for a few days to let me take what was coming to me. Her defense of me pushed away friends she might've otherwise kept. I damaged the commerce she relied on to prosper.

{~}

My mother trained people to fight. In addition to acting as a sentry and scout for the Iris tribe, this was her trade, and I assisted her when I grew beyond boyhood. My wanton belligerence aside, there might've been demand for her services if the Iris tribe wasn't averse to the concept of violence. I could count the few sentries we had on my hand when I was four. My mother and I managed to survive in spite of the disdain. If you wanted to learn to shoot a bow or make a trap or use a knife, my mother was the woman to see.

Keysha Baton made no attempt to conceal her weapons. Her technique and her passion for the hunt were unmatched. She was an artist just like the rest of the artisans, but they shamed her anyway. The plight of the Iris tribe troubled her beyond her own status. Seeing the tribe for what they'd become was painful for her. Despite a determined connection to nature, the Iris tribe was stubbornly removing themselves from the primal struggles of this world.

Whenever tribesmen came to learn from her, they usually had trepidation about the woman herself as well as the services she offered. She'd made peace with the reality of the situation. Training of hands to hold a bow or a knife wasn't the challenge my mother faced. Training the minds behind them was what required her patience.

Among the Iris tribe, fighting was discouraged as a matter of practice. Complex rules of protocol and discourse and debate moderated behaviour. People assumed that violence had no legitimate justification or positive outcome. A member of the tribe never need to fear beatings or imprisonment. Those were barbarities attributed to other tribes. Instead, infractions were dealt with through social privation or revocation of commodities, or in drastic cases, banishment.

This was the lens through which the Iris tribe viewed my mother and I. Her duties as sentry notwithstanding, her craft put us among the lowest of the low. My mother bore the brunt of this shame. I was viewed with pity, a charity case, but Keysha had committed the original sin of having a violent nature to begin with.

My mom never let insults keep her from her capabilities. I'm sure they tried to get her to slip, to lash out, but she was too disciplined to lose control.

I didn't share this self-discipline from the start, unfortunately. Perhaps as a young boy I couldn't have been expected to. Taunted or ignored by my peers, I wrestled them to the ground. Most of the time they hardly resisted me. I was a disgrace to the tribe, a person to be shunned until the Council could officially banish me. I know in my heart I blamed my mother sometimes for how the tribe treated us, but their behavior was never her fault, of course.

I grew older and learned how to play the game. In a tribe filled with determined pacifists, I thought a violent man had a shot at being king. I trained hard, putting on muscle, and more than a few of my fellow tribes-folk began to fear me openly or behind denying eyes.

In those days, I was perilously close to being banished. The reason my banishment didn't came to pass was because of the only person I could call a friend other than my mother.

Mages were known to the Iris tribe. Seer Sages, born among us to heal and speak prophecy, but the title was laid to rest in the decades before I was born. The artisans possessed a variety of minor mage skills which they employed in unique ways to aid in their work. Three generations prior, there was even a Warrior Shaman. The Iris tribe had sworn to renounce violence because of the Shaman's dying request. They became peaceful to honor his brave sacrifice, and honoring they were.

A new Seer Sage was born in the Iris tribe, a hand of Moons before my own birth. When I was a boy, the Seer Sage Tehsyn treated me kindly. She was an outcast as well, strange as she was. Technically the title of Seer Sage was a high honor, but the venerable role was burdened by mystery. The Iris mages suffered ailments of varying descriptions which accompanied their power. For her part, Tehsyn wasn't able to speak. She made signs in the air with her hands instead. Nobody could decipher her words until she learned the lettering of written language. From then on, she shaped the characters in front of her with glowing blue energy and wrote as though the air was her papyrus.

She scared people, too, I think, just like I did. I know the other children were uncomfortable with her pristine dresses and her inability to vocalize except through glowing communiques. I guess it never occurred to me to be afraid of her. I poked at her floating blue letters with a curious finger and it tingled. We looked at each other and grinned.

So in retrospect, there's no question in my mind as to why the tribe never went through with banishing me. The Council was willing to incur my mother's wrath, but they'd avoid the wrath of their celebrated Seer Sage until their hair went white.

The Iris tribe dabbled in philosophy and language, prided itself in cultural progress, but we also had tradition and custom we were inordinately attached to. The pageantry was harmless enough, but a specific custom made Tehsyn's life miserable.

The Seer Sage was obligated to marry whoever the Council chose for them. This ensured there was no conflict among the tribe for the honor affecting entire generations. The Council entered weeks of strenuous debate and consideration. The talks included Tehsyn at times, but others they didn't. She hated the process. I know the Council made efforts to appease her, but there was no way they were going to let her choose the person she wanted to choose.

{~}

I ran barefoot across the mud through the tall grass like an animal. The blue afternoon was invigorating, and I wore nothing except a loin wrap. The Sun struck the bronze of my skin and I inhaled the wild air. My knife was at my hip, but I wouldn't need the blade where I was going.

Tehsyn raced ahead. She'd look back at me, but then she was off again. I chased her down the deer paths and tracked her like a doe. The subtle incense clinging to her dress struck my face like a drug. I was proud of my strength as a runner, the swiftest in the tribe, but Tehsyn darted ahead of me with unconscionable ease.

"Where you headed, 'Syn?" I called breathlessly when she vanished over a hill. "We gotta be halfway across the valley by now."

I jogged to a stop at the mossy bank of a stream. Tehsyn sprang from her hiding spot and knocked us both in the drink.

The rush of fresh water was sublime. The late summer runoff was clean and cool, and the bottom was sandy and free from sharp rocks. I looked in Tehsyn's eyes. She moved closer to me, and I could see the mirrored reflection of myself in the bright green vibrance of her gaze. She placed her hands against my chest and pushed away, somersaulting in the stream. When she resurfaced, her dress was in her hand. She tossed the wet fabric towards the moss at the edge of the water.

The grass rustled beside where the dress landed, and several people emerged. The frowns of the Iris Council lined up before us, fully attired in ceremonial garb. The Confidants held wooden herding staves, the only armament they permitted themselves. A bearded man named Axial stepped forward stiffly. He snatched Tehsyn's wet dress from the ground, holding the garment in front of him. His face was growing redder by the second. He seemed unable to put words to his fury. A Confidant named Hos'Tei wasn't having any trouble.

"You profane this Council and this entire tribe!" she admonished us.

Tehsyn stood in the stream with her arms crossed over her chest. She made no signs with her hands, but the look on her face didn't need translating. Feeling compelled to defend her, I laughed as rebelliously as possible.

"I see you meant no harm, honored Confidants. The Seer Sage will consider your apology. The tribe may show understanding when they discover the Council has betrayed her privacy."

I held a hand towards Axial for Tehsyn's dress. He bristled at first, but then he handed the wet cloth to me reluctantly, and I passed the dress to our Seer Sage. My friend pulled the hem over her head as briskly as possible. Her hands free from her attempted modesty, she signed vigorously.

"What will you do?" Tehsyn asked the Council in glowing blue letters. Nobody mistook the aggressive slant of her characters.

Hos'Tei spoke for the Council these days.

"The Council has voted to banish Vilkir Baton at dawn. His offenses will no longer be overlooked."

Tehsyn shook her head. She signed again. "I Foresee him passing the Trial."

I reacted with shock to her statement.

"Tehsyn," I whispered to her. "You wanna get me killed? You know there are easier ways to break up with me, right?"

Tehsyn shook her head. "Vilkir kills the Demon Bear."

Her letters began to fade before the truth of the matter dawned on me. When the last Shaman of the Iris tribe died, he outlawed violence among the Iris tribe. Along with his standing order for pacifism, he left instructions for whoever desired to become the next Shaman. The rules of the Trial were painfully simple. If the Iris tribe was in need, a brave hunter must go kill the Demon Bear, thereby becoming the next Warrior Shaman. The liturgy was stored among the fairy tales, a myth from a past generation perpetuated as allegory for the children. The Demon Bear, if he even existed, was half the size of a mountain, everyone knew that. Attempting to kill such a fantastical notion was like trying to shoot an arrow through the moon.

Confidant Hos'Tei seemed to soften slightly after the Seer Sage's bold assertion of my fate.

"I'm not a woman who's quick to ignore what's been Foreseen," she began. "Nor are any of the Iris Confidants, I can assure you. Yet the thing you speak of shakes this faith to the core. If you love Baton–" she looked at me. Apparently considering the possibility made her nauseous. "–Then allow him to be banished. He could find a pleasant life, perhaps where his brutish ways would even fit in. But what you propose, Seer Sage," Hos'Tei shook her head. "His trial may end in his death."

Tehsyn signed into the air. "If Vilkir doesn't return by the end of Spring, I'll marry whomever the Council chooses." She looked at each Confidant as they weighed the value of her concession.

"When Vilkir returns, however," she continued, "I'll be marrying the new Warrior Shaman of the Iris tribe. Either way, you'll get your Spring wedding. Is that clear enough prophecy for you?"

The Confidants spoke in hushed, concerned tones, but Tehsyn and I were ignoring them. I looked in Tehsyn's eyes again. I know I had anxiety and questioning on my face. I frowned gently, doubting myself.

Tehsyn moved forward and kissed me.

A wise friend or mentor would calmly explain to me that I was totally under Tehsyn's control, and I was helpless to do anything but concede to her will. I'd have agreed wholeheartedly, but the advice wouldn't change how I felt about her. I looked at Tehsyn, and her eyes spoke volumes to me as she doodled a blue bear with her finger.

"Yeah, 'Syn," I laughed, "I hadn't forgotten you signed me up to kill a giant bear." I was smiling, but Tehsyn's emotions were starting to show as water appeared in her eyes.

"I hope he's lived a good, long life, 'Syn. And I hope your tent is big enough for the rug."

{~}

The dignitaries of the tribe and a group of interested spectators appeared in the morning to see me leave. My mother was among them. She controlled her emotions as she handed me a knife and a bow. Early in life, I discovered Keysha's faith and devotion towards the Seer Sage rivaled my own. She believed I'd get through the Trial successfully, and I think she held back out of pride. Tehsyn was escorted protectively by Confidant Axial, a blank expression on her face. The entrails of a goat were draped around my neck, the custom for banishment. Tehsyn protested, but the Confidants remained firm. Barring my triumphant return, I was banished from the Iris tribe.

"Go die to that bear," a voice said. "You were never one of us."

I wasted no time hanging around. I began a run which carried me away from the tribal encampment and towards the wide open grasses of the plains. I shrugged off the goat entrails after a few meters and tried to ignore the smell they left on my shirt. The early dew soaked my leggings, but the rising sun was warming the air and the exertion was freeing after the tension of the night before. I headed for the mountains in the distance where the bear was rumored to make his home. I intended to see Tehsyn's wedding dress.
{~}

I searched the Wilds for four Suns and saw no signs of the Demon Bear before I came across his tracks leading to a canyon. Over those Suns I found two fistfuls of wild carrots, trapped a rabbit, shot a pair of pheasants, and collected a humble pile of mushrooms and berries. I created a storage cache from rocks and placed the rabbit hide and the feathers inside instead of using a makeshift pack to carry the materials with me. The edible items I wrapped in leaves and tucked through my belt alongside my knife.

I paused for a moment to stare in awe at a footprint as I chewed on stringy sustenance. In recent Suns a gigantic paw had pressed against the muddy ground, hinting that the bear weighed more than I cared to carefully contemplate. If the paw-print had been filled with water, I could've taken a bath. I willed my limbs to steady themselves, and I climbed the left edge of the canyon entrance. Having gained a higher vantage point, I moved cautiously ahead.

I heard the Demon Bear breathing before I spotted him. His rumbling snores indicated he was taking an afternoon nap. When I crept closer, a vast mound of steel-gray fur arrived in view below me. The lump of ribcage rose and fell as the bear slept. I moved swiftly and silently, and the bear's snores continued.

I dropped down from a ledge and landed directly on the sleeping bear's enormous head. I plunged my knife through the fur of his neck and tried to find the skin. The bear gave a groan and rolled over, forcing me to leap away or be crushed by his bulk. As my feet hit the ground, I spun to brandish my weapons. He opened an eye to look at me.

"Hey!" The bear said. His voice was groggy. "A new Shaman finally managed to get himself born!" he said cheerfully. "Nice to meet you. Took you an extra generation or two. Did the Iris tribe stop breeding its best women or something?" He blinked at me a few times. He pointed to the canyon ledge with the claw on his left paw. "Pretty brave of you, jumping down here and poking me like that.

Name's Kiffu-San. And if you'll excuse me, this nap isn't gonna finish itself." The bear closed his eyes and resumed his snoring.

I staggered backwards, puzzled. I looked down at my knife and then back at the bear. I considered another attempted murder and I shook my head. My quest had been a fool's errand. I cleared my throat, hoping to get the bear's attention. The snores ceased abruptly, and he opened an eye to look at me.

"Um, excuse me, mister bear-San. I'm not a Shaman, not yet. To pass the Trial I'm supposed to kill you. If I don't, then I can't return to my tribe."

Kiffu-San made noises and I braced myself for the bear to attack me. The noises continued, and I realized the bear was laughing. Kiffu-San rolled back and forth on the ground, shaking the canyon with his belly laughs. When his laughter came to an end, he wiped a tear from his eye with a gigantic paw.

"Your old Shaman," Kiffu-San said with a mixture of mirth and sadness in his voice, "What a scamp. Hadn't seen him in a while, I was sad to hear he'd passed on." The bear gave a couple of straggling chuckles. "The man always did have a fine sense of humor."

I furrowed my brow. "Does this mean I'm not supposed to kill you?"

Kiffu-San barked and scoffed at me. "Heavens, no, boy. Take it easy, you passed the Trial. You were brave enough to find me and wise enough to give up on the rest."

The change of rules didn't placate my ambitions. "The tribe won't believe me. They'll think I'm lying to them."

The bear reclined cleared his throat with a thumping noise. "What does your tribe call you there, fella?"

"Vilkir," I replied dutifully.

"You and I, Vil. We'll find us a way to fix you up, don't you worry none," the bear assured me. He seemed to be struggling with whether or not he'd get to keep sleeping if he convinced me that everything was OK. I think he gave up. I was making things too awkward with my wide-eyed staring.

"Guess we can get moving then, lad. You ever hear of the Rose tribe?"

I nodded in response with my eyes narrowed. The Rose tribe was known for guns. Good ones, like the Jurisdiction used. The Rosean gunfighters were legendary in the Low Hills.

"The Rose tribe is gone now," Kiffu-San said bluntly. I was surprised at the news. If the Rose tribe was in trouble, the rest of the tribes were certainly on hard times.

"You mean they fled or like... gone, gone? From Jurisdiction raids?" I asked speculatively.

Kiffu-San shrugged. "I used to try to protect the tribes. Especially before the blasted Tribal Wars. When they turned on each other, I kinda gave up for a while. That was when I became partial to the Iris tribe. Your former Shaman was my friend. Those were decent Rounds, and they flew by too fast. Now the Jurisdiction is movin' in on the Low Hills. Movin' in hard. There's only so much I can do on my own. Glad you're here, Vil, it's your turn, now."

"My-" I began. I was unsure of how to refer to Tehsyn. "-the Seer Sage of our tribe said she'd Foreseen me becoming the Warrior Shaman. Did you know about her?"

The bear smiled. "Clever girl. I'll wager she's pretty, too, from your expression."

I tried not to turn red, but I don't know if I succeeded. Kiffu-San seized on my weakness. He rolled until his paws were beneath him and hefted his massive form from the ground before lumbering in an arc as he studied me. He was so large that my eyes blinked at his outer edges in disbelief. I could've stretched my arms across his face barely grasped his furry ears. Part of my mind insisted what I was witnessing must be part of a dream. Kiffu-San let me slide towards bewilderment for a moment before he brought me back with the subject which was holding things together for me.

"So you leave your tribe, you come face down the Demon Bear, all for this Seer Sage of yours?" He raised a furred eyebrow and followed with a sideways grin. "The situation is more severe than I thought." He gave a chuckle and began heading for the entrance to the canyon. "Come on, Vil. We need to investigate an old cache of mine. The right weapon is hard to come by, and you're sorely in need."
{~}

As a member of the nomadic Iris tribe, I knew my way around the Low Hills, but traveling with Kiffu-San revealed parts of them to me I'd never witnessed. When we found signs of the tribes, fire and destruction had visited as well. Pillaged fields and empty long-houses punctuated the landscape. Wherever people remained, they surrounded their camps with metal barricades and sharpened sticks. Kiffu-San sniffed at the air with his wide nostrils, shaking his head back and forth. Tensions ran too high for hospitality.

The bear tried to lighten the mood. He tilted his chin in a way which gestured towards the rest of his body. "Feel free to climb up and have a look around. No naps back there, though, or you'll make me sleepy." My eyes grew wide. I tentatively grasped a handful of the bear's gray fur while I walked next to his elbow. I felt his amusement as he relaxed his arm. "Go on," he said. "Won't bother me."

I climbed up the bear's shoulder using the furry hand-holds,. and I found myself sprawled in the thick carpeting of his back. He began walking again and when he spoke I felt the vibrations underneath me.

"Another Sun's travel, perhaps," he said.

"Until we get to the Rose tribe?" I asked.

Kiffu-San's ears wiggled as he shook his head. "Not the tribe, no. Only Sylviarg, the tribal seat. A birdie told me the place is abandoned now, which serves us just fine.

I swallowed, imagining myself looting the dead like a bandit. I couldn't grasp what we'd want with an abandoned tribal seat that would be worth the journey. Perhaps we'd find guns, I thought, and the idea brought another kind of anxiety. I knew enough about guns to realize I wouldn't know how to use them. I doubted the bear was well versed on the topic.

I let these thoughts slide as I grappled with the new experience of riding on Kiffu-San's back. He seemed indifferent to where I sat or stood, and the gentle shifting as he walked was stable and predictable. The feeling reminded me of being a passenger on a big wagon. I walked to each of his four corners and looked towards the horizons. The motion began to make my stomach churn when the morning wore on. I dropped to the ground and began a steady jog to keep pace with Kiffu-San's loping stride.

The bear eased his walking slightly and began to speak to me again.

"The Rose tribe was chock full of Shamans, once. I don't know if they ever labeled themselves as such. Mages, that's what they were. Earth mages, like yourself. Eventually they got distracted by their guns."

The exertion of our trek kept the melancholy I was feeling at bay. I responded to the bear with conviction.

"The Iris tribe would've known if I was a mage."

Kiffu-San came to a stop. He sat down with a significant thud. Before I could react, his two huge paws were around me, lifting me from the ground. He placed me in front of him like a doll he was readying for a tea-party.

"Yo, Vil," he began. "Who you gonna trust these Suns?" He looked directly at me with his enormous eyes as he casually scratched his rump. "Your tribe, who doesn't think you're cool, or me, who does?" The earthy smell of his fur was intoxicating. He exhaled a rush of air which sounded like an entire team of horses. "What about the princess you have a crush on? What does she say?"

I blushed at him before I found the words. "She's not a princess, Kiff, she's a Seer Sage. And we're gonna get married. But she never told me I was a mage."

"Ah yes, my apologies. Seer Sage, water mage. A tidy rhyme."

I furrowed my brow. "So Tehsyn doesn't know I'm a mage because she's a water mage?"

Kiffu-San laughed at me, but he wasn't cruel.

"Oh buddy. She knows."

The bear released me, and I found myself standing on my own. I felt betrayed by Tehsyn for a moment, but Kiffu-San was studying me closely and I realized I had no reason for angst. I'd never asked Tehsyn if I was a mage. Perhaps she always assumed the fact was obvious to me.

I looked at Kiffu-San. "Why wouldn't anyone tell me?" I asked him.

He shrugged. "I'm sure they had their reasons. You can probably guess better than me."

I pictured Axial and Hos'Tei plotting what to do with me, and I decided there was no surprise that they'd keep my talents a secret.

Kiffu-San groaned and stood up. "I'd love to stop and chat, but we gotta keep moving if we wanna get you back to your princess bride."

{~}

I knew we were close to our destination because the signs of battle were fresh. The trees and hedges and fields were torn up by bullet holes and tire tracks. The corpses of Regiment soldiers were a gruesome sight to behold. It was the first time I saw a Jurisdiction soldier. A meaty smell of death prevailed in the area. I began to suspect we weren't after guns when we walked past a wide selection in the possessions of the dead.

We reached the rise in terrain surrounding the heart of Sylviarg. In a previous configuration, the stones had been long-houses. Chunks of gray rock were strewn among rent earth. I realized my footing would be treacherous as we tried to climb the mound, so I boarded Kiffu-San's back. Dirt and stone shifted beneath the bear as he worked his way up the hill to the heart of Sylviarg. We began to see human remains which weren't Regiment soldiers, the fallen gunfighters of the Rose.

At the crest of the hill we came upon a wide crater boring down through the hill. This place seemed to please Kiffu-San. He signaled with a grunt for me to climb down. I leapt away but I didn't anticipate where I'd be landing. The steep slope caused me to tumble downward for a few meters before I could gain any kind of footing. Kiffu-San walked soundly behind me, his weight pressing into the soil.

As we drew closer to the bottom of the indentation, I noticed a glimpse of olive green peeking up from the brown earth. A chest buried here. Whatever made the crater had exposed the chest to fresh eyes. I knelt and brushed the remaining dirt away from the lid. The characters were written in another language, but they were close enough to my own for me to read them.

"Property of NATO. Who the hell is NATO?" I asked, tapping gently on the metal lid with my knuckles. "He or she must be pretty important to use capital letters like that."

Kiffu-San furrowed his eyebrows, trying to remember. "I'm not sure the labeling means anything. It's what's inside that counts."

The latches were completely rusted away, but I managed to pry them loose with my knife. When I finally pulled the lid away, a sucking sound told me the container was sealed around the edges.

The inside of Master NATO's chest was pristine, and I could see why he or she had been chosen. I wondered if NATO's family would be looking for their missing belongings. The chest was precisely lined with uniform black velvet. What rested on the velvet was curved sinuously and artfully, shaped by a craftsman whose means I couldn't identify.

The steel comprised a beautiful weapon, but there was a strangeness to the blades. Everything about the Sylviarg crater was strange to me. I looked around in bewilderment for a moment. The chest held a fixed set of curved daggers attached to a handle so they could be held together by a closed fist. The claw-weapon was fashioned with metal bearing a smoky varnish on the surface in order to dull the shine. When the bearer grasped the handle, the claw allowed for slashing or stabbing attacks. I looked at Kiffu-San.

"Go ahead," he said. "Should be fine."

The way in which he said "should" caused a chill to run up my spine, but I reached for the claw anyway. I placed my left hand in the weapon and grasped the handle by instinct. I stood up and tested the weight and balance. The claw reminded me of a bow, the weapon I was used to holding with my left hand.

Kiffu-San's chuckle was becoming familiar to me. "You've almost gotten the puzzle with no explanation. The Sylviarg Paw isn't a melee weapon, Vil. It's a mage-bow."

I looked down at my hand. Four wicked blades protruded from a frame near my knuckles. "I don't see a bow string or arrows anywhere," I told the bear. "I suppose I could craft them, but I don't see any place-"

The bear cut me off. "No need. A mage bow is hybrid technology."

I looked at Kiffu-San. My fingers made their way to the pointy fangs of the Sylviarg Paw. I felt the sharp tips. Perhaps I was dreaming.

"A bow shoots arrows, dude. Why are you telling me this is a bow if it doesn't shoot arrows?"

Kiffu-San grinned at me, toothy and wide.

"Arrows in a quiver are limited by the size of the quiver, the curve of the wood, the cleave of the arrowhead, the stiffness of the feathers. Arrows from a mage, though-" He declined to finish the sentence, leaving me to ponder for myself. He licked his lips with his pink tongue. The action reminded me of a normal, man-eating bear, and I took a step back.

"Are you telling me I can make up arrows? From nothing and nowhere, just because I'm a mage?"

The bear gave a non-committal shrug of agreement. "Sounds about right. We'll iron out the details later."

I was too practical to go along with his preposterous claim. The so-called Demon Bear was one thing to me, real enough as Kiffu-San was, but conjured arrows were beyond my patience. My mind rebelled, and I rebelled with it.

"What a bunch of hogwash. We came all the way here for this? Are you gonna leave me here if I tell you this is complete foolishness?"

Kiffu-San shrugged. "Nah, but then you wouldn't be Shaman, either. So best of luck getting hitched. Might as well at least try it before I start calling you names."

The bear was smarter than he looked. The goading about Tehsyn worked perfectly, and I held up the Sylviarg Paw defiantly. "Alright, then. Hocus-pocus. A-la-kazam."

Kiffu-San wasn't smiling at me for once. He sighed.

"Try to concentrate, hombre. And try to have a little faith, at least, while you're at it, or this isn't gonna work. Your own belief is the first tool. Much as I wish we were better connected to the world around us, everything starts inside us. Has to."

The Paw was already feeling like a bow to me. The metal was balanced and couched in my grasp. I could sense each axis, the way I did when I lined up a shot. Above and below my hand were the vertical 'string' where I could nock an arrow. To the front and the back went the horizontal path I wanted my arrow to fly along. The claws of the Sylviarg Paw became the sights of a mage bow.

The unexpected happened unexpectedly. The feeling was faint at first, but a glimmer appeared near my right fist as I held the Sylviarg Paw. I pictured myself drawing back on the bow, and the arrow coalesced. The sight of the arrow hovering in front of me was unlike anything I'd ever witnessed. The mage projectile was a column of blurry energy, the air around it wavering like heat radiating from a stone. I released my grip, unnerved by what I was doing.

The energy shot forward, but the mage arrow scattered in separate shafts which faded away and failed to meet any target. Panic rose in me, and I almost dropped the weapon, but I knew the blades would puncture my foot. I felt the bear paws grab my midsection as I lost control of my limbs. My seizure began.

{~}

I awoke with a horrendous headache, barely able to move.

"What happened?" I asked feebly. I sensed Kiffu-San was nearby. The warmth of the thought reassured me slightly.

"Seizure," the bear mumbled. He was half-asleep and his head was facing away. I swallowed.

"I need water," I said, trying to gauge my condition.

Kiffu-San sat up. To my surprise, he handed me a filled waterskin. The gulps I took helped my head a measure.

"Will I be alright?" I asked him tentatively.

The bear patted the ground next to him and invited me to pillow in the fur of his belly. I acquiesced. His warmth made me relax.

"Nobody's ever really alright, Vil. But you know what? Sometimes that's alright."

Chapter 15
Tehsyn tells of: "The Stag, The Dragon, and The Vision"

"You appear to be healing soundly, but are you still having those nightmares? You need to relax. I'm baking cookies that'll fix you right up."
-The Seer Sage

I awoke in the middle of the night with a jolt like a bucket of water was dumped in my face. I was growing accustomed to the burdens of the Seer Sage. Foresight arrived to me in forms as numerous as the stars.

Vilkir was in the Wilds, gone from the Iris tribe for nearly a Moon, but I was relatively certain he hadn't died yet. His fate wasn't the cause of my current anxiety, in any case. An unknown stranger was trying to reach me on a ley-line of universal understanding. I've never tried to explain the ley-lines to anyone. A mage either knows them, or they don't.

I knew the stranger was trying to communicate with me. The stranger was suffering, and they wanted me to help, wanted me to be the hand of the Guards themselves, I alone would suffice, the drama, I know. You could call the feeling Foresight if you wanted to. You could call it a lot of things.

The unfathomable distance was what perplexed me about the request for assistance. I cleared the sleep from my mind, and I tried to comprehend how far away the stranger was from my bed. I concluded that I'd have to travel across numerous leagues, swifter than any waterfall if I were to be of use. I thought of the horses the Iris tribe kept and bred. Fine animals, but the journey I was contemplating would lame even the best of them. A cold weight started to form in my stomach. The risk appeared and I accepted.

The summoning of unknown entities is always a dangerous business. In the realm of mages, a title bears little meaning compared to power and skill. Anything capable of receiving arcane communiques has a will of its own, and if this opposes another, the struggle could prove to be extremely hazardous. Whoever summoned me was desperate, and they'd passed their desperation to me in the summoning. I expressed my need for swift travel use the same language. I'd widely suggest that no mage attempt the things I'm about to describe.

The first step is making contact with the flow of energy around you. Breathe, feel, flow, clear your mind. To me, this is most easily done among the trees. Living anchors channel a complex web where the desired connection may occur. Test each and every leaf, each and every stem, the wide branches, the vivid haze of moss on the hard surface of bark.

Send the correct form of pulse. This is the trickiest part. Don't appear hostile or harm the delicate transmission network. If your casting is deftly completed, the signal should emulate the message. In my case, I was making a sincere request for aid.

When I made contact with him the Unicorn Stag was skeptical about me, I could tell. Far off as he was, his energy was faint. He didn't speak to me in words so much as a wide array of energy fluctuations over a broad spectrum. Nevertheless, he began making his way toward the Iris encampment, slowly at first, then transitioning to a purposeful bounding. I met him in the darkness of the forest before his lone spiral antler could be seen by a member of the tribe.

I trusted the Stag wasn't a demon, but I didn't know how he felt about my mission at the moment. I leapt to his back assertively before I could lose my nerve, and I spent a few minutes struggling to adjust to the perch. His body was a flawless combination of equine and cervine features, but his piercing eyes and his sandy coat trimmed with silver triggered fear of the unknown. I'd seen a humble shrine erected in his honor on the outskirts of a village in the Low Hills. The children called him "Saint Audubon" and left him apples, claiming he could talk to the birds. If Saint Audubon decided to abandon me in the Wilds, I was in for an inconvenient walk home. Best if I could placate the animal in every possible way. I soothed his joints and his muscles with flows of energy and handed him seed cakes over his shoulder as we made our way south.

Dawn broke, and the Stag increased his pace. The fantastical creature moved with an urgency which became hypnotic. We rushed over the surface of the landscape's features, greens and browns melting together in front of my eyes. The Unicorn and I were at peace with the Wilds, but we rejected passive stillness. We careened through a wide-open clearing and I studied the bobbing antler in appreciation. Few wild predators would be foolish enough to give chase to such a robust animal. No hunter had ever defeated the Unicorn Stag's keen senses or the thousands of Rounds worth of instincts blended in his own by right of his unlikely birth. The fact that I was granted a voyage on the hart-steed was a divine honor, the favor of the Guards themselves.

An entire Sun passed as we traveled. My body complained in the form of bruises and blisters as the morning wore on towards afternoon. I continued to pull seed cakes from my belt pouches, but the Unicorn Stag never missed a step. He moved like an animal who can see without looking. I could feel him sense each footfall, a connection between hoof and the earth beneath.

When we approached our destination, the Stag pulled to a stop with a snort. The abrupt halt nearly threw me head-first past his antler. Saint Audubon shrugged with annoyance and I slid to the ground. I wove words in the air in glowing blue, pleading my case with the Stag so he'd wait for me while I worked. I have no idea if he was able to read the written characters, but my intentions were clear.

Even clearer was the Unicorn Stag's disdain for whatever he smelled in the trees ahead of us. He stomped impatiently. When he began to shake his antler at me, I knew the time had come to leave him here and hope he'd either return to me eventually or I could summon him again. He deserved the rest and the task ahead of me gave him the opportunity. I wished I could rest as well from the arduous journey but there wasn't any time. I let myself stretch and lean against a tree trunk for a few moments. As I watched the Stag, grateful for his conveyance, he purposefully scratched an "X" on the forest floor with his hoof. A meeting spot, apparently. The monarch of the Wilds would go no further.

The tree beside me was one of the few left intact at the edge of the copse. I made my way forward through the splintered wreckage of fallen trees. My surroundings were intensely quiet with my own steps replacing those of the Stag. The Sun was fading, and I heard breathing before I saw my patient.

The sound was ragged and cavernous, a gusty sea breeze whirling through rocks and seaweed at low tide. I went through a moment of groping blindly ahead before realizing that the firm darkness was actually what I was looking for.

The dragon's scales were a midnight blue, almost black beneath the moon-shade of fallen branches around him. Where the lunar light reached the dragon, he reflected a subtle brilliance. He lay on his side and curled up as if he wished his egg were still around him. I placed my hand against a nearby wing and I felt nothing but pain. The sensation caused me to pull my hand back abruptly. I moved around the length of his tail as I attempted to avoid stumbling against him in the dark woods. I didn't have much light to go by, but when I reached his belly, the damage to the dragon became clear.

I could've crawled inside the jagged wounds made by the Jurisdiction's artillery cannons. A mess of dark dragon blood covered the loam, but I couldn't see liquid pouring from his scales anywhere. Sharp points of bright bone appeared where his ribs were broken. The dragon clung to life. From what I could tell, his wing was crushed by his crash landing. I needed to maneuver the appendage from underneath him if I wanted to set the breaks, but I'd begin by seeing to life-threatening injuries first.

I drew several potion bottles, tourniquets, and cutting instruments from my belt and then realized they'd be totally and completely useless. I took a breath and placed my hands against the dragon's shoulder, humming cadences of ancient hymns.

I never attempted a mage-healing on such a grand scale before, no pun intended. I knew there was a possibility the process could kill me if I took it too far. Using energy on the dragon would deplete my own existence, and I needed to be sensible in my actions. Powerful results always rested in the hands of the Guards.

Fresh pain assailed me as I entered my trance. I suspected the dragon's blood loss was slowing, but the damage to his body was extensive. I marveled at his biology. The wonders of his unique physiology had surely saved him from death. His scales and his ribs were dense as hardened steel. I pictured what the dragon would be like if he were whole again. I began to knit back together the pieces of him which were vital. His agony lanced at me, but I soothed him away. I began to repair his heart and his lungs, and I did what I could for his belly.

The work was exhausting enough when performed on a human or an animal. On the dragon, the drain on my resources was multiplied by a hundredfold. By the time I was sure the dragon could survive his injuries, I was getting lost. My consciousness was entangled and his pain was becoming my own. I was nauseous and slightly confused about my own identity. I'd succumb soon, never waking from my trance. My body would cease to function eventually, devoid of all guidance. I broke the connection with my last gasp of self discipline, collapsing against the cool, smooth scales.
{~}

When I awoke, the breathing was with me. I began to realize the breathing had been with me the entire night. Had we always breathed as one? I'd fallen into a dreamless sleep, breathing along with the dragon. I shook my head and tried to pull my mind away. I didn't want my breathing imprisoned in midnight blue scales. Despite a keen drowsiness, I felt normal enough, but I was wary of residual consequences. I examined my efforts with as much detachment as I could manage.

The dragon was several Moons from being healed, but I suspected he'd live. Infection was absent and I felt no badly set bones, though I couldn't be sure the flesh or scales wouldn't scar. He slept peacefully despite the pain emanating from him in waves. I laughed to myself about potion bottles as I returned them to my belt pockets. I'd normally hand them over to a patient with injuries this severe, but in order to treat the dragon I'd need casks of the stuff. I didn't think Saint Audubon would take kindly to being hitched to a wagon.
{~}

The Iris tribe was probably in a panic over my absence. I realized I'd never told anyone where I was going the night before. The Council would assume I went to find Vilkir.

Let the curmudgeons cry to the Seven Hells, I thought. Nobody had the guts to come after me anyway, except for Vilkir's mother, who trusted me enough to let me be. The Council would vent their anxieties about me as they sat at their looms and drank their shitty teas they spiked with liquor. I'd make a perfect topic of half-cocked conversation today. I couldn't wait to be righteously admonished for my unseemly disappearance when I returned.

I found the Unicorn Stag loitering by the spot he'd scratched for me. He was refreshed and amenable enough to a return trip, and we departed for the Iris camp. I thought about my birthright and my tribe as I left the downed dragon behind. I felt bitterness and resentment and I carefully considered them. Certainly a forced marriage was reason to be upset at the Iris tribe, but I had a deeper grievance with my people than antiquated nuptials. The Iris was a leaf, pushed around by the wind, only the breeze was becoming a gale. Uncouth as Vilkir may be, he had the spirit to stand against it.

Several hundred meters from where the sentries kept eyes on the trees, I bid my goodbyes to the Saint. I didn't need the added attention he'd bring me. I was hoping to resume my daily routines without a scene about my absence.

{~}

"Did you find him?"

Hos'Tei asked me the moment she spotted me.

I'd gotten to the entrance of my tent with only a confused glance or two, but the Confidant's question rang like an accusation before I could disappear.

I wrote curtly towards Hos'Tei. "That wasn't my task."

She walked closer to make the conversation private, shooing away curious onlookers with a dismissive gesture of her hand. I invited her to enter the privacy of my tent with mild reluctance. I'd best smooth this over so I could rest.

"Where were you?" Hos'Tei pressed me.

"A creature needed my help, an ally, perhaps," I signed thoughtfully.

Hos'Tei frowned. "I know your marriage isn't fair, but you must understand. The process exists for the protection of the Seer Sage. Not every Seer Sage has been so-" she paused, looking for the word which might stir the frown from my face, "-formidable." I stared at her. "Nevertheless," she concluded, shifting her feet, "You shouldn't be alone and away from the wagons. It isn't for you to decide who the Iris tribe makes alliances with."

I shrugged. "The Council could've made an exception. But they didn't. And healing is my craft, Madam, specifically ordained by the Iris Charter. You know the tenets of that Creed well, I assume. As Seer Sage I'm not confined to patients of anyone's choosing."

I could see Hos'Tei would only be satisfied by an apology or concession. My unannounced midnight departure would bring trouble beyond just her. She'd take my story to the Council. Hos'Tei was in an excellent mood during those Suns, however. She was quite confident Vilkir had been lunch for the Demon Bear.

"You'll meet with the Council as usual, you're aware." Hos'Tei left my tent with a smirk. I'm sure she meant to seem agreeable, but the expression was gloating.

I turned back to my quarters. The Seer Sage had a luxurious tent by the standards of the Iris tribe. Woven blankets and Vilkir's softest furs were everywhere you looked. Carved wooden chests were colorfully lacquered and interspersed with a collection of art and jewelry. My bed and sitting places consisted of downy cushions placed on the carpeted floor.

I usually kept my work tent near my living tent. The workspace was several times larger and shabbier, the interior filled with the exotic hazards and stains of my profession. I thought about concocting salves and potions and I shook my head. I needed to clear my mind, and I didn't want to deal with the mess of the work tent. My assistants would be glad to have a day without prodding.

I let myself relax. I brewed a pot of tea on a charcoal brazier. When I removed the boiling water, I placed incense in its place. Smoke filled the room with a subtle cloud before I doused the coals. I stirred the tea while the herbs were steeping and I removed my dirty clothes.
{~}

I settled on a cushion, taking a sip from my teacup, and my mind went immediately to Vilkir. The turn in thoughts was such an immediate process that I suspected Foresight, but instinct told me a personal emotion was at play. Nevertheless, the gray ceramic bowl in the corner of the room beckoned to me. Feeling fortified by my hot beverage, I decided to try looking for Vilkir. I'd been restraining myself from the act since he left. I didn't want him to think I'd lost confidence in him.

I set up the scrying bowl and a place to sit beside it. I poured clean water in the bowl and tossed the appropriate herbs on a freshly lit brazier. Burning plants mingled with lingering incense until the room was excessively hazy. I opened a flap at the top of my tent before preparing myself.

Incantations were supposed to go along with the scrying. Incantations were supposed go along with everything, actually. I learned early in life that being unable to speak presented an additional challenge if I attempted to follow the sacred texts the Iris Seer Sage. I experimented and discovered the words were mostly decorative. Seer Sages in the past had preferred an audience to boost their status with the tribe.

What truly matters to a mage is on the inside. I tried to clear my mind and unfocus my eyes as I looked at the clean water in the gray bowl. The person I was looking for wasn't in the water. The water was a conduit, and I reached beyond.

When the Vision began to appear, I was immediately filled with anxiety. The walls and voices were completely foreign to me. I contemplated breaking the connection for a moment, but I decided against the idea. Perhaps if my scrying led this to appear, then there was a reason, may the Guards show mercy. I focused on my energy and my technique. I knew my imperative was to conceal myself.

The Vision stabilized. I was inside a building like a castle, and I was looking directly at a tall man. He was leaving the door of a room, presumably his office, and closing the door behind him. I wasn't sure why he was speaking, but I know the voice belonged to the tall man. The man wore a red velvet robe and his silver hair was tied away from his face. The medallion of the Jurisdiction hung serenely around his neck. The opulent placard next to the door confirmed my initial assumptions about him. I suspected 'Executor' was a powerful title among the Jurisdiction. My anxiety spiked even higher, but I steadied my energy patterns. The Executor's eyes narrowed slightly, and his footsteps halted for an instant. I flowed through the scene around him, evading perception. I took several muted breaths. The footsteps moved on.

A set of doors at the end of the hallway opened of their own accord, and the Executor stepped through them to the square chamber beyond. I marveled at the precision of the image on a steel rimmed display screen. The little room was very odd, and as the doors closed, I was alone inside with the Executor. I began to sweat. He placed his hand on a sensor near the display. The chamber gave a subtle lurch downward, and the Executor folded his hands over his chest. My panic rose. I almost sighed with relief when we came to a stop, but the tiny-room display indicated that we were further down than the lowest basement was supposed to be.

The doors opened and I followed the man, continuing to watch him from the scrying bowl in my tent. We entered a sprawling underground cave. Uniform electric lights were artlessly attached to the rock above us at intervals, illuminating the natural corridor. After a few hundred meters, we were confronted with a formidable steel door. The device reminded me of a vault. The Executor drew a key from his robe, inserted it, and turned it with a clank. Gripping the steel hatch-wheel on the outside of the door, he spun the handle several times to the left.

Steam billowed from the doorway as the seal was broken. I resisted the urge to cough, knowing I wasn't truly inhaling the steam. I expected the Executor to turn away or cover his face, but he didn't feel the need. He moved around the door and stepped through the threshold.

The lighting inside the vault was dim, but I could tell the cave was expansive, much larger than the hallway. The floor was flat, dark stone with multiple tiers. Reddish walls curved to a twisting dome overhead and stalactites clustered in the center of the ceiling. I had difficulty taking in the details of my surroundings. My focus was drawn to the center of the cave.

A circular pool of molten lava was set in the stone of the floor. The sinister orange glow accounted for the dim light inside the cave. A figure basked in the lava and rested against the edge of the pool. I thought he was a charred corpse at first glance. Thin bars of linked metal protruded from his shoulders and draped over the edge of the pool like a tattered cape. When he opened his eyes, I nearly spilled the scrying bowl in my lap. I tried to retain my composure.

Guard dammit, I thought. He can see me, I know he can. The eyes were glowing red and they matched the lava. Nothing was peaceful or friendly about him. I thought for sure the blackened man would warn the Executor. I'd bring death on the Iris tribe for my idle curiosity.

Just as I was about to sever the connection, the blackened man in the pool began to speak to the Executor as though I wasn't listening. My confidence returned slightly. I was only looking at them through a ceramic bowl, anyway. What could they do to me? I steadied my breathing.

"To what do I owe the honor, Magnare?" the blackened man began.

The Executor narrowed his eyes. "Who was down here? Who told you my name?"

The blackened man laughed. His mirth was a horrible sound. The open mouth was a like a serrated void, and it mocked the Executor.

"Please, Fleuro," the blackened man said. "I know a Fleuro when I see one. If you desire to willfully misjudge me, then by all means, do so at your own peril. The pleasure will be mine."

The Executor was scowling with a sour calm. "You've been shut away down here for ages. Since before the Devisors formulated my predecessor. You're a relic, Faehr-Dun. What could you possibly know about the world? You're a relic who should be glad we permit you a modest retirement."

I was glad I couldn't feel the sweltering heat of the cave through the bowl. The two fire mages were testing each other. I half expected to see them engulfed in flame, but this was a dance of a different kind.

"I've been down here a while, indeed. How long has the Sovereign lain silent?" Faehr-Dun asked bluntly. The question made the Executor uncomfortable, but he kept his expression neutral.

The blackened man continued. "I could ask why you're here, Fleuro, but I already know." He rapped his charred knuckles against the rim of the lava pool. "I know about the Sovereign. I know you can't make water mages serve in your ranks." His sadistic crevice of a smile was a stiletto of the abyss. "Don't be down on yourself, Executor. Even the Sovereign couldn't sway the water mages. Death before dishonor, I suppose." Faehr-Dun twirled a finger in the lava pool. "Or maybe these are all guesses. What could I possibly know about the world?"

The Executor stared back at the blackened man for a moment. His hand traveled to the medallion on his chest.

"The Sovereign hasn't awoken in the entire time you've been down here, Faehr-Dun. Close to three centuries now, I'll wager. Since I was a boy," he said quietly.

Faehr-Dun shifted in his pool. He rested his elbows on the stone rim. "Sounds like our Sovereign is taking quite a vacation." He gave a sharp laugh. The sound was disarming, but it was singed with undertones of malevolence. He added a pause afterward in order to gauge the Executor's anxiety.

"I hope you understand, Magnare. I don't work for the Jurisdiction," Faehr-Dun said in an amused voice. The Executor grew visibly tense at the challenge in the blackened man's tone.

"Before you decide to create a fireworks display, you should know that I work directly for the Sovereign. No-one else." He slid casually back down in the pool. His chin made a dimple in the lavea. He scratched an itch on his back. "But if the Sovereign was silent this entire time," he stood up in the pool. Magma flowed reluctantly from the surface of his torso and made a combination of glowing orange and cooling white ash. He waded forward and came closer to where the Executor stood. He studied the man in the red robe with glowing eyes.

"Out with it, Fleuro. What can a relic accomplish?" Faehr-Dun asked the Executor.

The Executor kept his features neutral, but I could picture him wearing a thin-lipped sneer over his projected deference.

"You were an assassin. After your- incident. Highly effective, if the stories are true. I need you to find your successor and do what you do best." he said.

"The Major?" Faehr-Dun replied, genuinely surprised. He reappropriated a smile which was the worst kind of enjoyment.

"But he has such pretty wings." He stroked the linked strands of metal on his own shoulders as if to emphasize the disparity. "I bet he was expensive. Why decommission a work of art?"

The Executor growled. He was an unhappy, powerful man.

"It's complicated," he began. "My daughter-"

"Ha!" Faehr-Dun interrupted in a mournful tone. "Say no more, boss. I should've guessed. Family is always complicated."

"So you'll do it?" the Executor asked.

Faehr-Dun gave a snort. "That depends. I built up an appetite lounging around."

The expression on the Executor's face showed amused disgust.

"I don't think you're hoping for a tray of cold cuts."

"No," Faehr-Dun shook his head. "They better not be cold."

"I see the rumors are true." Executor Fleuro folded his hands. "Inconvenient appetites. Is that why people called you the 'Fallen Angel'?"

The name struck a note with the blackened man, but Faehr-Dun tried to remain blasé.

"Can't speculate about the idiotic imaginations of idle peasants," he said.

The Executor wrinkled his nose as he turned to leave. "I suppose I'll be in touch, then," he said, not bothering to look back.

"Make them bathe! And no skinny ones!" Faehr-Dun said as the Executor pulled the steel vault door shut behind him.

The Executor was gone, but I remained inside the cave with Faehr-Dun. I couldn't remember deciding to stay. The dim light of the vault began to worry me. The blackened man was sinking back down in his lava pool, and he looked directly at me his red eyes. I was locked. I couldn't break my scrying.

"I trust you had an informative visit, Miss Sage," Faehr-Dun said. The horrid smile was back. My revulsion drove me to fight.

A splash of water was followed by the sound of breaking ceramic.

I opened the flaps of my tent to let the carpet dry while I tried to dismiss what I'd witnessed. The Vision was disturbing, but like the broken ceramic pieces of my scrying bowl, I was at a loss for how to piece everything together. I curled to ball in my bed and hoped nobody needed me.

Chapter 16
Lucien tells of: "A Shrouded Rendezvous or Two"

"Why the insistence on black and white? This Guard-damned cosmos was painted in shades of gray by the Guards themselves when humans were flinging rocks and sticks instead of assumptions and guesses. Throw away your chess sets, my friends." -The Shapeshifter Virtuoso

I held her close as she wept. She whispered to me about how the knit lace at the edge of my sleeve was the softest thing she'd ever felt.

I brushed the hair away from her damp cheek with my pale hand. I wasn't a monster, you know. She was a beautiful person despite all the bruises. I treated her with respect.

I wasn't even the reason she was crying, for Guard sakes. The Regiment soldier she'd been assigned as a Prize Mate was her personal nightmare from the start. By that point in her life, she sought whatever escape from the Jurisdiction she could find.

I earned a reputation among the Prize Mates when the "manufactured spouses" project was in its infancy. The men and women I met from among their kind were seldom fearful of me. Only a few shrieked and called me a demon. I found chasing after victims was rarely worth the effort when I had so many willing participants. The darkness and the blood-energy of the Prize Mates was acute enough that I was usually the one to start shrieking about demons.

I let my Prize Mate acquaintances live if the wanted to, but to be honest, they usually didn't. The blood-energies I chose were the most desperate. I was drawn to them as they were to me. We found each other because we both hoped the other person was the exact person we were afraid of.

So I bit her in the neck, of course. What else was I gonna do? She moaned in ecstasy before she lost consciousness from the blood loss. I drank her in and felt the power in her flawless, mage-infused genetics. My stomach throbbed as I filled my entire being and my heartbeat pulsed in response. I hit the peak of the euphoric high the Prize Mate blood brought me. I could feel my mage abilities returning with the influx of energy. Wholesale rejuvenation was a crucial part of my feeding process. I was going to have to improvise in order to escape the Regiment barracks I'd infiltrated to feed my urges.

I stared at her on the bed before I left. She lay peacefully on the finely threaded sheets, a dribble of blood on her shoulder the only sign of a struggle apart from her fading bruises. She may've led a brief, cruel existence, but she ended strong. On her own terms.

Plus, her blood was the proverbial shit, top shelf. I was so buzzed up on her that my usual transformation started itself. I could feel the pain in my bones during the shape-shift. Intoxicated as I was, the sensation barely bothered me.

My essence changed inside my body. My sinews and tendons and muscles followed. My internal organs resized and resettled and my mind gained an instinctive bent as I became my other self. I finished my changes just as the first Regiment soldier broke through the door.

I screeched at him before he could open fire. I flapped the wings which were hands and arms moments before. My fangs were bared, and I stared the soldier down with beady black eyes. Violent soundwaves from my vocal chords distracted the attacker and I rushed at him, barreling against his chest with my furry body. I tucked my wings to get through the doorway, but I was satisfied with my timing. I readied my shielding.

The shotgun blasts were cruel to my sensitive ears in the narrow hallway of the barracks. I sent sonic bursts over my shoulder and they bounced from the walls behind me, an attempt to compromise the effectiveness of the firearms. Tiny metal balls reached me in clearly defined motion, part of a lazy dream. The pellets bruised my wings, but their dark membranes held.

I whirled in the air until I was inverted, gripping the ceiling. I was trapped like a rat in a grain basket. The situation left me distinctly unperturbed. I'd spent a century or three at shadier parties, and this wasn't my first rodeo. The men of my family, the notorious D'Arsailles line, we were recorded in various histories across this planet. A few of those accounts were good, plenty were bad, but one thing is for certain- we aren't particularly fond of dying nicely.

Take my father, for instance. He blamed the tribes of the Low Hills for my mother's death, and the people there became his prey. I knew in my heart that the Jurisdiction shared at least as much blame for the arrows he found in her body, but blind vengeance doesn't pause to discriminate. My father was mad for concentrated power without my mother to dilute him. He ate all the vulnerable parts of himself until there was nothing left except tooth and claw and muscle and bone. I'll not speak the names they called him, nor recount the nights of torch-and-blunderbuss.

When the Wise Witch finally killed my father, I was right there beside the man, holding his hand as he died. He'd lost touch with humanity by then, attacking anything smelling of blood, but the man was still my father.

None of the Witch's magecraft could injure him. She resorted to tracking him with a pack of cats like the beast he'd become after he attacked a village. On the Suns when he could no longer retain his animal aspect, he was a weakened creature. His final transformation came to pass. The Witch hamstrung him with a silver dagger and drove her wand through his heart. I'll never be at peace with how my father died, and I don't think I'll ever forgive the Witch. Not in this life, at least.

Among the endless rows of industrial windows, a single window pane the Regiment barracks lacked a steel grate. I hit the glass with a stream of focused air compressions, tuning my energy pulses to a precise frequency. The brittle window shattered. I tucked my wings around me like a cartridge fired from a musket as I dove through the fragments. Once I was free of the window frame, only the Guards could stop me.

Sentries on the roof spat bullets at me, but sensitive as I was to the air around me, the guns yelled warnings to my ears. My wings were agile, intertwining with the night sky, and the bullets whizzed about their business unimpeded by my person. I made clear of the range of Regiment weapons only to see a cluster of Swarm drones give chase. I wasn't worried about the little flying machines, easy as they were to outmaneuver or confuse or destroy. In the arena of pressure manipulation, I was a refined player of taste and depth.

It came to pass that I escaped under cover of darkness, a natural result for the nocturnal predator I resembled. I needed my beauty rest, and perhaps a change of clothes. My next moves were going to be elegantly simple. Having fed, my truest need was sated. The time was arriving to focus on other things, like a new friend coming to town.

{~}

I arrived at the humble tavern far too early to be fashionable, but I was dressed to the nines. How can one prefer to remain a bat and not insult a master tailor? I wore a suit with a vest, and the same tie my father was wearing the night he died. The tie still had blood on it, but so did I. I carried a black cane with a sheathed blade at the tip. My mop of black hair was perfectly slicked in place above my thin face.

I walked through the door with the confidence of knowing I'd probably retain my handsome boyishness for another sixty Rounds, at least. The Prize Mates weren't alone in admiring a character as polished as myself.

I was overdressed for the venue. I wasn't looking to feed, only talk. I appeared in the tavern like a swan in the chicken yard. This was a backwoods town, and I embraced the place. Two things made this town appear on a map- decent whiskey and the lack of any sanctioned Jurisdiction interest.

Predictable drunks cast eyes in my direction, but the bar and the common room were almost empty. The place had electric lighting, but as tenuously as the power flickered, I was reluctant to give them credit for it. The majority of the light inside the tavern came from lanterns. The venue reminded me of an ancient time, a time I'd only read about, before technology and mages and the Jurisdiction made a mess of things.

Nearly everything in the inn was hand-crafted from wood. The lanterns and the stone hearth were the only obvious exception. Wooden mugs hung behind a wooden bar in front of wooden casks of ales and spirits. Wooden pillars were interspersed with wooden tables and chairs resting on a wooden floor surrounded by wooden walls. The bartender appeared at the edge of my vision. A wooden club dangled from his belt at close reach. The club was engraved with a series of crude letters.

"No Trouble," the letters spelled. I sat down at the bar. The look the proprietor shot me as he moved to serve another patron first echoed the unspoken sentiment of his makeshift weapon. I stared ahead at the casks, hoping the latest batch of questionable moonshine was smooth.

"What'll you be having?" the bartender's rough hewn voice interrupted my thoughts.

"Whiskey," I replied instinctively. "Better make that a double."

"Mind showing me coin?" he cocked an eye at me. "From the looks of those fancy clothes, you're good for it, but hey. Policy here."

I placed a gold doubloon on the bar. The oversized coin was worth more than the establishment earned in a fortnight. The bartender's eyes grew wide, and a grin ensued. The man was wiser than he appeared, and I studied him for a moment.

"This is for my drinking purposes," I informed him. He nodded affably. "I'll let you know when I'd like a pour. Now this," I pulled a second doubloon from my pocket, placing it neatly on the bar next to the first, "this is to make sure my friend and I are welcome here."

"You just point 'em out to me. You'll be the welcome-est anyone ever seent here. Care for stew? Ain't gourmet, but less gristle'n usual-"

I held up a hand. "I already ate, but perhaps my friend will when he arrives."

I looked towards the door. The tavern entrance remained undarkened by my expected company as I studied the room. I was acutely conscious of the gold coins I'd placed on the bar, but no one appeared to be taking undue notice except for the bartender, who began vigorously polishing his best drinking glasses, or at least the ones with the least grime. In the corner, man lay wedged against the baseboard cradling a lute with a missing string. I asked the bartender for a second pour of whiskey and strolled to a table near the man, placing the two fingers down with a clank. He immediately sat up and straightened his beard. I asked him what songs he knew, and he seated himself on a stool beside the whiskey. His spoken response was incomprehensible, but I encouraged him anyway. When he began to pluck and hum, I decided the tune was a fitting enough sonnet for the tavern. I placed chips of silver in a stray boot matching the lute-man's left foot and I sent him a bowl of stew to go with his whiskey.

The guy I was waiting for was always right on time in my book. He was impossible to miss in a place like this. He tucked his wings so he wouldn't brush his magnificent edges against the rough wooden door frame when he entered. He spotted me almost instantly, but he kept his countenance impassive in accordance with a soldier's discipline. I signaled the bartender as the winged man seated himself next to me.

"Major Michael T. Zeyus, I presume-"

My new friend stopped me with a hand gesture. "Your message said you know what happened to Nash. He's the only person who ever knew my first name, let alone my middle initial. He's the only one who ever cared."

I looked at the haze of gray stubble covering the Major's jaw. He was looking ahead at the bar, disinclined to meet my gaze, but I knew from the tension in his body language he was a cautious man. His gaze moved towards his glass of whiskey but he neglected to take a sip until my silence became an awkward burden. Anger was fueling the Major, and I needed to tread carefully.

"Yes," I said solemnly. "My name, first of all," a subtle dig at his interruption, "is Count Lucien D'Arsailles. I knew your friend and your lover, your Nash. He told me your name so I might capture your attention."

Zeyus drained his glass and the bartender refilled the contents as if the whole process was a coordinated maneuver. I watched him growl at the urge to immediately drain the whiskey from the tumbler again.

"A Count, you said?" He looked around at the tavern and his gaze lingered on the dubious lute player. "Place like this had me expecting a Duke or a Baron, or maybe a fucking Earl," the Major drawled at me sarcastically. "When did you meet Nash?"

He was looking at me. His question had left his humor behind, and I wasn't going to dance around him.

"When Nash discovered that the Jurisdiction was coming for him," I began, watching Zeyus carefully, "I helped him escape."

Zeyus blinked as he attempted to put together what I was saying. His hand twitched near the hilt of his sword, but to his credit, he didn't draw on me immediately.

"You're the bat," he said coldly. "You're the blood-sucking monster who preys on the Prize Mates. You're telling me that you killed Nash? That you drained the blood from the only person I've ever loved?"

This wasn't a man to bull-shit. I spoke quickly, shifting my grip on my cane.

"I saw his body," Zeyus was saying. "I saw the teeth marks on his neck."

When he saw the inch of Jurisdiction steel leave the sheath at the Major's hip, the bartender made himself conspicuously absent.

"Nash was slated to be killed by the Jurisdiction, Zeyus. He failed every polygraph test they ever gave him until he simply stopped lying to them. For him, there was no other way to escape. He wanted to live through me, instead. Please understand. He made a vow that one way or another, he wasn't going to die the way the Nobility wanted. I only followed his wishes."

Zeyus clung to his whiskey while he gripped his weapon. I thought the tumbler might shatter under the grasp of his indecision. He relaxed superficially, but I wasn't reassured.

"Why are you telling me this? What do you want from me?"

The calculating demeanor of a Jurisdiction officer had returned to the man, and I pressed my luck.

"You're not going to attempt to avenge him? As you've said, he was the only person you ever loved."

The winged man refolded his wings and swirled his whiskey in his glass.

"The thought of leaving your dead body on the crappy floor of this crappy tavern had crossed my mind." He took a sip. "I imagine that wasn't your angle."

"Avenge him by fighting the Jurisdiction. For Nash," I said. I dared to test the use of the departed man's name since I'd survived the truth thus far.

I could see I intrigued Zeyus. He raised an eyebrow at me. "What makes you think I wouldn't just hand you over to the Nobility? Talk like that is dangerous talk. You know who I am, don't you?"

I smiled a perfect smile right back at him. I think my charms were beginning to work. Either that or the whiskey.

"I know exactly who you are, Major. I know nearly everything about you. I happen to know the trouble you're in, too. Seems a certain someone is on the Executor's shit-list these Sun, and that's a Guard-awful place to be. I have personal experience. If I were exceptionally brave or foolish, I'd suggest you're AWOL right at this very moment. I'd suggest you've already betrayed a few loyalty oaths by sitting here in a disreputable bar with an unknown informant." I tilted my glass back and the whiskey warmed my tongue. I kept an eye on the Major.

Zeyus shook his head, but a smile was beginning to crack his stubbled face. "I've been on the outs before with the Nobility. I always found a way to make right again. Getting rid of me would be bad publicity and a major inconvenience, no pun intended. Morale is low enough as it is." His train of thought reached a fork in the tracks and his anger returned. The emotion was a constant I could probably rely on.

"Guards, maybe you're right, Dukey. Whole damn world's gettin' turned on its head. I've lost my spirit these Suns. The Jurisdiction's nothing but a Guard-damn cancer. I been a part of the bloody tumor too long." His lips twitched in the subconscious gesture of an angry man in contemplation. "Sure, I've considered it before. Striking back at those bastards. A fool's errand, Dukey. Futility incarnate. An act of suicide where they'd spin an explanation and cover it up. I've barely got a place to sleep if I don't return to the barracks, but I'm not sure I'm depressed enough to end it yet."

I straightened my tie with delicate fingers. "As it happens, that's precisely what I'd like to offer you."

Zeyus looked at me. His brow scrunched with his scowl. "What makes you think for an instant I'd have a slumber party with Nash's killer?"

I looked past the man and mirrored his frown.

"Perhaps it's the least I can do. In honor of his passing."

Zeyus stood up and drew his sword, but I knew the gesture was a sign of his grief and frustration. The bartender gave me a worried look, but his eyes drifted back to the gleaming doubloons, and he ducked behind a rack of casks. I waited calmly and patiently for my companion, as though brandishing a sword was how he always stood up from the bar.

"I better have a few more drinks, first," he mumbled as he re-sheathed his weapon. "For your safety."

I took the words as an acceptance of hospitality, and I nodded to him in a gentleman's affirmation. Another candlemark of drinking whiskey in relative silence led the Major and I to stumble from the bar and enter the dark forest beyond.

{~}

I lived in an abandoned manse. I guess I was the one who abandoned it. Everything above ground was abandoned, anyway. Paint peeled away from antique wood and the quaint architecture was rotting away. I didn't trust the grand staircase or the second floor balcony enough to traverse them on foot. The tarnished chandelier in the main foyer suffered similar ailments, and the elegant grandfather clock was liable to fall on your head if you attempted to study its design. I kept the grand piano in the parlor well tuned, but its back leg was sinking through the rotting wooden floor and the keys tilted upward at an odd angle.

Beneath the dilapidated manse was an extensive wine cellar, though the true purpose of the basement was rarely so one-dimensional. The entrance was like the sealed bulkhead of a ship, a circular vault-wheel style door and locking mechanism. In addition to a selection of wine, the underground rooms of the manse acted as a storage space for a variety of goods my wealthy family didn't want found, especially during the rise of the Jurisdiction. An eclectic stash of artwork could be found tucked away in the dusty corners. During recent Rounds, the space had served me as a comfortable living quarters. I pilfered or purchased modern amenities from the Jurisdiction during my infrequent visits.

Zeyus was still sleeping from the whiskey. I tidied up the place, placing his boots by the door to the chamber where he slept. I didn't have much of an appetite for regular food, but I'd recently acquired a dry pantry and a cold larder in hopes of having a guest. I put fresh bread to bake in an antique oven, and when I heard Zeyus stirring, I poured boiling water over coffee grounds and tossed bacon in a hot pan. A pair of eggs followed the rasher when his face appeared. He grunted in appreciation before sitting at the table. His hair and his feathers were rumpled, and he was only partially dressed. I smiled over the sizzling pan.

Life could be lonely, and sometimes death made friends.

"I ran a fever during my time among the Rose tribe. My body temperature hit 546 degrees Kelvin, according to the Witch's records. The healers couldn't put clothes or bedding against my skin without destroying the fabric, and I was delirious and becoming belligerent. Patience exhausted, they used leather blacksmithing mitts and dragged me to an empty fire pit. I was abandoned in the iron ring, naked as the day I was born, glowing like a coal and shivering in the ashes. Truth be told, it was the best sleep I've gotten since my family was murdered by the Swarm." -The Sorcerer Prodigy

We all felt a keen sense of loss when the dragon fell.

The Witch, the swordsman Rahn, and the Den Mother Lohise knew the pain acutely. Perhaps we were able to sense Chaeoh's plight because of our hopes relying on his wings. No reunion with the Wise Witch's husband or rescue mission for Rahn's enSlaved brethren would take place if the dragon wasn't able to guide the way. Lohise's pack and the Rose tribe would ponder their survival devoid of monumental assistance.

The bickering among the Rose tribal Council proceeded briskly. Generale Oakes was a combative negotiator. A list of separate causes were united in concern for the dragon. A rescue mission was slated to take place. Decisions transitioned towards personnel and equipment. I frowned as I readied the meager gear in my possession for the expedition. If the injured dragon was a trap, the chances of a return trip were slim.

Despite the risks, I was optimistic. The morning was crisp and filled with potential. The fighting column forming in the City of Old was formidable. The Wise Witch hovered above her pack of Ash Cats. Charlie stalked alongside me with her shoulder blades working like pistons by my left arm. The Witch and I had fed the red cat until she was sizeable enough to carry me. This fact spoke to the urgency of the mission. I was uncertain of the wisdom in granting Charlie a drastic increase in teeth and claws.

The animal in her surged in size before my eyes, snarling with newfound power as I poured fire around her fur. The cat I thought I knew was replaced by a more intimidating personality. The prospect of being carried on Charlie's back was mortally terrifying. I wished I was well-versed in horsemanship. Or perhaps cat-manship? I was bound to end up saddle-sore before we arrived where we were headed.

Across the square, the gunfighters of the Rose and the titan wolves acquainted themselves. I witnessed an excess of choosy sniffing as each wolf determined which rider they would accept. The gunfighters stood straight and gave sideways looks while they presented weapons for inspection. Melodie and Lohise sighed together when each of the titan wolves chose a human they'd attempt to tolerate.

The Den Mother and the Generale were traveling with us. The entire operation was deemed an excessive risk by the Rose Council as a result. The Confidants were adamant that we shouldn't take too many people or resources. We packed lightly and brought no horses or wagons.

The Wise Witch spent a few minutes convincing Generale Oakes to allow me to join the rescue mission. The Generale gave sound arguments against, saying I was better placed bolstering the defenses of the City. Ultimately, I think the Witch's hints about 'mage training' convinced Melodie I should accompany the column. Generale Oakes would keep a close eye on me, I was sure. She was already watching my mage-lessons with guarded jealousy, like an older sister attempting to determine how her little brother had earned such approval.

The Wise Witch herself didn't help matters much. Despite her apparent magnanimity, she was lofty and distracted most of the time. When the Generale attempted to ask the Witch about mages, the reply was like a recorded message.

"My dear Melodie. Eventually you and I will sit comfortably and sip tea. We'll discuss what life could be like for us. Right now though, my child, in these Suns, with the troubles we face, this isn't the time for such a nicety. Best if you be version of yourself you've honed and sharpened already, bold heart. I know you'll see this through. To whatever ends await us."

The Witch and I gave each other knowing looks as we read the Generale's pensive frown. The situation with the strange swordsman was another drain on the Generale's focus. By my estimation the Generale was enamored with Rahn, and furious with herself because of it. The way she looked at him reminded me of how I probably looked at the vision-girl I saw in the trees. My cheeks flushed a fiery red at the thought. I didn't have the right words to say to either of them when I was caught in the middle of their tense interactions. The journey forced us to awkward companionship. Much like mage-craft, romantic relationships were an area of study where I lacked expertise.

I overheard Generale Melodie asking Lohise to send extra titan wolves for carrying supplies. I think she immediately recognized her mistake.

"The members of my pack aren't your baggage animals, Generale. Perhaps you'd like to send a string of humans to carry food for my wolves?" The Generale gave a curt nod. Lohise grew slightly more sympathetic.

"I thought not, Oakes. One-to-one is how this'll work, if it ever does."

Twenty-one titan wolves accompanied twenty-one gunfighters. The unified cavalry included Generale Melodie, Den Mother Lohise, Rahn, Couress, Verekas, Trenz, Jerro, Corwin, Khuper, Hassadi, names I knew from among the pack and the Rose tribe. The Witch, Charlie and myself brought the number of vocal members in our company to forty-five. The Ash Cats joined us as well, numbering around a dozen. While we spent a half-Sun in preparation, their dark bodies haunted the ruined buildings of the City of Old.

I readied my improvised saddle which was sized for Charlie's back. She didn't look thrilled with the prospect, but she crouched and allowed me to equip the tack. I placed my leg over her gingerly. She tensed and stood stiffy, as if she wanted nothing more than to spring forward and free herself from the weight. I doubted any true cat would've willing allowed such a burdening to take place, but I kept my opinions about cats to myself. Charlie's pupils grew dangerously large as she contemplated her matted fur and the legs dangling against her ribs. Her stripes echoed a red and orange tiger, but the shape of her body and face were mountain-lioness. The Ash Cats looked like back-alley skirmishers by comparison. The Wise Witch's feline attendants distracted her attention, as did the prospects of fresh game to hunt, or fire to feed from. The Wise Witch issued specific warnings to me about Charlie, tasking me with keeping the red cat in line. I solemnly hoped the feral fire mage would never become a real problem. I could tell from the spring of her gait that she'd be happier to pounce on me than accept admonishment. I fed her a steady trickle of flame to keep her size from diminishing. The exercise became like shielding, a fundamental mage-craft. I'd internalized both by the time we rode out.

I said goodbye to the children of the Witch's village. Most were comfortable enough with the Rose tribe, but Erixe and Briin were anxious about my departure. The girl and boy remembered seeing my sooty face triumphant on the battlefield when they surfaced from the bunker after the Quints attacked the City. I didn't have the heart to tell them that I hadn't done much to earn victory. I leaned on the glory the dragon brought us. The admiration in their eyes was why I wanted to join in the dragon's rescue. I steeled my nerves and flexed my knees as Charlie sauntered among the titan wolves. She was unconcerned with their presence, which was of no surprise, but canine jaws and the air rushing through dark nostrils disrupted my focus. Charlie could sense my nerves, just like she could sense any kind of weakness. Her chuckle was a voluminous purr. She loped ahead to the front of the column and I clung to her saddle for everything I was worth.

We were heading south, but in the High Hills, snow had begun to fall over the forest. The white flakes melted away as the warmth of the ground defeated the chilling ambition of the atmosphere. We began to wind through the mountains. I soon discovered the High Hills were just that- hills. The Wise Witch nodded to Melodie, indicating ancient roadbeds and landmarks as she hovered ahead of us. The tip of her wand threw sparks like a beacon as she guided the assembled force.

We felt Chaeoh's presence in the distance. Nobody needed to stop and consult about where to head next. The energetic tempo set by Charlie over open ground caused us to spread in a scattered, roving band. The titan wolves chased the crimson feline beneath me like they were hunting a rabbit. Whenever we were pressed in tighter spaces in the forest, we stayed nose to tail in a closer formation, trotting swiftly on padded paws. The horses would never have made it. Our days saw more ground pass beneath us than I thought possible.

Midway through the second morning, morale took a turn for the better when Verekas spotted the Lucky Watcher. The Wise Witch rocketed through the air and gave chase when the vague streak of aquamarine bolted lickety-split through the forest. I was hesitant to resume our journey without the Witch, but the Generale ordered us to move on, saying that if she were as wise as her name implied, she'd catch up with us eventually.

Our trepidation about the missing Witch lasted through an entire Sun. When she finally returned, the sentries almost opened fire in the fading light. She looked exhausted, dropping her branch to the ground with a disgusted thump. No one dared to inquire about what had happened to the Lucky Watcher.

"It's him, alright," she began, her voice tired and her face flushed in the firelight. "I should've figured it Rounds ago. He had a tattoo on his back, looked just like that blasted rabbit." She sat down on a patch of moss with a grunt. Her voice grew softer, but nobody interposed.

"I don't know what's left of him, or if he even knew I was trying to communicate with him. Whatever trance he's in," she shook her head. "His obliviousness didn't stop him from running like mad," The Witch gave a nod of gratitude as Trenz handed her a mug and a food pouch.

"I wonder what he's running from," she said thoughtfully, biting a travel biscuit.

Chapter 18
Melodie tells of: "The Battle of the Downed Dragon, Act II"

"Life holds moments which have no capacity for peace. In those moments, no hot meals and no family members are coming for you, no shelter or medical treatment is on the way. Life holds moments which have none of the soft things and only the hard ones. Life holds war." -The Gunslinger Confidant

The life of a gunfighter is constantly tested.

I saw my share of testing by the time I became Generale. Fighting back against the Jurisdiction Slavers made me a combat veteran at a tender age. When my father fell and the tribe was forced into exodus, the hurdle I faced was impossibly high. The titan wolves and the Quint raid on the City of Old put two hurdles in my path.

And yet, until the Battle of the Downed Dragon, I wasn't truly put to the test as a commander. The Generale of the Rose is more than just a soldier. When the bullets begin to fly, the Generale is responsible for the entire tribe with their every choice.

I'd given orders in battle before. I'd seen men and women fall under my command. But when we fought for Chaeoh, my decisions became the fuel of nightmares for the Rounds to follow. When viewed through the lens of a battlefield, there can be victory. The lens of shared humanity is often less charitable.

Our enemy was an enemy I could comprehend. The Regiment rode against us with their entire available number. The ranks were loosely organized but heavily armed, determined to kill whatever they could kill. Considering that we were determined to protect Chaeoh, the complexity of combat fell in our hands. The Battle of the Downed Dragon forced me to choose sacrifice.

Lohise's aggressive example at the outset of the battle set the tone. I wasn't going to contradict her command while my gunfighters were relying on lupine conveyance.

We sighted the dragon's scales, the Marks after daybreak, around 0800. His dark blue form in the distance was like a boulder near the horizon. The Regiment column formed nearly parallel to our own. Eager foes rode towards where the lizard lay prone with a purpose, but their formations were scattered and undisciplined. I was of a mind to race ahead of the Regiment towards Chaeoh's body and defend the higher spot, but Lohise had other ideas. I gripped her steely fur with my hands and she rallied her wolves with energetic barks.

We charged directly at the line of Regiment riders while the Wise Witch covered us from above. She spun about on the branch, flicking her wand to stall the Regiment motorbike engines. Her free hand conjured a billowing cloud of smoke. Ash Cats sprinted below her and wove through the Regiment ranks before the enemy riders knew hostile forces were among them. The grey beasts pounced in unison on every Regiment officer they could find. And so it began.

Raspho threw fireballs to protect the flanks, preventing the enemy from surrounding the column of wolves as we pressed the attack. Down to the last details, we used the right plan if you looked it us tactically. This was exactly what we needed, outnumbered as we were. The titan wolves were superior cavalry compared to the motorbikes. The unexpected charge sent us crashing through enemy lines and left the Regiment in total disarray. The broad bodies of the titan wolves protected the gunfighters on their backs as paws collided with the advancing Regiment, upending machines and slashing meaty riders. When the impact of Lohise's initial collisions passed, I freed my hands and drew my pistols.

I marveled at the resilience of the titan wolves. Humans were embarrassingly frail. Thick hair and dense bones made a natural armor, but the Regiment was an enemy equipped with excessive numbers of guns. No matter how steady or sturdy, strength becomes relative when put to the test. The titan wolves were suffering casualties. I hadn't thought to bring enough doctors. An oversight, perhaps, but not my last.

The swordsman Rahn rode on the back of Couress. Together they made a breathtaking sight to behold as they led the charge with unmistakable flamboyance. The pair were flanked by the two Couress suitors, the would-be pack Alphas Khuper and Hassadi. Rahn wore next to nothing in the way of armor, and his blue tunic was the wrong color for a gunfighter of the Rose. I felt a twinge of jealousy for the admiration he drew from the gunfighters. The heat of battle redirected the emotion.

The boldness of Den Mother Lohise's plan carried immediate repercussions. The logic of her charge did nothing to dispel the pain of inevitable losses. Amika's mother, the future Den Mother Couress, fell to the earth when her body couldn't continue. Her presence and barking threats had drawn too much attention, and perhaps that was her intent. When I saw what happened next, I burned with ugly suspicion. Had Couress led the charge of her own accord, or had Lohise ordered her to the front?

In an instant, the titan wolf pack was united in grief and rage. Tensions existing between Hassadi and Khuper and the factions in the pack dissolved away as life drained from the titan wolf mother's eyes. Rahn tumbled from Couress's back as she went down, but he regained his feet.

The martyrdom of Couress would've still been a grave error on the part of the Regiment if they'd stuck to a disciplined and organized command structure. Instead, what began as a successful engagement by the forces of the Rose ended as a bloody massacre. The sprays of red were freezing in speckled burgundy on Rahn's arms and face.

I saw the Wise Witch flick her wand at Regiment soldiers, who jerked their bodies and went damnably still. If she could stall off a motorbike engine, I found myself thinking, can she stall a person? I shuddered at the thought. The damage from bullets was horrific enough, but bullets were right in front of you. Bullets were honest. The Wise Witch was melting brains inside of skulls. Perhaps dishonest death was painless, but as I watched the Regiment soldiers topple over like rag dolls with ad steam pouring from their ears, I couldn't help but wish they'd been granted a soldier's death. I told myself I had to win the battle at hand before wished kindness on the enemies of the Rose.

"War makes demons of us all," I muttered to myself. I reloaded as I watched the fighting draw to a lull. The fire mage Raspho was proving to be an asset despite his green demeanor. I saw him bury his face in his sleeve as he threw a fireball. My heart would've sympathized, but from my perch as Generale, my sympathy couldn't extend far. Perhaps eventually he'd bring himself to look upon the destruction he caused so efficiently.

On the other hand, the 'Hellcat' known as Gunny Charlie Urnstead was possessed by the opposite problem. I think the feline savagery worsened Raspho's queasiness. I'll grant that Charlie was merciful, but she wasn't taking any prisoners, either. She enjoyed putting Regiment soldiers beyond misery more than a person should, but I wasn't sure if she was really a person anymore.

The Regiment riders in the first wave were dead as doornails, but respite was only temporary. I tried to use the time as effectively as I could. Enemy riders were already visible on the horizon. Tourniquets were applied and bleeding was staunched in whatever ways we could manage. We regrouped in an empty creek bed between Chaeoh and the direction of the next assault wave. Several precious fighters were dead or lost, and several others were too incapacitated to fight in the next wave of battle. What remained was a skeleton company. Eleven wolves and eleven riders, when we were accounted for, plus Rahn, Ras, the Hellcat and the Witch. If the Regiment continued to arrive or if any Quints appeared I was prepared to assess our options for retreat. If we were going to continue the fight, we needed a new plan. Lohise and I sensed the burden of leadership lay with yours truly, the Generale of the Rose. Executing another charge like was less likely to succeed with fewer riders and a wary enemy.

"Swordsman Rahn," I found myself saying, "I want you and the Witch to draw the attention of the Regiment. Get them away from here. To the east." I pointed with my arm so there was no confusion.

"Fire mage Raspho," He looked wobbly atop the vicious red feline, but he nodded nonetheless. I knew he was conserving his energy. "I need you to hit them as hard as you can when they fall for the bait." I looked around at the gunfighters and the titan wolf pack. I spoke with a confidence I longed to feel.

"To each of you. To your grace in service of a higher honor ,and to your steadfast will. To the hearts of true warriors. Among the Rose, these are well known to each of us. These are 'The-Things-Which-Never-Cease-To-Be'. We fight on, we fight to the end. We do this so pack and tribe might survive in the face of a monstrous enemy."

My voice began a wavering crescendo. By the end, I was shouting with everything I had.

"I remain unmoved when fall in battle, sisters and brothers. I remain unmoved if stories are unsung as they were for the heroes we know. The Guards will know, and our souls will know! The others we care about in this world will know. The dragon Chaeoh must rise so our mortal enemies can fall. To arms, my brethren! Pierce these festering swine with the thorns of the Rose!"

"If the Jurisdiction ends up writing an epitaph for my tombstone, I hope the inscription reads 'Here Lies A Pain In The Ass.'" -The Frost Swordsman

As the Regiment bore down on me, my first thought was that she'd hung me out to dry.

Why even mention her name or her title? Anyone who'd witnessed the tension between us knew exactly who I'm talking about.

Several minutes earlier, when the Generale gave the order to distract the enemy, I didn't give her command a second thought. I wasn't exactly a battlefield tactician, and the plan seemed sound enough. The Generale was a natural leader. The Witch shot me a sympathetic glance I ignored.

I felt alone and exposed as I broke formation, but I clenched my teeth. The moment reminded me of when I was preparing to amputate a limb in the Slave Pens. I wasn't about to let my squeamishness surface now. The Wizard's estranged wife flew overhead on her silvery broomstick and left me far below. I plodded across the surface of the field feeling like the victim of a terrestrial tether. I checked the state of my weapon, trying to clear my mind. I jogged beyond the cover of terrain at the far side of the valley. My motions were bold and swift, a theatrical attempt to compensate for uncertainty. The death of Couress and the approaching din of the Regiment was threatening to unnerve me. I calmly reminded myself that I'd fight to the best of my ability. The cold logic spread to my bones.

My self-confidence stabilized, but the bullets started to fly. I cursed the Generale's name as I struggled to defend myself. I cursed her noisy, smelly guns and her stuffy armor. I cursed the lines by her eyes and the curved corner of her mouth when her frown fractured and became a smirk. The Regiment's barrage of gunfire screeched against the steel of my machete and hammered my vulnerable skin. Sprays of shattering ice made visibility poor. I poured energy to my shielding.

Melodie Oakes was a demoness who wanted me dead, I decided. She probably thought I meant to usurp her title by drawing the favor of her Rose gunfighters. She'd already dispatched an insubordinate Lieutenant with the aid of Den Mother Lohise. Maybe the Generale had every reason to be wary of a mage who could survive her bullets.

Perhaps I wouldn't survive, I thought as the projectiles came at me in a sideways hail of lead. That'd show her, I decided. I suddenly cared less about Melodie's motives. There were too many Regiment riders shooting at me. Perhaps I'd succumb in battle just like the titan wolf Couress who carried me here. I tried to concentrate. Perhaps I'd bend without breaking. The Wizard would be proud of me.

My thoughts were dragged back to Melodie as my desperation became existential. I wanted to hate the woman, Guards I wanted to hate her. I was bleeding badly by then and I decided this was her fault. I managed to stumble towards a rock substantial enough for me to huddle and take cover. I tried to hate Melodie Oakes for about seven more seconds before I realized bullets were no longer whizzing past the rock.

I crept suspiciously from behind my cover. I looked ahead and saw the most well-executed pincer maneuver a battlefield commander could ask for. The Generale flanked the advancing Regiment from two directions and used the high ground of the valley to her advantage. I could hear Melodie's war-cry from a half-league away. The titan wolves advanced and struck the enemy's center in a calculated wedge. The canines were agile and vengeful without the burden of their riders. Ash Cats filled the gaps between the wolves and dashed through the enemy ranks. The unpredictability of the four-legged assault produced lethal results in favor of the Rose. As the Regiment reacted, the remaining gunfighters made use of the higher ground surrounding the Regiment forces. Human allies fired their weapons to cover the titan wolves, but there were too many Regiment bodies. The element of surprise was being overcome by the number of guns at the Jurisdiction's disposal.

I felt cold as I watched the Regiment regroup and attack. This isn't the way that this was supposed to go, I thought. I told my body to quit bleeding everywhere. I wasn't about to allow defeat after the shit I'd put up with.

I ran at the enemy, but my delusional one-man charge was fairly inconsequential. No matter how defiant or optimistic I was, reality was going to take over. I managed to cut down a pairRegiment soldiers before bullets were hammering me again. I saw flashes of blue and I figured the Jurisdiction had bested me. I came to an end, but at least I ended as a warrior on the battlefield, and not a Slave in the Pens.

{~}

When I arrived to consciousness again, I noticed a crude attempt had been made to doctor my wounds. The pain was acute, and my limbs were restrained. The grass and blankets around me were pleasant enough, but the dampness of the dew and the rising light told me I was witnessing the morning after battle. A wall next to me was made of stones. The wall shifted, and I blinked a few times. I quirmed in discomfort, but then I realized the stones next to me were blue. That blue was a blue I knew. How had Chaeoh painted these stones the same color as him?

Oh. wW must've won, the thought struck me. My pulse increased, but I wasn't in the mood to appreciate what appeared to be victory. I wheezed and groaned, realizing I'd become accustomed to Westings healing me rapidly. I needed to be freed me from my restraints since I was probably awake. I cleared my throat.

"Hello? Anyone?" I asked with an unsteady voice in the cool air. I gave a growl of frustration, but I was interrupted when Melodie's face appeared.

Part of me was relieved to see she'd survived, but from the looks of her, she crawled out of hell's asshole. Her face clearly indicated that she hadn't slept. The Generale's armor was dirty and battered. I wondered if any of the blood on it was mine. I heard the Den Mother Lohise coughing nearby and. She had a copious amount of blood matted in her fur as well. Other than the pair of them, the morning was silent.

"Where's everyone else?" I managed to say when the Generale said nothing. She frowned slightly and blinked before giving me a tiny shake of her head. Back and forth.

Melodie Oakes was going to fall apart soon, I thought. With so much death and strain, anyone would. I cared about this woman, I knew. Not because she was the only human left in my life to care about. She knelt beside me and shuddered as she drew her belt knife with raw hands. I flinched back, but she slashed at my restraints.

I exhaled. "The Guards are cruel!" I winced when my wounds complained. "I suppose they've seen fit to spare us."

Melodie ignored my words with a distant frown. She hadn't won the Battle of the Downed Dragon by seizing upon bland aphorisms about the divine. "The dragon was asking for his healer," Melodie said. "I think he was tended by a mage."

The way in which she said the words made me think the Generale suspected me of more than I let on. I wondered if she was chagrined to see I'd survived when none of the others did. I shook my head gently, sitting up against Chaeoh's neck. "I'm no healer, Mel," I said, wondering how delirious I sounded.

"Here," Melodie said, handing me a leather flask. "Last of that stuff. Cheers."

I took a sip. The taste was burning and bitter, but the pain-potion mixture would ease my injuries. I studied the Generale's face and I knew I was lucky to be alive. I could feel the sutures in my abdomen. I lifted the bandage and peered down at where I'd been sewn up.

"Practicing your cross-stitch?" My brow furrowed. "Did you write your name on me?"

Melodie Oakes sat beside me against _____ closed her eyes. I clasped her hands with mine, but s_____ away. I helped her remove her damaged armor jacke_, her her own water flask. Melodie's hands were a mess ot ___ residue and dried blood. I tore a piece of my trousers and ins_____ _ taking her hand back.

Even unyielding strength requires rest. War requires peace. The victory the Generale had achieved came with a cost that the brave woman was unsure she should've paid. Melodie released her hair from its clasp and the densely clustered tendrils formed a thicket of sorrow. I jabbed the dragon behind us with my elbow, suddenly angry with the giant lizard. I said Chaeoh's name to see if he responded, and my pointed word echoed among the trees.

"You'd better be worth it, buddy," I grumbled.

I know the dragon heard me. Nobody could mistake his tremendous sigh.

{~}

The Generale was sleeping when Chaeoh decided to speak to me. She stirred slightly when the dragon's neck shifted against her.

"Can't stay here," the voice said from within the scales.

I dragged myself painfully across the ground towards his green eye.

"Can you fly?"

His snout wiggled. I deciphered the motion as 'no.'

"Can't stay here," he repeated.

I gave a nod of understanding. I frowned when I thought about disturbing Melodie, but she was already feeling around in the grass for her jacket. Chaeoh's wing was badly broken and the bones hadn't healed yet.He shifted his other limbs, testing each in turn.

A frosty bellow of pain sounded as the dragon rose, but he loomed over us unsteadily anyway. His tail dragged behind him on the ground, and his scales had a sickly pallor. The surfaces were dull where they should gleam and pale where they were freshly formed in the healing process. He shook his head in an attempt to clear the dew from his face. He swayed and trembled, his breathing ragged but he began to walk away from his crash-landing with blind determination. Hills and forests and their welcoming cover would put us further from Jurisdiction outposts where another attack could be launched. Navigation was a lesser concern compared to immediate safety.

Melodie walked briskly next to the dragon and the titan wolf to keep up. She'd managed to sustain fewer injuries than the rest of us. As we departed the ruined copse, I rode on Lohise's back, but the titan wolf was limping. She fought to keep up with the dragon's lengthy steps. After a handful of kilometers, Chaeoh needed to stop to rest, which was just as well for the Den Mother. She'd lost plenty of blood the Sun before, and the bulk of the food supplies had been scattered over the battlefield with the unspoken list of other casualties we'd sustained.

We pressed on, and I managed to sit on Chaeoh's shoulders to give Lohise a reprieve, but the need to hunt was obvious. Melodie was the only person with the strength and mobility for the task. She managed to scrounge together ammunition, and she crept through the woods in hopes of surprising game. She returned with a rabbit and a grouse, but compared to the size of the tummies she was feeding, the morsels did more to taunt us than satiate the hunger. With promises of another hunt in the morning, we extinguished the humble fire and attempted to conceal ourselves for the night. I volunteered to sit first watch. The others drifted in their separate stupors and left me to wonder how many Suns we could continue like this.

Snow began to fall as the light of the Sun departed. I tried to let the dim moonlight and cold air soothe me. The temperature should've felt enjoyable against the radiating heat of my healing wounds. I shivered in aversion instead. The fears of the Slave pen were still with me. I tried to conserve my energy as I prayed for the Guards to intervene.

I thought about the Witch, struck down before she could be reunited with her lost husband. I thought about the Wizard who would be forever alone. The idea didn't sit right. Certainly the Wizard would've died a long time ago if he was subject to the usual ways of nature. I wondered if Melodie had seen the mage woman fall.

On the other hand, I didn't need much imagination to picture the fire mage Raspho being slain in battle. The loss of him and his cat were a tragedy to match the fallen titan wolves and gunfighters. The feline may've been a hellish beast, but at least the creature fought the Jurisdiction. All the lives lost, I thought to myself, and for what?

I wanted to go back to the island. The whole world was for the damn birds, and the island was the only peaceful part of it. For a moment I considered asking Melodie to travel with me when Chaeoh recovered, but I figured she'd reject the idea. I knew the Generale would never leave her Rose tribe behind. Such a request would only anger her, and her anger at me probably hadn't cooled as it was.

The overcast black of the sky was frigid and opaque. The night crawled by. I reflected on how I made a particularly vulnerable sentry, injured as I was. If we were attacked I could do very little aside from waking up the others. While I struggled with my thoughts, a blue glow crept at the edge of my peripheral vision.

The Lucky Watcher was perched on a ridge in the distance, his posture vigilant. I smiled sadly, knowing the watery rabbit wasn't exactly the talkative type. Even so, the night was less lonely when accented with aquamarine.

"Hello, Szakaieh," I said to myself in the dark.

Chapter 20
A'Rehia tells of: "The Accursed"

"Misdirection is stronger than strength, always has been. What good is the fight if you don't know what you're fighting?" -The Sky Dancer

I wonder about the myriad of nuanced ways in which the Jurisdiction has harmed me.

I know this may seem myopic and self-serving, given the lives destroyed by the ruthless regime my father orchestrated, but I find it's easiest to look at things closely through my own eyes.

I think about the world I've seen which was exactly what the Jurisdiction wanted me to see. I wonder how much thought was spent to deter me from thinking. I wonder how much casual violence I've accepted as normal because of the skewed perspective of those Nobility butchers.

The raven Steffen knew and accepted a range of bad possibilities about me. He didn't wish to do further harm, nor let me escape back to my father's graces. He kept me pinned under his keen eyes. In the harshest terms, I was his prisoner, but I was a prisoner of the Jurisdiction my entire life. Steffen was a change in captors I mostly welcomed.

In truth, I was given nearly unlimited freedom under the watch of the Thunder Raven. I flew daily in the company of the striking gray bird. Towering storms shadowed him everywhere, and I became accustomed to the static crackle of agitated air that slid in his wake. On the occasions when he felt the need to resort to violence, the Thunder Raven lived up to his name.

I no longer saw any mystery in the Swarm avoiding the Witch-village. I didn't wonder to myself about why the harpies hadn't overpopulated their towers. Living and the mechanical pestilence alike relied on vital functions which could be impeded by manipulating prodigious voltage differences.

A threatening cloud of Swarm drones appeared in the Wilds on an otherwise unremarkable Sun, rising up like a malevolent ocean which blocked the horizon. The machines threatened to strafe us, but I gaped in awe as forked tongues of pure white bounced through them in a dazzling display of power. Twisted metal carcasses rained down across the forest.

Electrical destruction was a similar story with the harpies, though I think Steffen found their disfigured bodies more resilient than the mass-produced circuitry of the Swarm. Getting close to the bird-beasts disgusted him, but Steffen's talons were an efficient tool. I don't think the raven relished combat the way talented fighters did. I caught him playing with the clouds and coaxing blips of static in picturesque visions. Here was an artist conscripted by circumstance against the forces of evil. I shook my head. Had I heard this story before?

When the raven questioned me, I think he did so as much from genuine curiosity as he did because of a desire for actionable intelligence. He knew I wasn't going to be able to give detailed information about the grander schemes of the Jurisdiction. What little I did know I didn't exactly care to hide from him. He was more interested in how I'd become the person he saw in front of him. When I told him what my father had done to my friends, he wanted the story to be a lie, but the raven knew I was telling the truth. Whatever worries I had about being tortured by electric shock and compelled to comply evaporated when I saw the black sadness in his avian eyes.

A fortnight in the Witch's village brought me to a sense of contentment with the place. While the amenities were a crude adjustment, they were exotic compared to the urban landscape of Atlantium. The fresh foods that Leon and Jeriah prepared were splendiferous fare. The sustenance of the Wilds revitalized body, mind, and spirit, and each of the nooks and crannies in between.
{~}

Another Moon passed like a ship in the night. Steffen was growing increasingly restless. This was apparent to me in the Witch village among a great many other odd facts. Leon and Jeriah were waiting for word from the Witch or her scouts. Contact hadn't been made. A Sun would come when the Thunder Raven would no longer tolerate inaction.

I saw no sense in Steffen dragging me along looking for the Witch. I would've happily stayed with Leon and Jeriah in the village. The bird wouldn't accept argument over this point, however. I wasn't fearful that Steffen would harm me if I refused his wry suggestions, but they were still more than just suggestions. Air crackled with power around the raven. Perhaps I wanted a piece of it for myself.

I was growing accustomed to the tingle of static. I could taste the electricity around Steffen in the heated ozone. I flew in formation with the avian mage, cruising effortlessly in the pressure pocket he established. I was hardly an expert on geography, but after a day of traveling I was suspicions about where we'd end up at the conclusion of our trip.

"We're headed for Atlantium, aren't we?" I asked the soaring raven in front of me.

Steffen turned his head towards me. The wind ruffled the feathers on his neck.

"Not quite, Miss mage. I've a healthy disdain for the damage the Jurisdiction has wrought on this world. I don't plan to hand you over to them as an easy victim. We'll be stopping long before we're anywhere near that hellish city. My sources say the Wise Witch was headed south from the City of Old, accompanied by a rebel escort. Keep your eyes peeled for anything- witchy."

I pondered my instructions for a minute. I was alert but indifferent to the talk of another City. I posed a question to the raven by way of casual conversation.

"What's the 'Wise Witch' like? Seems she can do no wrong, the way Leon and Jeriah talk about her."

Steffen abruptly entered a dive. The maneuver was a departure from his tranquil flying, and I whirled about in panic for a second, looking for a threat. When I saw empty sky, I realized the raven had landed on a tree branch and was perched there, staring at the trees.

I landed next to him gingerly. I was clueless as to why an arcane creature was afflicted by my clumsy small talk.

"The Wise Witch-" Steffen began. "The 'Wise Witch' has a name." He preened a rumpled feather on his left wing with a dramatic motion of his beak.

"Her name is Jae'lin Fleuro."

My heart skipped a beat and mind reeled as I attempted to discern between connection or coincidence. The raven spoke to me, his voice crooning among the branches.

"The Wise Witch might be more knowledgeable than any mage alive, A'Rehia, but she's flesh and blood" He shifted his feet on the branch. "So yes, since I know you were wondering. She could be dead. The Guards know she's been on the Jurisdiction's shit-list for centuries. The likelihood of her death is higher than I'd like to admit." He stopped staring and looked me dead in the eyes. The effect was singularly unnerving, but he wanted to impress his words upon me. He proceeded with the desired effect.

"Jae'lin has her flaws, like anyone else, A'Rehia Fleuro. Don't be blinded by her the way people around her tend to be. Because if you are, Miss mage, you may refuse to see what I need to show you right now. And you, you more than anyone-" He prepared to take wing.

"You're gonna need to see this shit."

{~}

The wind shifted. A miser-ly autumn gale blew from the northeast and brought the cold and rain. My clothing was soaked, and I defended myself with a spiteful shiver. Steffen was annoyed by the weather, but the exposure posed a threat to my health. We stopped whenever I was numb. The raven kindled warming fires with wayward sparks.

I learned from watching him that guiding electricity was difficult to plan. The tongues of power arced and forked unpredictably even under Steffen's experienced mastery. The phenomenon of energy could be encouraged, but did Steffen actually have control? Did he possess the bolts, or was he borrowing?

In any case, I didn't die from hypothermia. That's the best that can be said for some Suns. The whole thing was a fairly miserable trip. Steffen's light-shows were the best part, but they couldn't distract me completely. I'd get warmed up and nearly dry only to realize the rain wasn't letting up.

We'd almost reached Atlantium, and I'd almost reached my breaking point. Fortunately, the sky cleared, and the dawn was warmer at the lower longitude.

I can remember when I remembered the dragon. I might've felt the traces first, but Steffen made us stop because he sensed the energy.

We landed on a branch. A trampled clearing below us was covered in blotches of dark mud. We looked down at the clearing in silence as we contemplated dragon tracks.

The tracks led towards the forested hills to the north. We'd overflown the Wilds with no sign of anyone. We studied the prints with palpable curiosity.

"Do you know anything about a dragon?" Steffen asked me.

"I-uh-" I stammered as I remembered the booming artillery in Atlantium. "Yeah. Outside the city. They shot it down. I thought it was gonna die."

The bird blew air through his nostrils and made a bending whistle.

"Trying to kill a dragon is like falling in love, kid. You think you know where the heart is, but that doesn't mean you're aiming for the right spot."

{~}

After seeing the dragon tracks, Steffen completely lost interest in the Wise Witch. This baffled me. I thought surely, if you're going to worry, discovering she might be in the company of a dragon isn't exactly a reassurance. I guess the bird didn't see it that way.

"I feel like I've been shivering for a fortnight. And for what?" I complained. I was fed up with wasted Suns of bundled floating. I was tired. My body was using energy to stay warm. "What in the hell are we even doing?"

Steffen glanced at me with a skeptical eye as he circled through his billionth banking turn over a thermal he'd been nursing for most of the afternoon.

"We're preparing," he said.

"Preparing for what?" I retorted. I began a wild spin just to repel the sheer boredom.

"For what's coming next," Steffen responded, indifferent to my anxiety.

I sighed and slowed my rotation. "I don't see how flying around in the same spot gets us ready for anything."

Steffen set a course beyond the thermal. I was happy enough to be anywhere other than that particular patch of sky, and I waited patiently for him to reply.

"Depends on what part of you you're preparing," he said. He floated through the trees before on the edge of a ruined stone wall.

I raised an eyebrow, understandably skeptical. "I usually prepare by asking 'is something going to try to kill us?'"

I landed next to Steffen, but the top of the wall was a precarious perch for human feet. I looked at the forest in front of us and saw stones. The rocks varied in shape and size. Trees and vegetation had overgrown the area.

"This is a graveyard," I whispered. "Why did you bring me to a graveyard? Are you trying to spook me?"

Steffen said nothing in return. I realized I was frightened by how frazzled the raven looked. His composure was gone, replaced by fear and uncertainty. He could barely bring himself to look at me.

I heard the wind shift and come whipping through the gravestones. The air whistled against twisted tree branches and grasping vines until the noise was an oppressive din. The unearthly rush of the atmosphere wailed at the Steffen and I. Leaves and dead branches hurtled towards us without warning. We dodged and dropped behind the graveyard wall.

"Peace!" Steffen cawed as loudly as he could. "It's me!"

"What the fuck?" I interrogated the cowering raven as my words cracked with panic.

He laughed nervously. "The Jurisdiction has a new project designation for her every few Rounds when an ambitious Nob or Dev tries to contain her or destroy her. She does have a name, though."

I peered over the wall, summoning my courage as my heart pounded in my chest. The noise had calmed slightly, and Steffen's claims of familiarity emboldened me. The Sun was beginning to set. Excellent, I thought. As if a graveyard and a crazy ghost weren't dark enough.

The object of my curiosity was rather fetching, this ghost, even though she was scowling right through me She glowed with a pale light that wasn't shining from anywhere in particular. The unsettled air around her haunted the brush of the graveyard. She drifted towards me like a gossamer mist, her gown threading itself with the fibers of the dusk.

Steffen cleared his throat.

"A'Rehia, I'd like you to meet the mage who originally invented the kiteknife. Allow me to introduce Ms. Chrysanthemum Fleuro."

The ghost laughed, a musical sound to match the voice that followed.

"Hi, Uncle Steve. Hadn't seen you in a while. I was beginning to think my False Priesthood were the only mages who considered me a worthwhile tourist attraction."

The raven resettled his wings and found his nerve. "Has the Jurisdiction been letting you rest in peace these days, Chrys?"

Chrysanthemum continued to scowl and her hollow eyes turned away with a flash of anger. "For a while, they did. But lately, I've noticed some idiots somewhere must've pissed them off again." I felt the tendrils of air swirl around me. I knew if I made any false move, Chrysanthemum would lock me in place or hammer me down or pull the air from my lungs.

I cleared my throat. "I wonder who they are? The um- idiots, I mean," I ventured.

"The Jurisdiction is pure evil, Chrys," Steffen lamented. "You can't blame a few scraps of humanity for fighting to survive."

The ghost remained perturbed. Her emotion manifested in a physical pressure.

"The Nobility discovered the kiteknives on my corpse when the Fallen Angel betrayed me. And now you bring me this Jurisdiction princess, wide-eyed as anything?" Her translucent fingers extended as ectoplasmic claws. "Girl, I should tear you apart."

Steffen drew sparks with his eyes and extended his wings. He'd recovered from his initial fearfulness. Perhaps seeing his niece again allowed him to recall her as a human girl. He let his feathers flair to their fullest spread, and a crackle of static in the air threatened to ward away attack.

"Come now, Chrys. You think I'd bring an enemy to your doorstep? I've witness the new happenings in these Wilds. We might be able to put up a real resistance again. Your mother-"

The ghost interrupted him. "I don't want to hear about my mother. She's been in denial for centuries. My father is probably the only person who could talk sense to her, and he's a Guard-damn looney-ass hermit. The crazy pair of them would be entirely their own problem these Suns, except for the part where they cursed the hell out of their daughter."

Steffen made a chuckling sound. "My sister is a piece of work, no doubt. Don't forget, she's the reason Charlie and I can't even hold a set of chopsticks."

Chrysanthemum wasn't smiling over his jest. "I'm sure you had a blast, amusing yourselves by signing up to become your own goofy menagerie. I think I've had enough of this miniature reunion, Uncle Steve."

I could see the ghost was gathering herself to drift away. The way she hesitated signaled to me that she was waiting to be persuaded. Steffen started to open his beak, but I jabbed him with my elbow and he squawked.

"Please, Ms. Banshee," I said. I surprised myself with my own volume. "I'm tired of being dragged around by this bird. Being dead is probably extra-boring. I know how to dance. Do you like to dance? It might not be not as good as TV, but it's better than being bored." I knew Steffan was watching me, but I kept my eyes on Chrysanthemum. The ghostly woman in the silvery gown captivated my attention. Her intensity prevented me from ever getting bored with her, but my lie was cleverly chosen. She gave me a look which made her eyes coalesce in finer detail. I hoped she didn't want to kill me. A sincere smile appeared on my scheming face.

"Who cares about the bird," I suggested boldly. "He can go."

Chapter 21
Sunderah tells of: "The Dark Dragon"

"I've written several sternly worded letters to the Jurisdiction. I don't imagine wasted stationary will replace teeth or claws, though." -The Bright Dragon

Another dragon was living in the east.

I could feel him, in the early Suns. Guards know why or how. The feeling was akin to being in the sun on a hot day, and having water drip against your shirt, except nothing is dripping and you aren't wearing a shirt.

He was cold and blue, I knew that much. He was so cold he burned. I didn't want to look for him, but I needed to know why he irked me. The thought of never seeing what he looked like gnawed at my resolve. I couldn't decide if there would be a kind of comfort in finding another dragon, or if I wanted to kill him. The distraction of the shifting icy sensation was abominably annoying, but indecision became unbearable.

I decided to travel. I'd go towards where I might find the other dragon, that Guard-damn provocateur. Besides, my cave was getting smelly anyway. My appetite had lulled considerably after feasting on lots of fleshy men, but I hadn't hunted since then. I was laying in a cave in the dark, lighting fires and imagining my loves. If I lay just right, perhaps they'd appear in my mind.

But alas, I couldn't ignore the other dragon. What an inflated sense of self-worth! Oh, how I cursed him for pulling me away from memories of my loves! I blackened the walls of the cave in anger when I realized the faces of my loves were fading. I hated this world. I pictured myself ebbing away along with my memories.

My will to live wasn't particularly strong, but my anger was like a molten pressure cooker. I could feel the power building inside. I roared, and there it was, orange and alive and flickering. I stoked my rage and kept my teeth bared. This entire world was going to pay for what it did to my loves. The other dragon would serve me or slay me as a rival. I found both possibilities acceptable.
{~}

Later in the Sun, I left the cave behind as I slunk through the forest and shook the dust and the ash from my wings and scales. I was too disoriented by the bright light to hurry. Birds took flight to evade my passage. Obnoxious chirping made me swat my paws in annoyance. The birds escaped me, but branches snapped as they snagged my arms, and I thrashed in frustration. The movement made me feel less stagnant, but I was getting hungry again.

I hunted on foot, making a meal of a lean hart. The game was a pleasant change from Regiment grease-beef. When the deer was nothing except blood trail, I lifted away from the forest in earnest. I was feeling reinvigorated, my wings stretched in the sky, and I looped and spiraled with an eye slitted eye towards the horizon. Another dragon beckoned.

I traveled for Suns, not rushing to confront my quarry. I ate and flew for the pure enjoyment. The interloper in my private mourning wasn't about to rob me of the pleasure of patient brooding. I imagined how his scales would feel when my claws gouged at him. I'd make him regret tormenting me for so long.

I was an animal. I knew myself intimately and without thought. My senses were keener, and every instinct within me screamed with a primal urgency. The will to fight shouldered aside a will to flee as if my bones themselves understood my utter primacy in the food chain. My continued survival would come at the cost of rivers and rivers of spilled blood. I flexed my claws, ready to spill my share. I wondered if the other dragon's flesh would taste the same as my own.

Night was at it again, starting to kill off the light. Rain descended from the sky, stubbornly refusing to remove a scattered curtain from the sunset. The smell of humans reached my senses, but it wasn't essence-of-Regiment. A male and a female, possibly engaged in complicated mating rituals. The other dragon was near. I scanned the forest below for signs of him as I banked, and I began to glide silently. I smelled a canine odor, wet fur and raw meat.

I spotted the other dragon among the hills, and I looked for a place to land with enough distance to alight unnoticed. I snarled in disappointment. The pathetic beast was already injured. I'd find no contest in bending the dark dragon to my will. I contemplated making a few meals of him instead. Having flown across dozens of leagues, I decided to rest instead for an evening. The injured dragon wasn't going anywhere. His persistent chill had subsided. Besides, a short-stack of humans with a side of dog sounded like a breakfast I could dream about.

{~}

I awoke a few Marks before dawn, and I discovered I'd been disastrously wronged. I could feel the ropes binding my wings and limbs and snout. Vile, sneaky insects! I recalled the feeling of crunching bones. I woke my rage along with the rest of my body. I squeezed jets of flame through clenched teeth, but I couldn't burn away the ropes, and I couldn't move my head to look at my body. I started to shift. I decided the ropes holding me were puny and thin. Perhaps I was strong enough to snap the restraints.

A clawed dragon paw placed itself on my back.

"Easy, friend," Chaeoh said.

I wasn't going to be easy. The sound of the other dragon stirred my rebellion, making me thrash in earnest, but he was larger than I expected.

"Turn me loose and face me, you bloated skink!" I snarled against my fangs.

"I'm not your enemy, dragon-lady," came Chaeoh's calm reply.

"You captured me," I retorted. "You and those sneaky insects. Will you finish the job? Butcher and a coward? Or would you prefer I re-injure you first?"

He made no reply, but he settled to the earth near my flank. He was too close, and I couldn't wriggle free from the ropes. I could feel his paw on my back, but he was maddeningly gentle.

I hissed in showers of sparks. "You could at least feed me one of your humans. My tummy is rumbling."

I couldn't see his face, but I could feel Chaeoh shake his head in the dimness of the forest.

"Humans aren't for eating."

My entire body was wracked with cruel laughter.

"Tell that to all those skulls in my dragon-piles!"

Chaeoh didn't move. His voice became diminutive for such a sizeable dragon.

"Were you ever human?"

The question was confusing, at the time. Perhaps the other dragon was well versed in sneaky insect tactics. Suddenly, I was drowning in memories.

"Yes- I-" I'd lost my train of thought, and my eyes were leaking lava.

"My loves," I managed to say as I swallowed. How long had it been? Suns? Moons? Rounds? Time was twisted around. Images were disintegrating under the force of my discontent.

"I was human, Sunderah," Chaeoh continued. My pupils grew wide from attempted recollection. His scaled blue jaw moved as he continued speaking. "I'd forgotten. Forgotten everything until I realized I wasn't alone."

I sighed vehemently. I was tired, hungry and defeated.

"What happened?" I asked Chaeoh. I didn't care. The question was the only thing to say given the situation. The words were as meek as a dragon would ever get. I hated the unfairness. I was bound by more than just ropes. "My loves!" I cried, sputtering clouds of smoke.

I felt the cold drops of Chaeoh's tears fall against the hot, smooth bronze of my scales.

"Pain, my friend," he began. "Moons and Moons. Irons around my ankles, tossed in the sea." He moved away as he spoke, and I felt my bindings sliced away by a sharp claw.

"Down," he coughed, shaking the earth around us. "Way down. Down to the depths. Almost dead. Touched an egg." His scaly lips formed a mischievous grin. "Sound familiar?"

I crouched cautiously, circling Chaeoh in the forest, flexing where the ropes had been and exhaling puffs of fire. I kept my wings and claws ready for Chaeoh to make his move. I was no longer confident of my desire to kill the dark dragon, or even confident I could accomplish the task. I snarled at him and I seethed. I contemplated flying away and never looking back. But I had a few things I needed to know first.

"Chaeoh," I challenged him, chest forward and posture proud. He cocked a green eye. I sent a disdainful puff in his direction and put the question to him to see how he'd react.

"Do you know of any decent breakfast joints in this neck of the woods?"

Chapter 22
Vilkir tells of: "A Blue Heart"

"I get how 'casualty of war' isn't a particularly popular career choice for people, but I know a few folks who'd rather die on a battlefield than be at odds with their spouse." -The Warrior Shaman

I thought about Tehsyn the whole way home.

I wanted to leave the mage bow where I found the damn thing after my seizure. At Kiffu-San's insistence I securely lashed the Sylviarg Paw to my person with a few leather thongs next to my quiver and tried to forget it. The Iris recurve bow rested in my left hand instead. I'd sort out the mage stuff later.

I spent my time wondering what her dress would look like or what kind of flowers she'd put in her hair. There was no secret Tehsyn's favorite color was blue, but the entire palette of blues was far too broad a category. There were as many forms of blue as there were subtle cues in the Seer Sage's silent communiques. Thinking about Tehsyn became distracting enough for me that I almost toppled from Kiffu-San's back when he lurched beneath me. A laugh shook my legs following my desperate clutching at thick fur.

"Best keep your wits, Warrior Shaman. Riding a bear is a risky proposition, and getting hitched probably isn't any safer."

My hair drifted away from my face as I dropped to the ground. I jogged to get my blood flowing. Rebellious flakes of fresh snow accented the morning. The chill was significant, and my shoes were too thin for the weather. Summer leathers offered insufficient insulation and poor water resistance. Without Kiffu-San's furry body to keep me moving, I would've been hunting for a pelt. After another Moon, winter would fall on the Low Hills in earnest.

"Do you plan to hibernate soon?" I asked the bear.

Kiffu-San turned a casual eye. "I did enough sleeping over the last few winters, and to be honest, I'm kinda tired of it. Also, that's an offensive stereotype."

"What? But you said you- but you're- ah, nevermind."

A late autumn wedding was unusual. I desperately hoped the Confidants wouldn't push Tehsyn to delay the wedding until spring.

We faced the problem of finding the Iris tribe in the first place, nomadic as they were, but Kiffu-San and I were both experienced trackers. Generally speaking, humans are an easy animal to find in the Wilds, and any child knows the signs. From the spot of the camp I'd departed, we traced the hoof prints, wheel ruts and fire pits of the Iris tribe to a string of abandoned camps before we arrived at the edge of an inhabited site.

I'm sure we were spotted by the sentries, but I hadn't caught a glimpse. Stealth was part of their job, and Kiffu-San wasn't exactly an unobtrusive presence. By the time we reached the Iris populace, half of the tribe was already in motion, vanished towards the forest like a flock of birds disturbed by a badger. The people remaining in the camp were in the process of taking flight. Only the bravest of the Iris folk stood their ground in order to parley with the Demon Bear. The Seer Sage Tehsyn and the sentry Keysha Baton were foremost among them.

I almost tackled my two favorite women in the whole world, thrilled as I was to be home. I was certain that the happiest days of my life were in store for me. I'd face no more questions about my mother's place in the Iris tribe, or the Seer Sage's right to marry the person she'd chosen. The fact that I was that person was an overwhelming bonus. Kiffu-San placed his tremendous furry arms around the three of us and gave us a true bear hug. We hugged him right back, smearing our tears in his gray fur.

The rest of the Iris tribe watched our unlikely embrace with significant trepidation. The world of the Iris was upended. The bear terrified and intrigued anyone who witnessed him, as did the prospects of a new Shaman when only a handful of crones were alive who bothered to retell tall tales about the last one. I doubted that my fiance and I would be plotting to usurp power from the Confidants, but we gave no guarantee. In the Iris tribe, the arrival of the Demon Bear was the ending of an age.

The ursine lounged playfully in the grass and greeted the tribe casually. He made a show of being docile and benevolent, but his size and species left awestruck gawkers. Undisciplined youngsters approached Kiffu-San as he stretched and sniffed. The youths touched his fur and darted back to their panicked parents. After nearly a Mark of relative silence, a remaining Confidant stepped forward and greeted me with a wavering voice.

"We'll be moving for the rest of the S-Sun, Sh-Shaman. The Council orders- er- uh - they want you to meet them at the Sacred Stone."

The use of a Sacred Stone was to guarantee the safety of the meeting participants. Nomadic as the Iris tribe was, I hoped the people wouldn't witness a permanent split over the bear and the new Shaman. I knew we faced sunderings in the past. The various tribes of the Low Hills formed and reformed like dough in a baker's hands. I wondered if the Iris would take my return as a positive sign. I smiled when I thought of the piece of the puzzle which could make it so. The Iris tribe may not listen to a talking bear or a so-called Warrior Shaman, but they'd listen to a Seer Sage. The tribe would listen to Tehsyn. Only the foolish do otherwise.

I relayed tales about the mundane things which transpired on my journey as I helped Tehsyn and my mother pack tents. My belongings were already on my person, and in less than a Mark the Iris would vanish. When Kiffu-San informed us matter-of-factly that he'd have no trouble carrying the three of us as well as our belongings, we offered use of our horses to the rest of the tribe.

The Iris wagons galloping in the Wilds were thrilling and heartening sight to see. The Iris excelled at detailed banners and portable elegance. Artistry was on display as we careened through a grassy valley as smoothly as fresh-churned butter.

Today I saw the formations of the caravans with new eyes. I saw weakness, vulnerability, mortal danger. The carved wagons were never meant as war chariots. In my mind, the Jurisdiction was looming. I felt the shadow looming over the earth through instinct. No armor was found among the tribe, no weapons to fight. When the Sun came where the Iris tribe couldn't flee, the lesson we learned would be too much for anyone to bear. We made no consideration of an ambush, and no thought was given to the enemy who might lurk in the forest. The minor heartbreak I felt over my recurring realizations didn't come as a new feeling for me. The gloom warred strangely with my affection for Tehsyn. I watched her stand casually on Kiffu-San's forehead and tease him with honey-cakes.

Despite his playful game, Kiffu-San's tense body language echoed my thoughts about the Jurisdiction. Miraculous was how I'd describe the Iris tribe surviving the Tribal Wars. I thought of the limited incidents where raiders had killed or injured tribespeople. The events were traumatic, but they were nothing compared to the weight of war we'd avoided no matter the consequence. The Iris tribe traveled every reach of the Low Hills, and a few reaches beyond. The Seer Sages kept the wagons a step ahead of danger. My fiance's tradition wasn't painted faces and chanted nonsense.

Tehsyn knew wrongness like she always did. When I tried to share my concerns, I had difficulty turning feelings into words for her. By contrast, Tehsyn's blue letters always flowed perfectly with the right things to say. The best I could do was promise sincerely I'd explain everything later. Seeing concern creep through the contours of her face, I pulled a rakish smile across my own. You need to be coordinated to kiss a Seer Sage on a Demon Bear. I was a Warrior Shaman. Maybe I used mage-craft.

After a distinct lack of maulings took place at the Sacred Stone, we arrived in the new camp properly heralded by the dignitaries of the Iris tribe. The Council and the prominent artisans were resplendent in their ceremonial garb. I was peripherally aware of the rest of the tribe, clustered among the wagons, though fears of the Demon Bear kept the gathering from becoming crowded. Any questions I over whether or not the Council would attempt to delay the wedding were evaporating as I studied the camp. A celebration was imminent, anyone could tell that. Energy was in the air, and a smell of heady spice emanated from the cook-fires.

The clearing in the forest featured a stream, and the camp was close enough to the peak of a hill for us to see over the trees and the valley below. I suspected that other tribes had passed through the spot recently. The open vantage point offered scant comfort. I was nearly certain the brown stain in the tall grass where the wagons were parked was human blood. I pushed my cautious thoughts aside. The sentries were diligent. A few had even trained with my mother. I focused on Keysha and the honored spot near the stream for her tent, adjacent to the Seer Sage and her refined digs. A tented pavilion for the Demon Bear was strung across slender poles, but the shelter was woefully undersized, and a man was shaking his head in embarrassment and mumbling something about the metric system.

An over-eager child threw flower petals at Kiffu-San's furry legs. The Council was officially informing us that the wedding ceremony was set to take place before sundown. I was keenly aware of the Confidants' resentment, but nobody was brave enough to risk displeasing the Demon Bear and the Seer Sage. They looked at Kiffu-San as if a deity walked among them, and whatever they'd thought of me before, I was Warrior Shaman now.

My mother insisted on adjusting the Seer Sage's tents before she saw to her own. I pitched my tent near Tehsyn, but the animal skins were shabby and worn by comparison. A pair of artisans were already frowning nearby and rubbing their chins. I felt the excitement of imagining new stuff, but the feeling was decidedly secondary to having a new wife. Tehsyn had me, more likely.

"Have you written the minimum number of vows, yet?" Tehsyn wrote in the air in front of her with a mischievous grin.

I raised my eyebrows. I was unsettled as I wondered what the Seer Sage knew. I'd never tried to deceive her in any real way, always knowing she'd discover the truth. I had a taste, once, when a weaver's daughter was flirtatious. Needless to say, Tehsyn's commentary on the matter quickly dissuaded me from sneakiness. The Seer Sage didn't whisper her opinions in a tidy font.

We worked amiably, unpacking Tehsyn's things. The three of us were nearly delirious with contentment. I'm sure Tehsyn and I couldn't stop giving each other knowing looks. We probably drew a few eye rolls from well-wishers. Not from my mother, however. She opened a bottle of hooch she'd been saving for the occasion before the Sun even reached noon. The woman could hold her liquor, but she was insisting anybody who spoke to her share a drink. She took to loudly proclaiming in jest how she wanted to get rid of the alcohol before any grand-babies showed up.

With Tehsyn's responsibilities as Seer Sage consuming her life, she was always unusually independent from her parents, but they came to anxiously give regards to their famous daughter before the ceremony. The hugs we exchanged were perfectly pleasant, but Tehsyn's father gave his wife a sideways look when she steadied her balance by leaning against me a little too obviously.

I was starting to realize the wedding was gonna be bigger than both solstices tossed together. My mind reeled as I contemplated the food preparations. Pastries filled with meat or berries, grilled vegetables, soups and sauces, candied sweets, dishes readied over Iris fires. Brick ovens were placed in the morning and teams of bakers flocked to the central spot, banking the fires and readying their offerings. Appetizers got the mood going. No doubt ale and wine would follow.

The wedding of the Seer Sage, the arrival of the Demon Bear, and the appointing of a new Warrior Shaman were turnings in the history of the Iris tribe, and tradition dictated each be celebrated fully. Members of the tribe could petition the Council for reimbursement if in contributing to the festivities, but this was seen as a shameful act. The tribe offered foods, gifts and decorations as means to social status among their peers.

At an event like this, anyone need of material sustenance might receive largesse from the benevolence of the community. Left-over food, candles, clothing, and even unwanted matrimonial gifts were presented free for the taking. My mother and I were granted this kind of charity. I'd ended up with my longbow in this manner, although technically any weapons belonged to the tribe itself, subject to restrictive regulation. If anyone harbored thoughts about begrudging me the use of the tool, they'd be shrugged off in light of my new title. I pictured the fancy ceremonial weapons they'd probably make now, and I rolled my eyes. A bow was only worthwhile when it could put an arrow through a target.

I could hear the pipes and strings tuning up, and skins thrumming over drum heads. In an instant, the willing and the able became dancers and spectators in the wedding of the Sage and the Shaman. Closest acquaintances lined the avenue where Tehsyn and I would walk to the altar. Indications were made with whirling colorful scarves and bursts of flower petals.

I wore my cleanest buckskin trousers. My mother gifted me with a green suede vest she'd embroidered with symbols of the hunt. I didn't own much in the way of footwear, but I decided my leather moccasins had polished well enough to travel down the aisle. A leather belt with a tooled sheath for my knife was looped around my waist, and shining steel beads were tied in my hair.

My dubious finery made the bride look ethereal by comparison. Nobody except my mother was prepared for a new

Shaman to be wed, but the Seer Sage's gown was probably the subject of tense political and artistic drama for the past three Rounds. I thanked the Guards I'd missed the discussions, but the results were difficult to argue. Tehsyn was enveloped in gossamer sashes which the genteel blue lace of her bodice. The inner layers were form-fitting and accented her impeccably balanced frame. I'm sure her shoes were made for dancing at her own insistence. Each looked as if a stream of tiny jewels was woven together to adorn her feet. Her matching jewelry bore a similar opalescence. She was a striking burst of color in the afternoon sunlight.

Kiffu-San's furry elbow brought me back to myself as he nudged me in the ribs. "Don't forget to breathe, Mr. Sage."

The music shifted from movements of exuberant joy to a dignified procession before the musicians and dancers drew to a close and the entire clearing went quiet. The Iris tribe waited on baited breath for us to speak our part.

The altar was modest, but the aesthetics were ancient. We faced the tribe with a bow before facing each other. The ceremony was whatever we desired. Tehsyn reached forward and drew a blue heart that hung in the air. I knew she meant for me to speak.

"I'm the luckiest man in this entire tribe," I announced in a clear voice, leaving no question of my conviction. I had a hint of mirth in my voice. I felt an eloquent man would find words, but I let go of all the extras I was trying to remember.

"Yes, he is," Tehsyn wrote, dashing a tear from her eye with the edge of a detailed sleeve. Her gesture solidified the smiles in the audience before she continued. "The tribe is going to need him, our Warrior Shaman." The Seer Sage hesitated. Every eye awaited her graceful penmanship. "But not the way I need him."

She kissed me, and I found we were caught in a lingering embrace which was impossible to break. I wish I could say the wedding ceremony held additional substance or elaboration. I wish I could say I was able to speak aloud what love meant with poetry or statements of devotion, but I hadn't the proclivity for baring my soul in public. My wife and I were destined to resolve the details while we were wishing embraces lasted forever. The drums unleashed a festive fill, and the pipes and strings picked up the pulse.

"The path to peace isn't wide or straight or flat. Don't imagine a laden wagon will roll across roots or rocks with ease." -The Seer Sage

My betrothed wasn't a complete idiot, but he was silly enough to be endearing.

He didn't get any smarter when he became my husband. I love him dearly, and nothing can ever take that away, but I hoped his quest to find Kiffu-San would awaken the mage in him.

Instead, he quashed or fought his gift, or attempted to remain clueless. He carried his true self around as if he was suffering from a bad rash. With the weight of the Sylviarg Paw strapped to his back, he cringed as if a venerable mage artifact was still the goat's entrails.

I had to coax him and baby-step him. Despite his manly toughness, I knew no other way. I frowned playfully at him when he missed a dance step. He was staring at me again. When he kicked me in the toes, I wrote an expletive in cursive. At least he was reasonably handsome. Plus, he did have his eyes for the tribe, even after what they put his mother and him through. He saw the vulnerability. I knew he was a capable shot with a longbow, but we were going to need power beyond flinty arrows. The Iris tribe was gonna need a Warrior Shaman.

The bear and I were of a similar mind. Kiffu-San drew me aside during the festivities and told me about the first time my husband tried to use the Sylviarg Paw. I sympathized with the pains of being a mage, but I had no intention of letting Vilkir forget the truth now that he knew.

I'd kept quiet for Rounds. I never had a reason to force the issue until I decided to marry the man and make him the Shaman. I always thought Vilkir realized he was a mage. Speed and strength came naturally to him. He was instinctive, coordinated- dangerous. My face flushed pink. I suppose being married had its perks.

When Vilkir contemplated his mage-craft, his mind rebelled against it. I couldn't blame him for the struggle, especially if I wanted to help him overcome his limitations. The man wanted nothing more from life than to be a husband and a hunter. I knew he wanted those things potently, and with his whole heart. Much as the fact pained me to admit, the sentiments weren't going to suffice.

Later in the evening, when pillow talk turned toward the Sylviarg Paw, he willingly confessed his weakness. I knew he'd gained confidence from the respect his new title afforded him. He told me the touch of the Seer Sage was exactly what he needed to grow as a mage.

I didn't need Foresight to know he was full of crap and mostly just wanted to get laid, but if the glass has liquid in the bottom, I'm an optimist. So I tried to imagine he was right. We tried to free his mind. Our honeymoon was a walk in the solace of the forested hills. Our ultimate destination was the edge of a nearby lake. A Seer Sage learns a thing or two about energy and balance, and I shared them with my husband. With my hands on his shoulders, Vilkir attempted to shoot the mage bow, over and over. The process tore him up, mind, body and soul. I did everything I could to mitigate the damage. When he finally lost consciousness, I whispered prayers over his limp body.

Guard-damn the Jurisdiction! I thought to myself. The monsters were killing the man I loved and they hadn't even laid a finger on him yet. I soothed Vilkir's synapses as much as I could, but the healing of the mind is a delicate process. I was horrified by the idea that I might change Vilkir if I meddled with his head.

Our progress was protracted. I felt a glacier would outpace us. Guards, I was frustrated with Vil. I'm sure I lost my temper with him a few times. Every time I thought we were getting somewhere, he'd revert to his bad habits and poor technique, re-injuring himself. Vilkir's attempts at mage-craft turned the honeymoon to a tribulation which, bonding experience aside, I would've rather done without.

I can't say the trip was entirely unpleasant. The lake was as picturesque as any young couple would've hoped, and Vilkir as attentive and patient as he could possibly be, given the circumstances. When he finally fired a conjured arrow over the water, I wept freely and leapt in his arms to embrace him. He was staggering, but he didn't drop me. I made him rest for the remaining Sun and tried to help him relax.

Even as our Moon together began to feel more like a honeymoon, the Jurisdiction made its way to thoughts and conversation. Neither of us were ignorant enough to ignore the Regiment tire tracks or the Quint footprints littering the forest. Deep as we were in the Low Hills, Jurisdiction incursions were supposed to be rare. The Wilds were no longer a respite from danger.

"Do you think they built new outposts?" Vilkir asked me as he stepped over a motorbike tire print in the dry mud. I was already suspicious, and I nodded agreement, studying bullet holes in the tree trunks around us. I knew with sudden certainty that we'd find bodies if we continued walking. I grasped Vilkir's tunic, making him spin around to face me.

"Let's get back to the tribe," I wrote, pulling him close as I tried to keep the fear from showing in my letters.

He looked me in the eyes and he nodded. We left the path hand in hand. I led him back the way we came.
{~}

We moved away from the honeymoon lake. We traced the deer paths through open fields whenever we could, and we kept our heads down. When we found a tranquil part of the Wilds, we made a tiny camp and spoke in whispers. The walk cleared my mind.

"We need allies," I wrote diplomatically.

"We have the Demon Bear now. He can help us," Vilkir responded in a hopeful voice.

I nodded agreement before I continued to write. "He won't be enough. We need to convince the tribe that he isn't enough."

Vilkir rubbed the stubble on his chin. His beard made him look older, but I didn't mind. We were both older. A married pairing in the eyes of the tribe.

"Are you suggesting we find others from the Low Hills tribes? Would they join us? Or should we leave the Low Hills and seek help elsewhere?"

I shook my head. "I don't like the prospects of either option, my love, but Kiffu-San may know places we don't. He mentioned the Rose tribe."

Vilkir looked at me, and I remembered why I married him. He wasn't always bright, but he was sincere. He was carefully considering what he knew of the Rose tribe, I could tell.

"Looking for allies might not be safe, 'Syn. I know we'd be foolish if we didn't consider the guns. Rose guns, Regiment guns, they frighten me, I admit. I'd hunt any kind of game or fight any warrior in close combat, but firearms shouldn't be taken lightly. Much as I feel strange in saying, I can see why the Iris tribe has been running my entire life. We're frightened. And Guard-dammit, we should be."

I clasped my hands together and placed my fingers in front of my lips. When I brought them apart again, I drew a breath. My hand went to Vilkir's chest as my other fingers darted through the air.

"I know you're brave, Vil. You can face these fears like you do the rest. Can you be brave enough to frighten the Jurisdiction?"

{~}

Kiffu-San wasn't as much help as I'd hoped. The cagey bear knew way more than he was letting on, that was for sure. The weight of responsibility in governing the Iris tribe wasn't Kiffu-San's interest. He half-heartedly endorsed the plan to move west to the High Hills. The bear was downright evasive when I asked if he knew of any allies we might seek, or dangers we might encounter given our chosen course of action. When I brought up Kiffu-San's obstinance to Vilkir, my husband only shrugged.

"He's a bear, love. Who knows what bears think. Besides, I'm not sure the Sylviarg Paw would be enough to threaten him. That thick bear hide of his, I think we're stuck with him."

Sigh... men. So one-dimensional sometimes. No grasp of subtlety. The obstinance of the Council was a separate matter entirely, but at least I could count on a man-boy and his teddy-bear to back my plays.

The Iris Council initially concluded that traveling west to the High Hills was a terrible idea, which didn't surprise me. Fortunately, they also concluded that being mauled by a bear was a terrible idea. I closed my eyes and rubbed my temples. I had no intentions of staging any sort of coup. All I wanted was for everyone to survive the balancing act.

When the Council's decision was announced, the action began. Less than a fortnight after the wedding of the Seer Sage and the Warrior Shaman, the Iris tribe was on the move again. The fire pits, the latrines and the staking points would remain, but even these signs of passage would eventually be reclaimed by the land.

Vilkir patrolled the main column riding on Kiffu-San's shoulders. His colors, his route and his demeanor were similar to the sentries, a concept the people were familiar with. He shouted words of encouragement and caution whenever they were appropriate. I was glad he was finding his groove. I rode on horseback, surrounded by an entourage led by Keysha herself. I kept my eyes narrowed and I stayed as vigilant as possible. If an enemy threatened, I wanted to Foresee it.

"I made the acquaintance of a dragon, once. A minor one, if such may be said of any creature as rarefied as their kind. I'm afraid his name has been lost to history with the dragon himself. He was a scrappy beast, breathing fire and the whole lot. He kept a harem of nudes along with a treasure trove for bait. The Nobility eventually got tired of their underlings feeding themselves to him. I don't imagine they cared how many Regiment or Devisors he ate because of actual human empathy, but the drain on resources probably started showing up on a spreadsheet somewhere. The Devisors retrofitted a few Quints and squeezed them through the entrance to his cave. The resulting boots and handbags were in fashion among the Nobility for a Round or two." -The Shapeshifter Virtuoso

Michael Zeyus and I discovered that we were being hunted by none other than Faehr-Dun, the Fallen Angel himself.

Had I not been born into the esteemed role of Count, we would've been facing a complete unknown, but real-life nightmares are a bit of a family hobby.

In all the Rounds of the patriarchal D'Arsailles line, from my father to his father to a few fathers before him, the threshold of the ancestral estate was never breached by so dire a threat. The manse had been partially burned down, shot at plenty, and the above-ground section was captured numerous times. The grounds had seen murders and betrayals, resurrections and zombies, malformed incarnations, misguided arcane summonings. And still, the arrival of the Fallen Angel in the Year of Our Guards 517 JD presented an entirely different level of home-security breach. When the devil arrives at your door, you don't generally have time to speculate about his motives. The Major and I were near the tippy-top of the Jurisdiction's shit-list.

If this warped, malevolent fire mage wasn't the devil himself, he was a close associate. I was gripping the underside of a branch with my claws, and observed the interloper from the forest, my dark wings wrapped tightly around my furry body. The man, if you could call him that, was cracked and blackened from head to toe, like a charcoal briquette made from wet clay. My skin crawled as I watched him absorb the starlight around him. He blended seamlessly with the shadows of the night. The steel linkages implanted at his shoulders were the most easily visible part of him as they fanned behind him in a skeletal approximation of wings. The Fallen Angel had no interest in flying. He sauntered through the trees with limitless confidence.

Having seen enough, I dropped from my perch. My wings danced among the ferns as I worked my way back to the manse. I muffled the air around me to ensure sure my wingbeats didn't betray me to the careful ears of the hunter. The night was brighter than I would've liked, a clear sky up above, and I kept a perilously anemic altitude.

I finished my transformation back to human, and I was standing at the vault hatch to my underground cellar when I heard a window-frame splinter inward on the second floor of the empty manse. The glass and clattered through the dusty room.

Thoughtful footsteps moved down the main stairs, as if the intruder was taking his time to inspect moldy artwork adorning dilapidated plaster walls. A chuckle passed throughout the house. I heaved the basement hatch shut and spun the wheel.

{~}

A moment later an explosion leveled the D'Arsailles family manse. The sound was muted by the bulkhead above me, but the blast shook the dust loose from the ceiling in my bunker. What was left of the building caused distant wooden clinks and thuds as the splintered pieces resettled around the estate following outward trajectories. I turned around, and a shirtless Zeyus was standing in front of me with a baseball bat.

"I don't like this," he said.

I scowled at him like a tactician and a gentleman.

"I don't particularly like it either, comrade, but we're drawing our hand from a stacked deck."

"We're trapped like starlings in a shit-bucket, Lucy. This cellar, this whole situation. What the fuck am I gonna do with wings in here? Doesn't exactly play to our strengths, does it?"

I grinned at him. "Fortunately, my family had the foresight to accommodate for this contingency. We'll use the escape tunnel, for starters. But there's more to my plan. In a minute, we're going to open the door, Major. And then we're gonna trap this bloody monster and slay him, as he undoubtedly deserves. And then, I believe, we'll open a bottle of wine."

Zeyus snorted at me in amusement. "If it's really Faehr-Dun like you say, that's a tall order for a batty play-boy and an AWOL airman."

I stood at attention, mocking a military bearing before I relaxed to a confident smile. I had my doubts, of course, but I kept the uncertainty between the Guards and I.

{~}

The first step of my plan went swimmingly, but opening the front door was always bound to be the easiest part. I spun the wheel of the hatch counter-clockwise and the deadbolts disengaged with an audible clank. I pictured the blackened man on the other side, his exterior still smoking from the blast he created to dispatch the building. Sure enough, only a few moments passed before a hand grasped the handle. The hinges groaned as Faehr-Dun pulled.

Zeyus and I were on the move. I had difficulty convincing him that putting a javelin through the Fallen Angel's face the moment he showed his mug wasn't an advisable course of action. Fearsome a fighter as the Major was, I didn't trust he'd land a lethal blow.

We left through the escape tunnel, and I shut the passageway irrevocably behind me with an iron bar. Zeyus flew to manse's foundation to re-close the main hatch. I studied the ruins of my family's manse with academic curiosity rather than emotional attachment. Beneath us, the Fallen Angel was angry about the tables getting turned on him. I could hear him beginning to break things.

"Alas, so much for the wine," I lamented. "I'm glad I hid the '72 under the floorboards."

Zeyus' eyes remained un-amused, but he couldn't keep a smile from claiming part of his handsome jaw.

"What now?" the Major asked. "I'm willing to bet he'll break free before he starves or suffocates."

"He might," I agreed with a nod. "If it weren't for the Moses Box." I held up a remote control unit.

"Moses Box?" Zeyus asked, attempting indifference.

"This little beauty jiggers the main water valve wide the hell open," I said. Zeyus' eyebrows responded accordingly. "A vengeful flood is about to wash away the Fallen Angel's sins."

Zeyus laughed, but his posture was tense. I flipped the switch with a click.

"Let my people go," I said, placing the Moses Box in the pocket of my smoking jacket. I rummaged around in a different pocket and located a gold-plated pocket watch by the ticking sound it made.

{~}

Dawn wasn't far, and we waited companionably, the winged man and I. We both knew the site was compromised. The Jurisdiction would return for us. I managed to press Zeyus about the need to confirm Faehr-Dun's demise and salvage a few doubloons in the cellar, but truly it was the '72 under the floorboards that called to me most. I could almost taste the stuff, a vintage nearly as exquisite as the blood of a fresh Prize Mate. I flipped the switch on the Moses Box and we watched the Sun rise as the water drained from my cellar.

"Now would be the time for the javelin," I told Zeyus as we stood next to the hatch.

Zeyus pointed the tip of the weapon at the entrance. "What if he's locked the door from the inside?"

"I disabled the catch, but I suppose he could've repaired it," I replied. I grunted as I heaved the handle.

To my notable dismay, the hatch wasn't locked from the inside. The door opened quite willingly, in fact, at the urgent behest of an extremely damp, extremely disgruntled Jurisdiction assassin.

{~}

Flailing of limbs and threats of continued violence took place. I'll not waste any ink on the retelling of our skirmish with the Fallen Angel. Suffice to say, we won't boast of the encounter among our finer moments, Zeyus and I. I expected we'd wind up dead when Faehr-Dun gained the upper hand. The predictable dignity of dying didn't come to pass. If the Jurisdiction had plans other than an abrupt end to us, I tended to think an old-fashioned 'offing' was the preferred option.

The fiend trussed me to a branch like a pig on a spit. He did the same to the Major using a spool of steel cable attached to his belt for the purpose. I decided humanity was no longer inhabiting his shell of a body. I took stock of my numerous injuries, as well as the blood dribbling from my winged companion. Zeyus was unconscious from the fight, which I imagine was for the best. Faehr-Dun took hold of the branches and began the march to Atlantium.

"I wanna thank you, boys," he said with a smile. His breath smelled like burning paint thinner in a closed shed.

"I haven't had that much fun since last weekend," the Fallen Angel laughed.

"Had company for brunch."

{~}

We sought a Jurisdiction building near Atlantium, but I didn't recognize the site. I sensed the hidden bunker was a place of reverence. A narrow doorway and a pair of shoddy embrasures were barely visible from the outside where we stood. I wondered with a pang if I'd ever return to my own underground hideaway.

Beyond the metal door, the interior was occupied by stale air and darkness. Faehr-Dun placed us on the floor, and I heard the clacking of breakers being flipped. Miniature flames danced in front of the Fallen Angel to illuminate what he was looking for, but I was tired of craning my neck around, and I didn't see anything. He made a grunt when the place stayed dark, as if he was disappointed but he expected as much. Faehr-Dun wandered away in the depths of the foreign structure, and I was left in total darkness with the Major.

"You awake, buddy?" I asked Zeyus.

"Mmmf," came the reply. "You know he's gonna eat us now, right?"

"I believe another element may be at play. If we're to be dinner, why bother bringing us here?"

Zeyus pushed an irritated sigh in my direction.

"I dunno, Lucy. Maybe he keeps his favorite dining set in storage."

If this was going to be my end, I planned to enjoy every last second with this particular man, and I chuckled at him. I didn't exactly have anyone else around to die with, and it was no secret that I favored Major Zeyus.

"Nobody's ever called me 'Lucy' before," I told him.

"Yeah, well. Glad you got to fortify your bucket list before we become a two-course delicacy."

Distant creaks and groans in the underground outpost caught our attention, and we were silent as we listened to Faehr-Dun's footsteps returning. I assumed he'd activated a terminal inside the installation, and he proceeded to throw a switch near my feet. Lights came on all around. Fixtures flickered or sparked and failed from disuse. A dimness remained, but the room was in view, or what was left of the room, anyway.

Clearly a conflict had taken place inside the outpost. The chamber resembled a command center, but the rows of computer terminals where personnel had presumably been seated were battered or blasted to junk, and the surface of the main screen on the wall was riddled with bullet holes. Bony corpses were piled to the side, dressed in uniforms I didn't recognize. In spite of the mess, a thick steel safe along the wall looked newer than the rest of the furnishings. An industrial-looking throw-switch was attached to the side. Faehr-Dun shoved the handle against the contacts.

Despite apparent damage, the screen came to life. Light streamed across the dusty command center in gleaming rays where bullets had punctured. The backlit rectangle was as tall as Faehr-Dun, and after a moment of color fluctuations, a face appeared. The face was flawless. The eyes and nose and mouth were totally and unflinchingly symmetrical. The appearance was attractive, in a bald and featureless sort of way. The eyes were staring ahead, and the lips moved with uniform precision as a voice spoke though the room. Like the face, the sound was pleasant, austere, and devoid of identifying characteristics.

"Jurisdiction status: active. Planet optimization in progress." The floating face on the screen turned towards Faehr-Dun, blinking twice, unnaturally sluggish blinks which reminded me of a marionette.

"Greetings, Operative 51C. Present data for analysis."

I had a horrible suspicion about what I was witnessing. Even the Fallen Angel seemed tongue-tied. He cleared his throat.

"These two are solid mages." Faehr-Dun pointed. "Candidates for Conversion."

I mumbled to Zeyus. "I converted once, it wasn't so bad. I wonder if we'll end up Episcopalian this time."

The Fallen Angel was already slicing away the cables binding me to the wood. Zeyus sat up, looking at the face on the screen with significant trepidation.

My memory is fuzzy. I know we were standing in spite of our injuries. My limbs, my eyes, my entire body was no longer mine to command. My subconscious mind began to panic when I realized I didn't have control. The Sovereign was the authority. The pleasant voice crooned inside my head.

"Greetings, Convert 87A. Greetings, Convert 94B. Present data for analysis."

Chapter 25
Raspho tells of: "Dueling Mages"

"I'm not sure my stories will ever end. Or perhaps they already did. Am I dreaming right now? Are these real words I'm carelessly committing to paper?" -The Sorcerer Prodigy

I woke up. I was unsure if this was a positive development.

I was in a place unlike places I'd woken up in before. The room was manufactured in a way I didn't recognize. Never in my life had I witnessed such clean white tiles so uniform in shape and so perfectly placed, or felt such precisely machined stainless steel as made up the rails along the mattress cushioning my backside. The sheets were exceptionally thin and soft. I could feel the finely threaded bandages on the left side of my abdomen. Nothing about my body hurt enough to complain at me immediately. I attempted to gauge my own grogginess, and I wondered if any drugs were involved. My right hand explored across my stomach towards my left forearm, where a plastic tube was attached to my skin. My scattered wits managed to repress a panicked reflex as I reasoned that the device was probably a medical treatment. The Battle of the Downed Dragon had been a heinous atrocity.

I lay and contemplated the dark path I'd wandered down. Gore was becoming a source of trauma. I'd seen too much of it on the battlefield, and at my own hands, even. The mage in me felt coated in blood. I struggled under the throes of depression that assaulted me in the wake of the bullets piercing my body. The memories wouldn't let me be at peace. I wept and perpetuated my own bleary state. I let the tranquility of the room cradle me. I couldn't say what dissuaded me from sleeping for a minor eternity. Whatever energy I had remaining was consumed by repairing bullet wounds and grief, and yet I didn't want to slip back to blackness until I discovered where I was.

Apart from the tube in my arm, I wasn't restrained, but I didn't feel like moving, either. I moaned my apathy and mild discomfort aloud and looked around the room with great determination. The medical facility was spacious and featured a barred window behind my head, but the walls were unflinchingly bland, and the effect made my stomach turn. Too much flawless white tile everywhere, I decided. The wall held a steel door with a face-sized window. From the angle of my bed, I couldn't see anything other than painted gray. I decided I wanted to peer beyond my domain in earnest. I gathered my wits and began to test my limbs.

Nausea assailed me. Climbing from the bed was going to be a process. My suspicions were solidifying despite whatever drugs were in my system. Given the set of circumstances, I could only theorize that I'd be captured by Jurisdiction forces. I was certain if I sketched diagram of the facts, I'd guide myself to an identical conclusion. No other hypothesis would bring me to this alien place. I was confounded by the Jurisdiction's efforts at keeping me alive. Maybe I was facing torture. The prospects should've frightened me, but a dripping liquid next to my bed was attached to the tube in my arm. My focus on empirical data was fuzzy, at best. I scowled and made a grunt as my bare foot touched the cold tile.

{~}

The door swung away abruptly, and I looked up. A man with silver hair entered the room. His fine robe and medallion reminded me of wealthy merchants I'd seen during festivals as a boy. Those foreigners had traded in jewelry and perfume and expensive fabrics. I realized with a jolt I was witnessing the Jurisdiction Nobility on vacation among the primitive heathens.

"I bid you pleasant morning, young Sir," the robed man said. I opened my mouth to reply, but my face didn't formulate the words.

"You've been granted the honor of a meeting. My time is precious, and you'd be wise to accept. My title and my name are known. In fact, I'm the Noble Executor of this fair city, Executor Magnare Fleuro, to be precise. I was informed you're Kilnborn, by lineage. A Noble line. Free-spirited, you see. Although by way of introduction, you must enlighten me as to your first name."

I stared at the Jurisdiction Executor with his silver hair. This was it, I realized. This was what a real enemy looked like. This was a Nobility fire mage, the same kind who wanted me dead. The Jurisdiction killed my entire family, and now a person to blame was standing here next to me introducing himself. Despite the rage starting to boil inside, I couldn't see a reason to withhold the basic fact of my first name.

"Raspho Kilnborn," I said in a tone of voice that was as dead as my former relatives.

The way the Executor sniffed in response told me he'd identified my animosity, like a fox waiting at the back door of a rabbit warren.

"I imagine you're upset about the past, Raspho. Anyone in your shoes has every right to be simply, well, over the moon. However, the Jurisdiction is vastly more complicated than you might imagine."

He began to pace methodically by the foot of my bed as he spoke in careful sentences, keeping his eyes angled towards my face.

"Not only did I refrain from killing your family, my boy, I'd like you to be my Protege, Sir Raspho. You and I, we're naturally suited for Noble work. The arcane arts I could teach you, Kilnborn! Subjects and techniques no other mage has mastered."

He grew tense, as if the awkwardness of my personal tragedy was an obstacle to be navigated with tangible finesse.

"As for your family, I know those among the Nobility who are hard-set against the idea of allowing foreign mages to align with the Noble cause of Jurisdiction. Regrettably, these families hold sway with the Devisors. Together a number of political operatives did conspire and commit the grave offenses against you. I spent Suns at the records console, and gleaned the identity of the person who ordered an Operation for the Swarm to attack your family's farm."

He tapped on the steel door. The entry opened by unseen mechanism, and a wheelchair rolled across the tile bearing the Executor's captive.

The man's arms, legs and torso were bound to the chair. Only the wheels of the chair were free from the strips of white cloth. A gag was wrapped around the bottom part of the man's face, and his panicked eyes and thinning hair were his only distinguishing features. He made noises of protest ranging from whimpers to muted yells, but the Executor ignored him.

The sight of the helpless man was a shock, and I sat up and pushed my legs over the edge of the bed. My head spun, and I hadn't determined the extent of my injuries beneath the bandages, but my adrenaline assisted my efforts at alertness. Executor Fleuro pushed the wheelchair in front of me. When the captive was positioned to his satisfaction, he reached in his robe and drew out a steel dagger. The Nobility fire mage gracefully offered me the handle with an open palm.

"Go ahead," Executor Fleuro was encouraging. "Take your vengeance, Noble Kilnborn. You certainly deserve it."

I felt sick to my stomach. My wounds burned and my body and my mind attempted to judge their own viability. Too soon, Magnare Fleuro, I thought. You've overplayed your hand. No way was I going to stab someone on the say-so of an admitted member of the Jurisdiction Nobility without a reason to trust them. I shook my head and frowned, refusing the dagger.

"Justice," the Executor said. He stabbed the man in the chest with a casual gesture, as if he was returning a book to a shelf. I watched the blood soak through the cloth bindings in horror. Executor Fleuro continued to speak to me as if nothing were amiss.

"He was guilty, you know. Badly guilty. I hope your hesitation was a product of Noble mercy rather than weakness or foolishness. No matter," he pulled the dagger free and wiped the blade clean on a fresh white towel. "You aren't properly trained. Ours world is a troubled place, Kilnborn. I imagine you're learning that's the truth. I could let you run along and try to live your life, boy. But if I did, I wouldn't be able to prevent the Devisors like this man from killing you, eventually. And I wouldn't want to see that happen. I really wouldn't."

Executor Fleuro smoothed his robe and cracked his neck as he dared me to believe him.

"Due to my concern for your safety, as well as my respect for your talents, I'm taking you under my wing as Protege. As a renegade mage in the Wilds, the Nobility and the Devisors would be a threat to you and anyone you care about. As the First Protege of the Executor, on the other hand–" he raised his eyebrows in suggestion.

I was feeling dizzy. A wave of the sensation had struck me intensely. I dragged my eyes away from the dead man in the chair, but I couldn't bring myself to meet Magnare's gaze or that smile.

"Could I have a glass of water, please?" I asked.

Magnare nodded, feigning amiable hospitality. "Of course, Noble Kilnborn. I'll send your nurses right away. Nice ladies like these happen to be exceptionally attentive. They'll see to your every whim." He winked, but I pretended not to notice. He made a gesture with his hand, and the wheelchair holding the corpse of his victim rolled back through the door of the room. The Nobility fire mage performed a dignified bow and left me to war with myself in the Jurisdiction hospital bed.

{~}

I lay my head down on the pillow to cushion my thoughts. What an abysmal mess you've found yourself in, Raspho, I thought. In the corner of the room, a glass eye kept silent watch over my bed. I knew the Jurisdiction had me in its clutches. I had no way of knowing if Charlie or the Wise Witch were even alive. I had no way of knowing if anyone was alive, except me. I looked at the bandages on my side. Was being alive even the best option?

I fought back panic, but the liquid next to my bed was dripping again. I reached across my body for the tube in my arm, but I was too late, or perhaps I was right on time. My vision began to blur, and I guess I forgot what I'd been so unhappy about the moment before.

I laughed when the trio of nurses entered the room. Their perfect hair and their white uniforms and their painted faces were suddenly amusing to me. The ladies strutted and tittered and called me 'Young Master Kilnborn.' I grinned at them and drooled on myself. Fake nurses, a fake Nobility fire mage, a fake room. Ah, what the hell, I thought. Naps were always nice.

{~}

When I awoke again, I was in a real bed in a different room. I was drowsy and still bandaged, but I sat up. The room was eerily uniform, just as the hospital had been, but the walls were painted off-white instead of tile. Below my bed, maroon carpet covered the floor. A window to the courtyard was set in the wall. I was several stories above the ground, and I took in the view of Atlantium for the first time. I'd never seen a Jurisdiction city before, and I had nothing to compare it to except the City of Old and the lifeless ruins. Needless to say, the ambition and the scale of the technologically advanced architecture was a sight to behold. My fingers itched to sketch a diagram, but I was saved from the thought by a knock at the door.

When I grasped the handle and turned, Executor Fleuro was standing there..

"I hope these quarters are acceptable," he was saying to me as I froze and stared at his robe. "Come to my office so that we can chat."

He left me no time to prepare. I gathered he intended me to follow him, so I swallowed and began to walk. I felt rushed and uncoordinated as the tall man strode rigidly ahead of me. The medical garb I was wearing was flimsy and misshapen, and although there were few people present in the hallway, I felt nearly naked compared to their pristine uniforms and Jurisdiction finery. By the time we reached the elevator, I was glad to be concealed from unkind glances in the foreign building.

The Executor's office was a pleasant solitude when we first entered, and I relaxed fractionally. The windows offered a unique and interesting view. A spread of rich foods and beverages was laid across a table. I looked at the Executor, and he gestured towards the items giving me tacit permission. I poured myself spiced tea and placed a piece of cheese and a pair of pastries on plate. Executor Fleuro seated himself behind his desk. I chose a chair across from him to consume my breakfast. A picture frame rested on the surface of his desk. Seated in the picture was the Executor himself and a teenage girl with black hair. A croissant slid from my plate and rolled awkwardly across the stone floor.

The Executor raised his silver eyebrows. "Do you recognize my daughter?"

My mouth was empty, but I swallowed anyway. I studied the picture and my mind raced. That was definitely her, wasn't it? I was looking at the girl from the Witch village who was floating through the trees, and she was looking back at me from the photograph as she attempted a fake smile next to the Executor. Was this a trick?

"I- I'm not sure," I managed to stammer.

The Executor shook his head and I could sense danger in the gesture.

"An insufficient response. Why don't you take a seat, Kilnborn."

I swallowed again and found my resolve. I did as Executor Fleuro said, sitting on the edge of the chair. I took a sip of tea to gather my thoughts.

"I can't be certain," I replied, finding an even tone. "I saw a young woman resembling her in the Wilds. The place was far away, over a fortnight ago. I have nothing to hide, Executor, Sir, but I doubt I could find my way back there from here."

Fire surged in Executor Fleuro's eyes as he smirked back at me.

"Don't underestimate yourself, novitiate. I know some effective cures for forgetfulness. And I certainly know cures for hiding things from me." The fire flickered, and he continued. "But never you mind, Raspho. The girl isn't important. I've told you I'll be your teacher, and I'm going to teach you."

I ate the pastry remaining on my plate. My Jurisdiction captor was already resorting to threats, but at least he made the attempt to soften them. I attempted to appear compliant, which seemed a logical course.

"Tell you what," the Executor said. His smile was sleazy as he shoved the expression on his face. "This is a big change for you, Ras. Can I call you Ras? No need to rush things. Let's go celebrate. We'll see a show, a sporting event." He held up a bony finger as if he'd spontaneously arrived at the idea. "I know just the ticket, an inspiring start to your lessons."

The Executor dismissed me to my quarters. I couldn't accompany him to a social event wearing a hospital gown. I was assured that a Protege robe would be waiting. Sure enough, the browns and greys and burnt sienna of a young Nobility mage lay on my bed. I frowned as I studied my bandages. I was seething with anger inside, but venting it was impossible. I didn't want a lapse in judgement to jeopardize my tenuous position. I took a breath and pulled the robe down over my head.

I adjusted the sash at my waist. A full-length mirror had been placed in the room for my use, a grander mirror than I'd ever seen. As I studied my own reflection, an object caught my eye in the corner of the mirror.

I was certain the wooden carving wasn't in the room when I'd first arrived. I turned away from the mirror to look directly, and my wooden tear-drop greeted me. I placed my hands on the chiseled surface and tried to keep breathing. Control yourself, Raspho, I thought. If I became a fiery disaster, the Jurisdiction would have me. I pulled away from the wood of the tear-drop, but my hands left scorched prints behind. I wiped my eyes with the flowing sleeves of my new robe.

I made my way through the Jurisdiction building to the Executor's office disguised as a Nobility mage. I knocked and heard the door unlatch, but the Executor remained seated behind his desk across the room. He was distracted by his holographic screen and he completely ignored my presence. I approached cautiously, intending to sit and wait for him to respond to me. My eyes went inadvertently to the photograph on his desk. I drew a sharp intake of breath when I realized the girl was gone. Only the Executor remained in the photograph. I asked the question before I could ponder the wisdom in it.

"The picture- the girl-"

I didn't complete the sentence before the Executor gave me a sideways glance. He interrupted me without a trace of humor

"What girl?"

I nearly stammered an incredulous response before thinking better of the admission. Continuing to insist on the delicate topic was a futile and dangerous path.

I was recovering from the missing girl when Executor Fleuro led me from his office. Was my imagination playing tricks on me? Was the Jurisdiction playing tricks on me? The man didn't have my best interests at heart, I had no doubt about that. Had I hallucinated? I tried to recall details about her and I swallowed. Her beauty was breathtaking, but Executor Fleuro frightened me. I didn't feel comfortable announcing to him how I might be losing my mind. I stayed quiet as we walked through the Jurisdiction hallways.

The polished sepia marble of the floors under our shoes was grandiose, as was the ambitious scale of the carved pillars surrounding us. I'd never witnessed modernized construction, and as much as I hated the Jurisdiction, I sketched a diagram in my mind when we reached the main concourse. Nobility fire mages and gray-coated the Devisors were in abundance in the central gathering area of Atlantium. Panes of angled glass were arrayed overhead, and sunlight streamed into the spacious forum. The Executor introduced me to several Nobility who devoured me with hungry eyes, and I kept my replies as brief as possible.

From the main forum we continued alongside the others around us. We entered an adjacent structure which was undoubtedly an amphitheater. Like the main concourse, the chamber boasted impressively high ceilings and marble floors. The center of the room was dominated by a marble ellipsis which served as a spacious platform for the ostentatious costume of the Master of Ceremonies.

A massive obelisk loomed over the end of the platform, reaching reached nearly to the ceiling. Cracks in the obelisk were glowing an ominous red, unwavering, unflinchingly uniform. Executor Fleuro led me to a place of honor among the cushioned chairs in the spectator area. The proceedings were beginning.

"Welcome, Noble Sirs and Madams. This Sun we have a challenge unlike any other. Undefeated contestants! A battle of primal wills! Who will climb the ranks and take the prize? Who will impress the Sovereign? Will they awake the sacred obelisk with their power?" The announcer was dressed in the grey of the Devisors, but his coat was embroidered with purple accents. Countless lights made him visually striking. His hair was molded in golden scales, and his smile was hungry. He danced casually to the robotic music pumping through the amphitheater. The assembling crowd chanted a phrase I didn't understand. The suave Devisor continued.

"The purest contest, folks. No teammates, no weapons. No mercy. A duel as it was meant to be. The only rule is that you have to win!" The crowd erupted with shouting and applause when the announcer finished his statement. I frowned as he introduced the mages. I wasn't comfortable with the direction this scene was going.

The mages on the floor of the amphitheater wore stylized versions of Nobility robes. The man and the woman looked to be a few Rounds older than me, and both had pale hair. The contestants waved to the crowd and began elaborate posturing, which left me attempting to suppress a giggle. The Executor gave me a look.

"Are you paying attention?" he asked. The question was ominous enough to stifle my mirth. When enough body language and color commentary had transpired, the contest began. I felt the force fields go up around the dueling platform, and not a moment too soon.

Fireballs rocketed around the amphitheater. The mages flung orbs of flame at each other mercilessly while simultaneously deflecting the attacks aimed at them. The fireballs careened away and against the waiting force field which protected the onlookers. The woman changed her tactics, scoring a series of hits with fast attacks which burned marks on the front of the man's robe. He roared with pain and conjured a flaming sphere bigger than any fire I'd ever witnessed. He swung the conjured attack like an orange wrecking ball. She tumbled to the side, but the fiery attack spread outward when it hit the marble floor, and the flame scorched the fabric of the shoes she was wearing. She grunted, but I sensed she far from conceding. From the roar of the crowd, I gathered that scorching your opponent's clothing was the objective of the sport.

Executor Fleuro hollered in appreciation. He was wearing a smile more genuine than any I'd seen in the Suns since I met him. For a moment, he reminded me of a farmer from my childhood enjoying a game of Bases. He caught me looking at him, and his joy immediately reverted to a knowing frown. I tried to keep my eyes forward even though I wasn't sure if I wanted to see the mage duel.

The man and the woman were sweating profusely, and breathing laboriously. Wide torches shot from their palms, and they pushed at each other with the flames.

"Ah. The crowd loves a good tug of war," the Executor intoned. "Not a very efficient tactic, I'm afraid. Are you listening?"

"Hmm?" I responded. I hadn't been listening. The flames were hypnotic, and the crowd noise was deafening. The Executor sighed in disgust. I knew I'd hear it about my inattentiveness later.

The duelist man could conjure more extensive quantities of fire, but the woman was faster at maneuvering. She got him with bursts he wasn't ready to block. He fell to the floor before the bell rang. A pair of Devisors moved to take his charred body away on a stretcher. My heart sank, but Executor Fleuro made a 'tsk'-ing sound.

"His shielding wasn't completely useless. He'll probably live."

I knew my face was pale, but I nodded and rose from my seat. The Executor stood with aplomb before putting his hand on my shoulder and guiding me to the exit of the dueling amphitheater.

When we re-entered the main concourse, the noise of the crowd was left behind, and he spoke to me again.

"I used to be champion, you know."

I didn't know. I also had no idea what to say, so I raised my eyebrows at him.

"Ten Rounds in a row," he continued. "They put an eligibility limitation in the contests because of me. You can see how I became Executor." I don't know what he expected from me. I tried to look impressed as I gave an empty nod. His self-distracted smile and his passion for mage duels filled me with dread.

"In the time of my retirement from the amphitheater, they've had nothing except middling piss-ants trying to make a name. The Nobility always want to rise, just as I did. But those Enforcers you saw, they aren't true duelists. I dare say, nobody in this generation has any talent to speak of. Until I found you, Noble Kilnborn."

I stopped walking. For a split second, I'd had enough of this charade. I forgot my tactics and I forgot my fears. I asked the Executor what was on my mind. He seemed eager to respond to my change in disposition as I allowed heat to enter my words.

"Why would you train your enemy? I don't even know how many Regiment soldiers I killed in that battle. It was horrible. Aren't people in the Jurisdiction gonna want payback? Won't I be arrested or put on trial?"

The Executor laughed at me, but I didn't feel any better.

"I would kill a thousand Regiment idiots myself," he began, "if it meant having you as Protege, Raspho. No trouble, provided you prove yourself a willing student." He cocked his eyebrows at me. We knew the threat beneath his words, but he plastered the truth with pleasantries for the time being. I swallowed and nodded.
{~}

The following morning we were scheduled to depart from the city of Atlantium. Our destination was the Executor's private estate beyond the city limits.

Executor Fleuro waited for me at the door to my chamber. I'd been instructed to bring nothing except my Protege robe, but I had no other belongings. I knew better than to inquire about what happened to the Keenwood Staff. We began walking after only a nod of greeting.

"You'll be with me each Sun. Yen-thirty until two-thiry, no exceptions. We'll travel to my estate for training purposes. Laurelei will prepare accomodations when we arrive. Have you ever ridden a Pegasaur Drake?"

"A what?" I asked him uselessly. A set of doors opened up in front of us at the end of the hall. On the landing platform beyond, a sky-blue dragon was sunning himself. He opened a curious eye towards me, and I must have been visibly shaken at the sight of the creature because the Executor didn't hesitate to place his hand on my shoulder as he proceeded forward to the Pegasaur Drake. I gaped at the sweep of wings and the scaled body we were about to board. I was attempting to imagine the livestock required to feed the Executor's pet when he motioned impatiently towards the front saddle. The seat was covered in a waterproof cushion, and I strapped myself in according to the Executor's instructions. He took the rear seat, a couple meters behind me, behind where the drake's wings met the shimmering body.

"His name is Oh-Four-Three," the Executor said. I sensed a distinct lack of compassion for the magnificent animal. His tone of voice was better suited to speaking about a machine rather than a living being, and the numerical identifier reinforced the impression. The Pegasaur Drake turned his head back to look at us. He had a curious energy in his eyes that reminded me of a puppy, but when he saw the Executor, I noticed a subtle melancholy beyond a puppy's years. When the fire mage Fleuro grumbled in displeasure, Oh-Four-Three flinched and shook beneath us.

"Oh-Four-Three?" the Pegasaur Drake surprised me. He spoke his own name posed as a question.

Executor Fleuro made a dismissive gesture with his hand, and I could feel Oh-Four-Three crouch and tense his body. We rose from the earth in pulses, and I took note of how steady the Pegasaur Drake was. My eyes bulged as I watched the building recede beneath us.

"You can feel it, can't you?" The Executor said as he watched me.

I frowned, steadying myself on the saddle's arm-rests, and I turned my head. "Feels like we're flying."

The Executor returned my frown, and I immediately regretted frowning to begin with. I turned forward again, and the expression struck me in the back of the head.

"That seems obvious, so don't waste my time talking about it. I can't afford to be a moron, sadly. What else do you feel from the animal?"

My eyes lit up, I imagine. 'He's like the Mammoth the Rose tribe uses,' I almost blurted, but I caught myself lest I betray my allies.

"A steel reactor," I said. "Next to his-" I swallowed. "Next to his heart. I feel it, Sir. The Drake must be powerful."

Executor Fleuro nodded. His eyes lit up too. I didn't like the connection. I told myself I shouldn't light up my eyes anymore.

"A micro-fusion reactor," the Executor clarified. "When it comes to the biosciences, the Devisors recently opened a whole new world of possibilities. Not to mention the next generation of Quints. The Pegasaur Drakes are gaining popularity among the Nobility, but the Devisors think the creatures are inefficient compared to automated hardware. I'm telling you military secrets, Raspho, but you should know. I want you to fully understand the futility of resisting the Jurisdiction. However, if you prove yourself among the Nobility," I returned his eye contact. "You could hold sway here."

I nodded to his words, and I didn't have to fake it. The idea was something to consider. Would joining the Nobility allow me to find justice for my family? Could I make the Jurisdiction less monstrous if I were on the inside?

I was still pondering when an imposing stone mansion appeared among the trees. I knew immediately who the owner of the building was.

"Oh-Four-Three!" our mount announced. The Pegasaur Drake touched the ground with a gentle jolt, rebuking my tumbling thoughts and punctuating the Executor's silence. A ramp opened from the Pegasaur's elaborate saddle, and we rose from our seats.

The front steps of the building were a few paces away. I found the shape of the edifice to be unwelcoming, and the woman standing by the front door didn't help matters. She kept her arms crossed, a frown firmly planted on her face. Her dark hair was laced with gray and slung in a bun, and she wore the practical smock of a servant, but she carried no deference in her demeanor. With her left hand, she led a goat on a length of rope. Just as was beginning to wonder who was greeting us so icily, the Executor cleared his throat.

"Hello, Laurelei," he said.

The curtsy Laurelei returned us was stiff enough that I thought I might cringe. I remembered him saying this was the woman who would prepare accomodations for us. Studying her now, I wondered if she was going to poison us. The tall Executor in his flowing robes strolled past me, and I knew beyond a doubt that the man had considered duplicity. Whether it was Laurelei's life or another, Executor Fleuro held leverage. This woman was the Executor's Slave, but her face spoke plainly of her objections. I wondered if this was the direction I was headed.

As I passed Laurelei, I tried to give her a kindly nod as we watched Oh-Four-Three and the goat. I think she may have picked up on my sympathy, but she shot me a look which said sympathy and kindly nods were unwelcome under the whims of the Executor. The Pegasaur Drake nuzzled the goat affectionately before he grasped the creature in his jaws and gingerly broke his dinner's neck.

"A softie, this one," Laurelei explained as she stepped forward and placed a hand on Oh-Four-Three's shoulder. The Drake ate the goat with impeccable manners. The woman searched my face openly, as if to make up for the hard look she'd given me. She gestured with her head towards the front door, and we headed inside before we faced the Executor's displeasure.

The inside of the Executor's mansion held a full-scale replica of the dueling platform I'd witnessed in Atlantium. Laurelei wasn't smiling, but I sensed she refrained from open disdain in the Executor's presence due to self-preservation. She opted instead for a muted scowl.

As a serving woman, she stood next to an ornate sideboard and poured tea while we toured the practice amphitheater. The

Executor indicated the lack of force field or seats for spectators. My heart rate began to increase as I sipped my tea, and I thought about how the hell I was gonna survive this asshole.

I don't think I'd pieced together my entire strategy over cups of tea, but I did learn how to duel afterward. I had to. When a fireball is sent in your direction, you don't have time to consider what to do. You have to react, and you have to fight back. You have to do anything other than burn, although burn I did, many times over. My robe offered a measure of protection from flame, and Jurisdiction medical treatments were nothing short of miraculous, but Executor Fleuro was sadistic. He showed no concern for the pains of my body. My mind was holding the mage skill he coveted, and he wanted nothing more than to coax my power forth and bring it under his control. Sun after Sun we threw fireballs at each other in the stone practice room, until the whoosh of fire echoed in my dreams. When the task before him was shaping me as a mage, the Executor was a motivational teacher. My rage over the death of my family and my naive inexperience were fuel for the budding Nobility loyalist he hoped to create.

Laurelei arranged gourmet sandwiches for us on the sideboard. I never knew if she'd chosen the recipes or if the Executor had dictated the menu. In either case, the food was a variety I'd never experienced, and without a trace of poison.

Executor Fleuro was a virtuoso. He could manipulate fire precisely as he created breathtaking displays of red and orange. His conjured flames were tightly controlled and fed with steady continuity. Complex spirals and scattering geometric patterns were only his warm-up exercises. If the man had decided to be an artist instead of a power-hungry autocrat, he could've saved everyone a lot of hassle. I suppressed thoughts like this with a half grin whenever Magnare really got going.

{~}

I settled in a routine as the Suns ticked past. Neither Laurelei nor the Executor spoke to me beyond our prescribed time together, and loneliness often gnawed at me, but the privacy of my relatively pleasant quarters was becoming a familiar retreat. The books the Executor provided for me occupied my evenings. I studied the Jurisdiction and the history of mages. The bulk of the information was clearly propaganda which flattered the Jurisdiction, but truth could be gleaned from the spin.

For example, I discovered that nearly the entirety of the Nobility were essentially the progeny of the Wise Witch herself. She was the Mage Subject Double-Oh-One, a millennia ago, Ms. Jae'lin Fleuro. Her DNA held the components for mages, and the Jurisdiction Nobility stored and copied and used the code for centuries in order to produce all the mages they wanted. A few of the Nobility, like the Executor, even took the last name 'Fleuro' as a matter of convention, having themselves been born from the womb of a surrogate with no parents other than the Nobility and the Devisors. The name 'Fleuro' didn't even belong to the Witch, originally. It was her first husband's last name. I wondered if the man or the Fleuros before him had ever known what a legacy would be attached to it via their widowed daughter in-law.

When I learned of the Prize Mates, I spent several Suns trying to deduce whether or not Laurelei was a Prize Mate herself. She was certainly beautiful, but her tendency towards frowning and the shape of her face didn't match the descriptions of Prize Mates given in the official texts. I eventually gave up on speculation. I could conceive of no polite way to ask either Laurelei or the Executor about the nature of their relationship.

{~}

The Sun was wash-Sun again. I was wearing the extra robe the automated Jurisdiction clothing service provided. Whenever I returned from the Executor's estate I'd find a waist-high cart with a plastic bin in the corner of my quarters which held a modest selection of the clothes I required. I scrutinized the laundry cart when the device first appeared. I saw no handles anywhere, and I couldn't seem to make the wheels roll if I pushed against it. I remembered the dead man in the wheelchair, and I shuddered. The cart didn't need handles. The un-Guardly power of the Jurisdiction was more than enough.

I thrust my sweat stained practice robes in the laundry chute. I doubted Executor Fleuro paid any attention to the management of my wardrobe. He probably told the system that he didn't want me to be naked and that I needed practice robes. I was content enough where my Jurisdiction apparel was concerned. Fashion statements were the least of my worries.

I remember it was wash-Sun because I remember the whole Sun. Those twenty-four Marks might've been the most pivotal in my entire life, though I wasn't actively involved in the pivot. I recall I spent the first half of that wash-Sun in ignorance, and the remainder bleeding profusely.

Everything started in the practice amphitheater as usual. Actually, everything started with wash-Sun, but my mind drifts towards the real action. Executor Fleuro had a gleam in his eye that wash-Sun morning, and he wasn't fooling around when he flung fire. I matched him at his game, redirecting the blazes and adding my own. I moved the chess pieces where I could make them go. My final lesson with the Executor went swimmingly until the knife appeared.

I was struck in the back of my left shoulder. The tip of the blade would've plunged through further and pierced my lung if my shielding and my robe had been absent. The blade spun free instead, clattering to the floor beside me and leaving a deep gash. I had a sense that my life was spared. The lapse in concentration caused me to falter in my mage duel with the Executor. Rampant fiery energy caught me unaware and knocked me flat against the amphitheater floor, scorching the hair from my arms and face. I grunted and tried to remain conscious, reaching with my right arm towards the odd knife lying next to me. When I twisted my torso, I roared in pain, but adrenaline sustained the motion. I looked for the hidden assassin who'd attacked me during dueling practice.

I didn't find him, but the imaginary young woman floated there, the girl from the woods by the Witch village, the girl from the photo on the Executor's desk. I shook my head.

"Shit," I muttered, looking at her. "Fine time to be seeing things." I studied her face, as breathtaking as I remembered, but she was holding a knife. I made the connection and my anger swelled inside, but the imaginary girl wasn't even paying attention. Had I done this to myself? I looked at the blood on my fingers and then followed the concern in her gaze towards the Executor.

My first thought was that the man had driven himself insane. He battled an unseen enemy, blasting fire in every direction. I nearly laughed as I thought about the Enforcers locking up their Executor in a Jurisdiction cell. As the dark-haired air mage watched, however, I began to realize she could actually see a figure fighting back. Ripples in the air around the Executor weren't the product of heat. As the horror of the situation began to set in, the unseen force grabbed the Executor, pinning his arms and legs, limiting his ability to strike with mage fire. A figure in a brown dress sprinted from the doorway and onto to the practice platform.

Laurelei wasted no time stabbing Executor Fleuro in the chest. The floating air mage beside me made an audible gasp. The serving woman pulled the kitchen knife from the Executor's chest and stabbed him again force and finality, knocking the fire mage to his back. Silver hair struck the floor with an ugly thwack.

Slowly, I told myself. I could feel the energy. The unseen assailant materialized as if I was hallucinating a nightmare. An ethereal woman in an ornate white gown stood beside Magnare's corpse. I looked around, my mouth agape as the blood began to soak the left side of my robe. My knee smeared red across the marble in a wide swath. I was surrounded by unknown entities, and the moment terrified me as much as it thrilled me. The Executor was dead, and these women were not exactly the Executor's friends. I doubted they were even part of the Jurisdiction. I swallowed when I realized I should speak on my own behalf.

"I'm not a part of the Jurisdiction. Please don't kill me."

The ghostly woman laughed disdainfully. Her malevolence and the unearthly sound of her voice were shocking.

"You were inside the Executor's estate, training with the Executor himself, in his personal practice space. Doesn't get much more Jurisdiction than that, sweetheart. I bet you Nobility cowards always toss loyalty and honor in the shitter in favor of self-preservation any time you get captured. A'Rehia here didn't have the heart to finish you. Killing you isn't personal, kid. Basically standard procedure."

The ghost almost ended my story, and with her chain of reasoning, I don't know if I could've held it against her. She gathered the air energy which would destroy my body and send me to rest with my family.

"Wait," Laurelei spoke. She trembled, and her hand was covered in the Executor's blood. She put her other hand to her mouth, overcome with emotion as she began to cry. The word was almost a whisper.

"Daughter," she said. The beautiful dark-haired air mage touched her feet to the floor , accepting Laurelei's embrace. A warm feeling filled my body. I wondered if I was experiencing mage-craft or a happy heart or blood loss. I missed my mother. I'd write this down eventually.

After a few tearful moments, Laurelei seemed to remember the ghost. She shook her head.

"Raspho was a captive here. The Executor wanted to use him as his duelist. I don't know where he came from, but he isn't from the Nobility, I can tell."

The ghost studied me, reshaping her eyes as piercing scopes. I gave a mirthful sniff laying on my side on the bloody floor. I was no threat to these women. I barely cared what they decided to do with me. They existed, though, these fantastic people, and the fact alone was enough to fill me with a minor euphoria to dull the pain. The imaginary girl was real enough, standing here like she hadn't descended from the heavens or my imagination. My head spun with the possibilities. The stone and the congealing blood were pleasantly cool beneath me.

I began to drift away. Laurelei and the girl and the ghost launched a calm discussion of my fate.

"Brothers and sisters, you fight for your tribe. You fight for your family and you fight for yourself. When you're fighting alongside your brethren in arms, there seems no righter place to be. But more often than not, things get mixed up on you. No easy answers out there are real ones, and the honorable high-road still has muddy ruts in the rainy seasons." -The Gunslinger Confidant

I inspected the slide-action on my remaining pistol. Its identical twin was lost during the battle. I lacked the energy to mourn the dead, let alone my equipment. Practical matters occupied my thoughts instead. My maintenance kit with its brushes and oil was among the lost supplies, so I cleaned the mechanism with a piece of my shirt. I hoped to the Guards the damn thing wouldn't jam on me again. We needed the pheasant I'd spotted earlier at the edge of the clearing. I was losing weight, and it wasn't for the benefit of my figure. Muscle needs protein, and animals need to eat.

I moved between the trees, my boots treading swiftly as my legs pushed against the earth in rhythm. My pistol coughed, and the pheasant dropped from the tree with a muted avian cry. I said a prayer of thanks for my dirty firearm and the fact that it hadn't failed us yet, but I knew the Sun was fast approaching. Even if ammunition was the only limiting factor, we were going to need support eventually. I pulled wild carrots and onions from the autumn loam nearby before I hiked across the clearing to our camp.

The obvious path led north. Chaeoh, Lohise, Rahn and myself were headed to the City of Old. We were still hundreds of kilometers from our destination, unfortunately. The paws of the titan wolves had carried us south when we decided to find the dragon. Our return trip was undertaken by an injured foursome who needed to stop and hunt due to lack of supplies. In addition to the ordinary dilemmas, I anticipated we'd be subject to any manner of opportunistic ambushes. The Jurisdiction would find a way to pursue us after the victory we'd managed to steal. As conspicuous as Chaeoh was, I had no faith the journey could be completed unmolested.

I was in a foul mood. Perhaps my disdain for the current situation warded away the bulk of the heartbreak I might've felt in the aftermath of the Battle of the Downed Dragon. I actively prevented myself from thinking about the lives that I'd lost. I didn't have the luxury of mourning if I wanted to see the mission through. I'd save my feelings for a ceremony in the City of Old, after we returned with the dragon. I didn't have the luxury of dealing with how I felt about Rahn, either. His presence had become a constant nuisance. Perhaps his intent was to distract me from darker thoughts.

I managed my intentions along the shards of this reality I could control despite my sagging morale. I saw to the corporeal needs of my three companions. As their Generale, it was my duty. I was the only daughter of none other than Sampsen Oakes. The effort I put in took its toll on me. I tightened the straps on my jacket and shivered against Lohise's belly in the autumn nights.

The concern on Rahn's face made me want to send a fist directly at his sturdy jaw-line. Whenever I snapped at him about his eyes following me around, he'd give me crap about how he'd seen people under pressure before, and how anyone in my position right now would warrant concern.

'What about Chaeoh,' I'd say to him. I didn't see his handsome hazel eyes glued to the dragon's injured ass through every waking moment. I didn't allow myself to be mollified by Rahn's patronizing or his glances. I wasn't an innkeeper's daughter who was getting the vapors over an outing in the woods. Unless the man was going to start pulling his own weight again, I preferred he keep his worried face to himself.

As the Suns dragged by, they grew perilously repetitive. We moved towards the City as much as we could. I hunted as much as I could. We ate as much as we could, and rested as much as we could. If my companions were in a competition to heal, the titan wolf Lohise was winning. The dragon was the slowest to recover from his wounds. I suspected prolonged travel might be making his injuries worse, but I knew nothing we could do other than push forward. I was hopeful Lohise would be able to help with hunting soon. Perhaps Rahn would recover enough to forage for himself by the time we reached the City.

Navigation occasionally warranted discussion. When we traveled south, Trenz had made a crude map of the journey. When I was confronted with her lifeless body on the battlefield, my grief and shock distracted me from looting her body for the scrap of paper which would've guided us home. I was becoming weary of the opinions about exactly where we were headed. I made it clear to the boys that Den Mother Lohise had the final say. Canines were attuned to the sprawling Wilds. In that nose I could trust. When the party passed break in the trees I recognized, my spirits buoyed. Only a bit farther, I told myself. Each of my remaining bullets fit in the palm of my hand. I inspected them each carefully and pushed them down into the clip.

We didn't sleep enough during those final days. We pressed on instead, knowing the destination was the only thing able to relieve the pain, hunger, and desperation we were feeling.

The morning was hazy. A fog clung stubbornly beneath the canopy of trees. We reached a ridge where the tall beams of the City of Old were visible in the distance on a clearer Sun. I stumbled over a root, and Chaeoh caught me with his good wing. I thanked him brusquely as my face flushed with red. I found a mossy rock and sat.

We made it. My heart rate was elevated, but I began to relax fractionally.

A sentry spotted us from the path ahead. Instead of hailing us, the jacketed gunfighter reined his horse in a tight circle and galloped away. I thought nothing of the maneuver, and I figured a proper welcome was in short order. Lohise tensed beside me. Her canine nostrils pulled the air, and she began to growl.

"Something isn't right," the Den Mother said. I frowned at her, unsure of what to say to her pronouncement. I looked at each of the members of the group. I made sure my pistol was ready, but the weapon was practically useless and I couldn't see much else to be done. Chaeoh was in rough shape, and Rahn wasn't recovering as fast I wanted. I knew my mind and body were at their limit. We were helpless without the Rose tribe. I grunted, peering through the mist. We approached the City.

At the bank of the river, I bore witness to a waking nightmare on the other side. A row of gunfighters stood behind a spiked barricade, pointing guns across the water at us and saying nothing. The flag of the Rose tribe hung on a wooden post at a limp angle above their heads. A scaffold beside the flag showed the unmistakable pelt of a titan wolf.

I stared at the display. Lieutenant Drak's voice arrived at my ears.

"Close enough, Miss Oakes." The Lieutenant appeared from behind the barricade. From his resplendent new armor, I realized he'd taken the mantle of Generale for his own. I studied the row of guns, and my outrage increased.

"What's the meaning of this?"

"You!" Drak barked as he strolled along the edge of the barricade. He paused after the first word. I crossed my arms. Chaeoh and Lohise and Rahn were tense at my back. None of us had been prepared for what we'd found at the edge of the City.

"You failed. Failed in your responsibilities to this tribe, Melodie Oakes. Failed over and over again. Your title of Generale became forfeit the moment you galloped off on those... beasts. Now that you've managed to get everyone killed, it appears, you return to the tribe you've wronged. And for what? Did our fine men and women simply get eaten alive by their hungry mounts? Do the titan wolves await a second feeding?"

I scowled and pointed a finger emphatically at Chaeoh. "Don't you see this fucking dragon sitting here? Don't you know what he means for us?"

Chaeoh was preparing an ill-advised demonstration. I heard him inhale. For a split second, I felt the panic of knowing that the situation was about to erupt in violence. Rahn placed a hand on the dragon's scales, and the injured lizard groaned as he quelled the frost-fire welling in his belly.

I fought the urge to shout or curse or throw my pistol. I couldn't conscience this betrayal by my tribe and my kin. I'd been relying on the idea of food and rest for so many Suns that the abrupt cancellation of plans left me numb. Rahn and Lohise tried to lead me away as I muttered obscenities, but I turned my head and stared back at the gunfighters. I wasn't finished with them yet.

"Where's Confidant Flin?" I shouted at their line. Drak didn't say anything, but his smile was worth a bucket of unsavory words. At the edge of the defensive fortification, I saw a mangled foot. The rest of the wheelchair followed. The old man's rifle lay across his lap.

"Just 'Flin,' now, girlie," his voice came to me. He cleared his throat and spoke, but his vitality was cracked and faded. "Other leg finally crapped out." Concern was written on his scarred face. I could tell that he wanted to speak, but he lowered his head, tugging down on the brim of his hat as he backed the chair away. Drak stood in front of his wheelchair as if he'd won a great victory.

"You're done, Miss Oakes. Go live with the wild animals you seem to love more than you do your own tribe."

I was at a loss for a reply. Gunfighters who looked at me sympathetically, but I doubted anyone would turn muzzle against their new Generale in order to side with the disheveled refugees across the river. Everyone had probably assumed I was dead, and even if I hadn't been, the tribe made their contingency plan clear. When Drak took over, most of them were probably hoping to avoid the hostile reunion.

I wanted to give a speech to drive home my anger and disappointment. I should've tried to make them feel the proper amount of guilt for betraying their true Generale, but the words died in my throat. I put a hand on Lohise to steady myself.

For the first time in my life, I turned my back on the Rose tribe.

{~}

We receded back to the forest and we managed to construct a crude camp, but none of us wanted to speak about what happened. The spot where we stopped was probably too close to the City for safety, but I'd lost the willpower to care. If the gunfighters of the Rose tribe decided they wanted to finish us, perhaps it was for the best. Dying had begun to sound like a lot less effort than the other options.

I heard a rumble from Lohise which denoted her aggravation.

"Our pack is lessened. Rahn will gather while I hunt, won't you, Rahn?"

The mage's battered machete had been eaten by the battlefield, but he had a decent knife I'd salvaged. I knew his torso was healing, but he nodded gravely. He rose from where he was seated with a lurch. The duo walked towards the woods to begin their foray. I was left looking at Chaeoh's sea-foam eye, and I shook my head.

"Maybe I can barter with the tribe for supplies," I reasoned.

Chaeoh's eyes surged with greens in response.

"Nothing to trade, girlie."

The use of Flin's affectionate nickname startled me. I didn't know if I liked it or not. As the dragon spoke to me in encouraging words, I found myself fighting back tears.

"Why should fox trade with rabid dog?"

I sniffed. "Not much of a fox right now, am I?" I pulled my pistol and tossed it on the ground in disgust. "The damn thing uses bullets, you know."

The dragon was closing his eyes for a nap as if conversation was boring for him. I said a prayer to the Guards for Chaeoh to recover from his injuries since we weren't traveling anymore. He was going to need a lot of meat. I sent another prayer for Lohise's luck with the hunt. When I thought the dragon had fallen asleep, he mumbled another sentence.

"Bullets, yes. Multitudes of bullets, a singular Melodie."

{~}

The loss of my tribe was devastating. I tried to avoid thinking about my people. I fastidiously looked after my meager material possessions instead. Filthy as I was, I pulled my armor off and attempted to wash everything I owned in a nearby stream, including my body. I fished a sliver of soap from my pack and stripped down despite the cold air and the frigid water. The lather was thin, and the scent of Rosean soap made me remember too many things.

I didn't feel the need to inflict modesty on myself. I sat naked on the bank of the stream by the side of the sleeping dragon. I pulled my armor jacket across my lap and found a knife, cutting away the stitches which held the embroidered sigils of the Rose to the back and chest of the garment. I almost tossed the patches in the stream, but I stuffed them in my pack instead. I hung my underclothes and armor on Chaeoh's scales to dry.

I took no pleasure in being left alone with my thoughts as I wrapped myself in a blanket next to what remained of our campfire. I poked at the embers to distract myself from what had transpired. I wished I'd let Drak die, I told myself, but there was guilt and shame attached to the thought. I wished Flin fought for my rights as Generale, but what could a lone old man have done? Perhaps he tried. His status as Confidant was gone. I doubted my question would ever be resolved. The dragon was right. My pride prevented me from stooping to Drak's mercy. But a stubborn nature was only the half of it. Forcing my return could mean waging war against my own people, a path I refused to travel. I pledged to myself I'd stay away from the Rose tribe.

{~}

Lohise returned to the camp several Marks before Rahn. The evening was stretching through the trees, and Chaeoh's scales had lost the glow of the Sun. I was in my smallclothes, still wrapped in my blanket as she approached. The footsteps in the forest woke the dragon beside the stream. I snagged my pistol from where I'd left it on the ground.

I tucked the gun away when Lohise's furry face appeared. She dropped the better part of a deer by the fire, which captured Chaeoh's attention. He looked to the titan wolf for permission to eat, but she was otherwise distracted. Lohise sat across the fire from my blanket and lifted her nose to the stars. A resonant howl took my ears by surprise. The blue dragon and I looked at each other.

Lohise's howling continued She pitched to different notes, mourning her lost pack members, but her song carried a request. This became clear as I stood and added wood to the embers of the humble fire. I retrieved my clothing from Chaeoh's scales, but the forest around us had filled with gleaming eyes. The dragon didn't appear anxious, and I didn't bother to reach for my pistol.

The remaining members of Lohise's pack rejoined their Den Mother around us in the forest. None of them were much larger than ordinary timberwolves. I wondered how Rounds they needed to grow, and what age they reached adulthood. I noticed with relief that Amika was among them. Her prosthetic leg was a bittersweet work of art, now. I sighed, knowing Amika's safety was probably the insistence of the doctors. None would stand for her execution after the time and effort spent to heal her.

Perhaps Drak was right. Perhaps I loved the wolves like I loved my own tribe. But here they were, the only thing left when my Lieutenant had betrayed me. With the titan wolf cubs nuzzling from every side, I almost felt right again for the first time since the Battle of the Downed Dragon. Chaeoh echoed my sentiment as he hummed a tranquil tune. When I'd been thoroughly sniffed, the cubs wasted no time investigating the dragon.

"Eat the deer," Lohise barked. The words pulled me from my puppy-love reveries.

"What?" I replied.

"I'm talking to the dragon," the titan wolf said. "I want to keep the pack safe. This lizard-beast can protect us, but only if he recovers. For now, he must eat."

Chaeoh raised a scaly eyebrow.

"Eat the deer," the Den Mother repeated. "Before the cubs get after it. They're looking lean, in my eyes. The moon and the hunt are lusty lovers tonight, my friends."

Rahn tells of: "The Dragon Tribe"

"After I left the Slave Pens behind me, I found I hadn't escaped the horrors of the Jurisdiction. I continued to yearn for freedom, just as I had inside the Pens. Fighting the Jurisdiction was simply the next bend in the river, and everything drifts downstream." -The Frost Swordsman

When the Rose tribe rejected us, I changed almost immediately. I don't know if my change was physical or intangible, but I know I was different.

The Wizard might say that a mage was finally awakening again when the heaviest trauma of my wounds had receded. For my part, I know the Rosean betrayal of their Generale was a trauma which added to the rest. I had no way of separating the mage in me from the emotion of it all. I had no division between the arcane and the tangible anymore, or any space in my life between the occult and the mundane.

The pain I was feeling in my torso faded to a dull throb, and the damage remaining was either a scar to live with or the knitting of flesh which could benefit from increased movement. A primal strand in my being had been plucked again, and I was resonating in places where my injury had muted the amplitude. When we I realized the safe haven for survival was no longer an option, my insides turned to ice. I know Chaeoh felt the power in my touch when I placed my palm on his scales. I never knew the dragon's respect until he'd refrained from killing the man who usurped Melodie's leadership.

Lohise could sense the difference. The nose of the titan wolf was too keen to miss the consequential shift. I think her furry ears perked when she saw the determination in my eyes. The Den Mother was testing me, and I tested myself. We needed food. The existential concept became our unspoken priority. The wolf and I could agree on rumbling bellies telling us a story as ancient as stories themselves.

"I'll trace north-west. I smell deer," the huge wolf informed me, "And I intend to feed the cubs, for certain. Do you remember the plants you've been eating?"

I nodded in acknowledgment to the wolf. Unfortunately, I'd become excessively familiar with the earthy taste of cooked roots.

"Pull as many as you can find, and look for signs of game. Once you're familiar with the area, Melodie show you how to make traps."

My face flushed with red when the titan wolf trotted away. Clearly she didn't expect me to hunt or kill an animal. She assumed I was no more capable than a child. Perhaps she was correct, but I couldn't shake the feeling that the Den Mother had underestimated me. I might not be carrying a gun or a bow or a machete, but I'd been trained by the Wizard of the Waves, hadn't I?

A squirrel danced across a branch above my head, taunting me with his chattering as if he could sense my thoughts. I felt my aura when I studied my energy in the peaceful forest. The edge of the aura was cold, and I poured my focus towards the pain. The sphere around me expanded, enveloping the mocking squirrel. He chittered faster, his breath making tiny puffs of steam. Frost crept over his fur. When I realized what I was doing, I knew I didn't want to make the creature suffer.

I roared. My raised voice filled the forest. In a rush of white, water molecules changed states and coated the trees and the underbrush. My squirrel-cicle struck the ground with dense thunk.

I was trembling, and I centered myself. I couldn't stop thinking about the faces of the frozen Jurisdiction Nobility that Chaeoh left in his wake when we met. I began to shiver after my trembling died. I was tired, hungry, wounded, but my self-satisfaction over my accomplishment began to feel like a crisp refreshment of fresh-melted snow flowing through my veins. I placed the dead squirrel in my makeshift gathering bag with a grin. The woods were quiet following my display, and I stepped carefully across crunchy leaves.

"Here squirrel-squirrel," I said, whistling towards the trees.

{~}

The creature I spotted wasn't a squirrel. He wasn't any kind of game, I was sure of it. A Regiment soldier was here, traipsing through the Wilds. He didn't bother to move carefully. I could've stayed hidden, but after a moment I decided to show myself. I could've recognized those double-chins and that big-ass crowbar anywhere.

"Captain Crowbar!" I said, stepping from behind a tree.

The towering ogre whirled around, looking in my direction. He gripped the cast iron bar with both hands. He didn't appear to have a gun which was surprising, but what surprised me even more was the fear in his eyes. When he saw who I was, relief flooded his exaggerated features.

"Good Guards, Knife. What are you doing way the hell out here? I figured you for dragon-fodder, boy." The Regiment officer shook his head. "Don't suppose you got any victuals? My rations and supplies went tits-up in the skirmish."

I probably shouldn't have offered the man anything, given who he was, but I was intensely curious about him.

"Got myself a squirrel," I replied, lifting the crude gathering bag to indicate. "What are you doing here yourself, Captain? Are your boys around?"

The Regiment soldier glanced nervously towards the trees and spat juice from the plant-drug he was chewing.

"The duty we pulled, Knife. She was a Guard-damn shit-sandwich from the get-go, a raw-deal if I ever seen one, but the whole mission took a weird turn. Even by Regiment standards." He shook his head back and forth. "Really went sideways on us, Knife."

I sensed he wasn't keen to say anything else, but I placed my gathering bag on the ground and began choosing sticks for a fire. The gesture was enough of a kindness that it kept the man talking, which was exactly what I was hoping for. The Captain sat down by my pile of sticks and held his crowbar across his lap defensively.

"I don't even know where to begin if I ever get a debriefing. Evil is runnin' amok in the Wilds these Suns. I don't think the boys are gonna make it." He was shaking his head back and forth as if the gesture was becoming a twitch he could no longer control.

"I don't think they're gonna make it, Knife."

I swallowed as I attempted to summon a passable approximation of empathy. The Captain clearly believed he had the upper hand despite his fears of what else might be in the woods. I knew my mage skill would even the odds, but the Regiment was frightening to me, in truth. Memories of killing Regiment soldiers from the back of a titan wolf came to my mind, but I hadn't seen a machete since. I struck my flint and coaxed a tiny flame.

"Tell you what, Captain," I began cautiously. The Captain raised an eyebrow. I'm not sure I'd ever spoken to him with real confidence before.

"Once we eat this squirrel, let's go find my friends. I'll see if you can join up with us."

The Captain scowled.

"I haven't survived by being dumb, Knife," he reminded me. "How do I know your friends won't off me? Regiment grunts can get treated real rude-like by zealous freedom fighters."

I shrugged, feigning indifference. A play on my part, and I figured I'd succeed.

"Only an offer. Otherwise you'll be alone with whatever you and the boys encountered."

The Captain considered this but he hadn't taken the bait yet. "YOU were alone," he said to me. "You're not afraid of anything *strange* in these Wilds?"

I shook my head. "I haven't seen anything, Captain. My friends are camped close to here. Few as we are, we could probably use the help."

The Captain continued frowning. The best lies have truth in them, but even so, I began to doubt the Regiment man would go along with my plan.

"We'll see, Knife. Just cook up your puny-ass squirrel. I bet those loafers back at the barracks are getting prime-rib tonight. Guard-less ass-munchers."

{~}

After consuming the entirety of my freshly killed squirrel, Captain Crowbar relieved himself on what remained of our cook-fire. The desultory act plunged us into a dark forest. I was acutely aware of his presence and the smell of urine-soaked embers. I led the way back to Melodie and Chaeoh. I thought of how they'd react to the Captain and I didn't like his odds. My mind raced as we crept through the trees.

Our pace increased, and my eyes adjusted to the night. A solid half-moon and a clear sky proudly displayed the heavens, giving us the light our travel required, but much of the forest floor lay in impenetrable shadow. The unknown depths of the Wilds surrounding us grated on my nerves after the Captain's warnings. I listened to his clumsy footfalls behind me as we moved. I mentally chose the direction I'd approach the camp.

The dragon got him first, and I acknowledged the winner of my imaginary wager. A dragon paw was at least as effective as whatever restraint I could've improvised. In a flash of blue scales, Captain Crowbar was on his back looking up in bewilderment. Dragon claws pinned his arms to his sides. He didn't even struggle, beyond attempting to recover his wind.

"Guard-dammit, Knife!" he said when the daze of the impact had passed. "You maybe could've mentioned you made nice with that dragon!"

Lohise and Melodie were scowling. The expressions were a cross-species mirror of each other. Lohise spoke first.

"Regiment scum calls you by name?" the titan wolf asked. I noticed the titan wolf cubs were tentatively peering at the scene from behind the bushes. The Den Mother refused to allow me any distraction.

"Rahn!" she barked. "If you'd like us to leave the pair of you unharmed, you'd better explain why."

I shrugged, genuinely unsure. This was probably the worst response I could've given.

"He might have information," I growled.

The Captain sensed what was happening.

"Information? Oh sure, I'm an open library! The Jurisdiction can go fuck themselves, mates, ater the shit the boys and I just stepped in."

I rubbed my chin. Lohise and Melodie seemed to weigh the value in the Captain's frank admission.

"What happened to your boys?" I asked.

Captain Crowbar exhaled. "Woof," he said. "Straight away with the tough questions. But you got it, boss,"

He exhaled again, and I heard a genuine sigh. Even Chaeoh relaxed his grip while we settled ourselves for the tale.

"We were sent after a specific tribe which was rumored to be in these parts. We started over in the Low Hills. Now, no offense, but most of us Regiment don't give a rat's ass about what tribe is what. Y'all are Normies to us, and we don't much care for humans who ain't Prize Mates. But this time, Command was real specific-like." The

Captain swallowed. "And we found them. We found the Iris tribe. That we did."

He closed as mouth. He wanted nothing more than to stop telling the story. His lip was trembling. I think he may've never told a soul if nobody had pushed him. Veteran soldiers sometimes refuse a telling of wartime events. A person can repress trauma. I couldn't blame him for it.

"A bear," he began to speak. I saw a tear escape across the curvature of his bulbous cheek. "A Demon. Must've been. You couldn't shoot it. You couldn't do anything. We tried and tried until we had no more bullets. And the boys-" he shook his head again.

"The boys don't hide real good."

I was caught in the drama of his telling, but his suffering seemed to amuse Melodie.

"And you ran like a coward?" she asked him.

"Ma'am. I'm an officer. Somebody's gotta carry a full serving of brains."

Melodie snorted. "What good are brains if the only thing you do is follow Jurisdiction orders?"

This seemed to stump the Captain. He went quiet.

Chaeoh had watched the conversation as he held the man captive. He rumbled his opinion.

"Kill."

"I'll second the motion," Lohise joined. Melodie handed me the heavy crowbar.

"You wanna do the honors?"

I accepted the weapon, but I looked at my three companions, considering how bloodthirsty they were. Captain Crowbar, however, took the sentence fairly magnanimously.

"Ah, well. So it goes, Knife. Had a decent run. Saw some battles I prolly shoulda died in, anyway. Woulda hda to train a whole new crop of boys, which sounds like a whole new pain in the ass. I seen better Suns. No Prize Mate waitin' or nothin'."

He continued with his self-pity as I raised the crowbar over my head. Before I swung, I had a thought.

"Captain Crowbar," I said sharply, halting his self-requiem.

"What?" he replied, annoyed that I hadn't executed him yet.

"How old are you?" I asked.

He frowned at me as though my question was a dumb thing to ask, given the circumstances.

"Almost to retirement, the ripe age of nine. Climbed out of my tank as tall as I am now, Knife. A bit gooey, still, of course. Took night classes. Soldierin' and whatnot-"

His voice trailed away. I lowered the crowbar and looked at Melodie.

"I don't know-"

The two bangs startled me. I flinched and dropped the crowbar. I hadn't even seen Melodie draw the pistol and she hadn't blinked. Chaeoh released the Captain's body, and I didn't want to look at the bullet holes in his broad forehead. Instead I kept my gaze focused on Melodie. With the things she'd been through recently, I attempted to understand.

The rogue Generale holstered her smoking weapon and cleared her throat.

"Hey pups. Who wants first taste?"

Her savagery was frightening, but I was clear on who she cared about. Her concern wasn't for a Regiment officer who I had a history with. Much to my continued shock, Melodie walked to where I'd dropped the crowbar and picked up the weapon with ease. She put her hand on my shoulder. The gesture felt flirtatious, but I was careful not to assume too much about the troubled woman. She never broke eye contact as she spoke in a voice intended for Lohise's cubs.

"I hear the Regiment is extra-tasty. Filet mignon for wolf-lings like you."

The titan wolves were making odd yipping sounds, which I realized were giggles. Melodie gave the rusty crowbar a thoughtful twirl.

"Oh, so you find Melodie's human words amusing, do you?" Lohise commented. Her claws dug against a patch of moss. She sprawled her lupine body and showed her teeth with a cavernous yawn.
{~}

The next Suns found the former General and I working on terms akin to friendship. The matter of Captain Crowbar's death faded. I held no grievance over her actions, and she held no grievance over my hesitation. We both knew both things, and we both knew it.

As a mage, I could feel my power. I lent energy to Chaeoh and the healing he was able to achieve was nothing short of miraculous. By dawn on the third Sun, he was testing his wings for flight. By the end of the week, we knew we had things we needed to do. We needed to free the Slaves of the Pens. We needed to return to the island. I needed to tell the Wizard how much we needed him. The matter of the missing Wise Witch, whom Melodie presumed dead, might also interest him. I wondered how the Wizard would take my insistence that the Defiance wasn't done with him yet.

The dragon and I couldn't leave Lohise and her cubs behind when we left for the Slave Pens, and there was obviously no way Chaeoh could carry the entire pack. Chaeoh assured us he'd solve this problem. Nobody knew what to make of his confidence. We hunted and waited. His proclamations grow frequent, but no less mysterious.

"She's coming," the dragon would say.

"Who?" we'd reply. "Who's coming?"

He'd snake his head back and forth and snort through his nose.

"She is."
{~}

She reminded me of a hawk as she landed. Nothing to her, really. Wings and talons and appetite. Her demeanor was merciless and focused. She made Chaeoh look like a clumsy iguana by comparison. She sauntered towards us, her smooth bronze scales glimmered in tune with every step. A regal grace enveloped her which the dark dragon lacked. I decided she was probably sizeable enough to carry a person, but I doubted the wisdom of such an endeavor.

"You serve this foolish dragon?" the bright dragon asked Melodie and I when we rose to greet her. I thought that dragons were short of words, but the bright dragon proved my experience with Chaeoh to be a fallacy. I almost replied yes, we serve the foolish dragon, but apparently Melodie didn't agree.

"We're each our own, here," she said. "How may we address you?"

I wanted to grin, but the bright dragon seemed dangerous, unstable even. I was trying to signal to Chaeoh that his arrangement wasn't going to work. I wasn't prepared to leave a ruthless apex predator protecting the precious pack of titan wolves.

"Sunderah," she replied, breathing a plume of flame to demonstrate. Dear Guards, I thought, she literally breathes fire. I didn't know everything about wolf cubs, but I was pretty sure you shouldn't breathe fire on them.

I realized I was overthinking the situation. I looked at Lohise and Melodie, awaiting their judgement. They were in their element as they greeted the new dragon. Perhaps they saw a potential ally, or perhaps they saw another she-beast. The woman and the wolf sized up the dragon as though they did this sort of thing professionally. The dragon bared her fangs in return.

A moment came when the bright dragon relaxed fractionally, but I could feel her. We'd adhere to Chaeoh's arrangement.

{~}

The bright dragon and the Generale remained with the wolves when I climbed up Chaeoh's shoulder. The next two Suns rocketed by like clock-work. After what we'd endured in the aftermath of the Battle of the Downed Dragon, the rescue of Slaves was a pedestrian cake-walk. The difficult part was witnessing the physical and emotional condition of the Slaves themselves. I'd almost forgotten. Almost.

I slew a Regiment soldier. Chaeoh slew a couple more, but the rest of the Regiment stationed near the Pens lacked the usual blind courage which drove their kind to action. They activated a Quint to come after us, but the machine was outdated and poorly maintained. A hydraulic leg seized up and the war machine toppled over with no convincing from the dragon or myself. Chaeoh's claws shredded through the fencing of the Slave Pens.

We were left with a complicated matter of looting and logistics. I counted a hundred and fifty-seven free people, as bundled and provisioned against the winter as we could manage. They

organized around a sense of awe over Chaeoh, and I tried to see things as they would. I wanted to make camp before winter fell in earnest. We'd escort them to Melodie and Lohise. Our best estimate was that the return journey would take until the end of the Moon.
{~}

Sunderah and Lohise were annoyed when they sighted the caravan. Even Melodie sighed and looked perplexed by the mass of ragged humanity that Chaeoh and I had freed from bondage.

Melodie gripped the lapel on the jacket I was wearing. I sensed another woman might've given a hug or thrown in a 'glad you're alive.' I immediately realized how foolish the thought was. Melodie Oakes wasn't another woman. I thanked the Guards, most Suns.

"What are we supposed to do with these people?" she asked me.

"Do?" I replied, allowing myself a strained laugh. "They're just people, Mel. They do them. You do you. Or if you like, you can do whoever you want, really, but that requires negotiation." She tried to frown, but to my delight, she wasn't succeeding.

"Here." I handed her a package.

Melodie unwrapped the supplies. She shook her head back and forth, whistling through pursed lips. When she met my eyes, an intense connection made me shift my stance. I felt like I'd just handed an addict their fix. I knew how Melodie felt about being unarmed. When she'd seen the new machete strapped to my back, her hand drifted absent-mindedly towards her empty holster.

The gunfighter woman had what she needed. I found pistols and ammunition I was confident would fit the weapons. I brought cleaning and maintenance kits, and against my better judgement I'd allowed several of the freed Slaves to take possession of other firearms we found. Upon learning this fact, Melodie's gratitude for my gift was immediately cancelled.

My status with the woman was constantly in question, but Melodie took to the fledgling gun-holders with a fierce sense of responsibility. Twice she warned me that she wouldn't tolerate violence or abuses among the Freed People. If things got out of hand I knew someone was gonna end up digging one of her slugs out of their leg. I watched her confiscate firearms I'd doled out with a firmness of authority in her voice. The power of the former gangs held sway. Melodie made sure everyone was clear on her identity. Fortunately, the supplies of food and fuel were looking steady, and the task of constructing a camp in the forest was a task most of the Freed People undertook with pragmatic motivation.

We'd Freed them, hadn't we? Lohise and Sunderah's looming teeth made excellent reasons for the peace to be kept. Had we only made fangs the new bars of the Pens?

I shook my head. No, I thought. They're free to make their own way now.

"As are you," Chaeoh chimed in, startling me. My stomach did a turn. Were my thoughts that obvious? I stretched my shoulders and my wits, testing myself.

"We'd better tell our plans, then," I told Chaeoh. The dragon cleared his throat and raised his head, grabbing the attention of the entire pack. Even Sunderah acknowledged him. A cluster of eyes large and small greeted the dragon. I was braced with emotion, and I nodded at Melodie. She wasn't exactly joyous, but she accepted the attention.

"Two Suns from now, kindred spirits."

The dragon chuckled. He began to hum a soothing tune. When we were all sufficiently mesmerized, he brought the song to a close.

"We're off to see the Wizard," Chaeoh informed his audience.

"A certain self-hatred accompanies any sort of defeat. Hate is well at home on a battlefield, but what if defeat confronts us in the colosseum of love? Drive the chariots forward, brave contenders. No retreat." -The Gunslinger Confidant

As Rahn's body healed, so did my anger at him. I knew I wasn't feeling the right feeling, the feeling I was supposed to feel, but nobody else was left in my life, so everything felt like his fault.

He had every right to hate me after my orders on the battlefield nearly got him killed. The fact that I'd stitched him up and made him endure this cruel world alongside me as I scraped together small game in the Wilds barely seemed a mercy. But his blue eyes held no animosity I could detect- only sorrow.

I had to confront him, eventually. Giving voice to my anger started to feel like the only way I could ever work through my problems with the forlorn mage-man.

I cornered him by the trees. A barrier of thorn-brush next to our main campfire hemmed the area. He was sitting with a mug of weak tea which had gone cold Marks ago. I was in need of a topic, so I dug down and found it.

"Power, mage skill. Why do you swing a chunk of metal around like a Guard-damn barbarian? Hell, I could shoot a twenty-two before I was even potty trained. All you do is sit and stare. Get up!"

Sad eyes were the only response again. He wasn't gonna do it. Part of me wanted to start cursing at him and never stop. I felt hollow and on edge, and I wondered if I truly thought he was weak. He was depressed, pathetic, stagnant, but his calmness was far too frosty and far too unflappable for my taste. The thickness of his crossed arms and the heavy muscles of his torso were at odds with a gentler nature.

I didn't know what else to say. I shoved him and drew a pistol. At least when I did it he reacted enough to stand. I imagine he could see how badly I was trembling. His machete was strapped to his back, and he made eye contact as he reached deliberately for the hilt of the weapon.

"I've chosen my path," he said. What kind of stupid shit is that? I segued to the other reason I was angry with him, and the thought triggered my rage.

"Then fucking teach me something!" I roared, squeezing off a succession of shots. Sprays of ice and the sound of metal ricochets answered. Rahn and I were at odds, and I wasn't going to back down this time. The dance was beginning.

My entire life, I'd been shooting targets. Plenty of them were moving, and aiming was always instinctive. The weakness of a turkey or a deer or a man is innately obvious. Your subconscious can rationalize your next actions in a split second, and the memory in your muscles can bring force to bear. But attempting to find the weakness of a mage is like trying to scoop barbecue sauce from the bottom of a filled punch-bowl.

When my first clip of nine-millimeter rounds clicked hollow, I reloaded. My practiced eye attempted to avoid Rahn's machete, but when he offered no metal for my bullets to meet, the projectiles didn't strike his flesh. He looked directly in my eyes and walked through his footwork as I aimed for each of his limbs. He probably could've rushed or lunged, but he left only an insinuation.

"If I reach you, you're going to get sliced by a full meter of tempered Jurisdiction steel."

I started to feel the dream-like substance of my own aura in spite of myself. Perhaps my strength was apparent because Rahn's aura surged noticeably when our duel was enjoined. He pressed against the exposed skin of my collar like the impending chill of winter. His face remained an impassive frown, and not a whisper passed his lips.

I was soaked with sweat by the time I shot every bullet I could find on my person. Chaeoh was roaring in a language I could barely understand. The wild ricochets of our quarrel hadn't exactly created a safe environment, and apparently they stung against the dragon's flank. I tossed my pistols aside and flung myself at Rahn. He dropped his sword.

Honest fighters didn't use the stance and posture Rahn displayed. Here was a man with no rules of engagement and no sense of discipline, a combination of callous knife-fighter and a clueless monk, but he definitely fought dirty. I was gonna knock the crap out of him.

I discovered I couldn't make contact. He offered nothing of himself to hit, even when I did hit him. My knuckles were frozen and bleeding and the Guard-damn frown on his face was still completely identical.

I stalked towards the spring, kneeling to inhale fresh water. I needed to cuss, but my throat was parched.
{~}

The following morning I made strong tea and threw my hair in a bun. I remembered to bring the crowbar.

If Rahn thought he was gonna fly away on a fucking dragon and leave me with all his asshole refugee friends, he was mistaken. I had a discussion to initiate.

He didn't look up as I approached him, but when I swung for his ribs with the cast iron bar, he parried the blow with a clang.

"Stop this!" he insisted, but I found his instruction had no teeth to it. No teeth at all.

The swordsman never cut my body. Instead, I was going numb. Numb from swinging at him, and numb from the impact of metal against metal in my arms and hands and mind.

I bathed in the stream when it was done, but I refused to concede. We sat at opposite ends of the camp and listened to Lohise growl at refugees. I sipped a cup of bone broth when the Sun ended. Rahn retired to his tent.

I waited until the witching hour. His tent smelled like ashes and mint rubbed against bare steel. The mage was awake. I sat beside his bedroll.

"Please talk to me," I asked him.

"Throughout the ages, many a humble soul has been gravely wronged by the course of human events. I ask often myself, 'Has the field-mouse been wronged by the hawk?' but I find no answer to the question which is satisfactory, and no comfort in crude analogies. Perhaps if the weight of these wronged souls were heavy enough, they might eventually tear the very fabric of reality itself." - The Frost Swordsman

An ironic thought was swimming in the cold water around my mind, but I couldn't place my finger on its clammy skin. Chaeoh and I were soaring down the coast of the island. When we hit the sand of our destination, Westings and the Wizard of the Waves listened intently as I recounted what had transpired with the Jurisdiction since departing their company. The Wizard's interest lay solely with his missing wife.

"Did she survive?" he asked, not bothering to mask the desperation in his voice.

I shrugged and shook my head slowly.

"I don't know, Mr. Wizard. Generale Oakes listed her among the fallen. I didn't press her on the details."

The Wizard's fury surged, and his voice crescendoed.

"Pretty Guard-damn important details!"

I scowled back at the man. I realized I was less awed by him than when I last stood in his presence. The pleasant company and the functional clothing of the Rose tribe made the Wizard look like a mad old hermit, and my patience for his eccentricity was wearing thin after my flight. He was wearing a dingy blue bathrobe tied at the waist by a length of hemp. I admit, the fabric was finer than anything I'd ever seen him wear, but with the bags under his eyes and his odd figure and his thinning hair, he looked completely unprepared for human company. I didn't relish the words I needed to speak, and I attempted to make them sound as if I wasn't patronizing him or lecturing him.

"Your wife didn't know you were alive, Szakaieh. Hundreds of Rounds have passed, and your wife was more than free to risk herself in battle. I'll not take the blame for any confusion about her whereabouts after that un-Guardly scene. Where were you during the Battle of the Downed Dragon?" I heard Chaeoh snort.

"Why didn't you go see her, go help? Why don't you come help now? I know that you know what's happening. You knew about her. You let her think you were dead this whole time."

The Wizard sat down on the sand with a dazed look on his face. He cocked an eye. For a second, I was afraid I'd gone too far with him, and perhaps I had. A melancholy smile cracked his weathered face.

"Not this whole time, mind you. After the Torpedo Incident, it took me a few hundred Rounds to pull myself back together again." He turned an eye in my direction. "Westings never talks back to me like that."

The tree scoffed. "It's wiser to abstain from incurring unpredictable weather events, I assure you."

I pressed my luck. I felt my aura pulse as if a battle trance had begun. I snarled at the Wizard. I wondered if my social skills were a characteristic I was learning from my new friends. Melodie and Lohise entered my thoughts momentarily, and I wondered how they were faring in the High Hills. I hoped they were eating well. My concern translated directly to the here and now, and I felt spurred to act. The aggression I directed at the Wizard was fueled by sincere emotion, and a colder logic. I knew this might be my best chance to get the man to see sense.

"You're gonna come help us now, Mr. Wizard. You're gonna help find your wife, and you're gonna help fight the Jurisdiction."

His response was surprising. He was shorter than I was, so he wrapped his arms around my midsection. He pushed away from the hug after a moment, but he'd left his walking stick fall as we embraced, and I offered my arm when he seemed unstable on the sand.

"I very well might," the Wizard conceded. He studied the surf, and the water lapped against his toes.

"I have serious problems, though, Mr. Le'Del. Not just imaginary ones. Becoming a rabbit and sleeping through fortnights, these aren't voluntary for me. I'm not sure how far I can travel from the ocean and remain human. It took so much time to become myself again after I was destroyed, I-" he took a few measured breaths. "She would've been furious. I needed to withdraw. Pick up the pieces of myself. But most importantly, perhaps," The Wizard placed his words in an eerie calm as the waves and the tide waited for his voice.

"I don't know what to say to her, Rahn." He looked in my eyes. "What do I say to my wife about Chrysanthemum? What about our daughter?"

Chaeoh was listening, and he began to shake his massive head back and forth. I knew he'd have his own thoughts on the Wizard. The dragon's stillness was deceptive, and when he moved, he grabbed my attention in a heartbeat.

"You need to be fixed," the dragon said. His insight was obscured by the brevity of his words. Despite this, the statement unsettled the Wizard. I sensed a current of energy I didn't understand. Chaeoh had said the Wizard was broken, I reminded myself, and he probably wasn't referring to bones. I swallowed, wondering what a dragon-remedy for Wizard-ailments would be.

"I can't find the power I'm seeking," the Wizard began tentatively. "Any information I've gathered has been of little use, and the bulk of the scholars argue it's only a myth. Nobody is willing to risk their reputation to declare the facts. The British didn't seem know, the Spanish didn't seem to know-" Szakaieh looked as if he was striving to recall.

Chaeoh interrupted him.

"I do."

The Wizard's left eye gleamed with a burst of blue.

"You know where to find this arcane artifact I covet? You know the resting place of the Sorrow of the Deep?"

{~}

The Wizard of the Waves was in his element. I could see him gathering energy for the task ahead of him. When Westings began to tell us the tale, he listened as raptly as I did to the resonant voice of the tree.

"Once upon a time," Westings began, as many storytellers do. "Lived a pirate warlord. He was about as ethical as pirates could be, preferring bloodless capture or prisoner ransom and swift, painless execution as his means of operation. He remained a pretty dubious pirate, let's not forget, a thieving seaman possessed of a cold-hearted ruthlessness which keeps any pirate alive. Lore says his eye for ship-building and the subtle ways of the sea let him maneuver and fight against any ship who dared his waters, even the armada galleons which daunted more sensible captains. In the wake of his successes, he accrued a pirate fleet of his own, a fearsome flotilla here-to-fore unseen in ancient waters."

The tree stopped. He cleared his throat and scooped a splash of sea-water against his trunk with a branch.

"At the height of his worldly powers, he met a woman, as men are wont to do. She was a Slave's daughter, just a Slave in the fields herself, a homely woman by the standards of a burgeoning prosperity the pirate king was learning to associate with himself. He showered her with lavish affections and built her a fine house, a fortress unto herself for when he was at sea. She became an artist, a craftswoman who pursued whatever whims and fancies she desired. When the two were wed, the shin-dig was a pirate celebration heartier than any grogged-up sea-dog in attendance could remember. She gifted him with a pocket telescope, blown-glass in the shape of a spiraling cerith shell. The pirate king gifted his bride with endless bolts of blue and green cloth, the finest silks and linens and cashmeres, for she desired a cozy nursery for the child she carried. With the crafty telescope, the pirate could see impeccably over impossible distances, and the colors in the glass were said to swirl of their own accord. The pirate's wife gave birth to their baby boy in the Moons after the wedding. Their son was a true Prince of pirates, if ever oh-ever a-Prince was born. As for the pirate king himself, he began to rule as a true monarch might, establishing a semblance of order among the pirate towns and entreating with the Old Countries on behalf of a new people. Peace was difficult. The acts of piracy mixed poorly with the forts and enemy naval presence among the neighboring islands."

Westings twisted his entire trunk back and forth. I realized he was shaking his head, but the motion carried his branches along. The effect was dramatic.

"Ill-winds whispered, and malicious rumors began. From the moment of his nuptials, the power of the pirate king began to wane. His crews began to mutter about his wife being a 'sea-witch.' The other captains banded together, and traitors rose against him. One Sun, as he raised the glass telescope to peer to to the horizon, they stabbed the pirate king in the back. He was still clutching bloodied glass when they dumped his body over the railing."

The Wizard nodded. I hadn't expected a happy story. I stared at the waves while Westings finished the tale.

"His wife, the supposed sea-witch, was fairly calm about her husband's murder, by written accounts. She was calm as they tied her to the stake, calm when they kindled the fire. The bolts of blue and green cloth restrained her as she held her babe in her arms. The infant was disturbed, crying as any baby might, but much to the dismay of those who witnessed her, the mother comforted the child as they both burned away.

"Shhh little one," she said. "The Fates repay. Shhh now."

I shuddered, picturing the scene more clearly than I wished. Westings gave a sigh. For him, the tension in the story was gone.

"What happened after that?" I asked. As I spoke the words, I knew I'd been baited into asking the question.

Westings smiled.

"What say you, Rahn? Do the Fates repay?"

I leaned back, closing my eyes to block the light from our campfire. I could feel the twinkle of the stars across the sea.

"I imagine they do, or else you wouldn't be telling us this weird pirate story. And I don't know what this has to do with the Jurisdiction. What happened to the traitors who betrayed the pirate king?"

Westings looked genuinely pensive. I realized the story might not have a convenient end as I assumed.

"I don't know, Rahn. That sort of piracy became a thing of the past, one way or another. The Old Countries wiped it out. Wasn't pretty."

"The story isn't over yet," the Wizard said. He'd been thoughtfully sleepy as the tree did the telling, and I sensed he'd reawoken.

Westings appeared confused. "That's all I know, Wiz."

The Wizard shook his head. "The cerith telescope is an actual anomaly, Westy. Hoarded energy, untold quantities. Dubious in origin. Captured at the last by a pirate-king and a sea-witch in a blown-glass bauble, and lying out there at the bottom of the ocean somewhere." An insane smile mutinied against the lines of the Wizard's face.

"And now we have a dragon here who knows where to find it. The Fates do repay, they just take their sweet-ass time."

I could see him temper himself when he saw my rattled reaction. Like a passing buzz from last night's liquor, he sobered down from his arcane euphoria. He spoke quietly when he regained his composure, but a dark smile shone across his face.

"The Sorrow of the Deep, lads. A bit of worked glass so inconceivably distraught it could utterly destroy us. Ha! Gentlemen? The 'Wizard of the Waves' be damned if I let my fears get the best of me. The Guards know things get boring after a few centuries."

{~}

I imagine an expedition to the bottom of the ocean should've required planning. Perhaps a cache of supplies, or at least a brief mention of where we were headed or what was supposed to happen. The Wizard gave Westings the barest of nods and the next thing I knew we were clinging to dragon scales as Chaeoh dove. The speed at which the dragon was swimming made hanging on his back excruciatingly difficult, but my arms weren't ripped apart. I noticed the Wizard was grinning like a drunk. Neither of us were having any difficulty breathing. My chest felt the familiar lurch of knowing I didn't understand what was happening.

I certainly didn't understand how Chaeoh was supposed to find a dead pirate, let alone what was going to happen when we found the dude. My forearms began to ache from holding the dragon. The deeper we got, the colder the water was against my body, and I began to ache. When darkness surrounded us and the pressure became oppressive, my eyes felt like they were useless. The only thing I could do was to maintain a leveled sense of self and ward away any true panic. I thought I might lose the battle, but I noticed a hint of blue down in the dark.

The floor of the ocean was a hidden beach, concealed by the eclipse of the sea. The light from the blueish glass illuminated a solitary figure lying supine on the sandy expanse. The pirate king was wearing his jacket, an exquisite indigo blazer embroidered in silver. The dead man's bone hand was wrapped around the glowing shell, and the Wizard floated effortlessly towards the skeleton. The skull nodded as Szakaieh stared into the empty eye sockets. The Wizard pulled away the Sorrow of the Deep and the pirate king's loose finger bones scattered next to his hip on the bottom of the sea.

I thought about my time among the Rose tribe when I looked at the Wizard's face in the dark water. His expression reminded me of a gunfighter on the night of the memorial celebration who ate mysterious mushrooms. The Wizard's pupils were the size of saucers. He might've simply floated where was, stunned and rotating under hundreds of meters of ocean, but Chaeoh was impatient to get back to the surface. I pulled the old man towards the dragon by his robe, and he managed to hold a scale with his free hand. The Wizard held the Sorrow of the Deep in his other hand, and the skin of his fingers was beginning to turn an unsightly shade of blue. I frowned at his wide-eyed stare. I wasn't looking forward to medical malpractice when we got back to the island. Hopefully the Wizard would know what the hell he was doing.

Chaeoh breached the surface of the waves with a turbulent relish, but we were at sea, with no land in sight. He spread himself over the uneven surface of the ocean like a lengthy barge. When I looked to the Wizard to see how he was faring, it was as if I'd missed a total transformation. His posture was taller, as if he'd aged a few Rounds in the wrong direction. I knew his spirit was truly amiss when he turned and brandished a cutlass of teal blue water, the Sorrow of the Deep acting as its earthly handle.

I stared at him. I thought back to my moments like these in the Slave Pens. Was he the Wizard? Would he want to fight?

"Are you the Wizard? Do you want to fight?" I asked. I don't usually beat around the bush.

"Indeed, Rahn Le'Del, that I am," the man said, lowering his sword.

I twirled my machete and smiled. "And?" I pressed him. The Wizard didn't even pause to consider.

"Oh, yes," he said with charm in his grin. "Oh yes, indeed, I want to fight. I'm that pirate fellow, too, splendid chap. The man was understandably disgruntled when he no longer had a body at his disposal to exact his vengeance. As it so happens, I had one available for him, intriguing as the case may be. Or I did have a body, anyway. Until I decided to share. A pissed-off pirate warlord was the ingredient I needed to stabilize my physical form, which I suppose is what I wanted. Besides, I'm a one-man menage-a-trois. The ladies will love it."

He walked over to Chaeoh's tail with a sense of confidence which seemed incongruent with the Wizard I knew.

"I had a ship, once. A sailing ship. Made of wood and canvas and iron, and manned by Guard-damn idiots who wanted to drink poison and hump anything that moved. And now this is my vessel? Are you shitting me, Celesta?" the Wizard said shaking his head in disbelief at his fortune. "This creature is so magnificent that I wouldn't have dreamt of him in an eternity in Davy Jones' locker. And he isn't simply a sweet hallucination, courtesy of my own deprived mind. Celesta's love has brought me forth, as surely as I share in the strange hermit. I'm back in flesh and blood once again. Oh Celesta! Give my love to our only son! If the both of you could but see me now!"

Chaeoh turned his neck around to face the changed Wizard, and I studied the welling tears on the man's face reflected in lizard eyes. If the dragon found reason for comment, he gave no note. The Wizard strode towards Chaeoh's face and placed his hand on the side of the dragon's maw, gazing at his eye in wistful appreciation. The cutlass conjured from the Sorrow had faded, but he held the glass as though he'd never let the keepsake leave his hand. When Chaeoh tilted his head in interest, he displayed the glass to show its swirling blues and greens to the curious dragon. The Wizard spoke without turning away from Chaeoh's visage.

"Let's go find my other wife, Mr. Le'Del. Be she alive, or captured, or otherwise. Aye, she'll have due cause for being salty with me after my Rounds at sea, but the pirate king has already lost a Witch who was dear to him. He'll not let another slip away."

Chapter 28
A'Rehia tells of: "The Spirit of the Moment"

"I don't do drugs– at least none of the drugs I've tried. I think I'd be more inclined to do drugs if flying through the air wasn't like a drug. I suppose I could try to substitute for that feeling, but why would I want to? I'd rather get fucked up off the good stuff." -The Sky Dancer

"I don't get it," I told Chrysanthemum. "You really can't convince your mom you aren't dead?"

The ghostly woman who was my latest acquaintance winced and sighed at the question. She was using my first initial as a nickname. Nobody had ever called me 'A' before, and the novelty made me smile.

"First off, A, I'm pretty friggin' dead these Suns. Her Wise-ness thinks I'm a cruel illusion created by the Jurisdiction with the sole intent of driving her mad."

Chrys was dancing across the field to my right. She performed a flowing pirouette. I echoed her lead.

"Of course, if driving her mad was the Jurisdiction's mission, then perhaps 'Mission Accomplished' took place a long-ass time ago. My mom isn't a particularly haughty woman, but with the knowledge she's accrued, even a modest ego makes for one hell of a blind spot."

I touched the edge of Chrysanthemum's shimmering gown. The ghostly lace passed through my hands, but I felt a pressure like the air knew that the gown wasn't supposed to be air anymore.

"How did she make you a ghost when you died?" I asked.

Chrys closed her eyes and shook her head. "My father confessed. Though the Guards only know how the two of them pulled it off."

"What about your dad? Is he-" the awkwardness made me hesitate and the dance faltered. "Is he around?"

Chrys shrugged and stared out past my shoulder. She lunged in the air with vicious determination before gracefully completing her jete.

"I know where to find him. We've spoken to each other now and again throughout the Rounds. Been decades since I last saw him. I lost my patience with him the last time." She seemed uncomfortable, as if she'd finally found an outlet for the truth inside her which was pressed to escape. I surmised she was moved by a living reminder of her youth appearing in her graveyard.

"It's hard for my dad to see me like I am, A. I can't hold that against him after all these Rounds. But I'm not exactly planning a weekly brunch at the local diner, either."

I felt myself chuckle. "I think I sort of know the feeling."

We spoke at length while floating in the trees by the graveyard where we first met. Only two Suns had cycled since I was introduced to the ghostly Fleuro woman, but I was already becoming accustomed to her hollow gaze and her shifting form. Her "Uncle" Steffen, on the other hand, remained distinctly uncomfortable in Chrysanthemum's presence. I got the feeling he was staying discreetly within earshot despite his feelings. We spotted him hunting ground-hogs in a clearing, but Chrys didn't pay any notice to the gray raven. She spoke as though we were alone.

"I imagine you're wondering if I plan to fight the Jurisdiction," the air mage asked me in her wispy voice.

I shrugged. "The thought crossed my mind. Maybe it's just me, Chrys, but it seems like things are getting shaken up lately."

Chrysanthemum wrinkled her brow and put on a slim, noncommittal frown, but she nodded, conceding.

"My Uncle Birdie over there is right, I have to admit, A. Doesn't do any good trying to place blame when the shit is hitting the fan." Her lip curled in an approximation of a snarl, and her facial features became disturbingly skeletal. I did my best to not flinch as the air pressure increased.

"I've been storing power," she continued, "but I'm not gonna waste it willy-nilly. And for several lifetimes, that's what provoking the Jurisdiction has been. A waste."

I studied the lace on her garments. Chrys shook her head and began to pace back and forth. Her body language was unpredictable without footsteps involved, but Chrys' pensiveness was viscerally evident. The pressure around the edges of her sleeves coalesced in strands which curled and split and curled again.

"The Devastators are eating the earth, establishing a nearly endless supply of material resources. If the Devastators are running, whatever victories we could win on a battlefield will be practically meaningless. The rate at which the Jurisdiction replenishes their forces puts any rebellion at an inescapable disadvantage, even if the uprising could capture enemy outposts. We'll have to hit the Devastators before we hit anything else if we want to curtail the Jurisdiction's resources. How many machines exist and what forces are defending is anyone's guess, but I already know where we might be able to find one from the tracks they leave. We're gonna need reconnaissance first. Uncle Steffen might help us if we ask him. Otherwise it'll just be us. Sis? You with me, A?"

"Yes," I said, knowing I didn't doubt my affection for my newest friend. "I was hoping you might teach me to use the kiteknives."

Chrysanthemum raised an eyebrow. "You keep 'em sharp?"

I nodded hesitantly.

"Sharp things hurt," she said in her dry tone of voice.

I realized she was teasing, and I smiled in spite of myself. My smile caused Chrys to let the hidden grin appear on her face.

"Voila!" the ghost said with a flourish of a gesture. "You're a board-certified practitioner of the kiteknife, licensed in fifty-shades of dubious murder by the Americana Mage-ical Association. I'll get our resident notary Oon to ink a tattoo on your skinny midriff later. So everyone knows. An 'A' as big as you like. Now come on princess, let's get moving."
{~}

We couldn't find Steffen when we looked around for the raven, but once we left the overgrown graveyard in earnest he caught up with us.

"Care to join our youthful rebellion?" Chrysanthemum asked him.

Steffen made an awkward caw before answering. "A'Rehia isn't ready for this, Chrys. You're gonna get her killed. And no, I'm not going to join you. I'm going to try to track down your mother, who remains a formidable ally despite her- eccentricities."

Chrys snorted. "Yeah, I do remember getting killed isn't fun. Typical bird-brain. Probably still got a crush on my mom. Best of luck to you then, Uncle. Let me know if she lays any eggs."

I gave the Raven a wordless look of goodbye. I couldn't tell how he was reacting to Chrys or her verbal abuse. I don't know if he felt sympathy or disdain. I'm not sure if a bird's face can be concerned, but the feathers around Steffen's eyes furrowed in tufts of judgement.

The ghostly air mage was already floating away, and I caught up to her with gusts of speed.
{~}

The wind shifted. I studied the terrain with a pouty frown.

"We're heading back towards Atlantium, aren't we? Where are you taking us, Chrys? I thought the Devastators were west. We haven't moved towards the west, not even a click, as far as I can tell."

Chrys was distant, but I gathered this was fairly normal for a ghost. Not to say I'd met any others.

"Yes, I was wondering when you'd ask," she replied neutrally.

I raised an eyebrow.

"You weren't gonna tell me? What weren't you gonna tell me, Chrys?"

"My intentions were better left unsaid."

I found no animosity or pity in the ghost, I decided, only refusal. For the rest of the Sun, I wondered about our real destination.
{~}

When the following morning approached midday, my curiosity solidified to certainty.

The mansion estate was overblown in its bland opulence, and the property obviously belonged to my father. The tacky landscaping alone reminded me too much of the man. Even before Chrys began disabling Swarm drones, I never questioned where our journey had taken us when I saw the place. After we made contact with the enemy, our roles were defined. I'd neutralize the Enforcer duelist, and Chrys would neutralize my father. We'd rescue the servant woman held captive.

Chrysanthemum was my friend, but she was also a bitch. She didn't feel the need to tell me that the woman was my own mother, or that the mage I was supposed to kill was basically a hostage as well. Perhaps she judged I was overburdened enough with the consideration of my own father. She was right, but that doesn't make her any less of a bitch. When we reached the roof of the imposing mansion, I harnessed every wisp of courage I could find.

Laurelei's significance wasn't readily apparent, but I was overjoyed to discover my mother lived.

We couldn't decide what to do with my father's body. Mourning his death felt insincere, and we knew we shouldn't stay in the mansion. In the end, we placed him in the yard and doused his Nobility robes with bio-diesel from the garage before setting him ablaze. I turned away, unable to watch, but my mom wanted to see the ashes.

{~}

We put a tourniquet on the fire mage. Laurelei and I carried him to saddle of the Pegasaur Drake. The creature pointed his snout to the west. Laurelei guided us. She'd gotten to know Oh-Four-Three in the hopes she might escape her captor at the drakes' reins. The shifting winds of fate had granted Laurelei the exact boon she sought all those Rounds. The Executor didn't want his every move known by his underlings or his rivals, and I dared to hope that Oh-Four-Three was free from Jurisdiction tracking devices. My mother spoke sweetly to the Pegasaur Drake. The creature said his name with enthusiasm, and we departed the estate.

After several minutes of skimming past the treetops, we touched down in a tranquil part of the forest where Chrys and Laurelei believed we could hunt, gather, and tend to the mage I'd injured.

I felt a resurgent sense of joy when I thought of my mother. The woman I'd missed my entire life was actually alive. With all of my childhood speculation about her, you'd think Laurelei would've run amok of my expectations. She wasn't like I imagined, it was true, but she was a real woman, and she shared my physical features in subtle ways. Laurelei wore the plain garb of a servant, but she outshone her worldly trappings and labels. She located the medical supplies in Oh-Four-Three's saddle. She was touching my shoulder and saying the injured man's name was Raspho.

I felt a pang of guilt about causing the wound that Laurelei was preparing to stitch closed. She sensed this, but she didn't speak about it. Instead, her steady movements soothed away my anxiety. She was calm and careful, her hands cleaning and suturing the flesh I'd damaged. She hummed to herself as if everything was right with the world. Perhaps she felt guilty, as I did, and this was her way of atoning for the sins we'd committed. I wondered if she was trying to forget the feel of the knife in my father's chest.

Chrysanthemum thought we should kill Raspho, just to be safe, but Laurelei and I out-voted her. The ghost grumbled to herself about finding more fresh meat for "flesh-tanks" and drifted towards the trees. In particular, the Pegasaur Drake Oh-Four-Three was going to need the energy. Chrys launched a roosting pheasant in the beast's direction without pausing her diatribe about the inconvenience of corporeal sustenance.

Raspho was feverish and sweating throughout the night. He tossed and turned and uttered words about magecraft. He sank into a restful slumber by the time Chrys returned from hunting. Doubtless his peace was thanks to the drugs Laurelei had forced in him. I could tell the woman needed to remove a weight from her mind, and she'd been waiting for the moment.

"Thank you for the pheasants," she began, nodding to the additional bird Chrys placed next to Oh-Four-Three's paw. "I have an idea about where we should go next."

I could tell by the way Chrys stiffened she assumed this was her decision. We'd already overruled the phantom mage when we suspended Raspho's death sentence.

Chrys replied with a tight voice, but to her credit, she listened to what my mother had to say.

"I thought we were going west. The Devastators are waiting for some inspired sabotage."

Laurelei nodded to Chrysanthemum, but she didn't defer. "I was taken from my tribe in the Low Hills by the Jurisdiction, nearly two decades ago. They wanted me for my mage genetics, though I've never understood why. I'm not a mage myself." She frowned, and the expression reminded me of looking in a mirror.

"The Nobility were furious when the birth of A'Rehia left me unable to bear them additional mage-children. If you're fighting against the Jurisdiction, then I support you. If we can find my tribe, the gunfighters there could help you with your aims. I need to find my eldest daughter, Chrysanthemum. My two girls were lost, and now I could see them both together. The idea is beyond what I dreamt possible only Suns ago. A'Rehia, we need to find my tribe. The Rose tribe. If Samsen and Flin kept their vows and your half-sister lives, I want you to meet her."
{~}

Chrysanthemum objected to everything. She grew distant and irritable when it became apparent we'd head for the Low Hills regardless of her plan to seek the Devastators. Laurelei and I didn't have to hire a medium to realize we didn't want to be on the bad side of an unruly ghost. I'd only just made friends with Chrysanthemum, and I didn't want to see her leave us, especially when we needed her protection in the Wilds. When Laurelei sought sleep, I talked quietly to the ghost woman in the dark.

"Does it upset you that we're seeking others?"

I couldn't see her, but I could hear Chrys unleash a breathy sigh. She was excellent at those.

"People are complicated. Stuff gets messed up. The Jurisdiction always catches on. I've tried to refrain from getting involved with too many idiots over the Rounds. When I'm alone, life is simple. The only people I talk to are Oon and Duu, and Oon pretty much only communicates with animal noises. As bright as she is, perhaps the woman decided talking is a waste of time."

I stared through her. My was mind going in multiple directions. My thoughts breezed past a half-formed question before I settled on an idea.

"Are afraid of what people might think of you?"

She looked back at me, a soft glow in her eyes.

"The short answer, A, is of course I am. The False Priesthood had hundreds and hundreds of members when it was formed. They were all praise-and-worshipping like I was Aretha Fucking Franklin or something. The parties and the rituals they invented, they were a Guard-damn mess. The acts they performed on each other and the innocent lives disrupted became unconscionable. Do you know what it does to people? Thinking that death can be averted? Hoping that they, too, might grab even just a taste of that power?"

I stared at her. "What happened to the congregants?" I asked. I was unable to help myself but apprehensive about the answer. "What happened to the False Priesthood?"

Chrys shrugged and lowered her gaze.

"I took care of a few myself. The worst of the lot. A few ran away, but it was too late, regardless. News of reward money I posted was misconstrued before I could retract the offer. Instead of corralling my wayward flock, angry bounty hunters left carefully stacked piles of human heads at the edge of my graveyard. In the end, Oon and Duu made skeleton soldiers from most of the False Priesthood. I don't like to think about those Suns. The twin sisters aren't exactly saints, that's for sure. They usually listen to me, though. And without treating me like I'm some kind of Guard. Quite frankly, the pair doesn't take crap from anyone. I guess I sort of like that about them."

I brought the topic back to the task at hand, and I dared to propose a solution.

"When we locate Laurelei's tribe, why don't you wait until we go ahead and um- explain. I'll come find you when they're ready. That way you won't be as much of a shock."

Chrys arched an eyebrow at me. "Hard to prevent the inevitable, kid. And if you can explain what I am, then by all means, do tell."

{~}

When we reached the Low Hills and the shattered remains of Sylviarg, my mother was distraught at the sight of her former home. Chrys continued to be cross with the rest of the group for wasting time. Combined with Laurelei's fretting, the anxious sounds of Chrys's huffing awakened Raspho. He blinked at us dazedly from Oh-Four-Three's saddle as if he thought we were hallucinations.

My mother and I gazed at the remains of the tribal long-houses, but Laurelei didn't have the heart to search the ruins. Before a Mark could pass, the wind shifted. We took flight again.

The Rose tribe had journeyed west-ward, my mother knew, to the City of Old.

Chapter 29
Sunderah tells of: "Hungering Rebellion"

"I have many devotees among humankind. The hairless apes ardently adorn me with earthly splendors of every sheen imaginable. Such tribute is only fitting for a creature as divine as myself. I secretly admire the puny bodies and brief life-spans of my humble retainers. Their fragile little heads won't stay angry for nearly as long as mine." -The Bright Dragon

I made arrangements to grant my presence to the Wolf Mother and the Gun Woman. The Suns had eased my heated heart as I found myself living around other beings again. The wolf pups were my favorites, and I'll forever relish their playful attempts at the hunt. The grubby humans who were in residence were more of an acquired taste.

I grew bored after Chaeoh's departure. I found I didn't have the character of a conversationalist or a scholar. I couldn't remain sedentary, and I wanted to either hunt or sleep. Pretty normal dragon behavior, I can only assume. After strolling through the wide-eyed camp, I stretched my wings and took to the former.

I intended to bring down an animal beyond the area where the wolves and humans were already hunting. I didn't deem this a particularly difficult task. My olfactories and affinity for body-heat were keen. Instinctive sensations worked in tandem. Soon I'd know what was important about the world, namely what parts of it I could eat.

As I searched for prey, I discovered the Wilds were awash in beating hearts and sweaty uniforms. Regiment raiders were pouring through the edge of the forest. To my eyes, they looked like an overturned buffet line.

Scouting detachments had ventured through the trees ahead of their peers. I wasn't concerned with the scouts despite their closer proximity. The bulk of the Regiment flooding the area and the Quints escorted among the bikers constituted an overwhelming force. I was glad they were headed north-west, towards the ruined City, instead of north-east towards where my personal stash of cubs and humans was currently located. I started to think about which soldiers to eat first, and how many I could fit in my belly. I'd have difficulty flying before my appetite waned. In a moment of clarity, I decided I should warn the Wolf Mother and the Gun Woman.

Much to my delight, the Jurisdiction offered flying appetizers to go along with the main course. The prestige of dining options brought joy to my heart. The flying humans weren't nearly as beefy as the Regiment, but neither were the guns they used, and I didn't need to swoop down and crane my neck. The crazy bastards shot right up above the trees, nary an actual wing among them, straight into my jaws. Imagine that! I was so shocked I can picture the moment vividly, especially how it tasted. I should've spit out the batteries, though. My heartburn is bad enough.

The Wolf Mother and the Gun Woman preyed on Regiment scouts who wandered near the camp. We didn't want Regiment finding us and deciding to attack. I ensured Lohise that the enemies I encountered met with swift ends, and none were able to escape. I know the Gun Woman had her kin among the City, but we had no way to stem the tide of soldiers.

"Better them than us," I tried telling her. I couldn't decide if she agreed. When the Quints began shelling the area, our chances of defending the City dwindled even further. I gave a snort when I thought about the artillery. Damn things would hurt. Even in the deepest depths of rage and despair, I never became enough of a masochist to enjoy artillery.

I landed next to the Wolf Mother and belched with satisfaction. The Gun Woman was as tense a shrieking hawk while the Jurisdiction took the City. We could hear the Quint's cannons in the distance. Melodie's frown magnified along with each artillery barrage. When dusk began to set, she spoke to the Wolf Mother in a low voice and gave a concise lamentation of her former tribe and those in their care. The people of the City were either captured or killed by the time the light departed. We could do nothing except avoid their fate.

To that end, we broke camp and moved south before dawn. The cumbersome caravan angled to the west. Titan wolves were almost self-sufficient, but former Slaves led lives deprived of the skills they now required in the Wilds. The Wolf Mother and the Gun Woman worked tirelessly to aid in survival. I scouted and hunted and gathered dead wood. I lit bonfires to cook meat and heat bodies. Despite the efforts, progress was slow, and the refugees were suffering. Stray Regiment personnel were more likely to flee from the Wolf Mother than they were to attack. But one afternoon, we stumbled upon a Jurisdiction outpost.

The place looked like a hornet's nest was jabbed with a stick. Soldiers filed en masse from hidden bunkers. Bullets flew in sprays of metal pain. The humans on the ground were taking casualties which I dared not consider. The freed Slaves were a hardy sort, rallying admirably amidst the crisis. I noticed hairless paws clutching weapons as I dove at the enemy. The Wolf Mother and the Gun Woman focused on keeping young cubs safe. I didn't begrudge their protectiveness, but I wasn't fighting for the same reason. I wasn't a baby-sitter or harnessed beast-of-war. I fought for vengeance, and I fought for rage. I fought for blood and for meat.

I looked at my claws. The bronze curves were slicked with red. What had become of my loves? I thought. I thrashed my head in agony. No, my loves would never see me like this. My loves were gone, and I was here. I licked a claw. I tried to spit the stale blood out of my mouth, but it turned to flame.

The Regiment's bunkers were cleverly hidden, but not immune to dragon fire. Titan wolves gorged on the flesh of the fallen. The humans weren't keen on eating the meat of their kind, except in times of dire desperation. I felt the urge to argue that our circumstances might fit the definition, but I contented myself with finishing my meal and attempting to rest. My wounds throbbed painfully, and I knew energy for discussion was better used for healing.

Fortunately for the humans, the Wolf Mother smelled supplies inside the outpost which hadn't burned. The Gun Woman strung a rope around her waist and dropped through a hatch. Lohise and I waited for her on the roof of the buried structure. After several minutes of muffled shouting and gunfire, she gave a tug on the rope. The refugees pulled, and crates of packaged food and medical supplies arrived through the hole.

"They're gonna find us," the Gun Woman said later, when we were alone. She looked at my shining countenance without a trace of fear in her eyes. I had the urge to correct this frame of mind, but I quelled myself, and I tried to listen to her reasoning.

"The outpost has a comms console which was linked to the entire Jurisdiction network. Even when I blasted it, I'm not sure I disabled the entire system. The Nobility is gonna know what happened here."

I showed her my teeth. I let puffs of flame escape from my smile. The Gun Woman shifted uneasily, which was pleasing. The Regiment soldiers were my primary food source, and she was complaining about how plentiful sustenance might remain conveniently accessible. I cracked my neck, and I did the same with my razor-sharp knuckles. The afternoon blazed against my scales in a brilliant aura of golden light. I basked in the glory of the nearest star for a moment before I felt the need to reply.

"Let them come," I told her.

{~}

The interlopers thought they were being stealthy, but I was immediately aware.

I no longer troubled myself about the presence of the Regiment or the Squadron. The Quints were only a few wingbeats away as they concluded their raid on the City and I slept like a baby.

But the two fliers skirting us in the aftermath of the battle, that pair was a different breed from any of the others. The air began to smell distinctly odd whenever they were nearby, as if an aura had gone sour. I barely even paused to question whether or not they served the Jurisdiction. The two flying mages were enemies, through and through. Perfidy felt like an obvious conclusion.

The first of the interlopers was a Winged Man, I knew. The other was neither human nor animal, but a shapeshifting warlock who couldn't decide which organism he preferred. Both were undoubtedly swift. Two fleeting forms slipped through the forest around the human encampment. I knew I'd have difficulty catching either of the spies without planning an ambush. I imagined bruising my wings as I struggled to give chase through the trees.

And yet, if I could get close, there'd be hell to pay. Agile tricks wouldn't prevent a dragon from mangling their dainty wings with paws and teeth. I couldn't decide if I'd eat the bony bodies afterwards, or if the sour-ness would make me sick. I planned to decide on a menu after I'd had the last laugh.

The following afternoon, the Winged Man was bold enough to throw a javelin through my left wing. I pulled the splinter out with my back teeth and spat the metal away like a toothpick. The unprovoked assault had reinforced my growing determination to roast that particular human. The only question was whether or not I'd pluck white feathers from his bird-wings or eat him whole. I drove myself to a frenzy thinking about it. I pictured him dropping the bomb which killed my loves with his bare hands. I roared, which scared my humans a bit.

I continued the noisy display and stoked my rage like the bellows of a forge. I wasn't roaring because my physical body was in pain. In truth, the javelin was an insult rather than an injury. I was roaring because I was damaged inside. Unable to strike, I roared in frustration. I roared once again for good measure, a formal announcement of imminent vengeance.

"I never wanted to be knee-deep in this bull-shit. The Iris tribe is gonna suffer far too many casualties in the Suns ahead. Despite my grievances with the people I was born among, this isn't what I wanted for any of them. I wanted solid ground beneath my feet. I wanted a forest at peace, bountiful with humble offerings. I wanted what many simple folk want, but simplicity can be so easily taken away. Whether we were waylaid by our own faults or by the hinges of the universe itself, it makes no difference now. The Jurisdiction is a cancer of the spirit, malignant and deadly in its manifestation. Only the Wilds and the sturdy Bones of the Earth hold the power I seek to counteract such a foe. May my wife remain at the center of my thoughts and my heart. Without her, I'd become a bitter man, a man cursing the Guards for the cavalcade of death on their hands." -The Warrior Shaman

Kiffu-San knew exactly what we'd find whenever we headed west. Tehsyn was right, as usual. The bear kept his big mouth shut about important details when he wasn't yawning with it.

I dismounted from Kiff's furry shoulders and addressed him with as much annoyance as I dared. He was claiming he needed to venture ahead of us alone in an attempt to establish contact with another tribe. Kiff's absence would leave us vulnerable, and he couldn't say how much time his errand would take. Tehsyn was walking towards us from her work tent. An entourage of unsettled assistants trailed in the wake of her purposeful stride. She wasn't going to like what the bear had to say, and I didn't think I was, either.

"You're hiding everything you know, but you want us to trust your diplomacy?" My arms were crossed. My left hand tightened around the grip of the Sylviarg Paw.

Kiffu-San was unperturbed by my frustration. He was unperturbed by everything, I suppose. I wondered if attacking him outright would even bother him. Suddenly, I saw the enormous bear more clearly than I had before. Tehsyn's glance made me realize that I was late to the party. She'd suspected from the start that Kiffu-San might prove dangerous. His sheer size meant a minor tussle was easily life-threatening. The bear relied on an unspoken tension in a pragmatic kind of way, grinning at us while we fumed. His easy-going indifference and casual deference weren't an act, but they concealed his stubborn nature. I found myself forgetting the Demon Bear was a virtually indestructible mountain of flesh against which we stood little chance of prevailing in a fight.

If anyone was going to sway Kiffu-San, the negotiator would have to be Tehsyn. She stood with her hands on her hips, glaring at the bear. He studied her with his brown eyes and seated himself. His wide bottom hit the packed earth with a thud. In his frank manner, Kiff proceeded to tell our Seer Sage how he intended to abandon the Iris tribe. 'Syn shook her head at him in a devastating pendulum of condemnation. I though Kiff might actually concede, but my wife sighed and shrugged, writing the words for my benefit.

"The fates grasp in clouded water, love. We'd be ill-advised to obstruct their reach."

{~}

The bear bowled through the undergrowth with such carelessness a mere child could've tracked his passage through the Wilds. I frowned to see him go. I felt as if the shadows of forest grew taller in his absence. Kiffu-San would never be a tamed companion or a creature of the Iris tribe, I reminded myself. We'd get along without him, if it was required. My hands caressed the metal curves of the Sylviarg Paw.

{~}

One meal after another, the Suns progressed. Game was growing scarce, and meat was coming from our preserved stores. We needed to move in accordance with our usual imperative. We began to break camp. My anxiety about the bear's absence was in full force. I'd nearly lost hope of Kiffu-San's return when a lone woman stepped out from behind a tree. She didn't appear to be Jurisdiction, so I drew the Paw, but I didn't attack her. The full-length coat she wore pulled at a memory, but I couldn't place it. I called her out, and she nodded and showed her hands, a sign of parley. We walked to the edge of the camp, studying each other's body language suspiciously. When she held her arm towards my body, I was bold enough to clasp wrists with her in a warrior's greeting. Tehsyn appeared at the periphery of my vision. She was never one to miss a momentous occasion.

"Are you the leader of this tribe?" the woman asked in a straight voice with a bending accent. I cleared my throat to respond but her eyes drifted to Tehsyn, where they widened considerably at the sight of the exquisite blue fabric adorning our Seer Sage. When my wife began craft her blue letters, the visitor took a step backwards, judging her escape route to the woods. The woman in the long jacket regained her composure, but she was staring at the letters with her brow furrowed. I realized she might have difficulty reading our Iris dialect. I tried to project confidence as I offered 'Syn's greeting aloud to our guest in the language of trade.

"This is the Iris tribe, governed by a tribal Council, as any proper tribe of the Low Hills. This is Tehsyn, Seer Sage, and I'm Vilkir, Warrior Shaman."

"Mages?" The question came in a single word. Tehsyn and I nodded solemnly. 'Syn was writing in front of her, and she ended with a stylish question mark.

"What are you called, stranger? Where do you hail from?" I asked the woman when my wife completed the verbiage.

The woman in the long jacket seemed to absorb a great deal with her discerning gaze before she responded. She looked at the Sylviarg Paw. She looked at Tehsyn's colorful dress, and she studied our sentries and tribespeople who assembled near where we stood. When she replied, she used a military demeanor. I realized I was likely in the presence of a warrior more experienced than myself.

"Melodie Oakes is my handle," she said. "Formerly Generale of the Rose tribe. These Suns, I'm C.O. of the human battalion of the Dragon tribe." An awkward pause ensued. I looked at 'Syn. She looked at me. Neither of us had ever heard of a Dragon tribe. Melodie looked at us both. We looked at her. Nobody knew where to look anymore, so our guest decided to speak.

"Your uh, emissary, if you wanna call him that, met us over this ridge. I came here to see the truth in his words. I've made my judgment. I'm here to formally propose we join forces."

The offer caught me flat-footed, at best. Too much was present in the tangle of diplomacy that I hadn't unraveled. I needed to process, and I harbored misgivings about a stranger from a Tribe whose name I'd never heard.

"Kiffu-San has been gone for several Suns," I said. I didn't want to infer our guest had killed the Demon Bear. If that was the case, we were screwed, anyway. "What's he been doing this whole time?"

Melodie shrugged. "He's made friends. The kids feed him too many honey-cakes."

The shrug caused me to notice the bulges in her jacket near her hips, and I knew immediately she was packing. I made a note in my mind as I shook my head about the honey-cakes. The Iris Council was already beginning to convene nearby. Melodie seemed to understand how she'd need to introduce herself and let them discuss her proposal, but I also guessed she had no patience for this sort of thing. She took Tehsyn and I aside, whispering forcefully.

"Do I have assurances the two of you will support an alliance regardless of what your Council decides?"

I hadn't considered this possibility, but Tehsyn consistently transcended my social wit. My wife's frown met the visitor's gaze. She wrote five words in the air in front of her. This time, I didn't need to translate.

"Who's in charge?"

Melodie nodded.

"If push comes to shove, the dragons and your bear will undoubtedly have their way. I'm not sure any of us can change that. I'd question the sanity of anyone who'd wanna try. Den Mother Lohise and myself are the leaders of our pack and tribe. Your Iris tribe has a leadership of its own, as I'm aware. Total unity may be a lost cause. We want to serve a pragmatic common interest. Nobody wants the High Hills to fall to the Jurisdiction."

The mention of dragons and titan wolves made Tehsyn and I apprehensive. Iris tribal histories didn't look kindly on dangerous creatures. This was part of the fascination over the Demon Bear. In fact, super-natural beasts of any sort were considered an unclean abomination in the eyes of the Guards, but times were no longer clean, anyway. Running from danger indefinitely would cease to be an option. We'd be better placed with a little danger on our side. Besides, Kiffu-San put the 'super' in 'supernatural beast.' He'd crushed the norm already with his furry girth, if only by lounging around on it and eating all the rice-pudding he could find for most of a Moon.

In the end, Tehsyn and I assented to an alliance with Melodie. My wife's judgement was good enough. The Council was sluggish to acquiesce, but the arguments of their Seer Sage and Warrior Shaman made them realize the discord caused by refusal would be distinctly uncomfortable.

When the Iris tribe finished packing, we followed Melodie through the Wilds along the same trampled path Kiffu-San had created several Sunns before.

{~}

After spending time atop a bear's furry boulder of a backside, a nimble horse feels a diminutive mount. I admired the mare's fervor. Her ability to find footing among the underbrush was impeccable. We pressed on, and the Guards saw fit to test my station in life.

I raised the Sylviarg Paw with my left arm when I heard the snapping of sticks, a dozen meters from the trail. The metal thrummed with power. I touched the back edge with my right hand and prepared to draw.

A wolf, it was only a wolf. I relaxed fractionally, but I continued to peer down the sights. With growing alarm, I realized the wolf I'd spotted was standing on a prosthetic leg. The Jurisdiction! My mind yelled. I drew back on the Sylviarg Paw, I conjuring an arrow. The Jurisdiction made use of technology to replace flesh, this was known. The wolf was beginning a snarl, the gesture curling her lips. I felt the imperative to slay a clever spy before she betrayed our position.

In the split-sliver of time before I released my arrow, an event swayed the entire course of Iris tribe history. I'll forgo the impact to my personal history so I may focus on the true picture. I feel nauseated thinking about how grave an error I made. I intended death down the sights of my weapon. I tried to kill the spy. The dainty tips of Tehsyn's fingers found their way to the back of my shoulder. They graced my soul, touching all I was and all I might become. The destruction of a mountain was nothing next to this gentle contact point of timely affirmation. If anyone else had touched me this way, I would've felt patronized and dis-empowered, but 'Syn was my very heart and I needed her dearly. I never tried to keep Tehsyn away, never tried to shield myself from her, and she learned to guide me better than I could ever guide myself.

I let the arrow fly. The Foresight of the Seer Sage had altered the aim. I watched in cut-motion. The column of blurry energy raced towards the titan wolf cub from the silver fangs of my Sylviarg Paw.

As the projectile traveled forward, a groaning machine rose from the a hole in the forest floor and towered behind my target. The gruesome Quint was covered in algae and leaves and lichens, deadly camouflage for the dull steel of the artillery robot. How long the war machine had been crouching in a pit was anyone's guess. I heard the whoosh of hydraulics and the whine of servos as the Quint powered on, feeding ammunition to the forward cannons. The Paw's arrow ruffled the fur of the titan wolf's ear before it slammed through the front of the Quint's armored housing. The shot caused the mechanical arms to buckle upward. Artillery shells discharged through the branches of the trees in thunderous blasts.

In the next heartbeat, I was drawing back on the Sylviarg Paw again. The wolf cub with the peg-leg dashed away. The artillery alerted the tribe, and my people began to flee in every direction. I felt a moment of panic over being left alone to confront the deadly war machine, but Melodie was firing her pistols at the Quint before I could release another arrow. She knew where the machine was weakest. We incapacitated the ambusher. I put another blast through the circuitry of its fake brain. The Quint's mother wouldn't be getting an open casket.

Fortune favored the Iris tribe. The wagons made a clean getaway. But as they say, fortune can be an unreliable whore, no offense to actual whores. The point is, the first Quint wasn't the lone aggressor. Tehsyn and I took cover with Melodie, and we listened to the Quints come alive around us in the forest. This was no time to wonder how, or when, or why. The trap had been sprung.

"Will your people help?" Tehsyn asked our new friend in letters as clear and efficient as she could make them.

Melodie was remarkably calm and contemplative as she replied.

"People?" she shook her head. "People ain't what I'm hopin' for, sister."

As if to punctuate her statement, I heard Kiffu-San's ursine roar trumpet through the Wilds. The call was followed by the sounds of gunfire and groaning metal. A glint of light caught my eye, and I looked skyward.

Tehsyn was less amazed than I by the gleaming dragon. Perhaps she'd seen visions of it in her dreams. The rush of combat struck, and I realized we were going to overcome the horrible Jurisdiction creations. Tehsyn protected our position with a force-field as I returned fire. When I saw what the dragon could do, I became more concerned about the entire forest burning down than I was about the Quint projectiles Tehsyn was deflecting.

{~}

The Iris tribe took nearly a fortnight to regroup once the last of the buried Quints shuddered to a stop, but casualties were blessedly minimal. Melodie insisted we salvage as much as we could from the destroyed war machines, which prolonged the disorganization. Kiffu-San and the dragon were conspicuously absent after the fighting. I asked my wife if she knew anything, remembering the wolf before the battle with a rush of guilt. I kept the incident in my mind until we remade camp at the edge of the City.

I wondered how the Den Mother discovered what happened, but Tehsyn believes Amika simply told her. The titan wolf cub had sensed my intent to harm. Lohise wasn't as big as Kiffu-San, but compared to a human, this was a moot point. She knocked me backwards with her paw. The claws slammed against my leather armor and bruised my flesh, but I rolled back to my feet and drew the Sylviarg Paw. Lohise bared her fangs and brought her face so close that the blades of the weapon poked her wet nose.

"Enough!" Melodie shouted, but Tehsyn was at my left side. Her hand grasped my wrist, and the intent in her touch burned my skin. I let the power dissipate harmlessly. Tehsyn gave Lohise a firm smack on the muzzle. The enormous wolf's expression went from fearsome-and-intimidating to scolded-cub. I watched Lohise fight her own conscience. She defeated the reflex to tuck her tail, choosing instead to sit on her haunches in pained silence like a melancholy statue. We appraised each other, evaluating the tension and discontent.

"That asshole almost killed Amika," the Den Mother growled.

"He didn't," Melodie asserted. "The Seer Sage is his partner. Even if you don't like him, you can't deny the partnership or its power." The former Generale put her hand on my shoulder. The rough claiming made me distinctly uncomfortable, but I endured it.

"Besides, I imagine this Warrior Shaman of the Iris tribe would be willing to issue you a formal apology. Parley can take place. Reparations can be negotiated."

I didn't want to turn and look to my wife for advice. I was prouder than that, and more subtle. Tehsyn gave a nod of her head which was almost imperceptible. Despite our covert communications, I'm certain nothing got past the Den Mother. I cleared my throat.

"Den Mother Lohise, I do hereby apologize for my actions in endangering the safety of your cub. I'm sincere in my regret, as I genuinely desire no harm to come to any of us. We fight in trying times, and I was only attempting to protect my tribe. I'm prepared to do whatever is necessary to see this alliance succeed."

The titan wolf gazed at the Iris tribal insignia on my chest, but there was a sorrow growing inside her eyes. I imagine everyone else felt it, too. Melodie looked at the ground and rubbed her chin. Lohise began to speak.

"Our allies are too fierce, our trust too tenuous." The breakup was apparent in her voice. "My pack is reduced to nothing but pups.

We'll not stay in a war zone and be ground to meat. We flee to the safety of the Wilds. Would that I could stay and fight. I ensure the survival of my kind."

Melodie began to weep as she embraced the Den Mother's neck, but she hid her face in the steely gray fur.

{~}

As Tehsyn and I prepared to investigate the City, I wondered if we'd ever see Kiffu-San again, or if his goodbyes had been unspoken ones. Surely a dragon would show up eventually, since Melodie's tribe was purportedly named after their kind. The Bright Dragon was glorious, but I hoped to the Guards we wouldn't require her aid again.

The City of Old, as Melodie explained it, was the ancestral refuge of the Rose tribe, many Rounds before she was born. The place wasn't exactly a city, even, despite the impressive ruins. A City is made up of people, not hollow vestiges. Nobody had lived in the City of Old for hundreds and hundreds of Rounds. Much of the damage to the City had been done by time alone, but the site showed signs of recent conflict as well.

Melodie was grim, but she wasn't tense. She clearly doubted we'd find a residual Jurisdiction presence. Instead, she expected to find bodies. My throat tightened. We waded across a river and climbed the opposite embankment.

I thought a dragon awaited us, at first. The creature was pale blue. As I examined him, he seemed different than the dragon I remembered, thinner, perhaps. His head and face were shaped more narrowly than the Bright Dragon. He blinked at me with reptilian eyes, but his body language reminded me of a puppy. Melodie kept her hands near her hips, but she frowned at the odd dragon rather than drawing on him. Tehsyn smiled, sitting gracefully on the flat surface of an abandoned steel beam. The rust would stain her dress, but she crossed her legs to start her meditations anyway. I could feel the energy around her begin to clear.

"What do you think of Oh-Four-Three?" a female voice asked. We whirled to see a pair of women approach. The one who spoke was older, and her wavy hair hung about her shoulders. Her age was difficult to determine. She was accompanied by a young woman with black hair tied back as two tails. Neither appeared threatening, but Melodie went white with shock. I looked at Tehsyn for a clue, but when her meditation was completed, she simply clasped her arms around my torso in a hug.

I returned the hug while I watched. Melodie hadn't grown pale because the women were dangerous. She was tense because she hadn't seen her mother since she was a child, and now she had a half-sister.

Tehsyn sighed against my collarbone. The reunion wouldn't make up for the loss of Melodie's tribe or the departure of the Den Mother. Even as the women rejoiced about being restored to each other, I heard gasps of sorrow over the way life had transpired.

Melodie was correct to suspect we'd find bodies. Laurelei and A'Rehia led the way through winding barricades of broken concrete and steel to where the pyre was constructed.

The altar of the departed Rose had finished burning, but the embers still smoldered. A young man with blonde hair and a scarlet robe was seated on a piece of concrete next to the pyre, and he stared pensively at the ashes. He noticed our arrival, nodding in welcome, but he was reluctant to speak, and he kept his eyes downcast. Melodie called him Raspho. Kiffu-San wandered from among the ruins of the City without a how-do-you-do. He had a bored look on his face, as if he'd been waiting for us for so long that our actual arrival had become a non-event. I had some things I wanted to say to him, but I showed my respect to Melodie and her grief. I saluted the pyre with the Sylviarg Paw, whispering my words up to the Guards.

{~}

They told me ahead of time. They explained everything, and they were standing right there, totally insistent, and even so, I had difficulty believing them. The ordeal reminded me of when I first attempted to wield the Sylviarg Paw. My mind just didn't bend that way, and yet there she was. The translucent face of Chrysanthemum will forever haunt my dreams. I couldn't decide if I hated her or loved her. I was equal parts terrified and enticed by this phantasm, this human form which defied death. I knew the ghost was truly wrong when even Tehsyn was unsettled, which she certainly was. 'Syn was standing among the voices who warned of what I might witness when Chrysanthemum approached, but a warning is no match for wisps of white sending shivers up your spine.

I was beginning to get the sense that the Iris tribe had wandered into an unending nightmare when the dragon banked overhead and perched atop the propped-up skeleton of a squat building. Sunderah proceeded to preen herself, and suddenly everything seemed to be as it should be the world. The world was harsh, but the world had always been harsh. The pegasaur drake Oh-Four-Three nuzzled my hand, sleek and tame in comparison to the warlike demeanor of the Bright Dragon. My anxiety over Chrysanthemum was fading in the face of our new-found alliance. This was the Dragon tribe, after all. Was it any surprise that a banshee would seek such company?

{~}

Within Suns, we orchestrated attacks on the Devastators from the City of Old.

Chrysanthemum warned us that to do otherwise was to court disaster. Even if we managed to destroy the Devastators, an outright war against the Jurisdiction was a hopeless venture. We'd defend the City as long as possible and hope we secured a few Rounds of peace.

Melodie drew tentative plans for the City. She retained a personal knowledge of the damaged construction. Her first order of business was the excavation of the Mammoth's resting place. The machine was unlikely to ever move under its own power as it once had. Melodie could only restore partial function to the inner workings, but the buried relic was nearly as wondrous as the dragon or the ghost woman.

'Syn, Raspho, Laurelei and I spent the Suns aiding Melodie while A'Rehia, Chrysanthemum, and Sunderah attempted the raids. Absent any real knowledge of engineering, Melodie did her best with what she knew. A few of the Quint armaments were salvaged and mounted at ideal locations, but they were a precious smattering of firepower compared to a mobile force of the real deal. The small-arms which Melodie's freed Slaves had commandeered weren't going to be much help against armored death machines.

Upon returning to camp, Chrysanthemum was unable to contain her disappointment. The uncertain efficacy of sabotaging Devastators and our paltry excuse for a full military force were stressing her out, and she didn't care who knew.

"I've been cursed to live so that I can see everything else die," she told us, sulking towards the shadows to lick her wounds.

{~}

In the City of Old, I was delighted to make the acquaintance of the Thunder Raven. To my mind, the venerable bird eventually became Iris tribe's greatest asset, second only to the Seer Sage herself.

Steffen was looking for a Witch, but not just any Witch. Raspho was acutely interested in seeking this specific Witch. What was it about her, exactly, is beyond my telling. I gathered she was a mage, and of keen import. Raspho peppered the bird with clever questions, and Steffen cocked his head in thought.

"She's dead," Melodie said, interrupting the hopeful theorizing.

"I beg your pardon?" Steffen turned his head, looking at the woman sideways.

"You heard me just fine, bird. I wish that she wasn't. I want her back, too. But you're wasting your time."

Raspho and Steffen continued the search for their patron crone. I saw this as inevitable. Personally, I thought it likely she'd fallen. The confident assessment of a veteran gunfighter had an iron ring of truth to it.

The raven didn't like Melodie. My wife didn't like the raven. Between the people who didn't like the raven and the people the raven didn't like, I started to feel sympathy for Steffen. Syn's inexplicable disdain caused a minor quarrel between us.

"He's a killer," she'd say.

"I'm a killer, too," I wanted to respond, but I let the words die as a thoughtful growl.

When I saw the raven waltzing across Kiffu-San's furry belly, I contented myself knowing at least some of my friends were friends. I threw two berries from the edge of the ruins. The Thunder Raven

For the first time in my life, I fell prey to minor illness. I sniffled and shivered with fever as the first white flakes of approaching winter began to sift from the sky. I begged my body and my spirit to adjust to the bad energy nearby. Vilkir handled the situation admirably. The bone broth and the citrus weren't his purview, but crowd control was needed. A Seer Sage was immune to common illnesses, this was known. The Iris tribe was near panic upon discovering that I would be staying in my tent. Vil spoke to a gathering crowd about how I was in discernment over the future of the tribe, and the toll of the mystic process was a delicate burden. When I heard him outside my tent speaking to the Council in his firm voice, it didn't even sound like he was lying.

I recovered from my fever and resumed my duties in the newly established City of Old. A permanent residence was a novel experience for the Iris tribe. The people took to the endeavor with varying degrees of enthusiasm. Already we saw squabbles over the best turf or what should be done with the nimble Iris wagons. We decided on ground which would be designated for tents. The tents would be rotated to ensure nobody kept a perpetual claim to the preferred locations. This pleased much of the tribe, but a handful who held status or occupations which led them to believe they merited better arrangements could be heard at the Council meetings making measured demands.

The domestic struggles were interrupted by none other than the blasted Gray Raven himself. When he flew to the edge of the river, I spotted him through the trees. He had a desperate look about him. His mouth was open, and his feathers were ruffled. He flew directly towards my spot by the fire and my hand went instinctively to my belt knife. I'd plunge the metal through his feathery breast to end the wrongness if I could, I told myself.

Steffen pulled to a stop beyond my reach. His eyes went wide, as if he'd known my intentions. He perched on a steel beam and cawed for everything he was worth.

"We found her!" he kept saying.

"Who? Who did you find?" everyone asked him. I stared at him, letting their questions be my voice. He didn't reply to us, and his feathered body heaved with labored respiration. Despite his exhaustion, he had a self-satisfaction which made me hate him more.

The Iris scouts returned in less than a Mark. They carried a litter between them containing a shrouded figure. The fire mage Raspho followed, leaning solemnly on the Keenwood Staff.

I braced myself for a patient and directed my assistants. I needed preparations for any kind of surgery, but more importantly I needed strong black tea with a finger of firewhiskey before anything else happened.

The figure on the litter was an old woman. She was a Witch, by all accounts, and one who'd been in a battle by the looks of her. How she'd survived alone, or where she was found, nothing was ever clear, and Foresight wasn't gonna clear it up. I found clarity, however, as I cut away the sullied fabric of her dress. I saw a dying woman.

The situation called for forthright honesty. I spelled the words in front of my surgical apron and I watched them glow against the faces of Raspho and Vilkir in the infirmary tent. The two men reacted with dismay. I knew no chance the woman on the table would live. That she'd hung on this long was testament to some kind of a miracle.

Raspho swallowed his tears.

"Try," he said. Many say the same, and I nodded in assurance to him because I knew no other way. The Witch was unconscious, and I considered this a blessing. I chose my scalpel.

I didn't have much left of the Witch by the time I dug the slugs from her flesh. I could tell she could heal herself, but her body struggled in a un-winnable battle. Her insane longevity was a bitter testament to the power she wielded, and her waning aura was daunting to behold. I felt as though I basked in a collapsing star. I was uncertain of whether I approved of the nature of her mage skill, but my objections no longer mattered. The life of the old Witch was ending.

{~}

As with the Gray Raven, I wanted to reach for my belt knife when the Ghost Woman entered my infirmary tent. I was unsure the implement would have any effect on the delicate lack of substance composing her form. Her fake dress was immaculate, and I hated her unnatural beauty just as I hated the Gray Raven's cockiness. I didn't bother to write words. She'd say what she needed to say. In the candlemark before the Ghost Woman arrived on the scene, the bleeding Witch awakened, delirious with pain and determined to give her final words.

"Chrysanthemum," she whispered when she saw the Ghost Woman.

"It really is you, sweet-heart. Dear Guards, after so many Rounds. I want to leave this world behind. I'm afraid now, afraid of the pain, sweetie. Afraid of what surviving forever truly means. But dying like this, this is something I can't indulge. Not when I've found you again, my dear. Not when there's much work left undone. I'll stay where I'm needed, as I always have. The endless watch is yours already, Chrys, much to my denial, and to my regret. Nothing makes amends for what your father and I did to you before your death. I can't imagine what your- this life- has been like," Her cough was flecked with fire.

"And now I fear I embark on your path, myself."

I wasn't sure what I was hearing, but I knew I didn't like it.

"I'm taking the Witch," the Ghost Woman announced, as if she had every right in the world to impugn my ability and my authority as the Seer Sage. I nearly lashed words and told her, ungrateful as she was, but I was feeling pensive rather than

Chapter 31
Tehsyn tells of: "'The Energies Between Us'"

"'The synapses and neurons of a brain do not conjure a soul. A fleeting dance of thoughts and feelings does not define a consciousness. Humble thyself, mages all, and know thy power, O subtle sorcery! We are given one life, and one physical reality in which to manifest, but we are indeed one spirit when our precious life has passed us by. In love and faith, we strive to maintain the ties that bind. May we float along as a raft of refugees instead of sinking low amidst the turbulence of troubled waters.'" -The Seer Sage

The bird smelled like death. I didn't trust Steffen, and I didn't trust the apparition Chrysanthemum who was in the process of convincing A'Rehia that she was her ally. The two Elder air mages were ancient, indeed, but a Seer Sage knows power isn't everything.

I couldn't communicate the wrongness I felt. I tried to explain and rationalize for the benefit of my husband. Vilkir had difficulty understanding, and when I went to spell things out for him, the words didn't appear as if by Foresight. Nobody had dreamed the dreams I'd dreamed, survived the nightmares, the psychedelic hallucinations, the waking epiphanies. The closest I could get to the truth was telling Vilkir that the Gray Raven was 'a killer who smelled like death,' but my husband just wrinkled his nose at me and frowned.

"All I smell is feathers, Syn."

I let the topic rest and I tried to refocus. Nobody mistook my frayed nerves, and I'm afraid my assistants caught the worst of that, Guards bless their souls. They forced me to sit down and brought me tea, the sweet-hearts. The proximity of the Gray Raven and the Ghost Woman was literally causing my mind to deteriorate. I saw flashes of tearing flesh, trapped, vengeant souls in my mind whenever I looked at them. The two air mages were ambassadors of death, empowered by it, embracing it. The two of them absolutely reveled in it. Without a target for their cultivated bloodlust, they'd simply collapse. I wanted to run for the Wilds. I almost said as much to Vilkir. Whenever I thought of the Iris tribe mixed up with such unstable mages, I began to tremble. How much darkness should we align ourselves with? How far was my husband prepared to go in these trying times? Would I encourage each and every battle?

Even the dragon, savage as Sunderah was, rang of righteousness in comparison to the tainted air-mage energy polluting the camp. She slew her enemies cleanly, ate their flesh. Her vengeance was pure as the driven snow. By contrast, the Gray Raven had defiled his own nature, and the Ghost Woman defiled nature itself. How could one conscience such creatures? The dissonance drove me to distraction.

splattered the first one into juice with an arc of current from his tail feathers, spraying Kiff's fur with purple. The second, he turned his head and caught in his beak.

Demon Bear belly laughs echoed throughout the City.

belligerent. I could detect the life-force draining. I had a feeling the Ghost Woman and the Witch were family, and significant bonds flowed between the women. Chrysanthemum confirmed my suspicions as she whispered unearthly comforts to the dying mage.

"If it's what you want, mother."

I turned around and tossed my arms in dismissal, leaving the pair to their own devices. A few candlemarks later, the Witch and the Gray Raven and the Ghost Woman were gone. I was breathing easily again. Good riddance, I thought. If renegade mages wished to defy nature and provoke the Guards, then so be it. I was content they do so risking their own heads, and as far as possible from my Iris tribe.

{~}

Stories of the Dark Dragon were spoken among Melodie's people who had witnessed Chaeoh tearing through the fences of the Slave Pens. I gathered that the blue dragon was revered by dedicated clerics for this singular act. The Iris tribe generally agreed he was friendlier towards humans than his counterpart Sunderah, but the dragon Chaeoh spoke only in brief bursts, whereas the bronze seemed unimpeded by this eccentricity when she chose to bestow the sound of her voice.

When Chaoeh landed in the City with his two riders, I immediately recalled the feel of his scales against the sweaty palms of my hands. My memory didn't hold a picture of his broken form in the dark, but instead a complete image of every part of him in animalistic glory. He was looking healthy again, and the scarring on his belly was the only outward sign of the trauma which had nearly taken his life. The past history between us wasn't lost on him. He was surrounded by the people of both the Iris tribe and the Dragon tribe, but he spotted my shawl at the edge of the crowd. His wink was gigantic, but he aimed his eye perfectly towards where I was standing.

{~}

I was suffering under a plague of air mages. Chaeoh arrived bearing two intriguing strangers, but the newcomers weren't able to distract from my concerns over the Winged Man and the Shapeshifter who were spying on us from the trees. I was delighted to learn that the bronze dragon Sunderah also noticed our enemy's spies, but she wasn't able to read my written characters, so I spoke to her through Vilkir. Once we understood each other better, she extended her paw so I could place my hand in her own. A touch of the arcane between us was a link which required no words. We hatched a plan with devious grins.

I was supposed to be the bait, and Vilkir hated it. Why was he being so predictable? Hadn't he seen this script before? I insisted his presence would give us away. I refused to let him follow. He was in the process of delivering his predictably futile protest even as I donned the proper attire. One of the strangers who arrived with Chaeoh barged through the flaps of our tent.

He was an aging gentleman. He had thinning, unkempt white hair and striking blue eyes. I knew him for a mage immediately by the way the energy around him settled as if it were a pool of water. As I stood in our tent in my underclothes, the intruding mage and I looked at each other and much became clear.

"My wife-" he began, just as I wrote the words "Your wife" in front of me.

"Where is she?" he asked, and then he shook his head under Vilkir's savage glare. "Beg your pardon, Sir, Madame. I didn't mean to offend, it's just that-"

"She's your wife." I dismissed the apology. Vilkir handed me a robe, but the Wizard's presence was humble, and modesty seemed wasted on him.

The old mage nodded at us. "Name's Kai. My respects to you for what you've done. I've finally come to find her again, come to find my Jae'lin, and I find she may be lost forever."

I frowned at him, given what I knew. Did I dare tell the Wizard my suspicions about his daughter's plans?

"Her wounds were mortally grievous, Sir. Your daughter bore your lady-wife to the False Priesthood."

I let my words hover, and I tried to gauge his reaction. I hoped he might draw his own conclusions without the exact details spelled out for him. He'd have to ask the Guards if he wanted a full explanation. The tent grew awkward for a moment as I contemplated everything half-naked in the living space Vilkir and I shared. We had nowhere to sit, really, and I didn't know if inviting the Wizard to stay would've been the thing to do, anyway. Szakaieh was a riddle I hadn't pondered when I met him.

The man took the news of his late wife's certain death rather mildly. I tried to imagine how I'd feel if I learned devious mages might attempt to reanimate Vilkir as an inhuman monster. I wasn't sure if the calmness Szakaieh displayed was an indication he was at peace with what might come to pass or at peace with the drastic measures he'd need to take. He looked at me and spoke.

"I'm grateful to you, Ms. Sage. For more than the care of my wife. I'll leave you here and hope for peace."

He put on a knowing smile and executed a flowing bow, backing through the flaps of the tent.
{~}

I donned some sturdy trousers in a serviceable navy blue and a shawl woven from the colors of the forest which would protect my shoulders against more than just the chill. I summarily dismissed Vilkir's ignorant requests that I take armor or a horse. Bait was supposed to look vulnerable.

I calculated my odds. To our enemies, I was worth more alive than I was dead. I placed a tiara studded with sapphires on my head, a delicate bauble given as a wedding gift. I needed the Jurisdiction agents to identify my value. I took a gathering basket from my work tent, and I shared a kiss with Vilkir before giving Sunderah a fist-bump. I made my way to the foot-bridge which would lead beyond the City of Old.

{~}

Much as I loved my tribe and my husband, I felt much refreshed as I entered the Wilds alone. I savored the smell of the air and the vibrant colors of autumn. I'd grown weary of the stone and metal of the City. Our people were nomadic naturalists. The unchanging landscape of standing buildings made for foreign surroundings.

I'm certain my adversaries spotted either my tiara or my shawl before I realized I was being followed. I could feel the eyes. The unsettled feeling passed, replaced by the adrenaline of subterfuge. I kept my face impassive and my gait loose, ignoring the tingle of muffled wingbeats as I steadied my trek.

Sunderah was completely concealed by a disheveled warehouse, and I didn't see her coming. The lash of her bronze tail almost broke my legs when she leapt from behind her cover. I grabbed my shawl with one hand, shielding myself before peering towards the aftermath.

She had the bastards pinned, alright. The wounds were bleeding on her fingers as the dragon held the air mages down with her sharp claws, but the lacerations were far from fatal. The two men flailed, attempting to free themselves, and I immediately knew something was wrong with them. The eyes were too empty, and the motions too devoid of thought.

I grabbed Sunderah by the ankle before she did further injury. I must admit, this is not a technique for communicating with a dragon I recommend to anyone. I received a pointed elbow to the stomach for my interruption, but I'm a grown woman and a mage, and I bid the dragon hold steady while I worked.

When I went to my trance, Sunderah sensed what was happening. She acquiesced, although I could sense her desire for blood, a heat radiating from her belly. I reached for the Winged Man and I found he was already being grabbed by something other than a bronze dragon paw. The Jurisdiction air mages were subject to a mind overpowering their own, a gray hand grasping at the backs of their skulls. I gave a silent war-shriek in disgust and aversion over the violation of their souls. How dare a healer's empathic touch be corrupted for manipulative evil? The Guards would know of such trespasses, and I would bend their ears myself! I struck at the gray hands with every destructive energy I could draw to my aid. I felt the water and the earth beneath my knees rise and twist and turn to primordial soup, the power intertwining with my focus. I felt the beads of sweat condensing across my brow, my patients struggling alongside my effort. I broke the knuckles of the gray hands and drove them away until they faded.

When my first task was finished, I transitioned seamlessly to my second. Freed of the gray hands, these men couldn't be trusted without careful consideration of their motives. I was nearly as ruthless as the gray hands when I sorted through the endless conflicting pathways in their heads. I knew this was too much. I dabbled in unknown art I'd never dared. I felt the waves of power flowing to and fro, and I knew magecraft was a crude tool in the realms of the spirit. The energy rose as though the world might flood, and then sloshed from the heavens as though I'd stepped under a driving rain pressing back to earth. I was lightheaded, and I could tell I'd pass out soon. I tried to turn my hips away from the unconscious men when the connection started to distort, but they were dragging me under. Sunderah's mix of triumph and disappointment melded to a keen glare as I grasped her forearm, coaxing her to lift her paws from the trapped mages.

I looked around in a daze, blinking several times. I was incredibly thirsty. Where was my husband?

I toppled over like an empty decanter falling from a pedestal. A bronze dragon paw caught my body.

"The phenomenon of music can't be explained with just one album. You'd need an eclectic collection running the entire gambit. Compression, rarefaction, frequency, wavelength, nodes, overtones, harmonics, even what appears to be pleasant chance is quickly complicated. Musicians are clever conspirators in their own ways, but truthfully, the atmosphere itself acts as both instrument and composer for our soul's reprise." -The Shapeshifter Virtuoso

Her disdain for me was clear, but the Seer Sage let me live. A different person might've done otherwise. She had her fears, but fear wasn't what drove Tehsyn to free me from the Sovereign. I could feel her hopes for the future like waves on a shoreline crashing against the crags of my face.

I would've liked to taste her, thirsty as I was. The thought may seem crude, but I was overcome with a powerful sensation I find to be worthy of note. Just a teensy bite- I wouldn't even make a mess! I could be respectful. Her womanly figure wasn't what I was interested in, anyway, only the mystic red elixir within. The power would've been absolutely delectable, but I had no chance of sneaking a sip without risking life and limb. Vilkir seemed to share his wife's skeptical opinion. He probably trusted me even less than she did.

I tried to brush myself off, consider myself lucky. I'd survived the capture of my mind by the Jurisdiction Sovereign. The Guards knew the foul computerized entity cared nothing for my well-being, much less my wardrobe. The Suns under the Sovereign were like dreams I couldn't escape from, and my head hurt abominably. My corporeal self had been wielded like a disposable instrument for the better part of a Moon, and the worse part, too. I shuddered to think of the absent-minded torment lasting Rounds, and of the blood which could've been on my hands if the dragon and the Seer Sage had not put a stop to my fangs.

I cleared my throat laboriously.

"Your pardon, Mr. Shaman." I nodded towards Zeyus. His wings were starting to twitch, and his eyes opened. "Our injury and privation is no minor thing. I ask for water and humble food. I desire that my companion might not take further ill." I rummaged in my pockets, and I managed to produce a golden doubloon with a trembling hand. I grew dizzy when the light glinted from the shining surface of the coin. I had flashbacks of the dragon in the sun.

Vilkir's eyes grew wide at the sight of my liquidity, but he shook his head back and forth when I offered him a down payment. He gestured for a man bearing a pitcher and wooden cups. I drank the water gratefully, though the cold fluid left my insides aching. The

Sovereign hadn't seen fit hunt for the blood of a Prize Mate whilst the Jurisdiction's oppressive desires were behind the wheel. I was dehydrated in a way water wouldn't be able to fix.

I was far too weak to transform. Zeyus seemed even worse for the wear. The dragon's talons had slashed him badly, especially on his wings. Sorting his bloody and bedraggled feathers was a task he set himself to with a cringing determination. The Seer Sage took mercy, offering him a pain potion and the aid her assistants. The three of us knew she'd done enough already, and she wouldn't attempt to survey lesser ailments herself.

The dragon still wanted to eat us. Sunderah contented herself with blowing smoke from her bronze nose-holes in a sigh of regret. She stared us down as we struggled to cope with our injuries. Major Zeyus was determined, bringing bread to his mouth, but the Winged Man shook and shivered intermittently from the physical and mental pain he was feeling. When we finished eating, he wrapped and folded his damaged wings gingerly over himself, seeking sleep. I cushioned his head with a pillow, but I didn't dare put another blanket over his injuries. As I watched over him, I realized we were alone except for one other man. Vilkir nodded in acknowledgement when I looked to meet his gaze.

"We're going to need help. From both of you. You know that, don't you?"

To his credit, the gleaming metal claw was strapped to Vilkir's back, and not held in his hand, but I sensed his meaning. Compliance with his desire for assistance wasn't optional.

I shook my head to try to clear the cobwebs. My thoughts were blurry, with no mage-blood to feed upon, and the trauma from the Sovereign's presence was fresh inside my skull.

"How exactly do you think we'll be of any use to you?"

I got a raised eyebrow for my desperate words.

"Don't tempt me, Lucien D'Arsailles. The Record Keepers would need a full stack of hides to record your transgressions, I've no doubt. I'm not barbaric enough to execute you. But if you aren't worth anything to this tribe, then I'm not certain we can welcome you here."

I set my gaze on the muscled warrior. The kid had heart. I truly didn't wish to disappoint him, but I did want to drink his wife. Things were gonna get weird, even if I played my cards nicely.

"Very well, then," I called his bluff. I rose slowly and bowed graciously. "We're forever in your debt for our rescue, Warrior Shaman Vilkir Baton. My specific regards- ahem- to your Seer Sage. It is, however, as you say. We're of little use to your tribe. When my companion wakes, we'll not trouble you any further."

Vilkir snorted as if he'd expected my tactics. He persisted.

"Do you want vengeance? For what has been done to you?"

I could've lied to him. It would've required less energy to remain meek. I could've insisted I didn't care, which was part of the truth. Instead, I chose to let slip the rest.

"I shall have my revenge, eventually, Monsignore Baton. I assure. I wager Zeyus will take his pound of flesh. But to involve myself with you and yours," I shook my head. "I don't see the wisdom. Do you?"

I was fond of the Shaman, in spite of myself. Perhaps he was a finer chap than I'd originally thought. His next maneuver took my expectations completely by surprise. Standing before mine, Vilkir's splendid body rose head and shoulders above my thin frame. He knelt, smooth as anything, and he placed the Sylviarg Paw on the ground at my feet. His mahogany eyes looked up earnestly.

"I'm wise enough, Shapeshifter. Wise enough to see wisdom. For the boon of your rescue, I request you repay us with the boon of your presence, if only for a time. I'll do whatever is in my power to make it so."

I stared at him.

"If only friendship were a simple game, Shaman Vilkir, I would immediately accept your gracious offer. Touched, I truly am. However, I'm a loner by nature, you see." I glanced at Zeyus. "Loner plus-one these Suns." I tried to think of how I could explain my real reason for wanting to leave without revealing the critical blood lust which motivated my dinner reservations.

"Besides, I'm a mage with peculiar- needs. Ones which might trouble you in fulfillment."

The grimace across Vilkir's face looked like an irate wildcat.

"What sick needs, mage?" The Shaman crossed his arms. "I'd heard rumors about you. I was hoping you'd refute them."

I rubbed my chin and sighed, hoping the sound was thoughtful instead of completely clueless.

"Do you know what a Prize Mate is?"

Vilkir shook his head, indicating that he didn't. My mouth made a great many words as I attempted to remove the frown from the warrior's face. I considered the chances the expression might be stuck permanently.

{~}

As I finished my tale, I knew Vilkir would never be the friend he could've been in another life. I could tell from his questions. He shared much of his wife's disdain for magecraft which ran afoul of certain moral hurdles. He had difficulty accepting how anyone would willingly prefer death by pleasant exsanguination to the daily brutality of the Jurisdiction.

I could see him wrestle with his inner demons as he reached forward with his shapely arm to place a hand on my bony shoulder.

"We'll get you your fix. For now, Count D'Arsailles. I'll not torture an addict. Not when we've got the chance to strike a mighty blow together. We can't accomplish survival alone." A grin of anticipation spread across Vilkir's square jaw. I returned the expression, and took up the jest.

"The bards will yodle o'er your man-ly thighs for generations, Shaman."
{~}

"When deep autumn is nigh, I shall throw them the party of a lifetime."

"Lucy-"

"Now isn't the time to indulge in your whimsical fantasies, you Guard-damned crack-pot blood-sucker."

Melodie Oakes appeared uninterested in my delicate scheming. She wanted me to fight under her command. On a battlefield! Like an honorable gentleman! I don't know how she expected I would fall for such nonsense.

"A fabulous distraction, M'lady Warlord, I assure you. Whispered to the correct ears, my 'whimsical fantasies' should give you the opportunity you need to shooty shoot-shoot a gunny gun-gun wherever the hell you please."

Melodie shook her head. "If you've got a proposed target, out with it, Count. We hit three Devastators, but scores remain. We've yet to locate a Guard-damned one we can hit from here."

Zeyus cut in. "Take the time you need, find your next target. Hell, find every Guard-damn target. I'm gonna to need to prepare for this whole operation, too. A Moon, perhaps? Can we dance on that time-table?"

"A pair of fortnights?" Melodie lit a cigarillo. "Fair enough. Any longer feels flat-footed."

"Then we depart here at dawn."

The mood among the embattled resistance fighters gathered in our strategy meeting was grim. Even Sunderah seemed gloomy. and Her scales were losing their glimmer. Uncertainty and frustration prevented sleep when evening arrived. Everyone wondered if the war we'd found ourselves in was for naught. Did anyone truly believe we could defeat the Jurisdiction?
{~}

Unkind weather and unkinder circumstances caused breakfast the following morning to be an unhappy affair. We ate our biscuits and drank our tea in muted pensiveness. Partway through the food-based ritual, a boy approached the Iris Council table with a gathering basket in his hands. The boy was a former Slave who Melodie did her best to look after, the Dragon tribe, they called themselves. Because of the boy's origin, the Iris Council remained aloof as he entreated each of them about the contents of his gathering basket, but the fire mage Raspho fervently leapt from his seat and spilled tea down the front of his robe.

The wicker basket was lined with a square of cloth stained vibrant purple spots from the berries it normally held. Curled within was a tiny kitten, patterned like a tiger in orange and dark red. She was so teeny her eyes could barely open. I wondered if the baby cat would survive without its mother.

Raspho's intense behaviour towards the kitten was entirely irrational. Concerning, even. I sensed the Seer Sage tense as if the mage were ill. He swore the kitten already had a name, an utter impossibility given the recent birth of the creature in empty Wilds. He grasped the handle of the basket from the boy with fierce jealousy, nearly burning the child with a wave of heat rolling away from his robe. The boy began to cry, letting go of the basket. Melodie frowned at Raspho, rebuking him as if he were a younger brother. The fire mage was emotional, cradling his pilfered prize. Between tears and sharp breaths, he stammered what sounded a sincere apology. He fervently promised the boy could always see the kitten whenever he wished.

I'd already seen enough strange entities for several lifetimes. I had other things to do with my Sun. Zeyus and I looked at each other and departed from the mages with cursory nods. We were glad to be on our way, and I'm sure the City of Old was happy enough to see us go. I felt as though Zeyus and I could speak more easily without fearing that other ears would catch wind of the profound grief we both shared. To lose control is an assault where the damage is difficult to catalogue. The Sovereign had pushed us to the side, and when the Sovereign was removed, we felt an emptiness which used to be part of the whole. I began counting the Moons until I felt at ease with my entire self again.

"I don't want to get you killed," I told Zeyus as we hiked south through the forest. He had his weapons with him, and we'd been given supplies, but we knew the journey would require half a fortnight before we reached Atlantium's outskirts. I'd infiltrate the Regiment. If he joined, Zeyus would be spotted and identified. There was no sense in him following where I'd feed.

"I won't be anywhere near you. I have my own ideas."

I frowned, looking over at Zeyus, but he didn't return my concerned gaze.

"They'll kill you now, you know. Wouldn't you be better off taking revenge somewhere other than Atlantium? Perhaps a place you might not be instantly recognized?"

Zeyus shook his head. "The whole Guard-damned Jurisdiction knows who I am, but I know who Atlantium is. If I can get inside the inner Sanctum of the Devisors, then the Swarm and the Quints, the Bombers, I'll have it all, for a while. Long enough to make it count, anyway."

I drew a sharp breath. "You don't expect to live."

Zeyus shook his head, and for the first time he let the damage show on the surface.

"I'm going to leave a trail of blood to the heart of the Sanctum, Lucy. But no, I doubt I'll be making my way to any extraction points."

I reached to grasp his shoulder, and I looked at his face. He stopped moving, but the gesture clearly irritated him. I found myself at a loss for words, for once. We marched on in silence until I found the correct melody. The dirge was in a minor key, a D'Arsailles family composition, but I couldn't remember which distant relation had been the composer.

{~}

The Hidden Sashes presented splendidly for my re-emergence in the shadows of the Atlantium markets. My network of spies and accomplices among the Prize Mates had grown to beyond my imagining over the Rounds. In fact, such a preponderance of the Atlantium Prize Mates were pledged to the cause that the rest of them feared betraying "fang-scarf" sisters and brothers nearly as much as they feared the Jurisdiction.

I considered the power I'd accumulated with no lack of amusement. The Hidden Sashes were never meant to see the light of Sun. Before I met the dragons, outright rebellion had never been an option, not even remotely. Many of the Hidden Sashes could lose their lives as a result of my plans.

"We're ready, I declare for us," Vignetta said in a concealed corner of the Barracks cellar. A veil covered the bottom half of her face, but her eyes were brimming with intensity. She brandished a dagger to underscore the sincerity of her death wish.

"Are you sure, my dear?" I asked my brave co-conspirator. I wasn't sure had the heart for this. I was getting softer than a fuzzy bat.

She scoffed at my imagining otherwise. "We've been training for almost a decade, Count D'Arsailles. I've considered every scenario, hungered since the day I woke up in here. We can kill enough Regs. The bodies will clog the doorways. The confusion will work to our advantage. A number of the Prize Mates can escape. Others can kill until our blood mingles with the blood of the oppressors. It's only natural we should feel this way. We must give the chance, and the choice to make fate their own. It's what they've been waiting for."

"Please, Vignetta. Call me Lucien. You, of all people, and especially at this hour. It's an honor to have known you, sister. I'm sure you were a queen, once. In another life, perhaps. Perhaps you'll be that again, when your spirit is set free."

The tall woman clasped my hand in an earnest embrace.

"In this life, Count Lucien, let me be but a humble butcher."

{~}

The Barracks common areas were decorated in lavish fashion. The Sashes had insisted on the finest foods, luxurious distractions. The Prize Mates who held sway with their Jurisdiction spouses leveraged unison pleading to make it so, requesting exotic intoxicants and scandalous lingerie. Vignetta and I made a few suggestions we thought would make for the best tactics, but it was the Prize Mates themselves who ran away with the concept, and we made no move to constrain. The trap was set with convincing bait.

The party was billed as an Enchanted Autumn Ball, a halfway point between the fall and winter solstice. The air outside was losing warmth, but we wouldn't see snows yet at our latitude.

The Hidden Sashes were feeding my urges in the cellar, and when the night of the party arrived, I was already brimming with power. A lone final offering from the Sashes arrived. The woman was terribly fearful, aghast at the planned insurrection, and I alleviated her fears. My teeth sank through the pale skin of her neck. She drifted away and I left her at peace.

I grinned among the shadows the Hidden Sashes had conveniently placed around the room. The candles and draped lighting and dendroid decorations met the theme of the Ball flawlessly. I moved unnoticed behind a curtain, catching my first glimpse of a wide-eyed Regiment soldier. He'd finished his patrol in time to celebrate. The music began to lull him, luring him in.

Don't get overconfident, I reminded myself. The first few will be easy, but they'll catch on eventually, and trouble will begin. As I drifted towards another dark corner, I knew the Hidden Sashes were probably already concealing the dismembered corpse of the first guest. I watched an entire group of Regs enter next. The men were laughing, making crude jokes at the smiling Sashes. One of the ladies strutted forward wearing next to nothing and offered the soldiers a silver tray covered in rows of white powder. Make yourselves at home, gentlemen, I thought. Do a line or three.

Everything was proceeding as planned when I heard an alarm at the edge of the Devisors' compound. Dammit Zeyus, I thought. You should've kept the dance on the time-table! I whispered a curse as a number of Regiment drained away from the Ball. The Winged Man had added that extra heat to himself. I didn't have anything I could do to assist him without compromising the Ball.

While the alarm continued to drone in the distance, I felt a selfish glee. Zeyus' difficulty in sticking to schedule might've worked in favor of my favorite Prize Mates. A thinner crowd would notice the absences more easily, but the dwindling number of Regiment meant that our odds were steadily improving if an outright brawl erupted.

That moment arrived, of course. The Sashes saw it coming, thankfully. I witnessed the changing features of the Regiment soldier's face, twisted with kindling rage, and we anticipated the violence which would follow. He stood up from his chair, hurling his crystal goblet at Vignetta and grabbing a Prize Mate near him by the throat. His battle-buddy hadn't come back from the loo, and he'd been fed one-too-many sultry reassurances. The cocktails and the drugs and candlelight reddened his face, a countenance echoed by the entire table. I launched my furry body at him, wings wide, and I screeched for everything I was worth.

Bedlam ensued.

I bit necks, tripped legs, I blasted soundwaves until my enemies were senseless. If the blood of a Prize Mates was a fine carafe of mulled wine, the blood of a Regiment soldier is a dirty bath-tub full of lukewarm malt-liquor. The Hidden Sashes were hasty to use whatever sharp or blunt objects they'd acquired to finish off the groaning men. The dim air of the Enchanted Autumn Ball began to reek of fear and blood and murderous euphoria.

I wouldn't make any recommendations for general use in modern architecture, but a few big-ass dead bodies can sure as hell block up a doorway. The Regiment stored firearms inside the Barracks on a casual basis, and the Hidden Sashes were armed with more than clubs and shivs by the time Jurisdiction reinforcements arrived. The Regiment attendees of the Ball were dead, along with a handful of Sashes. We were trapped inside the barracks, and under constant siege. As we attempted to help the wounded and assess the situation, my thoughts went to Zeyus.

I muttered my thanks to the Guards when I saw Vignetta's blood-spattered face among the gathering Sashes. The remaining Prize Mates were starting to look in my direction. At this critical juncture, I knew Vignetta was twice the leader I had ever been. Rousing speeches were an art I'd always viewed with no trivial amount of scorn. Apathy and obscurity had always served my needs. Alas, I knew what the moment called for.

"Kindred of the Hidden Sashes," I began. My voice projected in the dark, among the flipped tables and bullet-riddled walls of the desecrated barracks. The power had been cut for almost a Mark. We conserved the flashlights and flares accordingly.

"I wish I could tell you that you've freed yourselves. For you've fought valiantly, and you've bled to for it. And yet, shapeshifting mage that I am, I don't control the world. I doubt if even the Guards themselves stoop from the heavens to do so now and then. You can tell by the sound of the artillery against the north wall of this building that the Jurisdiction hasn't forgotten us, here."

Determination was written plainly on pained expressions. I was emboldened to ask what I must.

"Your destiny now is entirely your own. I suggest a final place you should visit, if you have the strength to continue the fight. My dear friend has gone ahead already and made his presence known, and to provide a distraction. The back tunnel is how we'll go. Yes, Karen. Vignetta knows the route."

Murmurs of anticipation were spreading among the Sashes.

"Go and shut down the Swarm. Go reclaim your Birthing Chambers from the Devisors who made you as play-things. I suggest you destroy the seeds of the Regiment if you can, to stem the tide of reinforcements. As for the rest of what you find in the sanctum of the Devisors, I'll not instruct you on what to do with intimate secrets. The time is here for each of you. Think and act of your own free accord. You must come to terms with what you are, in the wake of servitude."

Vignetta turned to face the other Hidden Sashes. I thought for a moment that I saw her hand tremble, but she it by grasping the hilt of her sheathed dagger. No one would challenge her assumed authority. Throughout their lives, the Prize Mates were told what to do. As the Hidden Sashes, they'd finally chosen who they'd like to listen to. Vignetta unhooked her veil, revealing a jagged scar along the edge of her jaw. Her voice was barely more than a whisper, but nobody missed the words.

"Tear it down. Every scrap."

"Power condenses... power radiates. When everything else is said and done, life is just a chaotic transfer of energy. We've always been this way. Nothing will change the fact that we change." -The Sorcerer Prodigy

Pain awaited me when we entered the City of Old, but I preferred the sting to the numbness that followed. The injury inflicted by a vision known as "A'Rehia" was the least of my concerns, though the kiteknife gash dogged at me and sapped my strength. I tried to put on a strong face for her, even if she was an illusion. The levitating maiden was the only piece of the world I wanted to impress, but the drain of the world around me caused my projected facade to crack almost immediately.

I wept molten tears when we found the bodies of Erixe and Briin. I felt as though the loss of my family had repeated itself. Charlie and the Wise Witch were gone. The combined loss stirred a loneliness keener than the Keenwood Staff. I didn't care who saw me vent, or who might step too close to my fiery tantrums. The Guards needed to see what they'd done, even if I had to sketch them a diagram! The City was strewn with the bodies of the Rose tribe. We burned them to ash, just as I had my family on the beach. I was acquainted with the fierce gunfighters for a short time, but it was enough. Familiar lifeless faces put the horror of war on full display.

I was a shattered man. I'd been shattered since my family was murdered on their farm, and the fresh losses took the healing I'd done and tossed it all away. Was this the same spot, barely healed, or was I experiencing brand new damage?

My skills as a mage openly reflected my distress. I could barely light a candle most of the time, and I felt so weak I doubted I'd ever be myself again. Other Suns, the fire flowed from so freely and with such ease it felt like I could barely contain the danger I created. When the Wise Witch was taken away to the False Priesthood, I knew for certain the guidance I desired would never return.

I became withdrawn. I didn't trust myself, and I didn't want to hurt anyone. Laurelei kept an eye when she could. She remained gentle as she scolded me to eat or wash. Without distractions, I was distracted by my own trauma and grief. The sympathetic looks I got eroded my self confidence, and nobody offered any reassurances to accompany judgement.

Melodie and I had shared in the struggle of the Battle of the Downed Dragon. But seeing my face caused the gunfighter woman to remember what she'd lost. When she managed to put aside her own hurt enough to speak with me, I found her tough-talking and her dismissal of sadness and weakness to be nearly as jarring as the silence. I knew it was just her way of mourning. She stayed strong for all of us. She marked stones for Flin and Terche and Bonder, but not for Drak. The titan wolf pelt A'Rehia had pulled from the banner poles would've been gladly treasured for warmth, but Melodie flung the hide in the fire in a flash of emotion. A member of the Freed people didn't agree with her destruction, snatching at the smoking fur, but Melodie bodied the opportunist away. She cussed wildly before she found a measured tone of voice.

"This pelt represents a bitter chain of needless death," she said. "Would you wrap yourself in barbaric folly? Wear the skin of your brother or your sister if they happened to be furrier than you?" She swore again, a harsh string of creative terminology.

"You'll ask permission, from a titan wolf! I'll stitch together the hides of a million rats before I let a stolen titan wolf pelt keep anyone warm around here. The only place a titan wolf pelt belongs is on a Guard-damn titan wolf!"

{~}

A'Rehia and Chrysanthemum remained strangers in my eyes, despite having traveled and faced corpses together. I spent my time convalescing from the wounds I'd received. I heard scattered conversation around the cooking fires, and I remember the musical croon of A'Rehia's voice. On a full moon I'll never forget, she spoke to me when she thought I was sleeping, sincere apologies for knifing me. I spent many Marks feigning sleep after that, and her continued avoidance only increased the depression I was already feeling. Raw and vulnerable as I was, surely she'd noticed how entranced I was by her every facet. Of course she avoided me. The truth made me uncomfortable around her in a way I'd never experienced before.

A'Rehia and the ghostly air mage stayed in each other's company until the departure of the Wise Witch drew Chrysanthemum away from the City. Hoping the Witch would recover was a bittersweet tether, and I sensed A'Rehia was moody about her friend's departure. She began to spend nearly every minute of her time with her mother, Laurelei. Consequently, and to my secret delight, this meant I was graced by her presence.

"A boy found your cat?" A'Rehia asked.

My thoughts came back in focus, and I hoped I hadn't been staring at her clothing. Her voice contained the perfect amount of air rushing through perfect spaces. She resonated, and the sound struck my ears in places I didn't know they even had. The butterflies in my abdomen were going berserk. I swallowed. My throat bobbed as I struggled to respond to her question casually.

"Dude's name is Wohan. Charlie isn't my cat. He clings to his 'little sister' like a burr. Cat welcomes the company, but I'm tryna find Wohan stuff to do to occupy his time. He wasn't in favor among the Freed people. Scrawny as hell, and he doesn't like the gangs."

We were sitting on hewn stools by the cook fire. My heart pulsed rapidly because we were so seldom alone together. The wooden hovels we'd been living in were at our backs. Patched after recent warfare, the cots were cozy enough. Wohan shared my hovel, and A'Rehia was staying with her mother.

The air mage gave an accusing look. "He's always around here, doing chores for you and my mom. Do you make him work for you just to stay here with the kitten he found?"

"He's free to do as he pleases, but he's eager to please. I told him he's a Squire. Dunno if he'll ever be a mage or a fighter, but he likes the way it sounds, I guess. I convinced Melodie to teach him how to shoot when he's older. Tehsyn is teaching him the words and numbers Laurelei, er, ah, your mom didn't know."

She seemed to accept my explanation, but she cartwheeled to the doorway of my hovel. I stood in response, instantly wondering if I had any dirty laundry laying around. A'Rehia barged through the entry to my living quarters.

She didn't spare a glance for anything except the cat's corner. Charlie was still tiny, and A'Rehia bent over her crib, handing her a fire-warmed bottle. The whispering kitten seemed to prefer Wohan's company at least as much as mine, which was saddening, but I came to accept the way of it. Charlie was recovering from the pain, just as I was. I had too many other things to be sad about. Neither of us could avoid what we'd become.

{~}

A morning came when A'Rehia decided to dance.

I'm sure my jaw dangled. I sat gawking up at the sight of her. My trance broke for a moment, when her mother brought me tea. I probably blushed like a branding iron. Laurelei smiled as her daughter flipped and twirled above the ruins. Skirts fluttered in every direction, with only knickers preserving her modesty. She moved in a carefree way and captured every intricacy and nuance. I thought for a moment she'd lost her mind completely, and we were witnessing the result of a psychotic break, but if A'Rehia's dancing was a sickness I hoped it was contagious.

When A'Rehia finally landed breathlessly, Laurelei and I provided her with raucous applause.

"What about you?" she said. The question was unbalancing, and her slim hand on my shoulder threatened to tip me completely.

"You're a mage. Don't you need to practice?"

I shook my head. "Haven't been able to practice since- since my injury. Been messed up, inconsistent. I'm not sure what to do."

A'Rehia frowned. "That's why you practice. Only one way to fix it."

My mind and body were already preparing themselves for the effort. I listened to her confident deductions. I leapt to obey the Executor's daughter with a heart I'd never felt under the orders of the Jurisdiction tyrant who'd been her father. I already felt more stability inside even as I cautioned the ladies to step back while I did something cool.

I took a perfect breath and readied myself as much as I could. A rogue fireball winked into existence, reluctantly acquiescing to the whims of arcane manipulation. I felt the swirling tendrils, white hot heat. Instead of draining my energy, the pattern seemed to fuel it. I wasn't dysfunctional, only disrupted. In the flame, I found the purification of my own heart. The blazing glow found the sconces of my smiling eyes. I was becoming myself, again.

As I focused on my meditation, I forgot the spectators. When I looked away from the orb, Laurelei was nowhere to be found. The glow highlighted A'Rehia's features, but I saw an anguish in her eyes. A frown threatened to pull the corners of her mouth. My fireball rotated in perfect harmony. She turned away.

I let the fireball vanish as gracefully as possible.

"Your father-" I began. My hands fell to my sides. I noticed that they barely even trembled this time.

"I guess I understand."

A'Rehia recovered her composure to look again. She seemed to be fighting back tears. Her aura and her body pressed against mine.

"No, Ras," she said, but her frown was fading. "You don't understand."

I shouldn't kiss and tell, but she's the one who kissed me. I don't think I understood that part, either, but I decided I didn't need to sketch a diagram.

"If you leave traces of yourself behind after life and flesh have gone, let the evidence extend beyond your weathered bones." -The Gunslinger Confidant

Some Suns I felt like the hardest part of being in charge was convincing myself I didn't hate everyone.

Dear Guards, the Freed People were difficult. The insistence on the whims of scattered mobs and remorseless acts of violence left me shaken. I saw punishment meted with an un-holstered hand.

A new Council formed in the City of Old which held true to the only rules I knew for any tribe, overcoming the objections of both the Iris tribal Council and the gang-style leadership of the Freed Peoples. Perhaps I might've traveled a different path if I wasn't elected a Confidant, but the newly formed Free City chose me to join the governing body. The Seer Sage of the Iris tribe drew up the documents for the Charter after consulting with scrolls of animal hide defining tribal law in the Low Hills for generations. When no provision was made for the role of Generale, I held my silence. I'd allow my military command to die with the Rose. Even as a Confidant, I knew my loyalty wasn't with the Freed people, or with the Iris tribe, or even with the dragons themselves. I only knew what I was supposed to be fighting. We made no special accommodations for former status, but Vilkir and Tehsyn became members of the Council. Suspicious whispers began about how Tehsyn Foresaw the vote, but no one could offer any evidence of fraud or coercion beyond rumors I found mildly offensive.

Generale or no, I wasn't able to thrust aside the mantle of power. I went looking for firewhiskey, fighting voices echoing admonishment or request inside my head. Alive or dead, I felt souls who weighed heavily in those Suns. I was declared Sheriff of the Free City by the Council as their inaugural act. They granted me the power of judging who should be brought in for formal charges before the Council. With the Free City in its infancy, I was a crude but effective tool.

{~}

My favorite kind of assholes were the ones I could just shoot and be done with it. A need exists in this world for justice, peaceful community, and even clever murderers struggle to hide the blood. Brave souls whispered, and I pulled my jacket from the armor stand.

Rahn followed among the tents as we sought the culprits in the East Quarter of the City of Old. I would've protested an escort, but I knew his ears were frozen. His presence wasn't meant as a protective gesture. He'd gambled a stake in these people, his Freed People. He wanted them to know the authority of the Council was united as one, and sentencing for dire crimes would be unified and inevitable.

No need for trial, except by the Guards. Perhaps wisdom and mercy shone forth when the guilty attacked outright rather than stand condemned by the full weight of their peers in an orderly fashion. When the deed was done, Rahn spoke to the crowd gathering at the spectacle. He shook as the blood dripped from the blade in his hands, and his voice bent with emotion. He spoke as though children in every corner needed to hear him. He told the Free City of his hopes, and his fears. He told them how much he hated doing what he did, and he told them it wouldn't happen, not anymore. I returned wide eyed gazes with significantly less compassion, and I made sure to reload during the pauses in Rahn's speech, so the gesture was audible. I didn't hate what happened. In the moments when the crack and the jingle of spent shells rang in my ears, it was easier for me to still be on the battlefield.

The Council managed food and shelter. Better than the Jurisdiction ever had, Rahn assured me, but the City was a constant balancing act, and nothing ever went without complaint. A brave smile here and there was the meager reassurance I received from the Free People when I looked at their tattered clothing and shelter. The weather was only going to get colder. Twice, we'd needed to ward away the frost. Fuel and food were accessible, but the effort required meant we need to keep hands busy. People didn't always agree on the best approach, or the tasks available. The life of a Free City settler was different from a Slave of the Pens.

I hated arresting people. I saw enough suffering in the City to create a gray area in the ruins where I had no idea know who was guilty of what. I tended to blame the Jurisdiction for everything, instead. I'd haul people before the Council and let the other Confidants sort heads as best they could. In those moments, I held more gratitude for Tehsyn than I ever imagined possible. The woman always calmed me down and asked the clearest questions after she tended any- ahem- apprehension related side effects, of course. She had a way with rebels and outcasts. Where I saw disobedience and aggression, she uncovered misuse and unbridled passion. Tehsyn's script flowed through the air in due judgement, and penance invariably arrived with new direction.

{~}

A Sun came when I was called to inspect a collapsed tunnel in the guts of the City, beneath a ruined skyscraper. As the space was excavated, I recalled the Rose tribe had used the basement for storage. I'd taken to carrying the Regiment crowbar across my back, and I levered the tool to pry pieces of broken concrete free, joining in the efforts. When the rest of the digging team broke for lunch, I crawled through the reopened passage and entered the sealed-off room.

I dropped a chem-torch on the floor. The room illuminated with a dim, neutral white. The flare tinged the air with sulfurous smoke. I was looking at a collection of things that the Rose tribe had packed on wagons when they prepared to enter exile. The skins with our histories were rolled into neat piles. Artwork and trinkets and treasure, deemed too valuable to leave behind. Stacked in rows against the walls. The center of the room held the coup-de-gras, the centerpiece of the record-keepers long-house, the blown glass rose. The chem-torch scattered reds and greens against the ancient concrete ceiling of the buried chamber.

I felt the crowbar in my hands and I swung, wondering if anyone outside could hear me roaring. Shards of glass scattered through the air, and landed everywhere atop the useless hoard. I took a zealous breath and swung again.

I stalked away from the dig site, dragging the crowbar behind. I decided not to care about what happened at the dig site, anymore.
{~}

The state of the defenses and the ruination of the Mammoth stuck in my craw. We half-heartedly constructed wooden barricades, but everyone knew how useless they'd probably be against what was set against us. I led a few volunteers to dig through the Mammoth's remains. What appeared as catastrophic damage was limited to the cockpit. I was relieved to see valuable gear intact, but none of the hands who were around knew what to do with the machinery. I directed the Mammoth be cleared of debris, but when it came to assessing her integrity and getting her up and running again, I was at a loss.

I was alone inside the dimly lit interior of the superstructure, squinting at a cryptic technical manual, when a voice echoed down through the tube leading up to the hatch.

"Yooohoooo!"

The man sounded like Flin, and my heart wrenched in my chest, but the old Wizard appeared instead. His beard was too curious to stay away from the Mammoth, he told me, seating himself next to me at dinner the night before. I'd already insisted we didn't need his frail knees climbing the ladder, but there he was anyway, levitating in the entry shaft. He looked wide-eyed as ever and was apparently oblivious to how his robes were fluttering askew around his unsightly chicken-legs.

"Hells bells, Mel! Is this damn thing real, or did I eat the wrong mushrooms again?"

"Well if you do feel like your tripping, it seems you can float."

The Wizard laughed.

"I've heard if you get high enough, you'll never fall down."

I frowned and gritted my teeth, irritated by the Wizard's presence. He didn't seem to take this seriously with his lighthearted attempts at conversation. He smelled funny, and the cramped interior of the Mammoth did, too. I was beginning to think of an excuse to eject him, so I could concentrate. I sighed, but when I drew a breath to speak, he interrupted.

"Is that a fusion generator? I've never seen this machining setup before. How is it that the forge is so compact? Everything is run by a central operating system? Marvelous. Nothing short of pure genius, I mean, if you ask the right people. Too bad the Jurisdiction turned out to be such assholes, huh? I like to picture the early Devisors as a tribe of tinkering gnomes, essentially innocent in their boundless curiosity."

The Wizard ran his fingers along the wooden surface of the gunsmithing table. I began to consider him in a different light. He knew things, important things. Like the Witch did.

"You think you could get any of this working?"

The Wizard raised his frazzled eyebrows.

"Get what working? This big, dumb alliance? A few more of the pew-pew boom-tubes? My weathered old pirate schlong?" His eyes flashed an obscene shade of blue. "My apologies, a crude joke. May the humor be at my expense, not yours."

I rolled my eyes. He clearly hadn't answered my question, but I didn't think he'd forgotten, either.

"Well?" I prodded him verbally, but also physically.

He toppled from the stool in front of the gunsmithing bench in a dramatized response to my good-natured shove. He kept a sharp eye in my direction, smoothing his beard and drumming his bony fingers on the workshop table.

"I wish I knew what my wife thought about all of this, to be honest," he said sincerely after a lengthy pause. He peered at my eyes, but he was searching for more than my eye color. The blue glow of his irises was calming and flowing. Too calming. Entrancing, even. His hand danced sideways and flipped a switch I hadn't noticed. The hum of the Mammoth's cooling fans filled the room. He shook his head back and forth. Part of his beard strayed to the side, causing him to smooth the wisp with his left hand.

"I'll do it, Mel. Not for you. Not for anyone else." His eyes grew gentler. He cleared his throat. "Well, maybe for my wife. Or my daughter." He sat up straighter and his insistence returned. "But certainly not for me."

He threw a breaker. The contacts sizzled and sparked, and he thrust his hands into an abandoned pair of leather gloves. When he pulled the welding mask over his face, his white beard dangled beneath the shield. He picked up a pipe wrench, resting the tool against his shoulder. I knew the coils of the forge were beginning to glow within the Mammoth. His voice was muffled by the mask, but he was boomy in the enclosed space.

"For the Defiance, girlie."

{~}

I gave him his space for a few Suns, but my grace period ended when Vilkir made it clear we'd need more ammunition to train militia. I opened the hatch and descended once again to the inner floor of the Mammoth. Her sounds had resumed. I slept better with familiar ambient noises in my life. The Wizard was seated in a corner, stroking his beard, as usual.

"Whaddaya got for me down here?"

He gestured to the table. I could tell he was deep in thought by the frown on his face. I looked to where he indicated and I was immediately puzzled.

"That? You're down here making useless art projects? What is that thing, a ceremonial baseball bat? Where are the guns? Where's the ammunition? We need those, Wiz, to stay alive!" He didn't seem to hear, and my frustration spiked. I shouted.

"What have you been doing? Wasting time and resources? The whole City is gonna die!"

My volume must've gotten to him. He pointed, in his irritated way, towards a wall. A fresh hole had been bored through the steel of the Mammoth's hull. My entire fist fit through the opening and the blackness of the earth beyond yawned back.

"You? How?"

The Wizard looked exasperated, lifting his arm and pointing again.

"This thing? Really?"

The Wizard sighed aloud, returning to himself.

"Yes, yes. You thought a Wizard would make the same boring weapons that everyone else uses?"

I stared down at the metal club with new eyes. A large bead of colored glass was set in the end which swirled every color imaginable. The body of the club was mostly plain steel, and the handle was wrapped with black grip-tape.

"Where does- how does it-"

"Disintegration Scepter, Mel. Should run a few Suns before we need to recharge . More like a Moon if stored properly."

"Anyone can use it? Even if they aren't a mage?" I began to reach for the handle of the Scepter. The Wizard grasped my forearm.

"I wouldn't, yet. Hazardous prototype, and whatnot."

"You didn't answer my question."

The Wizard shrugged. "Better if the wielder is a mage. Not totally necessary. Mostly works like a gun, which I thought might make you happy. Holes galore. Wherever you point this baby."

He sat back against the wall of the Mammoth and squinted.

"But that's war, I suppose. Never really been my cup of tea."

{~}

From our sentry perches in the ruins, it wasn't uncommon for Vilkir or me to shoot down a stray Swarm drone or three. The flying machines were probably the best target practice any of us had other than hunting game to feed the hungry population. I had difficulty determining if the handfuls of drones coming in range were deliberate reconnaissance by the Jurisdiction or simply lost fragments of detachments operating elsewhere.

The line between target practice and a genuine threat was thin. When our perimeter scouts reported Swarm drones on the horizon, we were immediately wary. We took up arms and took battle stations, and battened down the hatches. This wasn't a drill, we told people, but with a concerted effort, we'd have a decisive victory. I couldn't picture the exact number of Swarm drones it would take overwhelm our defenses. With the dragons nearby, I didn't think that number existed. I took heart at the thought, but then Rahn handed me a set of binoculars.

My depth perception felt like it was distorted. At first, I decided the binoculars were a stronger magnification than I thought. I blinked when the Swarm came flowing above the trees and the hills of the landscape. The hum was different. I brought the binoculars to my face again. The aircraft were't Swarm drones at all. I yelled a garbled warning, but the battle had already begun.

The Nobility Airships were the cause of my confusion. Instead of rotors, each craft sported jet turbines. Instead of a receiver unit, each held a Nobility fire mage, seated in an open cockpit and invariably draped in red. The Devisors hadn't forgotten to put guns on the Airships, too, but the fire mage pilots lobbed fireballs with a casual grunt usually reserved for bowel movements.

My bullets weren't hitting the Airships. I growled in frustration. Projectiles vanished in a whoosh of flame before they could strike a target. Even the Disintegration Scepters the Wizard cooked up fared no better against whatever shielding the bastards were using. I watched a Nobility fire mage hover to a stop, pouring himself a drink from the sideboard beside his luxurious pilot's console. I gave him bullets, but my attack was impeded. My growl became vicious cussing. I reloaded as his crystal decanter clinked against stemmed glassware.

I was beginning to lose hope. I was hearing screams, and I inhaled the smell of burning flesh, but an inspiring rumble shook the City in spite of the destruction. The lash of a bronze tail flashed across the corner of my eye. The mage in my sights spilled his martini on the hull of his airship as the jet engine next to him exploded.

The Nobility regrouped, redirecting the raid to a vulnerable point in our defenses. We had difficulty taking cover due to the steep angles the Airships could take. The spread of mage fire left nowhere to hide, until Chaeoh's shadow fell over the battlefield. In a heartbeat, he was above me, using the entire bulk of his frame to shield from the onslaught. Gunfire and incendiaries crashed against his armored scales.

I heard a din like the breath of the Guards, and I knew our alliance within the City was holding. Tehsyn and the Wizard made a dome of glimmering water in to protect the children and the Mammoth when the Airships broke through. A pair of aqueous elementals patrolled the edge of the dome, expressionless in solemn duty. At the edge of my vision, I saw a tree move along the river bank, walking purposefully on stranded of roots. I blinked away disbelief, noting the tree appeared skeptical of the cold water. Adding to my shock, the arboreal scowled like a cartoon-ish nightmare. The Wizard was winking when I looked at him. The tree entwined its branches around a chunk of concrete and flung it at an Airship.

The altruistic phenomena hadn't produced the palpable rush of victory I was hearing. I detected a beat to the noise, almost like a creature was flapping a host of wings with precise timing.

"Oh my Guards," Raspho said, pointing towards the horizon. "Duu came back. She wants her target practice."

I doubted anyone had ever laid eyes on the machine the twin priestesses were operating, but the Wiz nodded and mouthed the word 'chopper'. The aircraft was antiquated technology, from a bygone era, unseen in centuries. In the time since those fabled Rounds, the Jurisdiction had warped the face of the world.

Duu sat in the cockpit of the helicopter. She waved saucily towards Raspho through the front window, and he returned the gesture apprehensively. Her mirth was dwarfed by the glee of her sister, who stood in the side bay of the gunship beneath the main rotor. The mysterious Priestess smiled with such ferocity that the full lengths of her sharpened yellowed teeth could be seen across the entire battlefield. She yowled, a ferocious announcement of primal urgency. Along with her yowl, she gripped the handles of the machine guns in front of her. The rotating barrels sprang to life.

Whatever shielded the Nobility Airships from attack was weakening as the fighting dragged on. Within minutes of the arrival of the dragons, the enemy began a full retreat, but it was unlikely any of our enemies would escape what they found in the City of Old. I watched Vilkir charge forward on Kiffu-San's shoulders, and I missed Lohise acutely.

A few Nobility mages survived the fighting, and I heard arguments about what to do with them. I saw a woman slaughter several prisoners, cut them in half with a Disintegration Scepter, before Tehsyn could disarm her. Afterwards, the injured Nobility were tied and bound, held in a tent with a sentry.

The dust was barely settled, but Rahn was at my side. He annoyed me with his public displays of emotion, but when the man decided he wanted to kiss me, I kissed him back, anyway.

"We're gonna keep this place safe, right?" he said, fighting back tears.

I frowned. For such a broad-shouldered hunk, Rahn was awfully emotional sometimes. The smell of sweat and blood and dirt was oppressive, but Rahn was limping, and I suppose I'd just kissed him, anyway. I gripped his belt with my arm around his lower back, and I let him put his weight across my shoulders.

"I doubt any other full-blown rebellions are hiring," I told him.

Chapter 35
Rahn tells of: "Crystallization"

"Death isn't a sign of weakness, and killing isn't a sign of strength. A worthy cause, on the other hand, is stronger than any blade or bullet will ever be. The battle for the body is brief and crude, but the war of hearts and minds is a graceful dance which spans every time and age." -The Frost Swordsman

When our improvised war band arrived at the burning outskirts of Atlantium, the place wasn't much of a city anymore. I heard A'Rehia gasp when she first surveyed the damage wrought on her childhood home. Behind her, Raspho clung to the back of the the Pegasaur Drake Oh-Four-Three, attempting to keep his face from turning green.

"Oh-Four-Three, Oh-Four-Three!"

The drake yelled an impassioned call to the injured city. Chaeoh and Sunderah nodded in approval of their lithe cousin. Melanie sat astride the gleaming bronze female, and Chaeoh's wide scales ferried the Wizard and me down the face of the continent. Ours was a bold counterattack. We knew what we'd signed up for, so to speak. With the two dragons and third of the City Council in Atlantium, I shuddered to think what would become of the Free City if none of us returned.

The rubble below us didn't provide much to comment about as we sought a landing site. Charred timbers wouldn't shelter anyone. Survivors had probably fled for the hills. Hopefully the killer Swarm drones were occupied by something other than hunting down escaping civilians.

The slums of Atlantium were rife with bullet holes and scorch marks. The Nobility weren't exactly known for patient clemency towards civilians whenever they perceived their power was being challenged. Conversely, the damage to the Jurisdiction strongholds at the heart of the city came as a surprise. Much to the relief of Raspho's stomach, we dismounted when the lizards touched down. Our feet crunched on caked dirt. Open insurrection had been unkind to the manicured lawn.

The footprints of the Regiment were everywhere, but I didn't see any bodies. Blackened concrete and twisted steel beams were the only remainder of the Jurisdiction edifice before us. The wreckage was strewn about, and I had a difficult time imagining how many buildings once stood. The Wizard picked up a fist sized rock near his foot, presumably jettisoned from its former location. He brought the rock to his nose, sniffing thoughtfully.

"Explosives," he said, a hint of approval in his voice. I realized the entire group waited on his next words. Oh-Four-Three and the dragons craned their necks to see his face. As for the humans, we each listened with varying degrees of skepticism to what the crazy old hermit thought we should do next.

"I sense we might be in danger," he said, frowning.

Melodie choked out a laugh.

"I'm glad you happened to notice," she said. Her body language left her holsters within easy reach.

"I wonder if anybody's alive."

Raspho's melancholy words compelled us to examine our options, but a voice responded from the ruins of Atlantium. Nobody could detect its source, and the unexpected sound caused the group to bristle with all manner of teeth and claws.

"You mean like, living people?"

An ugly laugh made us look at each other and adjust our formation.

"No, my dear guests. You probably won't find much fitting that description in Atlantium, not these Suns. But those boring hairless apes are pretty obsolete, anyway, don't you think? Mages and machines. That's all that matters anymore. I figured your cute little posse would understand the truth by now."

When the speaker showed himself, we gathered a collective self-control to resist leaping to the attack. His skin was charred from head to toe, and he was cracked, as though his soul had dried up and evaporated from his flesh. His eyes shone like stoked branding irons resting against the anvil of his face. Lengths of linked metal hung from his shoulders like a tattered cape. In each of his hands, he held a jagged tongue of flame. The controlled burn formed cruel, jagged swords.

The Jurisdiction apparently wasn't prepared to concede Atlantium without a fight. I was slightly dumbfounded by the Fallen Angel. I couldn't deduce why anyone would be determined to lord over a pile of rubble. Speculations about motive were useless. The truly frightening part about Faehr Dun was his unexpected existence. We were painfully unaware of the Jurisdiction's true capabilities.

Malicious fiend though he was, we might've defeated the Fallen Angel if the Quints hadn't held the edge of the city. A glowing red eye winked, and before I knew what was happening, mortars were falling everywhere I could look. A'Rehia bolted into the sky along with the three flying lizards, leaving Melodie, Raspho, the Wizard, and me attempting to take cover.

We made our way through a yawning crack in a concrete wall to avoid the barrage. The Fallen Angel was hot on our heels, his aggression beginning to show a hint of desperation. As he closed with us in the narrowing space, I parried a few vicious slashes, and Melodie's bullets left smouldering marks in his skin. The corridor prevented him from flanking us, and Raspho and the Wizard led the way to the subterranean heart of Atlantium. I sensed we were underground after a few hundred meters. The tunnels had no real light anywhere, only the blaze of the Fallen Angel's blades threatening behind us and the benign glow of the Wizard's conjured blue orb to lead us on.

The path forked several times. When dared to rush at him, the Fallen Angel vanished down a separate tunnel. The light of his fiery weapons was replaced by the intense anxiety of a dark uncertainty. In such a state, wariness is inevitable. A mage's survival requires a frame of mind beyond an animalistic fear. I was breathing heavily in the dark, listening to footsteps as I allowed myself to relax fractionally. I didn't want tension to disrupt my logic or technique.

When the devil sprang from a hidden corner, I didn't need to see him to know where he was. We were at the gates of hell, so I should've known better. The Guards didn't see fit to provide fair warning in any case. My blade bit him, but his returned the favor. The flash of Melodie's muzzles lit the chamber. The Fallen Angel roared and scurried back towards the shadows.

I cried in pain, falling on my knee as I felt Mel's hand grasp mine. She tried to joke, but her voice was hollow.

"Wounded again? Shouldn't you be getting used to it by now?"

I felt as though the flame had severed my leg.
Past injuries combined with my latest trauma in waves of pain as the adrenaline began to ebb. I didn't think I could put any weight on the limb at all, much less continue.

"I think you're gonna need more than your name to stitch this one, Mel. Favorite poem, maybe?" I explored my body with my fingers and they quickly returned, slicked with red. "Ugh. Manifesto, perhaps?"

I was losing too much strength, and too much blood. The severity of the injury was gruesome, and nobody wanted to admit the truth. The Wizard crouched by my side and placed a hand on my shoulder. Looking at his white beard, I felt as if time and space was suspended. I knew he was weaving energy. My wound wasn't improving, but I wasn't bleeding to death, either.

"My friend," he said. The words had a finality. "You should really know how to handle assholes like that. You had the best tutors money could never buy."

I heard a chuckle and a sound like the swell of the sea, and the Wizard vanished. I grasped towards him in shock and found only a damp robe on the dirt floor, the Sorrow of the Deep hiding beneath.

I stood up instinctively, not realizing the implications of the action. Raspho cradled a fireball to life, making the humble cavern visible.

"What–" the young mage asked, whirling around to look for the Wizard. "Where'd he go?"
{~}

We left the Wizard's robe behind in the tunnel after I thrust the Sorrow in a belt pouch. Melodie reminded me that my sentimentality didn't make a chunk of glass or a telescope any more useful to carry around underground.

We paused for a brief time, to see if the Wizard might reappear. Raspho was either meditating or scribbling things in the dirt. The fireball floating near his shoulder cast a flickering orange glow. When he stood, Melodie motioned for him to lead.

"You've got the light, my friend. The brains probably, too."

He gave a nod. I saw his confidence brighten, and he set off in a direction I hadn't even contemplated. I thought the irregularities in the stone wall had only been a shadowy nook, but they materialized as a pathway. Raspho's posture straightened under his robe, and I knew we had more than firelight as a guide. The tap of the Keenwood Staff against the floor and the shuffle of careful footsteps were the only sounds we could hear in the dank underground.

A chamber appeared. I noticed how damp the walls were. The Wizard would've shamed me for lack of awareness. I thought about the old man, running free, far from this broken city, his cares forgotten as he became the Lucky Watcher once again. I wondered if he'd soaked through the earth, become a part of everything, never to manifest as a distinct personality ever again. Perhaps that was what he wanted, and ultimately where he belonged. We'd see this through, with or without him, the whole Guard-damn thing.

For the Defiance.

We reached the top edge of a vast underground amphitheater, carved in the bedrock, I heard Melodie slide a pistol from her holsters. Raspho's fireball floated and intensified until we could view the entire space. A semi-circle of terraces made several levels, descending to the center of the room, where an obelisk towered over the rising echelons of the amphitheater. A host of sparkling stalactites on the distant roof made a natural chandelier, grand as the hands of any skilled craftsman could've managed.

The opposite wall was made from tall, pale slabs of marble. A white light blinked to life along the edge of the obelisk. The image of a hairless face projected onto the receiving stone.

My attention was captured by the towering face, but I saw why Melodie had pointed her weapon. People were seated in the amphitheater, staring at the face, the will to resist abandoned. Zeyus and Lucien ignored my attempts to communicate. To my belated shock, I was filing in beside the pair, along with Melodie and Raspho. The fireball extinguished, and the only light remaining was the glow of the face on the wall.

"You too, huh?" Zeyus mumbled at me through gritted teeth, and I almost sat on his wing. The Wizard wouldn't let himself be caught like this, I thought. He would've broken through the manipulation. Why couldn't I flow away from this grasp? Why couldn't I do as he'd taught?

The Sovereign was holding everything. The Fallen Angel sauntered into the room like he owned the whole Guard-damned joint. He lit a cigarette, leaning against the obelisk. The face remained impassive. If my features would've let me sneer at him, I might've done so. Faehr-Dun was stuck, just like everybody else.

The silence was deafening, and the passing of time was excruciating. My body began to ache, and I wondered how many Marks the others had been here. To my inexpressible disgust, the Fallen Angel began amusing himself by taking indiscriminate bites out of the immobilized crowd. A nip from buttocks, that guy's arm must've looked appetizing. I think it annoyed him when he got no reactions from his victims or witnesses. I thought I saw the face on the wall either frown or move an eye, but I suspected my imagination was attempting to relieve boredom. I began to think the Fallen Angel might actually be trying to get a rise out of the Sovereign. He was probably as at least as bored as I was. I couldn't decide if I wanted his ploy to work, but eventually the biting of fleshy targets seemed to go too far.

"Operative Fifty-One C," a calm voice filled the room.

The Fallen Angel laughed, his chin slick with blood.

"It's about damn time!"

"You'll refrain from damaging the equipment."

The Fallen Angel looked affronted by the remark.

"Me? Equipment? Never. A harmless nibble from the meaty parts, here and there."

The voice of the Sovereign remained neutral, but nobody mistook the authority it assumed.

"You may recall my disciplinary processing, Fifty-One C."

This caused the blackened man to grow pensive. His voice became husky.

"As if my flesh could ever forget."

"Trap status, set," the Sovereign intoned. "Accordingly, the dragons draw near. The sequence to raise Jurisdiction defenses has been initiated. And you," the face looked directly at the Fallen Angel. "You will go and compensate for the final variable. Travel to the surface and locate the air mage accomplice. Detain or delete the correct female. Have you received my communication, Fifty-One C?"

The Fallen Angel returned the Sovereign's unfeeling gaze with reluctance.

"Loud and clear, coach."

"Your disrespect has instantiated further tasks, Fifty-One C."

{~}

The mood was grim in the underground when the Fallen Angel was present, but the silence after his departure was a separate torture. Faehr-Dun gave an unhinged laugh before a metal door sealed the exit to the amphitheater behind him. The only thing I could see was the face on the wall. Looking, but never blinking, seeing everything, and feeling nothing at all. If I listened closely, I could hear the wind in the caverns above us. Or was the rushing noise I heard the combined sigh of a captive audience?

I couldn't move my neck or my eyes under the Sovereign's grip, but I could change my focus with immense effort. I relied on my peripheral vision. I felt as though I'd been sitting in the same spot for hours. When I saw a rogue blip of blue light, I was certain I'd begun to hallucinate. From the half-mad expressions a few of the other captives were wearing, I knew I'd end up brain-damaged before the end of a Sun. Even when I saw the Lucky Watcher, a part of my mind told me he was simply wishful thinking.

Whatever was remaining of the Wizard wasn't giant or powerful. A slinking rabbit perched atop the Sovereign's obelisk, apparently unnoticed by the towering face on the wall. He looked exhausted, sprawling on the flat panel with a yawn.

My wits came back to me like a cistern filled by a stream. Kill that thing dead! I wanted to shout to the Wizard. When I thought about how he'd saved my life in the tunnel, I felt sheepish for requesting additional assistance. What would the Wizard do in my place, I wondered? Was he trying to help?

I studied the rabbit on the altar, and I freed my thoughts as much as I could. The rabbit stood up and shook his ears as if he approved the gesture. His blue eyes were looking directly at me. I felt as though I could communicate, and the Lucky Watcher lifted his hind leg.

He was leaking- not just the contents of his conjured rodent bladder, but the entirety of himself. He dribbled down through the crevices of the obelisk. When I could no longer see any trace of the Lucky Watcher, my heart sank.

The face on the wall spoke.

"The scientist who built my systems wasn't a fool, and neither am I. She made certain to waterproof my circuits before she betrayed my cause. Director Jae'lin Fleuro never accepted the Jurisdiction. She couldn't accept her own creation. She ran away and joined the Defiance, perishing in obscurity, no doubt. Let the failings of such an exceptional mind be a lesson."

My mage senses tingled acutely, and I was barely listening. I thought I could feel the Lucky Watcher even though I couldn't see him. Pooling, dripping, running through cracks and crannies. He beaded across insulated wires and plastic sheeting, but as the Sovereign had indicated, nothing sparked or shorted or went awry.

I came to a realization, as I studied my teacher. Though the Sovereign gripped my body like hardening concrete, whatever mechanism had invaded my mind left places it couldn't grasp. My mage skill was something the Sovereign had never comprehended, never developed a capacity to catalogue or analyze. Truly, the Jurisdiction didn't understand the part of me that was a mage, and therefore it didn't know where to begin in order to attempt control. The water inside of the obelisk began to react with excitement, and I knew a moment of bitter clarity.

I yelled in anguish, and I pushed the Wizard. I made him freeze, made him spike, made him tear at everything around him as he coalesced to a splintering frost. The plastic membranes and insulated wiring of the Sovereign's obelisk were no match for the razor edges of vicious ice.

People around the amphitheater began to stir. Many collapsed, and the rest either sobbed or huddled against their fallen companions. The Sovereign remained silent, but the face on the wall left its mouth hanging open, and one of the eyes began to twitch.

"You can't destroy me," the face said, as Zeyus and Lucien embraced their freedom and each other. The Sovereign remained emotionless. I heard no desperation, only a statement of fact. I had no Wizard left to freeze, and no more power to use, but the face shone against the wall, and the amphitheater still held us sealed underground. Melodie kicked at the steel door with a booted foot before shaking her head.

Zeyus was studying the Sovereign's obelisk with a soldier's eye. I drew my machete, but his hand on my arm made me pause.

"That thing is right, Rahn. We can't kill it. It's networked to every Jurisdiction mainframe across the entire planet."

The winged man's affirming words did more to kill my spirit than any weapon ever could. My heart sank.

"So we'll never be free?"

Zeyus shook his head. "We can hope the mind-control unit in this cave was unique and too intricate to be easily duplicated. With any luck, we'll just be dying the old-fashioned way from now on."

{~}

Not every captive had survived. Without the Sovereign demanding the compliance of captured physiology, some simply lost the will and the strength to keep living. Others were so weak and traumatized that we saw no chance of them leaving this place under their own cognizance. Most of the unfortunate captives in the amphitheater were among Lucien's Hidden Sashes. The fighters come through Marks of desperate trials only to end up as drooling invalids. Lucien wasn't the leader or healer they needed. The renegade Prize Mates were fortunate Vignetta survived. I remonished myself for arriving at the thought too soon. Nobody would survive if we couldn't escape our underground prison.

The face on the wall faded away to nothingness. No departing words of mockery, no extended threats, only silence and darkness. I wanted to think the Sovereign was defeated, but I found no certainty in the thought. The disappearance only served to unnerve us.

We thanked the Guards over and over for Raspho as the unshakeable blackness of the sealed underground began to prevail. I had no confidence in my own ability to conjure light. The teenage fire mage created a fireball, warm and bright. The Hidden Sashes reacted fearfully at first to the spherical flame, but Lucien's coaxing convinced the survivors of benign intent. We huddled around, pulling shivering bodies towards the warmth.

Zeyus assigned himself to search the perimeter. I saw flashes of white wings in the shadowy edges of the room. He brought no words with him when he returned to the fire, so we assumed he'd found nothing of interest. Melodie and I stood to each side of Raspho while the Hidden Sashes conversed with Lucien and Vignetta.

I looked at Raspho, and he was staring at the flame. His eyes reflected the colors of the fireball, and I sensed the swirl of its fiery surface mirrored the swirl of his intricate thoughts. Memories and dreams mingled together and produced every shade of orange imaginable. I opened my mouth to ask him if he could sustain the fire, and then I looked at Melodie. As long as A'Rehia was outside, Raspho's light would burn.

"A highly efficient feedback loop," Raspho announced as if he'd heard my unspoken thought. "I give this a Sun or two, at current heat levels. I can sense enough oxygen down here, at least. That's a blessing."

Melody began to wander the dim amphitheater. I kept one eye on her, and another on the rest of the crowd. I couldn't help but show caution after what we'd witnessed.

"I feel a breeze," Melodie called back to the group. "It doesn't smell quite right, either. Matter of fact-" she didn't finish her sentence. I found my feet moving across the stone. Mel was walking towards me, but she had a strange look on her face.

"What is it?" I asked, growing tenser. She shook her head and I relaxed.

"Not a natural breeze. A mage is out there, making that breeze. I noticed another anomaly. Give me a boost."

I did as I was asked, baffled as I was. We climbed to the highest tier of the amphitheater, and I lifted Melodie to the ceiling on my shoulders. She bashed at the rock above her with the Captain's crowbar, and I could feel the ring of each savage strike through the twist of her thighs.

Melodie's legs around my neck kept me distracted from my thoughts, but before a Mark went by, we saw claws above us. I watched in puzzlement as dark knives flashed through the soil. Curved, heavy, black claws. What were they attached to, and where were they coming from? A pair of muzzles appeared in the gap. The first was much larger, but both noses had a pair of nostrils with fuzzy edges. A few more thrashes of dirt and a flash of gray fur, and Lohise's entire head appeared in the hole. She panted and sneezed the dust away before growling Melodie's name in triumph.

"We smelled mages, and we thought you might be down here. Kiffu-San is OOF- here too. I wish he would stop leaning on me like I'm an upholstered sofa."

She gave a snarl before she withdrew her head. Melodie hopped down from my shoulders at the sight of her friend, and I took a step back and looked at the hole. The breach we'd created was well above our heads, and I had no idea how we were going to get anyone out through it. I heard a raven cawing and the whoosh of feathered wings, and they made me realize where the flow of air was coming from. Kiffu-San's eye appeared, and it looked directly in my direction. The onyx circle of his eye was smiling even though I couldn't see the rest of his face.

"Step back, kids."

The bear had mumbled through the dirt with a foreign accent, but we all heard him.

Chapter 36
A'Rehia tells of: "Dragon Wilds"

"I think we can be free if we're really determined. The world holds plenty of possibilities. But power defines freedom, and minds define what freedom means. Are peace and freedom even the same thing? Has freedom been giving justice the ol' runaround?" -The Sky Dancer

It took me approximately seven seconds to regret my decision to team up with dragons.

I could've fled with Oh-Four-Three, poor feller. I don't think I've ever seen a pair of wings move with such haste. He was a gentle, sensitive soul, unsuited to combat, and the noises scared him.

I could've been snug underground with Raspho and the other humans. But instead, I was up in the sky with nowhere to hide when the guns began to fire.

The only thing I could do was contain the panic assailing me, at first. I heard a tremendous amount of noise. Dragon wings pushed the air near my body in turbulent, thumping pulses, but the sound of Quint artillery was totally disorienting. Explosions began on the ground as they fired, and we felt whizzes near our bodies as the shells flew at us. I hid behind Chaeoh until I found a measure of courage and confidence.

When Atlantium's ordnance installations arose from their hidden berths, I knew I had to act. I recalled vividly what had happened when Chaeoh attacked the city of my birth. I drew my knives to defend my friends.

The dragons saw the risk, destroying a pair of cannons and avoided the others. When my nerves settled, I saw the fight for what it truly was. This was the air I knew. Not the earth beneath us, or the sea to the east. This was the air I'd known, above the city I was born in, and I would be the one to decide what happened here.

The boom registered in my ears, and not a moment too soon. I pushed away from Chaeoh's belly with my feet as I looked for the sneaky shell. I saw metal spinning, following its trajectory. I felt the knife slip from my hand, and I pushed the air around it. The shell wobbled as the air resistance raked against the shining metal, and my knife collided with the housing, detonating the explosive payload. I shielded my eyes and winced. White hot shards of shrapnel attempted to tear through my leg. I looked down at the injury, trying to maintain my altitude. Ugly battles leave ugly scratches.

The Quints assembled in ranks as fast the dragons could destroy the war machines, and when they opened fire, the bullets and mortars came at us in droves. I realized how foolish I was when the barrages began. I took cover behind the dragons instead of risking a debilitating injury which could send me crashing to my death. I didn't trust the strength of my shielding against the unbridled firepower in the skies over Atlantium.

Chaeoh and Sunderah didn't react kindly to being fired upon, either, and I knew the dragons were growing desperate. Armored scales were showing ragged edges, and the fire-breathing had developed a hoarse, throaty sound. Before the fight ended, I was protecting the dragons instead of hiding, and I knew we had to get away from the city. Atlantium was a harsh teacher. My friends had seen enough of her.

I convinced the pair to fly away from the worst of the massing artillery with my stubborn insistence. Sunderah didn't take kindly to turning tail or any notion of retreat. I had no doubt she would've gladly died there in Atlantium, the bodies of countless Quints tangled in her fangs. I had to grab her ears to turn her away from the firing line.

When we made clear of danger, a feeling came over me which was new and invigorating. I was free, now. Free from the battle in the clear sky, but free from fear, and free from myself. I took in the splendor of the Wilds with new eyes, listening to the wind as it shifted. I pointed to a cove along the shoreline, and the dragons followed to the landing site, too battered to refuse as adrenaline began to fade. The blue and gold scales looked even worse as we maneuvered in. Sunderah managed to get her feet underneath her as she touched, but Chaeoh stumbled, sliding on his belly in the shallows of the ocean. He groaned, making no effort to regain his feet.

I spun and drew a knife when I heard a creature snort at the edge of the trees. I lowered the weapon when I saw blue letters floating in the air. Tehsyn sat astride the Unicorn Stag, her eyes closed. Her hands were pressed together in meditative concentration.

"You're late."

{~}

I watched for a few moments when Tehsyn began her work with the dragons. The scratch on my leg was bleeding, but not badly, and I didn't want to distract the Seer Sage from her work. I wasn't exactly among her favorite people to begin with. I needed to return to Atlantium discreetly, to see what became of those I'd left behind. I was tired, but the feeling didn't deter me from leaving the sandy beach and speeding though the trees. I managed my exhaustion by walking briskly when I was within a kilometer of the city limits. I was determined to keep moving, despite the complaining of my lacerated leg. The guns were quiet. The ringing in my ears told me this was for the best.

I hid from the Quints and the Swarm. My progress became tedious. I saw few signs of humanity left anywhere among the rubble. Static rode on the wind, and a chill to the air spoke volumes. I knew where I was going, even if I couldn't say why. When I ducked under an overhang to dodge the drones, a hand reached from the shadows and clasped over my mouth, pre-empting my war-cry.

I almost stabbed him again, right then and there, right through his silly red robe. But even with the dirt and grime covering him, I couldn't mistake Raspho's eyes. He smiled, and I tried to relax, but the knife in my hand was shaking.

"You didn't happen to park a dragon or two around here, did you?" he asked, continuing to grin as he released his hold.

"We could use a lift, or some granola bars, or a nap. Are you alright? We're a bit peckish after getting captured by a demon. I think your leg is bleeding."

I found myself speaking words I didn't know I had.

"This is no place for dragons. Chaeoh and Sunderah belong in the Wilds."

I shook my head and cleared my throat to find my confidence.

"And the Wilds belong to the dragons, now."

{~}

I wish I could report about how Atlantium fell to the Defiance. I wish we'd defeated the Jurisdiction, even just a little, and I could walk the streets of the city where I grew up in without fear or a disguise. But the place I yearn for, it doesn't exist anymore. The people are gone, and the people are what make a place, anyway. Atlantium, she's a hollow town now, even more hollow than she was when I knew her. Ranks of Quints stalk the streets with robotic dismissiveness, and the Swarm floats aimlessly above her in a noxious cloud. Even the Regiment refuse to enter the city limits, claiming the ruins are haunted, now. The truth in their claims is disputable, but I'm not privy to the details of Chrysanthemum's schedule.

I didn't know if I fit in anywhere. I didn't fit in with Atlantium, either, but at least she was familiar. Faced with the choice of how I should make a new home, I couldn't bring myself to do it. I wanted to be everywhere, and nowhere at all. Why settle for a piece of earth when you can move freely through the sky?

I traveled with Raspho and my mother for a fortnight, which felt like several Moons. Oh-Four-Three didn't mind carrying the two humans, but the entire trip felt dull and uneventful. We visited Raspho's farm, and the grave-stones of his family. I know my mother viewed the Free City as her home, and she insisted on returning.

I couldn't be bound by normalcy, not after the careening course of my life. When my restlessness peaked, I spent Moons where Zeyus and I traveled the Low Hills together. I had a falling out with Raspho one morning, probably over 'traipsing about without him,' and by pure chance I discovered the aging Major drinking moonshine in a village near the Free City. Once the Jurisdiction presence receded, a number of such villages emerged, and we sought and tasted whatever spirits each of them had to offer, thanks to a supply of golden doubloons stashed away by the D'Arsailles family line. I turned plenty of heads strutting though those joints in dancing skirts. I discovered I was glad the low whistles and predictable catcalls weren't my adoring boyfriend's style. I couldn't picture any jealous immolations, either. If I thought Ras were capable of that, I probably would've just dumped him.

Even the exploration of a burgeoning Low Hills was a pastime which couldn't last forever. On the final night of our travels, a brawl broke out in the tavern we were slumming at, fueled by old tribal rivalries. I had no stake in the outcome, only the thrill of the scene. I remember a tribal war-call starting up. The dolts never finished the words, because Zeyus kept flinging beer bottles. The moment sticks with me, because I remember a fleeting feeling of contentment as I somersaulted through the rafters of the bar.

The next Sun, Zeyus ditched my ass, but I couldn't blame him. Lucien and the Hidden Sashes were exotic and intriguing, and probably more fun than a teenage air mage who doesn't want to settle to domesticity. I thought about the Free City, and I realized I had no idea what intrigue had transpired in my absence.

I put off going back to my mom for as many Suns as I possibly could. I put off going back to Mel, 'Syn, Vil, Rahn, Kiff, Charlie, Steffen. I procrastinated and daydreamed, and I wondered if Raspho missed me, which of course he did. I snuck across the back bridge to the Free City in a heavy cloak, no fanfare or ceremony, and I ducked through the leathery curtain of the nearest tavern. The joint was a homely establishment, barely slung together with ancient concrete and fresh timber, but the bartender poured a mean ale.

The frothy mug tasted like spring. A crooked wooden skylight was set in the ceiling above the wooden bar, and the wind shifted beyond a thin pane of salvaged stained-glass. Perhaps the streets of the Free City would be my streets, eventually. For now, I'd buy her a drink and get to know her better.

Book 4:
Epilogues 1-2

Epilogue 1
Duu tells of: "Not My Worst Thursday Night"

"Notes? Why would jou want my notes? Notes won't drill any stupidity out of that stinking cheese-wheel jou call a brain. Wine and crackers are what jou should be after. Jou want my notes, fine. I hope they catch on fire when jou're least expecting." -The False Priestess

    I'm tired of friggin' dragons. What a pain in the ass. Dear Guards, what I wouldn't give for a juicy dragon steak to tide me over 'til breakfast. I don't care if the Jurisdiction retreated. What do I look like, an ethics professor? At least the Jurisdiction established predictable economic trends. You ever try keeping a sheep alive before? Didn't friggin' think so! The Wilds were never flowing with milk and honey and firewhiskey, folks. Hell, I'd retire if life was that easy. You don't survive around here without stepping on a few toes.
    For instance, when I go to my favorite bar, I like to carry a conspicuously large bong under one arm. I generally usurp control of the jukebox as soon as I step through the door, just to let everyone know who's in charge. If anyone ever objects to this state of affairs, I get to decide what part of their tender body I should jab with my wand. Truly, they've done me a favor and started my evening on a high note.
    Thursday nights aren't for getting drunk. I never get drunk anymore. It's too much effort, especially on a Thursday. Now-a-Suns, I drink because putting booze in my belly makes me feel sort of human...ish. Plus, at the bar you'll always meet a drunk person who can entertain you, free-of-charge. If they're nice, then chances are good they're real extra super nice, and if they aren't nice, then you can always break a cheap wooden barstool over their most convenient bony surface. Either way you end up with a win, is what I'm saying.
    Like I said, this was a Thursday night. But don't get me wrong, it wasn't my first Thursday night. Maybe if you were listening, you'd have a modicum of correct information lodged in that cheese-wheel of yours. I met an interesting dude on this particular Thursday. Definitely wasn't a Wednesday, I'll tell you that much. I probably shouldn't even call this dude a 'dude,' because he was a capuchin. A capuchin is a wee-monkey, in case you forgot you were part of an animal kingdom. I mean, he wasn't a chick capuchin, so I wasn't wrong when I called him 'dude'. Even if he was a chick, I'd probably still call him 'dude'. I'm not wrong often because I'm not a loser.

We do need to get back to this capuchin, this dude, though. I don't know why you made me wander off of my main topic in the first place. The dude was bright blue, for one thing. His misguided fashion sense prevented me from hating him. He was sitting on the bar and draining Manhattans with a piece of hollow reed cut from the marsh behind the establishment. Can you imagine? I almost high-fived him before I even asked what the hell his name was.

I introduced myself, and I reminded him I had full control of the jukebox. I asked him politely if he could refrain from piddling on the bar for the evening. I may be a woman of diverse tastes, but when it comes to food service regulations I don't fuck around. The cook in the back could throw together a half-decent taco, and I didn't want any monkey pee messing with the vibe. He assured me he'd use the loo.

"My parents called me Jahnny. I guess everybody else calls me Jahnny, too. People, at least. Not that I have any of those, anymore."

"Well, you certainly showed up to the right bar, then," I assured him. "I'll buy you a taco. What kind of dead animal do you want them to cover in cheese for you?"

He started giving me lame answers, so I threatened the waitress on his behalf. Jahnny seemed to think this was rude, and I do have a conscience. I felt guilty for mistreating the woman. I offered to fix her face in my lab and make her actually pretty. Nobody liked this solution, either, but I've always known that social skills are Guard-damn boring. I needed both of them to stop yammering about how mean I was, because I really wanted to hear this Guard-damn monkey's tale.

Fortunately, I'm rich, and I flung money at my new friends. I like them a lot, even if they're just a weird-ass monkey and a plain-ass waitress, and I want to be sure they like me back. I really just want to be loved and feared at the same time. But mostly, I'm at the point in this spectacular narrative where I just wanna know why there's a blue monkey sitting on the bar. If this furry whipper-snapper is a water mage, like I suspect, he'd be the best thing to come from Thursday night since a few friendly local assholes convinced a Pegasaur Drake to do keg-stands on the mayor's lawn.

So I says to him, I says, "Jahnny! Bruh! What's jour deal? Who jou gotta piss off around here to end up a talkin'-ass monkey?"
{~}

"The Swarm, they came to our farm. That's where my family lived. I only knew it was the Swarm 'cause-a scary stories from when I was a kid. I was surfin', an' I swam down the coast. Swam 'til I couldn't swim. Thought I was gonna drown. Lost count of the leagues of coast I passed. When I was gonna slip under the waves, I grabbed hold of a ship-wreck, lodged in the rocks."

The blue monkey signaled the bartender as his Manhattan drained away.

"The fear, exhaustion, they made stars swim in my eyes. My fingers clung against sharp barnacles. I told myself I was a coward, but I prayed my family might live, and I might go back to find them. The ship had probably been abandoned for centuries. A massive steel wreck, I never would've imagined it in my wildest dreams. I pulled myself from the sea to the slanted deck. I found a cold, grimy corner to cry in."

Jahnny tipped the bartender generously from a sack of coins next to him nearly as big as he was. I began to wonder where the monkey had acquired the cash that he was flashing around.

"I heard noises when I was trying to rest. The dawn was nearly upon the horizon. I assumed the sounds were ocean against the hull of the ancient vessel. When I gathered the energy to move, I realized I wasn't hearing the ocean at all. I was hearing footsteps."

"Jou know," I interrupted, "Jou might be the most interesting capuchin I've met on a Thursday night. This story is slightly above average, and I believe I'd like jou to continue."

The blue capuchin raised an eyebrow, but his mouth kept moving, so I didn't complain.

"The ship didn't have people. It had monkeys. Every size and description you can possibly imagine, swinging from the ceilings and sprinting through the hallways. I kicked and screamed when the hands grabbed dragged me below-decks. That's where they kept the machine. They held me down, made me one of their own."

Jahnny cleared his throat. His hairy fist jammed the straw against the ice in his tumbler.

"Looks like jou got away," I pointed at his money-sack. "Like a bandit, from what I can tell."

The monkey shook his head.

"Two Rounds, Ma'am. Two Rounds, I was on that ship. Never would've cared much for monkey-politics, but it was life or death. Robbed them blind, made my escape, except my family is dead. Raspho might've survived the Swarm, but the Jurisdiction was after him, I imagine. I love my brother, but he wouldn't make it two Rounds on his own with the Jurisdiction after him."

I cackled violently, and heads turned my way along the length of the bar. I was tickled pink by Jahnny's connection.

"Stick-boy? Jou wanna know where jou can find Stick-boy? I can help jou with that, my friend! I'll wager jou've enough coin to contract my services. I'll have my people send jour people an invoice so that Jou and I can focus on results."

The capuchin's eyes lit with cerulean. He leapt to his feet and shoved his Manhattan away with a foot.

"If you know about my brother Raspho, then please, Ma'am. Do tell, by all means. I've spent too many nights in bars like this. I'm gettin' tired of howlin' the blues."

Epilogue 2
Szakaieh tells of: "The Ends Don't Justify the Meanings"

"Who told you this isn't real? Just because somebody made it up doesn't mean it isn't real." -The Wizard of the Waves

A line of prisoners stood in chains behind the Jurisdiction courthouse, trampling the high grass at the edge of town. The drunks, the cheats, the ruffians, they were all present, and I stood among them in a hooded robe. My gray-brown garment was filthy, especially around the knees. The caked dirt was from my garden. The hood was generously cut, and it drooped over my eyes. Only my beard and my bony hands were visible. A Regiment soldier shoved me, snatching my cane away. Shackle-chains jingled the whole way down the line. Deprived of my cane, I had difficulty with my balance, but the other prisoners helped me along.

Inside the courthouse, the people of the town gathered and seated themselves in padded pews. The Jurisdiction chose to make a display of this weekly sentencing as a public warning. The Enforcers wore their bloodiest scarlet robes, and when the doors were shut, the Nobility prosecutors spoke to the crowd in dulcet tones. The stand for suspects was surrounded by iron railings. The floor beneath the iron chair was made of an iron grate.

If a suspect repented, they could be a slave for a while. If you refused to repent, the ash-catcher below your feet was waiting.

Slave labor was a pragmatic resource for the Jurisdiction. Prisoners were rarely executed. The suspects would invariably repent and beg mercy of the Enforcers in an attempt to reduce their sentencing.

"Mister Zachary, is it?" the Enforcer began. I sat at the stand. The man's name was Harold Hotfinger, Esquire. Personally, I begin my morning by drinking coffee and dabbling in a little light reading, but Harry spent his morning sending children to the factories.

"You stand accused of being a non-licensed hedge-wizard, Mister Zachary. We've records of how you've defiled the dirt with your green-thumbery. You may deem your actions inconsequential, but no-matter. A swift reprimand is due in response to your transgressions. Illicit magecraft of any nature rises beyond mere misdemeanor."

He stroked his goatee and scowled. I kept my head tilted forward in contrition and rose feebly from the iron chair.

"Your Honor, please. I do what I must. I wish only to help the people survive these harsh times. I grow a bit of grain, here and there. To feed the hungry."

Hotfinger smirked.

"I'm sure the Jurisdiction could find a more suitable use for whatever food you've been wasting on this miserable lot. I'm sending you to the laboratories, where the Devisors may identify the depths of your sins against the state, hedge-mage. You might see freedom, eventually, if my Devisor brethren deem you worthy of redemption."

Hotfinger touched the golden Jurisdiction medallion hanging around his neck.

"That is," he continued, "if you choose to repent."

I began to chuckle.

Harold wasn't pleased. His tone of voice became much firmer and angrier.

"I repeat myself only to your hazard, foul sinner. Do you repent?"

I muttered loudly when my chuckles had subsided.

"Holy shit, Harry. Of course I don't repent, you moron. You love this gig, don't you? Is that lump I see just your stupid robe or do you actually have a boner right now?"

Harold was secretly thrilled. For too many Turns he'd endured groveling Jurisdiction slaves in his presence without being able to display his true powers. The chance to immolate an actual target beckoned him like a siren's call. He called fire, throwing blazing heat. The red washed over my form in a searing torrent. My robe and my illusions were swept away by the cleansing inferno.

When the energy abated, Harry Hotfinger wasn't even paying attention anymore. He'd assumed I was nothing but ash. He lifted a glass to toast his Nobility buddies before the next prisoner could be brought to the stand. The crowd in the courthouse was murmuring about the fiery display. A spectator shouted, and the Enforcers noticed.

My titanium body was black from the soot, but my face was machined in a unique design I chose myself, a mask of my own creation. I was vaguely skeletal in shape, but geometrically rigid when compared to natural bones. The Sorrow of the Deep was lashed to my pelvis in a wire sheath.

I chuckled again. Harold and his cronies allowed their eyes to betray their hand.

"The long arm of the law has gotta be down-right exhausted by now, don't you think? Either too many bicep curls, or too much masturbation, I'll wager. What do you say we adjourn this session? Who wants to have a drink on the Jurisdiction? Civil-asset forfeiture, folks. Legal term I'm using incorrectly. Means 'if we're taking back the government, let's at least steal the booze.'"

The Enforcers attacked, but the brawling-scene thing is pretty passe, if you want my opinion. I'm not really tryna kill people these Suns, I swear. I know professionals who make a decent living at it, and I don't wanna cut in on their action. Occasionally guys like Harry damage themselves with their own ambition, but Harry needed a little assistance, if you catch my drift.

I walked towards the front row of pews when the eager townspeople finished looting the courthouse. Only one person remained behind. The cloaked woman hadn't budged an inch during the entire fiasco. She drew her hood back from her face.

The Wise Witch was carved from rosewood, and inlaid with silver. Her daughter had shaped her according to the patterns on her branch. Upon her re-awakening, my love pronounced herself mostly pleased with our efforts before she made a few minor modifications to her face and her shoulders. Her features were affixed in silver, but I knew the woman was grinning.

"I'm not sure you'll ever be my favorite husband, Kai. But if you don't disappear on me again, you might still make the top five."

CPSIA information can be obtained
at www.ICGtesting.com
Printed in the USA
LVHW091333040220
645810LV00010B/339